The Girl
From
The Cornfield

The Girl From The Cornfield
Gina Iafrate

Published by Gina Iafrate
Hollywood FL

Publisher: Gina Iafrate

ISBN: 1537370847
ISBN 13: 9781537370842

Cover Design: Gina Iafrate

Back Cover Design: Gina Iafrate

Originally published in the USA by Gina Iafrate
Hollywood FL

In Gratitude

My heartfelt gratitude goes to my husband, Mario, for his endless love and support as he watched me type away into the wee hours of the night. I am grateful to my grandson, Stephen, for his enthusiastic encouragement — believing that I would succeed in seeing this novel through to the end.

Chapter One
The Hiring

September 11, 1950

Giuliana was given no inclination that her life would take a sinister turn from this pleasant, early September morning. The announcement from the town crier the night before had motivated her to rise at four o'clock. With his loud trumpet, he had made the rounds on her street.

"Attention, town folks! Workers are needed to harvest corn! Orlando Alonza will be recruiting. Anyone interested needs to be at La Mesa Bifernina by six o'clock tomorrow morning."

Giuliana's alarm clock had startled her tired body. Driven by duty, she was working diligently to force herself up as the pain from the hard labour of picking dandelions the day before was shooting down her leg muscles. The temptation to crawl back under the warm covers and let the world go away was enticing. With reluctance, she forced herself out of bed. Her eyes glanced toward the window. It was pitch black out there. Where Am I going? She questioned with bloodshot eyes as she struggled to recall her intentions through the grogginess that comes from a lack of sleep.

"Giuliana? What are you doing?"

The tiny, muffled voice came from her younger sister, Triza, as she delivered her query from deep within the covers of the shared bed.

"I need to get there before everyone else," Giuliana whispered to

1

her sister.

"Who cares?" murmured Trizia.

"I know you don't! But, Mom and Papa sure do. You know how badly we need the money."

"Ugh, just go! And leave me alone to sleep in peace. Turn off that light too. You are so inconsiderate."

Trizia flipped over and brought her arm over her face trying to shield her eyes from the light. Giuliana rolled her eyes and quietly made her way down the stairs, barefoot, trying hard not to wake up the rest of the family. She noticed a dim light on by the landing. Puzzled, she forced her eyes wider, trying to compel them to adjust the break in darkness. To her surprise, her father was standing by the door at the bottom of the stairs. With a sweet, caring smile he greeted her.

"Good morning, Giuliana," he whispered. He was ready with his small knapsack on his back.

"Papa! Why are you up?" Giuliana asked, taken aback.

"I will go with you. It is not a good idea for you to walk that distance alone and besides, maybe we will both get hired if we are lucky," he said with a tired smile that had become all too familiar to Giuliana in the last few years.

"Okay, Papa. I am pleased you are coming. I could use the company on the walk. When passing in front of the cemetery, I admit that the only things that enter my mind are Grandpa's ghost stories."

"Come, my love. Let's go. You have nothing to be afraid of with me beside you."

He was always so reassuring, and Giuliana liked that.

"Of course not! Thanks, Papa."

Giuliana's father put an arm around his daughter's shoulders as they ventured out into the misty morning air.

The small Italian town they lived in had a population of thirty-five hundred people sprawled in between a cluster of stone and mortar homes from a rocky hilltop down to a circular valley. Here, in one of the descending structures, Giuliana Ferrante lived with her family. The Ferrante's consisted of her mother and father, Gioia and Ruggiero, a younger sister, Trizia, and her Grandpa Luigi and Nonna Rosa. The farmlands extended all around the town right up to the bank of the river Biferno, which dried up in the summer. The townsfolk that worked the fields travelled by foot to get to their destination every morning and returned in the evening after their day's labour. Cars were few and far between as the country roads were not easily accessible by automobile.

***

Giuliana and her dad walked two hours before reaching La Mesa Bifernina. Once they arrived, they were greeted by a long line ahead of them.

"Papa, have some of these people been here all night?" Giuliana asked.

"Looks like it," her father said with an audible sigh.

Giuliana and her dad merged into the line with some resignation. Almost immediately, many others began to shuffle into place behind them. Most were adults – therefore bigger, stronger, and more experienced than her – but dishevelled in appearance. Like Giuliana and her father, these townsfolk were desperate for employment, hoping to be hired for whatever work was available. As Giuliana studied them she calculated and cringed at her chances of being selected.

At the front, a fellow in his mid-thirties appeared and began addressing the line. His presence immediately silenced the murmuring of the restless crowd. His complexion was olive-toned, his hair - wavy black, eyebrows thick, and he had sunken greyish eyes above a long protruding nose. He was very well groomed, which demarcated him from the townsfolk in line in front of him. Giuliana heard someone whispering ahead of her.

"That's that Spanish guy she hired as her foreman."

"Yeah. I found out he is a character, all right," another replied.

Giuliana turned her head toward the voices to see two older women gossiping before her. One had enough hair on her lip to be considered a moustache and the other was both stout and squat. To Giuliana, the portly woman looked as if she might burst.

"More like a prick than a character, I would say," said the moustached lady.

"He is the son of Luca Alonza. I heard he married some woman while he was in Spain and came back here with his family after his father died."

"Oh, I see. Explains his accent," the moustache lady mused, stroking the hair on her lip.

"I heard he is well connected, that he found new buyers to export the corn to for that woman, Sibilla."

"Hush, hush, folks!" the Spanish man called out, quieting the few remaining whisperers. "We are only picking thirty workers today." The man had an aura of authority that came with his thick Spanish accent and imposing demeanour.

Anxiously, Giuliana stood on her tiptoes to rise above the women in front of her; she needed this job just as bad as anybody else. Her dad had lost his job months ago, just before her grandma and grandpa moved into her old room. Now the six of them all shared three beds in their modest house. Giuliana missed her old room; there was no more privacy now that Trizia was sharing her bed. They really needed the money now more than ever.

Peering through the crowd towards the speaker, she noticed a nametag hanging from his shirt as he slowly drew closer. Orlando. As Orlando spoke, everyone stood quiet - anticipating his selections. The man began going down the line, handpicking people out of the crowd. One by one, the selected men and women stepped aside, as relief replaced the look of despair on their faces. It had felt like hours passed before he stopped in front of Giuliana. She could smell his sweet cologne as he sized her up and down. It felt as if she were an animal at the community fair being assessed for purchase. She held her breath.

"How old are you?" he asked, shaking his head, incredulously.

Giuliana was frozen. After what felt like a second too long, she managed to regain her speech and squeak out her answer.

"Sixteen, Sir," she lied.

Orlando took a second look, analysing her begging eyes with his firm gaze. Her high cheekbones accentuated her thick lips. She was blessed with copious long brown hair, big brown eyes, and was busty for her age. The boys at school often teased her, but she would try to ignore them and focus on her studies.

Does he know I am lying? Giuliana wondered. His serious look lapsed briefly into a subtle grin. Giuliana felt fire on her face as her cheeks turned bright red.

"Okay, young lady," Orlando said, as he extended his hand toward her. "I am counting you in as our number thirty-one. I shouldn't, but I will make an exception for you."

"Thank you, sir," she replied as calmly as she could as Orlando pulled her out of the line. A wave of relief came rushing through her body forcing her to grin. Orlando turned to address the rest of the crowd.

"Sorry, folks. The rest of you can go home!"

Thank you, God. I am in! She could not believe it. At only twelve, she was hired to work in the cornfield. Dad did not even make the cut! Like a bunch of ducklings, the selected group followed Orlando towards a straw shack where two women were waiting. Giuliana left her father.

"Folks, this is Sibilla and her assistant, Liliana. From now on Lady Sibilla is in charge. I strongly advise you to follow her orders. Liliana will supply you with bushels and a scythe to cut and gather the ears of corn. Should you not be productive, you will be replaced. I don't need to tell you how many disappointed workers were sent home this morning. Have I made myself clear?"

Giuliana found his Spanish accent sweet, but his words stern and explicitly noted. All of the villagers nodded their heads in agreement – there was no need to oppose. This job would give them money, and money would buy them food. They were all here for the same reason.

Sibilla and Liliana distributed a small scythe and a large bushel to each worker. Both felt awkward in Giuliana's little hands. As they left the shack, Liliana accompanied the girl to the field.

"What is your name?" Liliana asked.

"Giuliana."

"Giuliana, I see. You seem so young. How old are you?"

"Sixteen."

"I see…"

Giuliana couldn't tell if she believed her.

"Sibilla does not want the workers to engage in conversation; this is why we put distance between them. There is limited time to pick the corn. Production is Sibilla's primary interest."

"I understand," responded Giuliana. "How old are you?"

"Seventeen."

"Oh! I thought you were older," Giuliana observed.

Liliana was tall and well developed. Her blond hair was tied back in a ponytail and her bangs covered her forehead. Above all, her blue eyes were striking, filled with kindness amidst her other features. Liliana gave Giuliana an encouraging smile and proceeded to teach her how to cut the ears of the corn before moving on. Giuliana liked her; she had shown sympathy. If she only knew how badly I need this job, she thought.

The rest of the workers were put immediately to their duties. Like Giuliana, they were all prepared to work hard. However, many had more labour experience than her. Even so, she was eager to learn and determined to keep up with them. The cornfield was immense, extending into endless acres of rocky and dry terrain. In the hills of Molise not many green trees grew since the drought had destroyed most of the lush vegetation. The surrounding area was full of yellowish weeds.

Not long after Giuliana had started working, Sibilla reappeared with further instructions.

"Remove the ears from the corn stalks, and leave the stalk intact for operation two. Once the bushel is filled, you will put this yellow tag on it. This is your colour. Place the bushel on your head and carry it to the end of the row. A wagon will bring the bushels to the main barn. We will then keep count."

She was intimidating and much less encouraging than her assistant.

"Yes, Madam," Giuliana hastily replied before putting her head down and returning to work.

"Here, take this." Sibilla said, interrupting Giuliana's labouring as she handed her a large brimmed straw hat. "You'll thank me later."

The sun was beaming unremitting rays as the morning

progressed with exasperating heat. The dry dust blowing from the corn was playing havoc on Giuliana's sweltering skin. The discomfort was unbearable, but she mopped away the sweat on her face with the back of her arm and continued on. The straw hat often flopped over her eyes, making matters worse, but Sibilla was right, she was thankful for any type of protection from the sun. Regardless, Giuliana knew her pale skin would burn in the relentless sun.

***

After a few days, Giuliana noticed that Liliana was assigning her to work further and further from the other workers.

"Why am I placed so far away, Liliana? We haven't finished clearing the south section yet," Giuliana worked up the courage to finally ask.

"I am only following orders. Here is where I was told to place you," responded Liliana.

Giuliana could not complain as it was Friday afternoon and she would collect her first pay by the end of the day and rush home to hand it to her grandmother. Grandma Rosa would finally be able to buy some decent food for them. Her mom, Gioia, did laundry and helped some of the town artisans whenever they called for her. This was the only other source of income her family had to live on. Her dad found a little work from time to time when someone called for help on the fields, but they paid him mostly with food, giving him produce from their farm or eggs from their chickens. That was such a treat for them since their main meals mostly consisted of dandelion leaves, beans, and cornbread, topped with any other ingredients Grandma would forage from the public side of the country roads.

It was two o'clock in the afternoon, nearing the hottest part of the day. Sweat was streaming down Giuliana's forehead and backside. Ignoring it, she kept ploughing on. The faster she filled her bushel, the more money she made. Her back strained as she bent while she swung the scythe down as quickly as she could. Suddenly, she felt something grab her back leg.

"HEY!"

Giuliana whirled around holding the scythe out aggressively in front of her. It was Orlando.

"Woah! Settle down there, Sunshine."

Orlando grabbed the scythe by the neck and lowered it from his face.

"How is my number thirty-one doing?" He laughed and smiled broadly.

Giuliana put her arm down and tried to conceal her defensive response.

"Fine, Sir. Sorry. I was. . . I was just startled," Giuliana was unsure of how to respond.

Orlando extended his hand, stroking Giuliana's long hair boldly.

"You don't have to call me Sir, you can call me Orlando. I like that better."

Giuliana didn't know what to make of it. But, in half-whisper she replied.

"Ok...Orlando."

"There! That's better! It sounds even nicer coming from your lips."

Giuliana felt uneasy, but nodded in agreement – secretly wishing him gone. He stared at her for a moment longer, and then, as suddenly as he appeared, he walked away. Giuliana let out a long sigh of relief. I do NOT like that Orlando guy, she thought, but soon shook her feelings and immersed herself in her work.

"It's celebration night," she muttered to herself out loud, "you're almost done for the day."

Not much later, a rustle in the corn made her turn. There was Orlando again, right behind her, and much too close for her comfort. He continued to advance with lustful eyes.

"Sir? Er…I mean, Orlando?" Giuliana said, backing away cautiously.

"Baby, it's time for my pay off!"

With one hand, he grabbed at her scythe and threw it on the ground, then grabbed her arm with the other.

Giuliana was frozen for a moment, but regained awareness with a start and began to push him away with the little force she had. But, he was stronger, and he knew it. Orlando lugged Giuliana's body closer towards him and then grabbed her other arm. Even if she were not exhausted from the day's work, her squirming wouldn't have had any effect. She was trapped, and she knew it. He threw her on the ground.

"Look, Baby, if I were you, I would cooperate. Don't you know who I am? No one refuses Orlando! Why do you think I made an expectation for little number thirty-one? You need to please me. It's all just part of the job, Baby."

"NO! NO! PLEASE!" Giuliana screamed loudly, thrashing her feet as he jumped on top of her. "Get away from me! Please! STOP!"

Her heart was beating so rapidly that she thought it might explode. Orlando kept her beneath him, trying hard to kiss her. She was kicking and biting him, and screaming when she could, but no one came – no one was going to come.

The ferocious animal was forcing himself on her without mercy. With one last desperate effort, Giuliana kicked hard, distancing Orlando just far enough for a moment. She rolled over and pushed herself to her feet and began to run as fast as she could into another row of the cornfield. She stumbled as tears smeared her vision, her head foggy. She was fleeing blindly. Giuliana could hear Orlando's heavy footsteps from behind, closing in on her. He lunged forward and grabbed her legs again. Giuliana fell harder this time and smashed her face into the ground. Her mouth filled with the taste of salt from her tears and bloodied nose, and her head throbbed harder than ever before. She forced her body to roll over only to see Orlando standing over her.

"Quite the fight in you," Orlando observed, towering over her.

She gasped in a mouthful of air to let out another scream, but it was no use. Her voice was gone.

"No," she let out a soft whisper, "please. . ."

Orlando came down on top of her again, and everything went black.

***

Giuliana awoke much later on the ground, alone, between the rows of corn. She did not know how long she had been there. At first, she didn't remember anything. Then, slowly the nightmare of recollection began. Her dress was torn, making her half naked, and her underwear was thrown by her feet. Looking down at herself, disgust engulfed her soul. Her dress was smeared with blood, and her body ached with deep pain. This monster had carved into her heart and soul, leaving her immobilised body empty. She did not quite understand what had happened to her, but she knew what had taken place was horrendous. Orlando was a monster and a menace and she was number thirty-one. Giuliana sat, crying in despair.

***

When no bushels had been delivered at the end of the row the rest of the afternoon Liliana began to get suspicious. She decided to check on the new girl. As Liliana appeared, Giuliana was still on the ground. Liliana took one look at her, and she immediately knew what had happened.

"I am sorry, Giuliana," she said softly, looking at her pitifully.

Without delay, she worked to get the girl to her feet.

Giuliana, embarrassed, could not conceal her dishevelled appearance. Her crying resumed uncontrollably.

"I'm sorry," Liliana said again, wracked with guilt, "I...I should have warned you."

Giuliana was stunned by her revelation but forced herself to regain composure.

"You knew? What do you mean? Why did no one stop him?"

"Orlando takes all the new girls that arrive here. You're just another one of his conquests.

I figured he was on to you when he ordered me to place you in secluded areas."

Giuliana listened in disbelief.

"What are you saying ?"

"He waited until Friday. He usually strikes soon after."

"You mean he does that to all the girls he hires? He needs to be reported! What about Sibilla, does she know?"

"Of course she knows."

Giuliana was enraged.

"She does not report him? Or fire him?"

"Giuliana," Liliana put a hand on her shoulder to calm her down. "We are out in the country. These folks are desperate. Most of the girls are grateful to have a job. They succumb to his advances and move on. You should do the same. Orlando has…he has even had his way with me. Afterwards, he does not bother you anymore. He always moves on to the next new girl."

Giuliana was appalled. As young as she was, she knew this was unacceptable. Now she found her thoughts consumed by the feeling that she had lost her dignity. How could she move on? The repulsion inside her was more than she could bear.

"Come on. You'll feel better tomorrow. Let's walk toward the creek. I'll help you wash up, get yourself together, and get you looking half decent before you go home."

Giuliana followed her; disoriented and incapable of reasoning for herself.

"I will walk you home tonight. Don't worry. As you know, today is payday; we will stop at the shack. Sibilla will give you your pay," Liliana tried to reassure her.

Giuliana was quiet for the rest of the trip home. She wasn't even sure if she wanted to go to her house. She was ashamed to face her family, but she had no other place to go.

Once she got home, she was relieved to find that no one else was there. She was in no condition to be seen. After making her way to the safety of her room, she crawled and hid under the covers. She felt cold and dirty, and she vowed to get even with that brute. No way would she allow him to violate or touch her ever again, or anybody else for that matter. He needed to be brought to justice. Until he was, she was not going back to that place.

Her mom and dad and the rest of the family would be home soon and would be anxious to talk about her first pay. This was the celebration they had planned. This is what they had been cheering for all week. Giuliana had taken the little brown envelope with the cash and thrown it in disgust on her night table. What a hard price had she paid for that money. The anticipated joy had been stripped away, and now it was dirty money.

Once her mom arrived home, she immediately called out.

"Giuliana, Dear! I am home. Where are you?"

Giuliana did not feel like responding, but her mom kept calling, leaving her no choice.

"In my room, Mom," she answered.

"In your room? Come down!"

But, she did not want to face her or the rest of the family. She locked her bedroom door and refused to come out. Her mother walked up the stairs and was surprised to find Giuliana's door locked.

"Giuliana, what are you doing?" her mother asked, pounding on the door and shaking her head. "Is something wrong? Open the door."

"Mom, I'm not feeling well. The heat was too much for me today. I just want to go to sleep. Please, Mom, let me be."

Her mother was disappointed. She shrugged her shoulders and decided to let Giuliana rest.

Not much later, the rest of the family arrived. Everyone was eager to talk to Giuliana. The first to arrive was her dad.

"Gioia?" he immediately inquired, after kissing his wife as she greeted him, "Where is our hard worker?"

"Hush, she is resting."

"Poor child of mine, I need to find work soon. It's my responsibility to support this family." Ruggiero shrugged his shoulders heavily while shaking his head.

14

"Have faith, Dear. You will," Gioia replied, giving him a peck on the cheek.

Ruggiero was a good man and loved his family. It bothered him immensely that he could not find work. Occasionally, he was called down to the hydro plant by the river Biferno. There, he did some maintenance work, but unfortunately that work wasn't often enough. He was a smart man who had been in the army and drafted to the war. There he had received his education: engineering skills and machinery maintenance. But, in this small town, he was limited.

Regardless of her family's intermittent pleading, Giuliana would not come out of her room for the rest of the evening. The family resigned themselves to her wishes.

***

The next morning Giuliana did not get up for work. Her mother was curious about her daughter's sudden change of heart. Her instinct drove her to check on her. When she opened the door to her room, Gioia came across Giuliana curled up in a ball wrapped in blankets.

"Giuliana, what's going on? You are still not well, Dear?"

Her face was pale as she trembled like a scared rabbit. With a faint whisper, she answered.

"No, Mom, I am not. I don't want to go back there ever. I do not like that place. It's not for me."

"No? I thought you liked it. You seemed excited. What changed your mind?"

"Mom, everything there changed my mind: the people, the heat, the dust."

"Fine, Dear. Although jobs are hard to find - if you don't want to, you don't have to go. We are poor, but with the Lord's help, we will survive."

Her mom relented quickly as she certainly didn't want her daughter forced to do something against her will.

Giuliana kept herself in seclusion for days. Her bubbly personality had turned into quiet sadness. Her family, especially her mom and dad, grew more worried and concerned.

"Ruggiero, I am going to summon Don Francisco to come and visit Giuliana. I don't like what's happening to our daughter. She is not eating, she doesn't want to go out, she has crying spells…she is just not herself. Something has taken place and she is not telling us."

"Of course, Dear. Don't waste any more time. Let's get the doctor," Ruggiero replied, concerned.

They decided to call the only doctor in town, Don Francisco, to see if he would have some answers and help their daughter snap out of this melancholy.

Chapter Two
The Doctor's Visit

When Gioia and Ruggiero called Don Francisco, he promptly obliged. Grabbing his little black bag, he made his way to their home. It was late morning and Giuliana was still hibernating in her room. Once she heard the squeak of her bedroom door opening, her blurred eyes spotted first the doctor and then the shadowed outline of her mother. Like a frightened kitten, she shivered and retreated further back to the corner of the bed. Her quick hands grabbed the ruffled blanket, sheltering herself as she tried to disappear. An uncontrollable fear from deep in her belly stimulated her to let out an outrageous scream.

"No! Don't come near me! Stay away from me! Mom! Mom, make him go away please!"

She turned her face to hide between the corners in the wall. The last person she wanted to see was a male beside her bed – doctor or no doctor.

"Giuliana, Don Francisco is here to help you. He needs to visit you and make you better! We need to find out what is wrong with you. You know how much we all love you, darling." Her mother's face was twisted with worry. Furiously, Giuliana pulled the blankets closer to her body.

"Mom. No! Send him away; he cannot touch me!"

Don Francisco turned to face Gioia, furrowing his brow.

"Let's step out for a moment and give Giuliana her privacy," he said, as he nodded for Gioia to follow him out of the room. The room was vacated as he softly closed the door behind them.

"We need to talk. Let's go downstairs. Ruggiero needs to hear what I have to say," the doctor said, solemnly.

The adults sat around the table in the small kitchen, there were five of them, including Grandma and Grandpa. Trizia was away visiting cousins in a nearby city.

"Folks," Don Francisco said, referring mainly to the Ferrante males, "I have not been able to get near Giuliana. She is deeply traumatised. Having not been able to examine her or question her, I cannot say for sure, but there is a high possibility that your daughter," he hesitated, looking at Ruggiero straight in the eyes, "has been molested."

"What?" Both Ruggiero and Grandpa Luigi jumped up. They looked at each other, with lion's faces, ready to attack.

"Please sit down. Calm down! Our first interest here is Giuliana's wellbeing. She needs to be checked over physically, as well as being reassured psychologically with tender, loving care. I will not be able to reach her. She is turned off by a male doctor – or any male – as far as I can detect. I suggest you call a levatrice. I could refer you to a midwife who is a friend of mine, Mrs. Zicardo. She has children of Giuliana's own age. She will be able to do a better job than I can at this time."

They all listened attentively. Grandpa and Ruggiero visually agitated were trying hard to obey the doctor as they sat on the edge of their straw chairs. Grandma Rosa was the first to speak up.

"Yes, I know the lady. As a matter of fact, she lives few doors down. She's from Bologna and has been assigned for service here. Giuliana plays with her daughters sometimes. We would be lucky to have her help."

"Good. That's all to our advantage. She might feel comfortable with someone she knows. I will speak to her and make my recommendation. Let's not delay. She cannot go on in this state."

The doctor got up to leave, patting Ruggiero's shoulder. "Stay calm. Mrs. Zicardo can be of great help."

It was Grandpa who responded this time, with sinister eyes and a furrowed brow.

"Doctor, I will tell you right now. If anybody out there has harmed my granddaughter, they've made a big mistake. They don't know who they are dealing with."

"I know, I know," the doctor replied, "but we don't know anything yet. Let's wait and see."

Once the doctor left, Grandpa turned to Ruggiero.

"We will not let anyone get away with this. Nobody touches my family, especially my grandchildren."

***

Don Francisco made his way to Mrs. Zicardo's place. He was a caring doctor and was emotionally attached to the plights of the poor town folks. Seeing Giuliana in her condition disturbed him immensely. She is definitely traumatised, the poor girl. He frowned at his own thoughts as he made his way to knock on the door of Mrs. Zicardo's home.

"Good day Renalta, I just took a chance to see if I'd be lucky enough to catch you at home. No emergency deliveries today?"

"Don Francisco! What a surprise! Come in, come in, please! What brings you down to the Borgo? Nothing serious I hope."

"I am not sure, but it could be very serious. I was over at the Ferrante's. Their young girl appears to be in a traumatised state. I need your help. I cannot go near her. She is very frightened."

The doctor followed Mrs. Zicardo into her living room and sat down next to her in a big armchair by the fireplace. The end of summer was delivering some cool breezes, and the warm fire was welcoming.

"Oh? I see." Mrs. Zicardo replied with concern. "Young Giuliana? She hangs around with my girls. She's very smart. She helps my daughters with their homework."

Don Francisco found her northern accent musical.

"I am glad. It's good that you know her. She may need your help badly right now."

"Really, what's happened to her?" Mrs. Zicardo was troubled by where this was going.

"That's what we need to find out. I cannot get near her for an examination. This is what I need you to do. I suspect she might have been molested."

"Oh, dear Lord! I hope not. She is such a good soul with a heart of gold."

"As you know, there are malicious people out there and they often target the best."

Mrs. Zicardo fell silent for a moment before meeting the doctor's eyes.

"Ok, Don. I will go as soon as they can receive me. I certainly want to help."

"Leave it for tomorrow; I think she has had enough for today. Give me the report and together we will come to a solution."

"I sure will, Doctor. Can I offer you anything to drink?"

"No, thanks. I must get going to visit my next patient." He stood up and motioned to leave. "Thank you, Signora Zicardo. I wish you luck and we will talk soon."

Mrs. Zicardo wished Don Francisco farewell and closed the door behind him. She brushed a hand through her hair shaking in anticipation. Tomorrow. Tomorrow I will give this poor girl all of my attention.

***

Giuliana remained in her room and wouldn't come down for supper again. Her mother patiently fixed a bowl of minestrone and brought it up to her, hoping she eventually would help herself to some if it were left unattended. The bronzing from her labour in the Mediterranean sun had not taken long to fade from Giuliana's skin. Her now pale face showed signs of malnutrition, and her two big sunken eyes glared, lost in fear.

Gioia had sent Grandma in her place to do laundry for some Artisans. She didn't feel comfortable leaving the house with Giuliana in such a morbid state. It rendered her restless and worried to no end. Plus, Don Francisco had advised her that Mrs. Zicardo was coming in the morning – she wanted to be there.

It was eleven in the morning when Mrs. Zicardo knocked on their door. Gioia couldn't have been happier to see her.

"Mrs. Zicardo, do come in please."

"Buon Giorno, Signora Ferrante." She greeted Gioia with a radiant smile. She was used to facing patients while bringing babies into this world. However, she knew her job also came with the occasional complications, and she was aware this visit could be a complicated one. Mrs. Zicardo was a professional and would not alarm Mrs. Ferrante or the rest of the family.

"As you know, I am here on the recommendation of Don Francisco. I want to see if I can help. Where is young Giuliana?"

"Mrs. Zicardo, I sure hope you can talk some sense into Giuliana. It's been ten days now. She spends most of the time in her room in the dark. We are worried sick about her. I hope she

21

will talk and open up to you because we have not been able. . ."

"Ok," Mrs. Zicardo said interrupting Gioia's train of thought before it could run any further. "Lead me to her and leave her with me alone. I will see what I can do."

Mrs. Zicardo was renowned for her cheery disposition and quiet resolve. Everyone loved her. She was a conventionally beautiful lady with blonde hair that fell to her shoulders. Her blue eyes gleamed with a constant hint of the loving care that she readily showed. Her frame was a bit on the stout side, but she stood with a straight back and impeccable posture that made her seem taller than she was and formidable. She was a single mother and her well-disciplined children respected her.

Leading the way upstairs, Gioia opened the door to Giuliana's room. They found her still huddled in a ball in bed.

"Giuliana, you have a visitor! Look, look who is here."

"Mom, please, why are you disturbing me?"

Mrs. Zicardo intervened, carrying on quite normally at first.

"Giuliana! What is going on? It's a beautiful day out there. Why would you choose to be inside? Lora and Sara have missed you dearly; they have been waiting for you to play your skipping games. Come on out. Let me see you."

After a pause, Mrs. Zicardo motioned to Mrs. Ferrante to leave the room before making her way towards Giuliana's bed. She put her bag on the bed and sat down beside her, carefully peeling the covers from the girl's head.

"My Angel, you are going to suffocate under those covers! There-there, let me see your lovely face. What is wrong my darling?" Mrs. Zicardo was stroking Giuliana's back affectionately. "Tell me how you feel. I am here to help you, Dear."

At first, Giuliana did not answer or respond in any way. But

Mrs. Zicardo was patient and knew that she just needed to keep reassuring Giuliana that she was there only to care for her.

"Giuliana, talk to me. We all need you. Your mom, dad, your grandmother, grandfather, even young Triza, they all need you. You don't have to tell me what's making you sad, but I promise I can help if you should want to talk. It is totally up to you, Dear."

Mrs. Zicardo remained there, in silence for two hours, caressing and gently petting her. Eventually, frightened Giuliana's head slowly started to move. Her hair, tangled, covered her blotchy, unwashed face. Mrs. Zicardo was pleased with this small act of progress.

"Ok, Darling, I will revive some life into you! Just stay there."

Mrs. Zicardo ran downstairs, fetched a white basin filled with fresh water and returned. She extracted a soft sponge from her black leather bag and poured lavender liquid soap into the bowl. She soaked the sponge and gently cleaned Giuliana's eyes and refreshed her face. Then, she took out a white jar of aloe Vera and lavender. Gentle strokes with the aromatic mixture helped sooth Giuliana's neglected face and skin.

"There-there, my beautiful girl. If you want, I can wash you up all over, and you will feel much better. Can I do that? I will need to change this water first."

"Oh no! No please!"

The girl forcefully pulled the covers over herself, defensively.

"Giuliana, I'll tell you what: I will prepare the water for you, and you will do it by yourself while I have a little chat with your mom. If you like, I will help you braid your hair after, once you are dressed. Why don't you put on your Sunday dress as well? It will please your family and make you feel better. And, if you feel up to it, you can come and join the girls and me for a nice plate of pasta! What do you think of that?"

She detected a sudden spark in Giuliana's eyes. But, just as quickly as the spark appeared, it faded away. Giuliana lowered her eyes and let out a faint whisper.

"I...feel so dirty."

"You must just try, darling. I promise you will feel much better." Mrs. Zicardo said quietly.

Pleased with her progress, Mrs. Zicardo ran down for fresh, clean water. She winked at Mrs. Ferrante in passing before returning upstairs.

"She is coming around," she promised. Although she hoped it was a promise that she could keep.

***

After a long wait, Giuliana was well-groomed in her Sunday best. The dress revealed her legs, which were blackened and bruised from her ordeal. Mrs. Zicardo glanced at the bruises for what seemed like a very long time before looking away without comment. With a new approach, Mrs. Zicardo asked,

"Giuliana, would you like to tell me what has been bothering you lately?"

Giuliana brought a hand to her mouth and began to shiver.

"Va Bene, Giuliana, it's ok," Mrs. Zicardo said with sympathy. "You don't have to tell me anything right now. Should you feel like it, you come and talk to me when you are ready. I am here to listen, Angel."

She kissed Giuliana on her forehead, picked up her bag and began to make her exit.

"I want you to promise me that you will leave this room and resume your mobility. Your family loves you. I know you love them too, don't you?"

Giuliana nodded with her head down blinking back tears. Mrs. Zicardo felt so sorry for her. It was too bad she had not been able to examine her but she preferred not to frighten her any further. Like the doctor, she too had a strong suspicion that something tragic had taken place with Giuliana. She hoped in time that she would come around and talk.

Chapter Three
In Search of Number Thirty-one

While Giuliana was struggling at home to regain her sanity, Orlando was assessing the cornfield in search of his new conquest. He had just gotten back from delivering corn to Spain. The load was delivered to the mill where it was then turned into oil. While walking through the field he took notice of his workers hard at their duties, but there was no sign of his fresh-faced number thirty-one.

"Hmm? Where could Liliana have placed her?" He mused aloud while continuing his search. Arriving at the shack, he spotted Liliana counting and weighing corn for the next load.

"Eh! Sunshine," he grinned, smacking her behind, "I don't see my number thirty-one girl on the field. Where did you place her?"

Liliana stopped her counting, visibly disturbed by Orlando's touch, presence, and inquiry. She spun around to face him.

"Why are you looking for her? After the job you did on her, you expect her to be here?"

"Eh, sunshine, what are you getting at? You know the girls love my touch. They should consider themselves lucky and privileged!"

Liliana's insides were electrified by his comment. She was not going to let this bastard get away with such delusions of his charm – job be damned.

"Look, Orlando, I think you are a sick, egotistical son-of-a-bitch. I happened to see the condition you left that poor girl in, and she was certainly not privileged or pleased by you."

A dark cloud passed behind Orlando's eyes. He stepped closer to her.

"Now, now. Watch the way you talk to me or you will go back to the field cutting corn!"

"I don't care anymore," Liliana replied, trying to hide the sudden fear that had come over her.

"What do you care? Do you forget that you earned your way into a promotion with your own charms?"

Furious, Liliana whirled around to smack his face but not before Orlando could duck.

"Yeah, you did promote me, in exchange for what? You took my body...my soul...my being." Liliana stumbled over her words as they finally found freedom, pouring from her mouth. "You disgust me."

"I think you forgot about how loud you were moaning."

Liliana felt sick.

"I was foolish to believe you cared. You tire fast and move on. You are an animal, Orlando!"

"Who gives you permission to talk to me like that? You forget I am your boss!" Orlando stepped forward and smacked Liliana across the face sending her sprawling across the floor of the shack. Liliana whimpered for a moment before regaining her feet and turning to look at Orlando again.

"You are disgusting!"

"Eh! She is sixteen! I tried to do her a favour, breaking her into the pleasures of life. You know the girls like that. You of all people should know that!"

"Oh yeah? All for this lousy job? You are a beast!"

Orlando brought his arm up ready to strike again when suddenly Sibilla appeared at the entrance. Immediately, he changed his tactic to his bounteous, sweet charm.

"Oh, Sibilla, glad you are here! I might have to get you a new assistant. Young Liliana is getting too mouthy and disobedient." He shot Liliana a stare with daggers in his eyes.

Sibilla, however, was unmoved by the remark.

"Look, Orlando, we are behind schedule. I have one hundred acres of corn to be picked and delivered by Friday. Liliana works efficiently for me; we have no time for changes right now. I suggest you get your own orders ready for your next shipment."

She gave Liliana a nod and quickly disappeared around the corner. Orlando's ego was visibly wounded by his inability to influence Sibilla. Liliana smiled back at the man.

"For your information, your number thirty-one never came back after you raped her. Yes, rape. That is what you did."

"What are you saying? I was trying to teach her the facts of life."

"Well, Orlando, the 'facts of life' did not register well with her. The girl never came back, and she vowed never to step foot in this place ever again. She despises you."

"Well, it's her loss. A new group will soon be hired. As for you, Liliana, Sibilla might have a use for you, but I certainly do not!"

"That girl you hurt, she is not like every other girl. I have a feeling this time that you made a big mistake..." She shook her finger at Orlando. "She is a smart girl, from a good family. They happen to have fallen in hard times right now, but I know for a fact she is well connected."

"What are you insinuating?"

"She might report you."

"Why am I wasting time listening to you." He retorted, walking away.

Liliana's nerves had gotten the best of her. She hated him. At only seventeen, she had been through plenty and was no longer afraid losing her job. Six months ago, she had found herself pregnant, and one of the town quacks had to perform the abortion for her. Liliana had barely survived, and her reward for her survival was to be alone in her despair, with no support from Orlando. Her pain from this loss was enough for her to want to hang him.

Later that day, Liliana was walking the field when she stumbled upon something on the ground. She bent over to pick it up, realising it was the hat given to Giuliana a couple of weeks back. It had holes in it and was smeared with mud and other debris. It was still in the row of the corn where the girl had been attacked. Tonight, on her way home, she would stop by Giuliana's house to return it to her and check on her well-being.

***

Gioia was sweeping the cobblestones in front of her home when Liliana approached.

"Good evening, Mrs. Ferrante. I am Liliana, the assistant at the cornfield from the Bifernina. I found this hat today; I think it belongs to Giuliana. I want to return it to her."

Gioia stopped her sweeping, intrigued, and looked up.

"Oh, hello. Yes, Thank-you." Gioia examined the hat. "That is hers. Do you want to come in? You can give it to Giuliana yourself."

"Thank-you. I would very much like to see Giuliana. How is she?"

Gioia put down her broom and quietly lead Liliana inside.

"She is coming along, but I must warn you, she is not her old self . . . would you happen to know what has taken place at the farm? She does not want to hear or be part of that place anymore."

"I see. It is a hard place to work. I don't blame her," Liliana said guardedly. "Can I talk to her?"

"Yes, of course."

Gioia escorted her in and called out to Giuliana to come down, but her efforts were ignored. Agitated from the embarrassment of her daughter's behaviour, she turned to Liliana.

"Liliana, let's go on up. She has been spending a lot of time in her room lately."

After leading her to her room, Gioia thought it would be best to leave the two girls alone. She purposely left the door ajar before heading back downstairs. Once at the bottom, her curiosity merged with her anxiety, leading her to tiptoe mid-way up the stairs. It was not her style to eavesdrop on their conversation, but she was desperate to discover anything that might solve the mystery of her daughter's change of behaviour.

Chapter Four
Liliana's Visit

"Giuliana," Orlando's assistant approached cautiously. "Hello, it's me, Liliana."

Totally taken by surprise, Giuliana, jumped up from her bed at Liliana's greeting. The covers came off her head.

"Liliana? What brings you here? I am glad to see you!"

Liliana lifted up the hat and presented it to her.

"This, I believe, is yours."

"Oh, that? Yes, it is mine. Sibilla gave it to me." Giuliana lowered her eyes to look down at the hat apprehensively. Liliana got the impression that the hat was a bad reminder.

"I thought I should bring it to you after you never came back. I have been concerned about you, Giuliana."

"I have not been out of the house much. I've been secluded in this room. I feel dirty Liliana . . . I cannot face my family or anybody for that matter." Her tears flowed freely.

"Giuliana, listen to me. You cannot go on like that. You need to get a hold of yourself. It was a bad experience, I know. You've had to deal with much more than most girls your age do. Have you told your mom and dad?"

Liliana sat beside her friend and sorrowfully wiped the tears from her cheeks.

"Oh, no! I cannot do that! Mom had the doctor and the midwife come. I did not say anything to them either. The doctor wanted to look, but I would not let him touch me. Mrs. Zicardo, she was nice, but I kept it to myself. I cannot tell anyone, Liliana. Reliving it gives me the shakes. I have nightmares every single night."

"Look, Giuliana, I like you, and I want to help you. All I can say is what I told you before: you are not the only one. You need to get a hold of yourself, and maybe together we can put Orlando in his place." The past began to come back to Liliana's mind. "He got me pregnant. I was traumatised. I could never accept having a piece of him growing inside me. I had an abortion."

"What? No!"

"It happened. He has taken many other girls. What do you say Giuliana? Let's stand together and put an end to his immoral actions. We can do this together, but you need to be brave and courageous. You will not solve anything hiding away in this room."

Giuliana was done crying. She sat up on the bed and held Liliana's outstretched hand. Liliana squeezed her hand.

"I must give you credit for not coming back."

Liliana had given her strength. Deep in her heart, Giuliana knew that everything she had said was right. She could not continue to live in seclusion. She needed to get over her nightmares.

"Liliana, you have been good to me. I should listen to you. What do I need to do first?"

"Tell your parents. You need to be checked. As painful as this is, you must do it."

"It's . . . it's just so scary."

"I know it is, but it needs to be done. Then, we will go to the police, and we will report him."

"You make it sound so easy. There is nothing I would like

better than to see him punished."

"Giuliana, besides being punished, we need to stop him. He cannot go on hurting girls like you and me and get away with it!"

Since the girls' conversation first began, Gioia had been listening from the stairs. She had experienced a multitude of emotions over the course of their conversation. Rattled, she did the sign of the cross. Goosebumps had crawled their way across the skin of her arms and back. Please Jesus, what am I hearing? Don't let it be true. She prayed.

In her room, Giuliana took a deep breath. She knew her friend was right; she needed to stop feeling sorry for herself. Liliana embraced her in a hug.

"Be brave. You are a smart girl. Don't waste life away here because of that man. Time is precious. Do what you have to do. You can count on me to back you up."

With that final assertion, Liliana got up and turned to leave.

At the sound of Liliana's sudden approach, Gioia jumped. Startled against her covert actions, Gioia almost fell down the stairs. She caught herself and rushed to get back into the kitchen. She quickly assumed what she thought appeared to be a well-constructed nonchalant manner. The conversation she had overheard had rendered her nervous as hell. She tried her utmost to appear normal for the girl's sake, but her body was jittering, which made her casual lean seem staged. Liliana entered the kitchen and extended her hand as she approached.

"Mrs. Ferrante, thank-you and good night. Giuliana will be fine, I can assure you of that."

"Thank you," Gioia answered, wanting desperately to believe the girl. "Thank you for stopping by. Can I offer you anything to drink?"

"No, thanks. I must run. Another day's hard work tomorrow! I need to get home to rest."

Once alone, Gioia began to pace back and forth while shaking her head. She was holding her chest with one hand, trying to contain her beating heart. Fearing the worst for her daughter, her mind careened through possible outcomes. A short time later the men arrived, followed by Grandma. Gioia had nothing on the stove. In her preoccupied state, preparing supper for the hungry troop had totally escaped her. Ruggiero was the first to notice.

"Gioia, what's going on here? Are we not going to eat tonight? I am hungry as a horse, and there is no sign of anything cooking. Where is our Giuliana? Don't tell me she is still up in her room?"

"She had a visitor, a sweet girl from the corn field actually, that's what kept me from making supper. Not to worry! I will have something on the table in no time."

Ruggiero gave his wife a peck on the cheek.

"Ok, Honey. In the meantime, I will go check on that Bambola doll of ours. Ok, my love? I will try to talk some sense into her. Maybe she will join us for supper."

"That will be great, Dear! You do that."

Once Ruggiero went upstairs, he found Giuliana washing up. We are improving - a good sign. He gave his daughter an affectionate hug and kissed her ruffled hair.

"Bambola! You are coming down to have supper with us?"

"Yes, Dad, as soon as I get dressed. I will help Mom with setting the table."

"Ay! That's my girl!"

Delighted, he gave her a caressing tug by her shoulder and darted downstairs to inform the rest of the family.

"Gioia, you said Giuliana had a visitor?"

"Yes. Liliana was up there a long time."

"Well, it must have done her good because she is coming

36

down. I was relieved not to find her under the covers. She is just washing up!"

Gioia smiled to her husband and contemplated a quick prayer. Please, please, God. Let things be good with our daughter.

***

The Ferrantes sat down for supper and all faces present were clearly pleased with the development that brought Giuliana down to dine with them. Grandma and Grandpa were particularly overjoyed, showering her with love and attention. They adored their oldest granddaughter. Giuliana was pleasant but not too talkative. Regardless, the four adults were grateful for the improvement and were not pressing her in any way. They knew she was a good girl. Whatever had shaken her up, they hoped that it would soon pass and their lovely Giuliana would be her old self again.

Giuliana moved her peas around her plate, preoccupied. The ugly secret sitting at the bottom of her soul was a burden that carved deeper and deeper into her being with each passing hour. She looked around at these four adults she loved and trusted most in the world. They seemed to be at her mercy, eager to please. They were hanging onto her every word and attentively watching every move. How can I bring myself to tell the truth? She wondered. They would be appalled and feel the hurt, just like she did. Giuliana took a deep breath and turned to look out the window. It was dark out there. For an instant, she had a flashback of the cornfield – dark and deserted. She could see Orlando's piercing grey eyes. She could feel the man forcing himself on her out of control. She could taste the salt from her blood and the dirt from the earth in her mouth. She quickly shook herself and started to chatter uncontrollably. She did not want to remember. The thoughts were just as disturbing as what took place. How ugly.

Maybe tomorrow it will be better with the daylight and sunshine. She would find the courage to tell her family then.

Chapter Five
The Tormented Mind

That night Giuliana's tormented soul played havoc on her already restless body. She tossed and turned, wrestling with her covers until streaks of daylight made their way through her window. Her tender mind was tarnished with many concerns: her young sister, Trizia, was due back in a couple of days, the school year would be starting soon, and the girls would be getting back into their usual routine. That meant Giuliana would have less privacy for the recurring nightmares. The hibernating in her room had to stop. Her stomach churned in misery. Liliana was right; she could not continue to feel sorry for herself. If they wanted to stop Orlando Alonza from hurting the town girls, they needed to act upon their shared secret. But deep in her heart, Giuliana was still a child. She had lived a sheltered life with her loving family. Another doubt surfaced in her mind. Liliana thinks I am sixteen; little does she know I have lied to them all. Maybe if I were sixteen, I would have more courage. Liliana had been the only one to show her kindness since that first day in the cornfield. I have deceived her.

The next morning Giuliana was deafened by the customary clanging noises coming from the kitchen. It had started earlier than usual. Giuliana, tired as she was, jumped out of bed and opened her bedroom window wide. The sun was bright, and there was not a cloud in the sky.

"Oh!" she exclaimed aloud, "What a perfect October morning." She breathed in the pristine air, invigorating her lungs with energy. Quickly she dressed and made it downstairs before losing her courage. There they were, having a cup of orzo with a piece of Grandma's homemade biscuit.

"Oh, Darling! Good morning! How nice of you to join us." Her dad greeted Giuliana while the rest of the family smiled in accordance.

"I will say!" Exclaimed Grandpa Luigi.

She took a seat as Grandma promptly got up to assist her with whatever was to offer.

"Grandma, please! Please, I don't feel like having anything, please sit down, I need to talk to all of you. It's taken a lot out of me to do this…" She took a deep breath and cleared her throat as her grandma returned to her seat. "Mom, Dad, Grandma, Grandpa, I don't know how to tell you this, but something terrible happened to me at the cornfield. Dad, that man Orlando, the one that hired me…" she choked, stopping to regain her breath, but uncontrollable tears inundated her face like a broken river dam. Giuliana could not go on.

Gioia ran to embrace her daughter, enveloping her in her arms.

"Oh! My darling, you know how much we have always wanted to protect you."

Gioia had not been sleeping well herself anymore after overhearing the conversation between Giuliana and Liliana. She had kept quiet, placing her feelings on hold. But now, with her daughter's outburst, she needed to face reality. The rest of the family jumped up to run to her side also.

"What? What did he do? Did he touch you?" Ruggiero demanded, his face livid in anticipation of that which he hoped not to hear.

"It was worse than that. I cannot say it," she responded with tears.

"You mean he molested you?" Luigi exclaimed in rage as he

began pacing back and forth like a crazy man. "We will take care of him, don't you worry."

Ruggiero, wide-eyed, pleaded with her.

"Tell me what he did to you, if you can, Darling."

"Dad, please don't ask me to describe it. The whole thing was horrible. I...I passed out. Liliana found me and helped me. That is why I never went back. I am having a hard time remembering. I just want to forget the whole thing." It was hard for Giuliana to convey the ordeal in detail to them.

"Oh! My Lord!" Grandpa and Ruggiero exclaimed while looking at each other like two warriors ready to attack.

Grandpa, infuriated, ran to get his hunting rifle. Ruggiero heatedly yanked open the kitchen drawers searching for the biggest knife he could find. He turned around, holding a butcher knife in his hand. Gioia and Grandma were screaming at the men. This was exactly what Giuliana feared would happen.

"Ruggiero! Hold on here! Where do you think you are going with those weapons?" Gioia intervened. "Do you want to make matters worse than they are? We will let the police take care of him."

Rosa was struggling to stop her husband from loading his gun, but Luigi was now mad beyond control. Gioia was also holding Ruggiero back, trying to talk sense into him.

"Ruggiero! Put that knife back! We need to deal with this without going crazy!" She turned to her father-in-law. "You too, Dad! Get rid of that rifle! You are scaring Giuliana even more! Stop being stupid! We need to handle this the right way!"

Giuliana, crying hysterically, did not know how to stop the chaos occurring in her house. Suddenly, from the top of her lungs, she called out.

"Grandpa! Dad! I should not have told you anything! Put those weapons away and stop it!"

They were blind with fury. The two ignored Giuliana and her mother's pleas and ran out the door heading down the hills of the countryside. They were going to find Orlando and make him pay. The women were now in despair, unsure of what to do next.

"Gioia, let's go. We need to run and summon my sons," Rosa ordered her daughter-in-law.

"Thank God they live close by. They need to stop those two from taking the law into their own hands."

In no time, Rosa was knocking on Raniero's door and Gioia on John's. John and Raniero lived on the same street a block apart. The hard banging on the door brought Raniero quickly out of bed to look out the bedroom balcony.

"Mom? Is it you? What's going on? What's the hurry? What's happened?" He sensed urgency.

"There is no time to explain. Get dressed! You need to go stop your father and your brother. They left armed to kill that Spanish guy at the Bifernina's cornfield!"

"What? Why?"

"I told you there is no time to explain! Gioia is getting John now. Please! Run! Before it's too late!"

Raniero made the sign of the cross and ran to join John. Gioia and Rosa were ahead of him already banging on John's door. John answered the door confused and full of questions. Raniero was the first to respond.

"Look, John, apparently those two bozos lost their marbles! Let's not waste any time! We have to stop them before they do something foolish. We need to find them."

***

One of the attendees on duty, Renato, saw the two wild characters approaching. He was puzzled and didn't know what to make of them. But, he knew they looked dangerously agitated. At first he thought they were hunters, but soon realised they were approaching for a much more serious matter.

Ruggiero and Luigi were fuming when they arrived at the farm. They were ready to take Orlando on. Luigi put a hand on Ruggiero's shoulder and with a firm grimace he ordered him to stand down.

"Son, it's not your job. I will take care of him. Until I stop breathing, I will always remain the head of our family, and as the head it is my responsibility to protect my family. You see this?" He pointed at his rifle. "Two bullets are going right through his eyes."

Renato saw the men talking. Maybe they are just in the wrong place. But that one guy is holding a kitchen knife! He called out to the men.

"You are on private property here, fellows."

Grandpa was the one to respond.

"We know exactly where we are. We are looking for the Spanish guy. Where is he?"

"You mean Orlando Alonza?"

"Yes, that's exactly who we are looking for?"

"Sorry, he is not here. He's gone on delivery, taking a load to the North."

"When will he be back?" Asked Luigi with an authoritative voice.

"Probably by Friday, I am not too sure," said Renato, with some caution.

Luigi and Ruggiero, disappointed, looked at each other. Grandpa nodded his head to leave. They certainly could not attempt to search for him on the highway. They did not own a car.

"What has he done? Why are you looking for him? Do you want to talk to Sibilla, the owner?" Renato had clearly gathered that these guys were really troubled by something important.

"No, no, we don't want to talk to anyone. Will wait for him to return. Please don't mention we are looking for him."

Renato nodded in agreement and waved them away. He did not like those two, but he figured Orlando must have been up to no good. He wiped the trickling sweat from his forehead as the father and son turned around to leave.

"Come on Son, let's leave this place for now. But I promise you, come Friday we will return."

"Papa, your blood is running through my veins. Anybody that hurts my family will pay."

On their way back, they ran into John and Raniero. Papa Luigi was the first to speak.

"What are you guys doing this way?"

"What do you think? Have you two gone nuts or something? You have scared all of us! Mom and Gioia are beside themselves, and Giuliana is hysterical! What's going on here? Have you two lost your minds?"

Raniero glanced at the knife in Ruggiero's hand. John noticed as well.

"For heaven's sake, Ruggiero, get that knife out of your hand! You can be arrested if someone sees you! We need to let the law handle things properly. You have both turned into a couple of lunatics!"

"Look you two, tell us what has happened," John piped in. "We will go to the police and have them handle it. Do you want to end up in jail for murder for the rest of your life? You, Ruggiero, did you stop to think of your daughters and your wife? And Papa, you are just as crazy! Do you want to spend time behind bars at your old age? Hot heads! Do you not realise the consequences?"

Ruggiero shot a look at his brother.

"John, it's easy for you to talk. This guy had the guts to touch my flesh and blood, my precious daughter. I tell you, he will pay! And Papa feels as I do."

"Eh! I am not saying he has to get away with it! I am with you! Of course, he needs to be punished, but let the authorities take care of him."

"John is right," said Raniero, "you both need to calm down and let the police handle the matter."

"It's not as easy as that!" Ruggiero was getting angrier. "Giuliana will be exposed. She will have to go through plenty once the town folks hear about it. She is scarred for life. My beautiful, precious girl!"

"Do you have a choice? Unless the whole thing is hushed up and we forget about it!" said Raniero.

"Are you serious? He has to deal with me," responded Grandpa Luigi.

"Papa, you have always been a sensible man. But I think at your old age you lost your brain! You are definitely making no sense!"

Luigi was still enraged.

"This guy is lucky he wasn't there. These bullets were ready for his eyes!"

"Oh my God! Papa, I cannot believe what you are saying. You will do no such thing. Our father will not turn into a murderer."

***

Gioia and Grandma gave a collective sigh of relief once the four of them appeared at the door. Grandma Rosa called out.

"Raniero, John, please come in and sit down and talk some sense into these two stubborn mules."

Giuliana was sick to her stomach and confused by the whole ordeal. She now remembered why she had chosen the darkness of her room day and night for refuge. She had been terrified of upsetting the family. Should I have kept my secret and spared them the grief? Maybe this is why the other girls have kept quiet? No... That is the easy way out. Her young mind was rustling with thoughts. Giuliana might have been only twelve, but her caring and loving nature was that of a much more mature woman. She remembered Liliana's words:

"I will back you up, the two of us."

Liliana is right. The two of us, together, can stop this predator and hopefully bring his abuses to an end. Giuliana bravely got up, wiped her teary eyes, and spoke to the adults gathered around the kitchen table.

"Mom, Dad, all of you. I want to do what is right. But first, you, Grandpa, and you too Dad, need to promise me that you will stop this nonsense of shooting and killing him yourselves! Liliana will help me, she promised. What he did to me he did to her also, and to many other girls. This is why we need to stop him. We will go to the police and report him."

Raniero, the oldest brother, spoke up.

"Of course, that is the right thing to do. Not the way these two clowns think. We certainly do not want a murder on our hands!"

"Yes, Raniero, you are right. Liliana seemed caring and genuine toward our daughter," said Gioia.

"We need to talk to her again then. What do you say, sweetheart?" he asked, turning to Giuliana.

"Yes, Dad, we should." She hugged him for reassurance.

She was glad her family had joined in support. They gave her strength. The heavy weight on her soul was lifting with newfound hope.

GINA IAFRATE

Chapter Six
The Testimony

The following morning Giuliana awoke to the gentle touch of her Mom's hand stroking her messy brown hair. She stretched her body, now reinforced with a sense of support and love. She greeted her mother with a faint smile. Gioia had been sitting there quietly observing her daughter for hours. How could that invader hurt my precious baby?

Giuliana sat up shaking her head, surprised but pleased to see her mom.

"Mom, how long have you been here? I didn't hear you come in. "

"It makes me happy to see you peacefully asleep."

Giuliana suddenly circled her arms around her mom's neck in a tender, loving embrace. Gioia held her daughter close for a long time as if her maternal touch could protect her from the cruel world outside the room. Reluctantly, she broke away as delicately as she could.

"Sweetheart, we are all glad and proud of you for wanting to report Orlando, but I know we must do one thing for your sake."

"What is that, Mom?"

"Sweetie," she took a deep breath, "you need to be checked physically. It's for your own safety. I could call Mrs. Zicardo, Dear. That would also serve to verify evidence for the police report."

"Mom, it's embarrassing. I don't want to submit myself to that!"

"Darling, Mrs. Zicardo is a professional. You will be fine with her. We must do it! Don't you agree?"

She gave her daughter a reassuring look.

"Oh, Mom. No. Please…"

"Believe me. I wish you didn't have too, but you must!"

Giuliana closed her eyes for a moment before looking back into her mother's, mercifully begging with her gaze.

"If you say so," she said, finally agreeing.

Gioia gave a big sigh of relief.

***

The next morning, Mrs. Zicardo arrived with her black bag.

"Good morning, Gioia!" She was smiling, as always, sending positive energy.

"Good morning, Signora. Please do come in."

Mrs. Zicardo came in swiftly, turning towards Gioia. With a soft voice, she began.

"Gioia, I am afraid I must have complete privacy with Giuliana. This will be difficult for her, but I promise I will use my utmost professionalism and care. I will write a report for Don Francisco afterwards. From there, he can pass it along to the chief of police."

Gioia tried to hide her shaking hands; they tremored from her nerves.

"Yes, Mrs. Zicardo. I know it's not an easy task. Giuliana is

50

trying to be brave. In your care, she will be fine."

Mrs. Zicardo wore an aura of lightness as she entered Giuliana's room. She approached her cheerfully.

"How is my favourite girl today? Look what I brought for you - some chocolates from Bologna!"

"Oh! Thanks," responded Giuliana, pleased.

"I am here to help, Dear. Whatever you confide in me will be confidential. However, I will need to report to the doctor in town for his records."

Giuliana nodded in agreement. Mrs. Zicardo, as gently as she could, went on with her questions and performed her examination, keeping Giuliana distracted at the same time. After the physical was over, it was clear to see her hymen had been torn and violated. Since she had daughters of her own and felt deeply for Giuliana, the findings disturbed her immensely.

"Giuliana, I am sorry that you had to endure this unpleasant check-up. This could bring justice to the pain you have endured at the hands of this man," Mrs. Zicardo said softly. She wondered if Giuliana was the aggressor's first or even last victim. This was not her first case, sadly.

"Yes, Mrs. Zicardo. My friend, Liliana will help vouch for me against this man. She was a victim as well." Giuliana seemed to reply to Mrs. Zicardo's private thoughts.

"Giuliana, I want you to know that brave girls like you go places in life. You will be fine once you put this behind you. You can come and talk to me anytime you feel troubled, Dear. Remember that."

With that, Mrs. Zicardo kissed Giuliana on her forehead. Before exiting, she turned to the sweet child one last time, choosing her words as delicately as she could.

"It's lovely outside. Why don't you get dressed and join my

girls to play outdoors? They are competing with their skipping ropes. You are good at that!" She didn't wait for a response, but smiled and closed the door softly behind her.

Gioia was downstairs waiting anxiously for Mrs. Zicardo. Walking back and forth, her out-of-control nerves foretold only the worst results.

"Gioia, my Dear," Mrs. Zicardo called out, interrupting the patrolling as she put her arm around Gioia's shoulder, "I am sorry to report what we already know: there are definitely signs of molestation. But, Giuliana is young, and with the right counselling she will put the event behind her and will be fine. She is a bright girl; let's give her some time."

Mrs. Zicardo tightened her hold as she felt Gioia's body shiver. The blow was too much for her and she broke down sobbing.

"Now, Gioia," Mrs. Zicardo chided, "you don't want Giuliana to see you like that. I know how you feel. For her sake, try to get a hold of your composure. You know she needs you now more than ever."

"Thank you, Mrs. Zicardo," Gioia mumbled, wiping her tears.

"I have to make a report for Don Francesco. With that, we can notify the police. We will have proof and you can then lay charges against the perpetrator."

"Yes, of course. I am sure we will."

***

Nothing was going to stop Ruggiero and Luigi's vendetta against the Spanish worker. After Gioia had relayed Mrs. Zicardo's information to the men, they were so agitated and couldn't wait to put actions in motion. Rosa did not trust the two of them to go out alone. She insisted that John and Raniero go along with them to the police station. In the meantime, Rosa and Gioia would get in touch with Liliana Manzana and her widowed mother, Agnes. It was imperative for Liliana to go along with Giuliana to the authorities. Of course, Liliana would come, as promised. She was eager to do her duty.

***

The Chief of police, Nicola Del Conte, was overwhelmed in receiving the large group of rowdy people. Usually, the town was quiet with nothing major to pursue. Two more police officers were present to assist in accommodating the group and to take notes during the interrogation. Nicola was in his late forties but still towered over his two assistants. His black uniform confirmed his position of power, especially with his pistol pinned at his waist-side. He removed his hat after saluting Giuliana's family. His jet-black hair was cut in a military style, accentuating the thick eyebrows that hung above his big, dark brown eyes. His grave features suited his position. A sharp pang of fear hit Giuliana's stomach upon meeting him. Liliana felt somewhat intimidated also. No, I am not going to let my young friend down, she repeated to herself like a mantra. She mustered up as much courage as she could and stood erect to assert herself.

When Nicola spoke, he seemed surprisingly gentle and caring. His assistants, Alfonso Romolo and Giorgio Marinaro, had joined the force from the army. They were two young men in their mid-twenties, both respectful and proud of the uniform they wore. This small collection of men accounted for the entirety of the police force that the town employed. Usually, the crimes they investigated were limited to people trying to steal a few feet of land from their adjacent neighbour, or thieving sheep, cattle, chickens and pigs in the leanest years. At this moment, the men's faces signalled a clear message of discontent. They would be dealing with a severe matter for the first time.

The Caserma consisted of a fair size room with two small windows. It held a long rectangular wooden table with high back bamboo chairs. There was a dim light hanging from the ceiling, which produced hardly enough light to work with. The marshal sat at the centre of the table with officer Alfonso at his side. He was ready to take notes, with pen and paper on hand. Giorgio stood beside Nicola, observing and supervising the family. The custodian had arranged for a few extra chairs for the family members to sit down on.

"I guess we will start with this young lady here," Nicola nodded, referring to Liliana.

Liliana stepped forward, trying hard to conceal her nervousness.

"State your name, please," asked Officer Alfonso.

"Liliana Manzana."

Slowly and methodically, the marshal interrogated Liliana, sympathising with her while using his utmost professionalism to put her at ease. Alfonso quickly jotted down the information. Everyone listened attentively while Liliana painfully recollected her ordeal under the tyranny of Orlando's control.

"Miss Manzana, please, in your own words and to the best of your knowledge, tell us about your relationship with Orlando Alonza," Nicola asked.

"Sir, I was hired by Orlando Alonza to work at the cornfield. My job was to pick the corn from the stalk, just like the other workers."

"Was there a relationship between you and Mr. Alonza, other than a work related one?"

"Yes, Sir. A few days after I started work, Mr. Alonza began to make passes at me. He had demands . . . and he stressed that it would be in my best interest to cooperate – that I would benefit from it all."

"In what way?" Nicola scratched his chin.

"I would be employed. My job would be lighter. . . but it required that I please him as he wished."

"Would you say the act of intimacy was considered consensual by yourself and this fellow? Since you accepted his advances and participated?"

"No, Sir! It was against my wishes and my wants, but I needed the job. He said if I did not please him then I would be working on the hardest jobs in the field, or be replaced! He said if I complied I would keep my job, and he would promote me."

"Oh, what kind of position would that have been?"

"An assistant supervisor," she replied, pained.

"That meant that you were in compliance and in agreement with his advances." The officer's tone was flat.

"No! No, I was not. He forced himself on me; it was totally against my will! When he threatened to fire me, I gave in." Liliana was fighting back tears. "You see, Sir, my Dad died three years ago. It is hard for Mom to leave the house. My younger brothers are twins only three years old, born just after Dad died. The money he left is not enough to feed the four of us."

"I see. This is why you submitted to the abuse, in order to keep the job?"

"Yes, Sir. It was awful. I got pregnant. Once I expressed that to Orlando he laughed in my face and told me not to repeat that mistake ever again. He slapped me violently. He kicked me and beat me. The day I told him, I was left bleeding on the ground."

The two policemen and the marshal did not seem shocked. In fact, they didn't so much as blink an eye. They had heard such gossip around town but it was never formally reported until now.

"Go on, Miss Liliana, tell us all you can," the officer encouraged. "I know this is painful for you. We are here to help." Nicola said in a soft tone.

Liliana, trembling, took a deep breath and let out a big sigh. Still fighting back tears, she continued.

"He forcefully grabbed my arms and shook me violently, hollering: 'I had nothing to do with it. Do you understand? You are nothing but a cheap slut.' That is what he said to me. He was trying to blame me. 'How dare you?' he said, and then he slapped me again. He said he would kill me if I told a soul."

"Did he approach you afterwards with more sexual demands?"

"No, he would only look at me with disgust. I was relieved, but I knew he had just moved on to other girls."

"Do you know for a fact that he molested some of the other girls? Did you actually see him? Did anybody else complain or report his misbehaviour to the management?"

"No, Sir. Most of the girls would have been too afraid to do so."

"What makes you so sure of that?"

"Because most of the town folk are desperate for a job! Besides, he would threaten them if they ever spoke out."

"Miss Liliana, you are assuming this. I understand clearly what he has done to you. Other than Miss Giuliana here, do we have other women that you know for sure that have been molested?"

"Not really, I just suspected."

"How did you come to this conclusion?"

"He usually made me assign a girl in a secluded area, distant from other workers. That is how I knew."

"You did not actually see him molest other girls, though. Correct?"

"No. Not until I found Giuliana beaten and tossed on the dirt. That's when I knew he had gotten to her."

"Did he ever talk about other girls to you, or of his intentions?"

"Yes. He often bragged to me of the girls he sought after. I feared for Giuliana when he instructed me to place her far away from the rest."

"Didn't you feel a certain sense of responsibility to warn Giuliana against Signor Alonza?"

"Yes, I did. But, I was scared to say anything. He would have beaten me up, or fired me!"

"I see."

Nicola looked over at Alfonso, who was scribbling furiously in his notepad. He looked up at his boss and gave him a nod.

"What happened with your pregnancy?"

"My Mamma had to take me to a Magara, a quack, for an abortion. It was in a farmhouse out in the country. The whole thing was so dirty... What I experienced nearly killed me. It was the worst thing I ever had to go through, but that is why I am here, Sir. No one should be put through the same torture. As for Giuliana, I want to do my part to keep her from ending up with the same fate. She was smart to not come back to work. You know, Sir, he was looking for her after he came back from his out of town deliveries. He called her number thirty-one."

"Oh? Why was that?"

"He usually hires thirty people at a time. I think Giuliana was hired for his convenience; the extra one."

The marshal had daughters of his own. He shook his head. With a masked look, he turned to his assistants.

"We need to get this guy at all costs."

He turned and put his arm on Liliana's shoulder in an act of kindness, showing protection and reassurance.

"Miss Liliana, you can be reassured that my Carabinieri here," he said, gesturing to his fellow officers, "and myself will do all we can to bring this fellow to justice. I am sorry you did not come to us sooner, and I am sorry for what he did to you. I am glad you came forward. I admire you and your friend's courage."

"I am sorry I had not spoken sooner. I care about Giuliana. This is why I am here, Sir."

"You did the right thing. I think we have all we need from you, Liliana. Carabiniere Alfonso has been taking notes. He needs you to sign the declaration of the interrogation."

Liliana, once dismissed, let out a big sigh. She walked head down, embarrassed to look at the people present. However, she felt as if a big weight had been lifted from her chest. It was now Giuliana's turn. Sitting erect between her parents, she was awash with an aura of courage and assertiveness that surprised her.

"Miss Giuliana, can you come forward please?" asked chief Nicola Del Conte with a pleasant smile of encouragement.

Without hesitation, Giuliana promptly stood up and walked to his desk. Gioia and Ruggiero looked at each other. Their frightened young daughter seemed strong and feisty. Her frowned forehead and poignant eyes showed determination.

"That Liliana girl has empowered her," Gioia whispered to Ruggiero.

Alfonso led her to the chair in front of chief Nicola Del Conte and Giorgio.

"Please, take a seat Miss Ferrante," said Giorgio in an amiable voice.

"State your name please," said Alfonso in routine fashion.

"Giuliana Ferrante."

"Giuliana," said Nicola, "you are here with a few members of your family, I see." He lifted his head to give a second look at the Ferrante clan. "Can you tell us, to the best of your recollection,

58

how you came into contact with Orlando Alonza, and him with you?"

"Sir, a job. I was looking for work."

"A job? Are you still in school Miss Ferrante?"

"No, Sir."

"How old are you Miss Ferrante?"

Giuliana looked at her parents and hesitated for a moment. She cleared her throat and held back for a moment, then glanced at Liliana.

"I am twelve years old, Sir."

Liliana gasped and brought a hand to her mouth.

"You are rather young to work on the cornfield. What made you seek work there?"

"My dad and I went together. I got hired, but he didn't."

"I see. Mr. Alonzo hired you – I am told – by making an exception to the number of workers he was supposed to hire."

"I am not sure, Sir. He said I was number thirty-one."

"Was he aware that you were only twelve years old?"

"No, Sir."

"How is that?"

"I was desperate to be hired. My dad has been out of work for a long time… we needed the money. When he asked me how old I was, I lied. I am sorry Sir, but I told him I was sixteen." Tears rolled down her face, beyond her control. Nicola Del Conte turned to Alfonso who was taking down the report and whispered to him.

"You underlined that? We are dealing with a minor here." Nicola turned back to Giuliana. "Miss Ferrante, can I call you Giuliana?"

"Yes, please do," she promptly replied like a mature adult.

"Ok, Giuliana. I know this is very painful for you. Can you tell us in plain words and to the best of your recollection what took place at the cornfield and how Orlando Alonza made advances toward you?"

"Sir, I never did see him much since I had been hired. The Friday afternoon I was working, I turned to find him behind me. He gawked at me from head to toe and then he went away for a short time. Soon he was there again with a strange look on his face. I thought, 'This guy is up to no good, what does he want from me?' Then, he jumped at me..."

"How did he force himself on you? Was he violent? Sorry, but do you mind describing it in more detail?"

Giuliana looked at the members in the room, and then turned back to the marshal to recall every detail of the event.

"He pressed his body against mine. I was shocked and uncomfortable. When I pushed him away, he moved behind me. I felt both of his hands grab my legs. I turned to strike him with the scythe, but he grabbed my arm and shook it violently. The scythe flew on the ground away from me. He tried hugging and kissing me... I fought him as hard as I could. At one point I got away from him and I ran. I screamed for help. But I lost my footing when he had caught up with me. He grabbed the back of my legs and dragged my body. I was face down on the ground. I kept trying to scream, but no one heard me, everyone was too far away I guess... After what seemed like forever, I lost consciousness. I awoke on the ground alone, in a mess. That is when Liliana found me. Even with my blurred vision I recognised the look of horror on her face, but I realised that she would help me. I remember that she knelt beside me and hugged me. Then she helped me up and took me to the creek to wash up before walking me home. Liliana was a Godsend. I was relieved to see her, and she helped me."

Nicola Del Conte rubbed his head but maintained a stern

expression on his face.

"Giuliana, I promise you, we will bring this fellow to justice. I am sorry for this whole ordeal and for having put you through this unpleasant recollection. You need to sign this declaration also, like your friend, and then we will move forward to do what we need to do."

The Ferrantes all listened attentively. When Giuliana was dismissed, Gioia and Rosa ran to embrace the child and to shower her with their love. She walked between them as they all cried together. Luigi was fuming, grinding his teeth back and forth and bouncing on his chair. Ruggiero's eyes were obscured by a frown.

"Papa, I can't wait to get my hands on this guy," Ruggiero threatened.

John put his hands on Ruggiero's shoulders.

"Look, brother, I know how you feel and believe me – my blood is boiling too. But, we need to remain calm."

"Guys, we are here now. These fellows are men of the law. They will do what is right," Raniero said in a calm voice.

Liliana made her way over to the Ferrante's. She hugged her young friend and looked straight into her eyes.

"Giuliana, you are one heck of a brave and courageous girl. I have to give you credit for not coming back to work." She squeezed Giuliana's arms.

"Liliana, you gave me courage after you told me what he put you through. I couldn't be afraid anymore."

"I was foolish... but now, together, we will stop him," responded Liliana, smiling back at the girl.

The Ferrantes glared in admiration at the two young girls. As they gathered themselves to leave, Luigi stepped aside with a strange grin on his face. He went over to Nicola Del Conte.

"Signor Del Conte, you have to do me a personal favour. You must allow me and my son to come along. I want to take a look at this guy and spit in his face. Can I have that satisfaction?"

"Now, Mr. Ferrante, let us take care of him. I know that you are very upset and I don't blame you. But leave him to us."

"You must allow my son and me to come! I just want to see him sweat when you handcuff him."

"No. Please, we cannot afford to do anything foolish here. I recommend that you carry no rifle, no knife, no weapon of any sort. I prefer you stayed away from the situation. Let us handle it by the rules of the law."

"Signor," Luigi pleaded, "I am a hunter. My son and I have hunting licenses. We are entitled at this time of the year to walk in certain areas of the fields. No one can stop us."

"Ok. Stay in your zone – that is all I am asking."

Luigi was a stubborn and old-fashioned kind of a man. He wanted so badly to be part of the action that would bring Orlando to justice and wasn't about to give up his personal vendettas that easily. But, he swallowed hard, thinking to himself. I need to see the outcome of this with my own eyes. I don't want any under the table deals here at my granddaughter's expense. Nicola, reading Luigi's mind, slapped Luigi firmly on the shoulder.

"Mr. Ferrante, we will get a warrant for his arrest and move in on him as soon as we can."

Chapter Seven
A Change of Season

Fall approached and nature was producing bountiful magic. Mantels of purple, yellow, and fuchsia were spreading vivaciously across the undulating valleys. The days were getting shorter, and the sun was hiding more and more behind the clouds. It had been many months since Giuliana had reached the last year of schooling offered in the small town, and since concluding her studies the fall no longer harkened a return to class. Without the promise of school, the season seemed oddly discharged of its usual energy. In order for her to continue her studies, it would be necessary to move to the big city in the province, but her family just didn't have the means for this to transpire. Ruggiero felt pangs of guilt. Often at night he tossed and turned in bed unable to sleep, worrying about the future of his family.

The arrival of cloudy, gloomy days meant Giuliana was often confined indoors. Trizia was still happily attending school and the house was decidedly quiet in her absence. Some of Giuliana's friends were fortunate to be sons or daughters of landowners, blessed with opportunities that took them to the city to further their studies or to take apprenticeships to learn a trade. Giuliana had no such outlet except the refuge of her room and her old books. Looking to find something else to occupy her daughter, Gioia had departed one morning to inquire about work with the seamstress, Beatrice.

"Signora, could you have Giuliana come and help you with your sewing? I wish to keep her occupied." Gioia asked over coffee.

"Sorry, Gioia, I don't have enough work here. She would be an extra body in the way, I'm afraid." Beatrice responded.

Gioia was disappointed. She knew deep down that if she had been able to bring Beatrice bottles of oil or a fine prosciutto, Giuliana's odds would have greatly improved. This was the way of things and had enriched the prospects of some of the others who came for coffee with Beatrice in the past. But unfortunately Gioia's family had no possibility for such lavish gifts to give away freely. Therefore, there would be no favours found here. Gioia wrapped up her visit and returned home. She would keep praying and hoping for life to get better. Gioia often confided in her mother-in-law when she felt overwhelmed.

"Mom, I can accept this misery but I certainly want better for my girls. My heart aches for Giuliana," Gioia said shortly after coming through the door.

"I take it you were unsuccessful? I suspected as much, sadly." Rosa, being the spunky mature lady, was quick to change her tone and drop the resignation from her voice. "Gioia, have faith. Our Giuliana is kind and a smart, loving girl. I am sure the good Lord has something great saved for her."

"Thanks, Mom. You are always positive; that's what I like about you! I sure hope you are right. I know Papa ridicules your constant praying but I am with you in this faith."

Gioia extended her arm onto Rosa's shoulder and smiled.

***

October quickly rolled into November. On the second of the month came The Day of the Dead. The heavy rain pounding on the rooftop woke Gioia earlier than usual. In the hold of this hallowed date, she knew a long and dutiful day lay ahead. She got up and peeked out her bedroom window. It was still pitch black outside. A drizzling, grey day seemed to be surfacing from the hilltops and rapidly descending onto the village. She could see the misty fog slipping in from the valley, lifting slowly to meet the dreary sky. She opened her window and bent over to look below her onto the street. Some of the townsfolk were already making their way to the fields, tending to their morning duties. Later, most of them would make their way to the cemetery. Today, the whole town would awake in a sombre mood, reliving the memories of their late loved ones.

The previous day, Gioia and her family had attended mass to joyfully reinforce their faith in honour of All Saints Day. But today, they too would make their way to the cemetery to pay tribute to the dead. Everyone from the town went on foot carrying their chrysanthemums, candles, and ornaments to embellish tombs and graves. The chrysanthemums were the flower of sadness in this particular part of the region. Regardless of the colour, the beautiful scent of the mums was heavy. These flowers were to represent the heart and soul still mourning in pain. By nine in the morning, a flow of people carrying their offerings of mums of every colour lined the street in a single procession. A lot of the women were dressed in black, mourning and reciting the beads in prayer. Their painful and lamenting tones could be heard in unison; murmurs expressing their sorrow.

The dark, thick clouds in the sky had ceased their downpour temporarily. The heavy rain had been relentless the night before, as if in preparation for the day. Trizia had woken up in a sweat; she was having nightmares. The night before, Grandfather Luigi and Grandmother Rosa had been telling ghost stories around the fireplace. Both Giuliana and Trizia loved story telling by their grandparents, especially the spooky ones.

***

"Grandma, please! We are done with the evening prayer. It's story time now!" Trizia implored that night.

This was their usual form of entertainment. Sometimes Rosa would recount stories of departed ancestors. Both Giuliana and Trizia were interested in the past lives of their relatives who had passed onto the other world. That night, Giuliana asked her grandmother a question.

"Grandma, do you think our old relatives are in heaven, purgatory, or hell?"

"Oh my Dear, your great Nonna Maria was a good soul. I am sure she is in heaven," her Grandmother replied with a laugh.

"I am glad, Grandma! You know the nuns? When they preach the Catechism they always say we need to do good actions, otherwise we go to the fires of hell or purgatory for a period of time to pay our penance and then pass into heaven."

"I know, Dear. If you are a good Christian and follow the Ten Commandments, you will be fine." Giuliana's grandmother was patiently explaining this to the girl while quietly wondering what was inspiring such a conversation.

"I know, Grandma. But sometimes it's hard. If we miss mass, it is a big sin. If we eat meat on Friday, it is a sin. But I suppose we don't have to worry about that as much because we have no meat – period!" Giuliana said with a wry smile.

"You love thy neighbour as you love yourself and don't do onto others what you don't like for yourself. Then, you commit no sins," her grandmother continued.

"Ok! Ok, Rosa!" Intervened Grandpa Luigi, "Stop brainwashing these girls with your sainthood preaching. Some of it is all hogwash." He waved his arm to silence Rosa and turned to the girls with a smirk on his face. He lowered his voice to capture their attention. "Look, girls, I've got some stories for you that will wake you up from your sleep. These are real ones. Forget about the nuns and the priests at church. They just want to keep you intimidated."

With that, Grandpa got his turn. He and Rosa always seemed to be in competition with one another, but he had a way of seizing his granddaughters' curiosity. His stories were different. He provided bizarre occurrences of the past that transpired in the old town and around the cemetery. Trizia found it scary but intriguing. Giuliana, although twelve, always managed to still be captivated by Grandpa. Listening to his stories was fun.

"Grandpa! Ok, tell us!" Trizia egged him on, listening with her eyes wide-open.

"Don't go telling them scary stories, Luigi!" retorted Rosa. "They are not funny! I don't want the girls disturbed with your nonsense ghost stories, especially tonight. We are going to the cemetery tomorrow!"

Luigi laughed, ignoring Rosa's comments. Giuliana and Trizia were ready to listen. After all, Trizia thought, I am sharing the bed with Giuliana. There was a comfort to be had in that, to be sure. But, even so, during the night Trizia had woke up shaken and screaming from her grandfather's haunting ghost tales. She turned to her sister for consolation.

"Giuliana, wake up please! I want the light turned on. Please, please! This awful skeleton is trying to drag me into a well!"

Giuliana jumped up to turn the light on. She found her younger sister terrorised with freight. She was pale as a ghost.

"Trizia, you imagine things. There is no one here!"

"Giuliana! You cannot see him because he is a ghost! He was pulling me in this dark place with dirty water. I was going deep down!" Trizia remembered, breathless in her relating. Giuliana put her arms around her, trying hard to reassure her younger sister.

"Trizia, you are dreaming. Look! We are in our room. Everything is fine." Disoriented herself, with half-shut eyes,

Giuliana continued, "Go back to sleep Trizia, and let me sleep too. There are no ghosts. Grandpa just made those stories up to amuse us."

But that night Giuliana did not feel so sure herself. The room did feel spooky. Grandpa's tales really had intensified the mood around them. The plans to spend the day at the cemetery added to the disquiet. Giuliana recited a silent prayer for courage while stroking her sister's hair. Before long, Trizia was snoring with total abandon. Giuliana, having drifted off herself, was again awoken by noises. As she concentrated on listening, her ears were overtaken by the heavy rain that was hitting the shingles. The windows were rattling from the fury of the wind blowing. At this time of the year, Grandma would always say that the west winds from the mountains were battering up the town with a vengeance, taking no pity on the sinners within. This is a night for the dead to celebrate thought Giuliana, as she lay huddled against her sister. Sleep soon fell upon her.

When Gioia woke, Ruggiero had long departed with his father and their dog, Spinella. They were addicted hunters – rain or shine, they would be out there. Gioia gave her body a good stretch, but it was aching everywhere. There was no heat in the house. The cold and humidity had settled in all her joints. However, as tired as she was, she knew she needed to get up. Chores were waiting for her. The ironing for Mrs. Zicardo needed to be done before heading with the family to the cemetery. She saw Grandma's bedroom door wide open – she was out already. In all likelihood she was gathering the snails that came out from last night's rain.

Rosa, with a deep white plastic pail and an umbrella, was indeed venturing along the country road picking snails. She would cure them in water for a couple of days and then wash them clean. They would make a nice soup or salsa gravy for pasta. Her endeavour would act as the family's meat replacement.

Gioia, now done her delivery, had been paid few liras. This allowed her to grab some milk for the family. When she got home, her daughters were still asleep. She bent over to kiss them gently. She hated to wake them, but they had a busy day ahead.

"Eh, sleepy heads! It's time to get up! Look what I have for you," she held out her container of milk, "I will toast some cornbread on the charcoal and you can have some breakfast!"

Pieces of bread and milk in a bowl wasn't much, but Grandma always mixed a little white grain flour with the corn making the bread softer and much more palatable. It was a rare treat for the family.

"Oh, Mom! Can't we stay asleep longer? We are tired," moaned Giuliana.

"Do you forget what today is? Your poor grandmother has already been gone for hours, and not to mention Papa and Grandpa! Come on, my sweet angels. How often do you get the treat I have here for you this morning? Milk and toast!"

At this repeated announcement the girls jumped out of bed to start their day's events. Although Giuliana was not crazy about the trip to the cemetery, she was excited about breakfast. The praying with the beads, the ordeal of ritual, the obedience that was expected – she secretly detested it. But she knew she was left with no choice in the matter.

Grandma cheerfully made her entrance with her loot in hand.

"Look, Gioia! Girls! Come and see what I have. These creatures are enough for three days! My pail is full! They were out on the grass by the roadside – everywhere! Good thing I went early." She put her pail down, and the snails began to crawl outside in a futile attempt at escape. The girls giggled as Grandma kept scooping them back where they belonged. She was not going to let them go anywhere after all her hard work picking them.

***

Later, the girls, Rosa, and Gioia left for the cemetery. Papa and Grandpa would meet them there. They too had left at six in the morning, but to hunt. Ruggiero and Luigi had happily gone together on a search for rabbits, birds, or whatever wild creature they could find. Every now and then they would find few grapes throughout the farmlands. These grapes were not ripe at the time of harvest. The farmers, in order not to ruin their wine's taste, had abandoned the slight crop and left the small globes on the vine. Although they were either mushy or half dried, the two men did not care and were grateful for the small bounty. It would be a treat for the family when they went home with their knapsack full.

By nine in the morning, Gioia, Nonna Rosa, Giuliana, and Trizia – as well as their neighbours – were on their way to the cemetery by foot. The rain had created chaos, leaving the country road soggy. The small creeks that ran down the valleys were overflowing and wild, making the river at the base expand three-times its normal size. La Bifernina was running ferociously, dangerously carrying debris and broken branches from the storm the night before.

Ruggiero and Luigi, on their hunting expedition, were staggering as their heavy boots became caked in sticky, reddish clay. The bottom of their pants and socks were wet. Ruggiero turned to look at his father, seeing fatigue line his strained face.

"Papa, you are dragging your feet. Listen, I don't know about you, but I say we should give this up. It's crazy to continue in these conditions." Ruggiero put a hand on Luigi's shoulder and motioned with his head to turn around. "Let's go."

"Son, are you turning into an old nun? If you prefer to join the girls at the cemetery then be my guest! The murmuring and the recitals drive me insane. Let your mother and the girls do that."

"Papa, I had promised Gioia I would be there," Ruggiero said.

"Son, I will feel satisfied only if I have something to bring home," Luigi sighed.

"Believe me, I know. But the few grapes I picked will have to do for today."

Luigi looked out and studied the area around them before responding.

"Let's give ourselves another half-hour and then we will turn around. We will drop our fuciles off at the Masseria on our way to the holy place." Luigi said, gesturing toward his rifle.

Ruggiero bowed his head in agreement.

"Whatever you wish, Papa."

"Son, I know your mother and Gioia are brainwashing the girls about all this praying and blah blah blah about an afterlife. But, believe me Son, once you're dead, you are dead. Dust to dust…"

"I think it's nice that Mom and Gioia teach the girls to believe in an afterlife," Ruggiero countered, "I choose to believe that myself. It makes me feel better. I suggest you keep your thoughts to yourself or Ma will be angry at you!"

Luigi waved him off.

"I have been in the war. I have seen so many of my friends shot down dead. I remember lying there, huddled beside many of them as they died. My heart was torn. My eyes were blind from my tears. I implored the good Lord for them to rise, but they lay there solid as stones. You become hard when you lose so many friends…"

"I understand Papa. But today we must go along with the girls. Today is a day of prayer for the dead."

Spinella was running ahead of them with his ears perked up, nosediving everywhere while her tail wagged from side to side. Despite the dog's excitement, his smelling and sniffing were not yielding any results for the men. Luigi had always commented on how alert his dog was. Sometimes, he sacrificed his own supper to feed the dog. Spinella was his faithful friend. She was white, with a couple of black spots on his neck and ears.

"Son, the dog has found something," Luigi pointed out as Spinella suddenly froze in place.

"Papa! Papa, look!" Ruggiero exclaimed. Spinella started barking and then took off running like the wild winds from the mountain of Matese. Ignoring the treacherous cracks in the descending valley, the dog ran uncontrollably in a chase.

"She is on to something!" Luigi exclaimed. "I know my dog!"

Chapter Eight
The Chase

On the other side of the hill, Nicola Del Conte and his men were also on a wild chase. They had made their way to the cornfield with a warrant to arrest Orlando. When they arrived, Orlando was already at the wheel of his tractor-trailer ready to take off for the Alps. It was going to be his last corn delivery of the season. The marshal and his men approached the vehicle cautiously. Dressed in their formal uniforms, the marshal sported an impressive hat and had his revolver hooked at his side. His face donned a severe brow.

On their advance, Orlando's heart skipped with a jolt of panic. It was easy for him to overpower women, but he wasn't too confident when surrounded by men of law. With an aura of authority, Nicola approached the vehicle flanked by his men.

"Are you Signor Orlando Alonza?"

Orlando rolled down his window and looked at the marshal and his men with scrutiny. He was choking on some form of a response, but his voice wasn't coming out right. Before he could get in a proper reply, Nicola Del Conte spoke again.

"Will you step down out of your vehicle, please?"

Orlando, sitting up high above them, was not used to people telling him what to do. His nastiness kicked in as a defence mechanism.

"Eh, you jerks! I suggest you get out of my way or I will run you over with this rigger and make three pizzas out of you." His

73

motor was running. He did not appreciate being ordered around.

"Boys, get your weapons in position here," ordered Nicola. At his command, Alfonso and Giorgio pulled out their revolvers and pointed them at Orlando. Nicola spoke again calmly."We have a warrant for your arrest. You would be better off cooperating or we will take you in by force. Come out with your hands up."

Sibilla had appeared, shocked by the sight of the police. She approached them sensing trouble brewing. What's the situation here?

"I am Sibilla Lalonde. This is my property. I run this place. Can you please tell me what's going on here?"

"We have a warrant for Signor Orlando Alonzo's arrest. We need to take him in," Nicola replied, still eyeing Orlando.

"Oh! What has he done?"

"We are not at liberty to discuss the accusations. Our job is to take him into custody."

"Orlando, come on down! Get out of that truck!" she ordered. She quickly moved on back to her duties, extricating herself from any of the drama her workers might involve themselves in.

Reluctantly, Orlando came out with a malevolent smirk on his lips. Giorgio and Alfonso immediately grabbed him and tightened handcuffs around his wrists.

"Good job, Boys," said Nicola, as he patted the two Carabinieris on the back.

Giorgio and Alfonso took a deep breath of relief, but a moment too soon. Orlando pushed off Giorgio and ran like lightning towards the woods at the edge of the field. He had been an accomplished runner in his school days and the winner of many local races – this was just another race he would have to win.

Puffing, Orlando's legs kicked high and fast down the muddy terrain that he knew well. He muttered curses to himself about

Liliana; somehow he knew she was a part of this. He was relieved when he glanced over his shoulders and saw that the pursuing cops were having a hard time navigating the uneven, rocky terrain behind him. They had their weapons in hand but were in no habit to shoot and kill, especially from behind. Nicola was having the worst time compared to his men. Being close to fifty and overweight did not help his situation. The two younger policemen were doing better in their pursuit.

"Do not shoot! Do you hear me? Do NOT shoot!" yelled Nicola from the rear.

"Can we shoot a warning? It might scare him!" Alfonso suggested from ahead.

"Yes! Do it!"

The two bangs from Alfonso's pistol were totally ignored by Orlando. Having now reached the base of the valley, Orlando stopped, shocked and confused. The river was flowing rapidly. To make things worse, the mist in the air blurred his vision.

"Damn handcuffs!" he was muttering to himself in anger. He could not even wipe his eyes. He shook his head like a wild beast trying to toss the sweat and moisture from his face, but his gestures were not clearing anything. What the hell is this? A river? Or has God turned it into a sea? Son-of-a-bitch! Orlando was getting discouraged. Now, seeing the condition of the river, he was not so sure about his decision to escape. He yanked his hands in the cuffs as hard as he could one more time. If I could only undo these handcuffs... He was a strong swimmer and had crossed the river many times over – but only in its normal condition. He turned around to look back. The police were way behind yelling out his name. And now, he could hear a dog barking as well. Fear was starting to engulf Orlando's entire body; his legs began to shake. The dog's bark was getting louder and louder. Where on earth is that dog coming from?

***

The policemen and the chief were still in pursuit. Nicola was breathless. His muddy boots were getting heavier with every step from the sticky clay that opened up craters in his wake, making the chase more and more difficult. Giorgio was the first to hear the barking of a dog. He turned his head to look. There, on top of the west hillside barking away at them was a dog. It did not seem like a tamed dog. The other officers took notice as well.

"Stop! Guys! You might have some help here…depends what kind of dog it is. Stand still for a moment. If he sees you running he might jump us!" ordered Nicola. His men obeyed, relieved to slow down to a stop. They had lost sight of Orlando behind the valley.

"Our guy cannot be too far ahead. The river makes a sharp turn after this hillside. With the rain last night, there's no way it can be crossed. We will catch up to him," Alfonso said to his chief.

***

Ruggiero and Luigi had just approached the ridge of the Valley when they observed their dog's fixated behaviour.

"Oh yes, she is up to something big, Son. I know it," said Luigi, puzzled.

The dog had now stopped on the ridge of the hill turning back and forth waiting for her owners. All she needed was instructions to move forward. Once Luigi and Ruggiero reached the dog, she was whining, begging to be given the go-ahead. The craters of the valleys were deep, but the dog could leap. It would seem that she was conscious of the limitations of her two beloved owners. Luigi looked down the steep valley and turned to his son.

"Ruggiero, my eyesight is not as clear as yours. I see three blurred figures down there; can you make them out?"

"Yes, Papa. I see! We need to get closer. It looks like men in uniform. I will be damned! If it isn't the Carabinieri! The chief and his men!"

"What on earth are they doing down here? On The Day of the Defunti?"

"Yeah, they are usually at the cemetery. That's strange."

The dog wailed for their attention. Luigi patted her on the head and motioned Ruggiero to descend, testing his footing.

"Papa, where are we going? Do you want to have a heart attack scaling these craters?"

"I am curious; I want to know what or who these guys are chasing."

"They are hunting - just like us."

"No, not all three of them on this day. They are out here for a serious matter."

"Papa, let's turn around and get to the cemetery. We promised the girls we would be there, and it's getting late."

Ruggiero looked up at the sky. The sun was peeking over the highest ridge behind the clouds. He was concerned about his wife and daughters. He should be with them by now.

"Papa, let's go."

"I am a hunter - not a mourner. Praying with those beads is not for me. Let your mother do my part. The later we go, the better. I am not abandoning this. Besides, I want to know what's going on ahead of us if these men are here."

I cannot leave him behind. Ruggiero glanced at his watch; it was eleven in the morning. "Papa, we are leaving in half an hour."

"Ok, Son. We will."

Spinella had no problem jumping the lush terrain where some running creeks had formed. For her owners, however, it was certainly a frightening challenge.

***

Nicola and his men had reached the open field to the river. Orlando was way ahead by the riverbank. He was walking back and forth, assessing where it was easier to cross. He remembered coming here and climbing the highest rock with his buddies in the hottest days of July. The rock was ten feet high and served as their diving board. At the base, the green whirlpool water swirled in circles. While they used to race and fight with it, now, right by the rock, the water pulled down in full force. Orlando spotted la morgia del bagno: The rock of the bath. He looked down at his wrists, bruised and bloodied now, from his constant pulling and struggling. As his morale was failing him, tears were blurring his vision. He climbed to the rock in a fog and looked down to see the water beneath him doing circles. The high caps on the riverbed were just as menacing.

He heard it again, the loud barks of a dog. Did those idiots get a hunting dog to chase me? He turned his eyes to look up to the sky. The heavens looked grey and gloomy, loaded with clouds that would soon resume their downpour. The sun had totally disappeared. He took a deep breath to strengthen his lungs and then closed his eyes. He shook his head as if to wake up, but his brain was not being rational. The universe around him had ceased to make sense; everything seemed to be against him.

***

Luigi and Ruggiero were out of breath when they caught up to Spinella, who was barking at Nicola and his officers. The men hushed the dog and extended a handshake.

"Signor Marescialle, what brings you down here?" inquired Luigi.

"What brings you two here? My men and I are doing our job. Aren't you out of your boundaries?"

"It's hunting season. My son and I have been hunting – but with no luck. We were ready to call it quits when my dog headed this way. We followed."

"You have a serious dog here. We were relieved to see you two appear." Nicola looked at the dog that had been calmed by her masters.

"Oh, Spinella? She is the best and has such strong senses. She doesn't miss anything, and she obeys my orders well!"

"Sorry guys, we cannot waste time. We must move on," said the chief of police.

Ruggiero and Luigi were ready to turn around when Spinella took off like a jet.

"Spinella! Come here! Stop it! Turn around and get over here!" Spinella turned wiggling her tail, barking louder as if imploring her master.

"Ruggiero, she's got something," exclaimed Luigi.

The crew stepped forward struggling with their heavy boots. Once they reached the ridge on top of the valley, they looked down below.

"Papa! Take a good look. Do you see what I see?"

"I see a person, but I cannot distinguish the rest clearly."

"Forget the valley though, look over there!" Ruggiero pointed up. "Papa, high on top of that diving rock, a fellow appears ready to jump!"

"Jump?"

"Is he crazy? Jump from there, and that will be the end of him!"

While the two looked on, the policemen and Nicola were observing. They too watched in shock. Orlando was at the very top of the rock ready to jump.

"Good Lord," exclaimed Nicola, "We must stop him!"

"He is handcuffed and the river is uncrossable," said Giorgio as he studied the current. "Do you guys know what's at the base of that morgia? The ritornello! If he jumps there, he will be sucked right under by the current!"

"We must stop him!" ordered Nicola. "You guys get to him; try to talk some sense into him. Get him to surrender calmly."

Giorgio and Alfonso were well trained, but the last serious crime that had taken place here was a few years back. Two men had lost their lives trying to cross the river due to a robbery. Giorgio shook his head and whispered to his partner.

"This guy is certainly trying our strength and experience."

"I know," responded Alfonso. "One lousy guy somehow escapes the three of us? Wouldn't go over well with most people…"

"Don't worry. We will get him one way or another. Our chief should let those hunters help. The five of us will close in on him."

***

Orlando had reached the very top. He looked out below him. There, the raging water was furious and threatening. Back at the cornfield, this place was described as the forbidden zone - a death trap. He turned around bewildered. What other direction can I go? He spotted the chasing group getting closer with the dog leading the way. His brain shut down, his feet felt heavy, his muddy shoes were sticky, and his hands were still unmercifully handcuffed. His mental state was one of defeat. His bravado had abandoned him.

"They are not going to get me," he muttered to himself.

The policemen had reached the base and called out to him. Orlando moved slowly forward.

"NO!" the policemen yelled.

Orlando enjoyed the feeling of the cool wind against his face as he propelled himself forward, until this sensation was replaced by a stinging smack from the water. A jolt of energy electrified his body. He was in the whirlpool. I will let myself twirl around with the water flow. Then, I will make the escape under with the returning churn. He wiggled his legs with all his might, pushing his torso in motion to help execute his manoeuvres. But, his legs rejected the command of his brain. A strong force was sucking them down heavily as if some monster at the bottom wouldn't let go. He fought and fought until his body was pulled under. His lungs continued to gasp for air. The force pulling him down sapped the fight out of him until he fought no more.

***

The Marescialle and his men, along with Ruggiero and Luigi, had watched Orlando jump. It was only in this dramatic moment that the truth of whom they were pursuing struck Luigi and Ruggiero with a tremor. They had no way of fully comprehending what had taken place before their eyes. Every summer, crazy young swimmers had raced with the dangerous whirlpool, but the condition of the river on this November day was severe. It didn't necessary mean Orlando hadn't survived, but his fate seemed doubtful to all who watched on.

Nicola and the officers reached the riverbank with Ruggiero and Luigi on their heels.

The chief lifted his hat and spoke.

"Boys, we will search from this side to see if we can spot him walking down along the bank. I seriously don't think he made it across. I certainly don't want either of you crossing these mad waters today."

"It sure must have been fate for us to find ourselves in this part of the land," Luigi commented, still wide-eyed from the realisation.

Ruggiero began to speak, shaking his head.

"The area right at the base," he pointed out, gesturing widely, "is highly dangerous. Not many people would survive. The current pulls you in, right into that funnel."

They all looked down flabbergasted. The water circled in rapid chaos.

"Good heavens," said Luigi.

They could not see any sign of a body. Occasionally, there would be branches and rubbish roaring within the white foam of the high tides, so they continued their walk along the riverbank. There was no sign of Orlando, on foot nor in the water.

"Has he fooled all of us?" Nicola repeated. "How can he have disappeared just like that?"

Spinella kept whining. She was not moving as fast as she should have been. After a while she proceeded, sniffing with her head down in every bush, checking out anything of interest along the way. Ruggiero and Luigi, taken with the excitement, had forgotten all about their family at the cemetery. Ruggiero glanced at the time; It was now one in the afternoon.

"Papa," he called out, "the girls are waiting for us."

"I know, Son, but this is important. Have you forgotten who this guy is? What this shmuck has done to our Giuliana?"

"Papa, believe me, I cannot wait until these guys catch him. I want to have that satisfaction also."

"The girls will have to wait. This is more important."

Nicola and his men were starting to get discouraged.

"Eh, guys, do you think there is any chance he got away?" asked Alfonso.

Nicola stepped between them and put his arms on their shoulders.

"Don't get discouraged men. We will get him soon, not to worry."

Chapter Nine
The Cemetery

The priest had ended his blessings and the faithful were placing their flickering candles in the tombs of their loved ones. The prayers and the recital of the rosary were over. Gioia and Rosa, with the girls, kept anxiously turning to look at the gate entrance hoping to see their Husbands arrive. So far there was no sign of them. Since the service was over, most of the people were starting to disperse.

"Mamma Rosa," Gioia called out with a frown on her face, "I am concerned. It's getting late. Why are Ruggiero and Papa not here yet?"

"I wonder myself. I know Luigi hates the ordeal of the cemetery visitation and what goes with it. I am surprised at Ruggiero though. He is not one to disappoint the girls – or you for that matter."

Giuliana also had been fighting her uneasiness, but for Trizia's sake she tried to remain calm. She held her hand gently and kept amusing her by pointing out the photos on the marble slabs of the tombs of the departed souls.

"Look, Sis. This girl looks young. I thought you had to be old to die?" Trizia questioned her older sister.

"Not necessarily. Sometimes people get sick, or it's just their time to go. It all depends on your destiny," Giuliana replied.

"What's your destiny?"

"Mine, you mean? Or in general?" Giuliana asked.

"Yes. Both. Yours and mine. Do you think we will die when we are really old?"

"I sure hope so. Trizia, why are you thinking about death? We are just starting life. I know this is a sad day to go through. After all, we are here to concentrate on our loved ones, but just be grateful! We have Nonna Rosa and Grandpa with us. We are pretty fortunate!"

"I know, Mamma and Papa love us, but I think Grandpa and Grandma love us more," Trizia said with a smirk. "Why don't we pray for God to give them a long life? I could not bear losing our grandparents."

"Oh Trizia, don't worry. Nonna Rosa is strong and witty, and Grandpa – with his drive – is far from an old man," Giuliana reassured her.

Trizia believed her older sister. With a brighter grin on her face she smiled up at her.

"Come to think of them, where on earth are Papa and Grandpa? They were supposed to be here." They had not been paying attention to the timing. Since the sun had been hidden all day, it looked dark already.

With serious concern, the women waited but the men never walked through the big iron-gate. The curator was clearing the spent candles and gathering his tools, ready to close for the night. Once the girls had accosted Gioia and Rosa, the women had stopped their gibbering prayer and tried to conceal their worry, but Gioia's nerves had gotten the best of her. She finally spoke up.

"Something has happened to them – I don't like it. I have a knot in my stomach. Ruggiero has never disappointed me like this," said Gioia.

"Gioia, stop thinking the worst! That old husband of mine is probably chasing some rabbits. You know how stubborn the mule is! Once he gets his catch his pride is fulfilled. Only then will the hard-head return home," said Rosa.

"Grandpa doesn't like to spend the day here, he told me. He is probably doing everything he can to avoid it and is keeping Papa with him," said Giuliana. "They will show up at home with some good hunting!"

Not a soul was left roaming the cemetery anymore. Rosa, walking briskly, tried to control her anger.

"Ok girls, we better be on our way before they lock us up in here. I will deal with that husband of mine when I get home! He has been disrespectful to his parents and our dear departed. He is a bad influence on his own son!"

"Now, now, Mamma Rosa! Calm down. I am sure Ruggiero felt duty-bound if his father didn't want to leave," rationalised Gioia.

"Don't I know that? Luigi, He is the culprit," she answered indignantly.

"Oh! Grandma stop. You keep bickering at Grandpa. He loves all of us, and he means well," responded Giuliana, like a mature adult, in defence of her grandpa.

"Oh yes, he has you girls wrapped around his finger. But wait 'till he deals with me when he comes home!"

The four women arrived home after navigating the treacherous road once more. The house was dark on their return; there was no sign of the two men.

"Mamma Rosa, do you think I should go fetch the brothers again to go look for those two vagabonds? They have been gone since early morning – now I am starting to panic," Gioia pensively suggested.

As soon as she said that, they heard footsteps outside their front door. Rosa, boiling in anger, walked to the kitchen window and opened it to peek out. She saw Spinella whining and wiggling her tail. Luigi and Ruggiero were outside conversing with the shoemaker across the street.

"There they are! Both of them!" Rosa exclaimed, much relieved but also angry.

"Grandma, please don't start at Grandpa! I am sure he has a good explanation for not coming to the service," Giuliana warned.

As she said that, the door opened and Luigi entered.

"Hello! How are my favourite girls?" There was no response from his wife. "We are home!"

Giuliana and Trizia burst into the kitchen and ran to hug him.

"How are my precious granddaughters?" he asked, stretching his arms to hug them both.

"Grandpa! We were just about to send our uncles to look for you! What took you so long? Why didn't you come to the cemetery?"

Before he could answer, Gioia barged from the pantry carrying some food to warm up for supper.

"Papa, where is Ruggiero? You got us all worried waiting all day!"

"Gioia, we found ourselves in a different hunting situation. Wait 'till we tell you Ruggiero is looking after Spinella. He will tell you! We couldn't leave! Where is that wife of mine?"

"Papa, Mom is furious. You'd better have a good excuse for not showing up! You know how important it is to Mom for all the family to be at the cemetery to pray together. It wasn't the same without you guys. Mom likes to initiate the rosary in sequence. We could not do that," said Gioia.

Luigi brought a hand up to straighten the strands of hair covering his tired face before answering. Suddenly Rosa appeared like a thundercloud ready to unload. Luigi usually greeted his wife with a peck on her lips, but in observing her face, he was discouraged.

"Rosa!" He called out to her. She turned her back furiously without responding.

Ruggiero walked in with his hands up, and then began banging his chest with his right hand.

"My culp, my solemni culp," he greeted his wife and the girls, humbly admitting guilt. "Sorry guys. You have every right to be mad. We were caught in a bizarre situation."

Luigi interrupted him.

"Ruggiero, please, before you explain anything, see what to do with your mother. She is not speaking to me."

"Papa, now you sound like a teenager. Do I have to fight your battles with Mom?"

"She despises me! Do you think she lets me speak and explain?"

Rosa, in her sombre mood, was fretting in the kitchen by the fireplace while getting the food ready. She had boiled the snails and now was frying the garlic with parsley. She would add some tomatoes later from her preserved jars. A delicious salsa would be ready for her homemade spaghetti from corn and white wheat flour. The aroma was hitting Luigi's nostrils rendering his hunger uncontrollable.

"Rosa, please. Rosa..." Luigi was doing circles around her, imploring her affection. She gave him nothing. He shook his hands down and resigned. "Lordy, Lordy, touch my wife's heart."

Once they sat around the table, Rosa, ignoring her husband, turned to speak to Ruggiero.

"Son of mine, can you please explain to me why you never showed up to our service?"

"Mom, Papa should explain it to you."

"No Son, I don't want to hear from him. I know he would do anything to avoid a religious service. He dragged you along with him to commit a sin the day of our dearly departed!"

"Mom you are not being fair! Before you act so harsh, let Papa explain. I am telling you, you are being hard on him. We were duty bound."

"Rosa, let me tell you what we encountered just when we were turning around to leave," Luigi began, trying to change her sullenness.

Gioia reached out, lightly tapped Rosa's foot under the table to motivate her in compliance. Rosa gulped a fork full of twisted spaghetti in her mouth and eyed her daughter-in-law with a smirk and glare, letting her know she wished to see him suffer longer. Then reconsidering, she spoke directly to Luigi.

"Ok, you old goat. I shouldn't be speaking to you, but for the sake of our children here you'd better have a good explanation."

Luigi, animated, gave a soft laugh.

"Rosa, while we were out Spinella discovered something, and she would not turn around! We followed, thinking she was after some rabbit - only it wasn't a four-legged animal, but a human being, in handcuffs, running like a desperado. He was trying to get away from the marshal and the policemen." He flashed his eyes and glanced around at the women. "Guess who it was? Guess! We struggled, wet and muddy, to reach the ridge. Ruggiero spotted the marshal and his two Carabinieri chasing the breathless Spanish guy; the cocky Romeo. We were about to turn around and be on our way. But, Rosa you tell me: after our discovery, how could we leave? Tell me?" Getting excited, his voice became louder. "Do you know how much I wanted to kill him myself? We are hunters! The marshal and his assistants are not used to those hills and valleys, plus the creeks and land craters that have sprung up from the downpour. Ruggiero and I could navigate it like the farmers do. The guy got away from them! The marshal didn't even object to our presence on the scene. Actually, I think they were glad to see us with the dog. Spinella was a big help."

"Yes, it was Spinella that gave the guy a chase for his life," explained Ruggiero.

The woman listened stunned. Giuliana's ears perked up. She held her breath and stopped eating.

"Papa, he got away?" she asked, holding her fork upward like a weapon.

"He climbed the diving morgia. Spinella was ready to go get him up there. He was right on the edge… I never thought he would jump in there - handcuffed even! The whirlpool is unforgiving. The river was a menace to cross. Right before our eyes, he disappeared. I am sure he got knocked off."

The woman listened, perplexed. Gioia cleared her throat.

"He drowned?"

"We don't know," answered Ruggiero.

"He was nowhere in sight when we got to the base of the river," said Luigi. "We left the marshal and the police there. They were still looking for him until dark."

"Oh! Honey!" Gioia put an arm around Ruggiero in sympathy.

"And my Rosa here gets all stirred up because of the cemetery service. How could we leave? Especially with our dog. We had a hard time getting her away," exclaimed Luigi.

"Sorry girls. Tomorrow, if the marshal and his man are out there, we will be there with them," said Ruggiero.

"Yes, Son. I am with you. I will have no peace until I see this guy caught dead or alive. Spinella will lead the way."

"I am sorry, Luigi. I understand how much you care for our family," apologised Rosa. She got up and approached Luigi, putting her hands on his face and kissing him tenderly. "You cannot blame me for wanting you with us."

***

Out by the river bank, Nicola Del Conte, Alfonso, and Giorgio, still searching, looked at each other discouraged. It was getting dark. It had been a disappointing and hard day. The fog was lifting, the air was getting unbearable, the humidity penetrating their bones. A fine rain was drizzling, leaving their hair and clothes drenched. The sky was dark with no moon in sight. Nicola's achy knees were buckling under his wet uniform.

"Guys, let's call it a night. We will resume tomorrow morning. We are shivering. If he is out there, he cannot get far," said the chief.

"No, he cannot get across for sure. He has to remain on this side," said Alfonso.

"We'll get him, soon enough," retorted Giorgio.

They turned their backs to the river and the steep valley.

"Ok, fellows, we have a ways to go. We have to climb these hills back on foot and make our way home," said Nicola as his breath ascended, visible in the cold air.

"Thanks, Sir," responded Giorgio. "I hate to admit it but since this morning I have no energy left."

Chapter Ten
In the Whirlpool

Orlando's lifeless body was swirling around beneath the water. The current was having its way, tumbling the corpse like a garment in a washing machine. At times it pulled him down and at other times it pushed him upwards. But, mostly Orlando remained in the depths of the current as the narrow water funnel eagerly pulled the cadaver into its dark abyss. Then, suddenly, there was a calm release. Branches from broken trees that had been pulled along in the swollen river seemed to be dancing in an erratic circle to the musical roar of the waterway. The dead were to rest on this night, after the day's celebrations and visitations. Orlando was now among the unrested souls between the doors of hell and purgatory. His family wouldn't miss him.

***

The next morning Sibilla was the first to arrive at the farm. There sat the truck with its door open and its engine off. There was no sign of Orlando. Strange, she thought. He would have been long gone. What has he been up to now? Have those Carabinieri kept him? She mused quietly to herself, pulling her woollen sweater closer to her body. There was frost on the ground and a cool chill in the air. She walked toward the farmhouse where the fireplace had been earlier lit, in an effort to keep warm while the clock kept moving toward late morning. There was no news of Orlando. Her patience was running out. Sibilla did not know that

Orlando would never drive her corn to Spain again.

***

The next morning, a sombre Nicola Del Conte reluctantly met with his men to resume the ordeal, which had been abandoned the evening before. The terrain was dryer and the hills less slippery. They felt encouraged. However, once they reached the river, they were set back again as once more the tides were high and menacing. The foamy caps were wildly dragging broken branches and debris along without mercy.

Nicola pensively placed a hand on his forehead.

"Guys, there is no way anyone can cross this river. I don't think he could have made it to the other side. Let's concentrate the search on this side of the riverbank. My intuition tells me he is probably hiding motionless, not too far ahead."

"He must feel hungry and defeated if he has been on the run since yesterday morning. The cold of the night must have taken a toll on him. I doubt if he could have gotten far. We will soon come upon him," said Giorgio.

"The Electric plant is not too far ahead. Maybe he is hiding around there," contributed Alfonso.

"I suspect that too," answered the Marshal.

***

A violent rush of current had caused chaos in the whirlpool and Orlando's body had jolted out of the churning turmoil by the suction power of the current. His body had been going downstream. The workers at the Hydro plant had opened the big steel doors, allowing the water to turn the turbines that produced electricity for the region. Orlando's body had glided along only to be stopped by the iron grate that held back debris. There, he was slammed horizontally against the coated steel fence. The sunrays were causing a reflective glare on the polished fence and that was what guided the watchman, Roberto Gambari, supervising the area for his final shift, to take a second look. But before his eyes could adjust, he heard voices and turned to spot three men in uniform. He was interrupted by the intrusion and his attention moved to the officers whom he recognised. He needed to warn them that some of the area was totally restricted. They needed to be guided to safety.

Nicola and his men had made their way onto the grounds of the hydroplant. The watchman looked at his watch. It was seven-thirty in the morning and he was still on duty until eight. What are these guys doing here at this time? I am tired and looking forward to my sleep. He was impatient to go and rest. At a snail's pace he walked over to greet them.

"Good morning, Signor Marshal, Signor Carabinieri. What brings you this way?" he inquired, trying to be civil and hide his annoyance. They shook hands in greeting and the Marshal spoke first.

"Roberto, we are here searching for a fellow. He escaped from us. It happened yesterday."

"You don't say? From the three of you? Who is the fellow?" he asked, with an amused chuckle. "Come on, it cannot be."

"He is a runner from Madrid. He knows how to negotiate these hills much better than we do. It's a shame to say it, and embarrassing for us. Unfortunately, he did get away. Have you seen him around here, or heard anything strange during the night? He is a fellow in his thirties, handcuffed, medium height? Black hair. He was wearing dark blue pants, white shirt. He got away just before noon."

"What has he done anyway? Or am I not allowed to ask?"

"We would rather not say. He has been accused, and we need to take him into the province city of Molise."

"No, I have not heard or seen anyone," Roberto responded, furring his brow. "I have been on duty all night. Have you seen the river after all the rain? I can tell you, crossing to the next town is simply impossible. If one would try, definitely one would not survive."

"Especially if he was handcuffed," said Nicola.

"Wait a minute," Roberto retorted, removing his hat. "You are telling me he was handcuffed? Let's check the grate before the turbines. Drowning corpses are usually held up there. If he drowned, that is."

He walked, leading the way toward the location with the men in tow. The roar of the water was deafening as they approached. Curiosity had reenergized Roberto's interest.

"I don't know," he shook his head, "If he had made his way around here I would have heard him. I walk the grounds often when on-duty. It was pretty quiet during the night, except for the river."

"We need to do our duty, Roberto. It's our job to scrutinise the area entirely before we move on," responded Nicola.

"I understand. I will tell you before we waste time, let's look at the grate. I have been here a long time. You know those briganti that went to rob the cows from that family on the other side of the river? That is where they got stuck when they drowned with the poor cows and their loot. They had a bag of eggs, cheese, and soaking bread in their backpacks!"

"I remember that," said Nicola. "What a shame, in a way. I felt sorry for them. See what hunger makes you do? They were desperate to feed their family. With this fellow, it is a different story...I am not going into it further," said Nicola.

"Ok. Guys, we are here," announced Roberto.

The four of them intensively observed the deep green water, murky and scary. George was the one to spot something first.

"Oh! My God! Look, guys. Do you see what I see of there bubbling up?"

He was pointing to what seemed to be a leg or foot.

"Where? Where?"

"Bent over. You see under that branch over there?"

With his arm stretched and pointing out, George was gesturing wildly in his excitement. They all assumed an attentive mode, holding their breath until they saw it. A human foot was bobbing up and down with the current. Then, there appeared another with a shoe still on.

"That must be our man," said Nicola.

"It must be," responded Giorgio. "Where else could he have gone . . . considering?"

Lucky for them, the electric station had a telephone, which was rare in the village. They informed the authorities from the province to come to the rescue. Orlando's body was eventually fished out of the water and in no time the all town was privy to the news. No newspaper, radio announcement or television was to assist in word travelling, but by word of mouth, everybody knew.

***

Sibilla mourned.

"What do I do now?" She brought her hands to her head. She knew he had been up to no good, but she had ignored it all.

Liliana felt a pang of sorrow going through her heart. She wanted him stopped and punished, but not drowned in that

97

unforgiving whirlpool.

Giuliana was in her room when the news came upon her house. She was dressing up to go to the church service with her mom and grandma. The priest was saying a mass for their departed. The whole month of November was their devotion. Grandma had brought some eggs to the priest a few days ago to pay for his service.

Gioia and Rosa had gotten the news. The lady across the street, Rosaria, had leaned over to the open window and had called out to Rosa.

"Eh! Rosa, Rosa," she shouted loudly, "have you heard the terrible news?"

Rosa quickly walked to her window, opened the louvers wide open to face her neighbour.

"The Spanish guy - you know the one that was the foreman at the big farm on the corn field? He worked for that woman, Sibilla. They found him drowned by the hydro plant."

Gioia overheard and ran to the window, tripping over a chair to join in on the gossip and the unbelievable news.

"What? Are you sure?" The Mother and Daughter-in-law looked at each other and made the sign of the cross. "Oh my God. Really?"

They chitchatted with the folks and retreated to their kitchen.

"We need to deal with Giuliana. We will tell her gently," said Rosa.

"Mom, without disrespect, I know you are our matriarch, but I would like to break the news to Giuliana myself before we leave for church."

The three of them would go by themselves. Their men had left already to resume the hunt with Spinella. Rosa had resigned herself to not to get into an argument with Luigi regarding church services. He was definitely setting a bad example for his son. But this time she would forgive him since they were on a mission.

"Gioia, we will leave them alone. Let them go," she had said the night before. They had left the house at six in the morning.

"Who knows if they heard the news? They are out there in the rocky valleys," Rosa said to Gioia.

"Let's not be concerned about them now. We need to deal with Giuliana."

"Yes. We need to tell Giuliana for sure. We will break the news to her gently," said Rosa.

"Mom! Let me handle my daughter."

GINA IAFRATE

Chapter Eleven
The News

"Good morning, Mom. Good morning, Grandma," greeted Giuliana cheerfully with a peck on her favourite people's cheeks.

"Giuliana, Dear, we are almost ready to leave, but before we go your Mom has some news to tell you."

Curious, Giuliana turned to her mother.

"Oh? Mom, what's the news? Good news, I hope," she said, twisting her head sideways attentively.

Gioia protectively put an arm around her shoulder.

"Dear, we have just heard from Rosaria from across the street, that they found Orlando dead – drowned in the river by the electric plant. I wanted to tell you before we leave the house. I am sure the whole town will be talking about it."

"Oh! Dear Lord," Giuliana embraced herself. "Mom, I am so sorry," she said as she started crying. "I just wanted to stop him from hurting other girls and be punished by the law, but Mom, I never wished him to drown! I feel so bad... Oh, Mom! It's awful." Giuliana turned to look at her grandmother. "Grandma, honestly I never meant it to end it that way for him."

"I know, my angel; I understand how you feel," her grandmother replied as she loving hugged her. "I am not so sure your grandfather feels remorse. Don't forget, he was ready to kill him with his own rifle."

Gioia, seeing her daughter upset, continued trying to pacify her with kind reasoning.

"I know, Dear, none of us wished him that kind of death. I am sorry it happened that way. Come on, we are going to church. We will pray for his soul."

After all, they were Christians. Gioia wanted to protect her daughter the best way she knew how. She looked up to implore to heaven. Please God, don't let my daughter blame herself for his death. They gathered their prayer books and beads and headed for church. Grandma proceeded with tender care to place a shawl over Giuliana's shoulders.

When they entered, the place was full. The priest was not at the altar yet to commence the service. While waiting for his appearance, they could hear whispering among the parishioners. The noise resembled buzzing bees fresh out of their nest. As they moved along the pews to find their seats, Giuliana noticed the people close by staring and murmuring. Giuliana's eyes were red from crying. Embarrassed, she pulled the shawl lower to conceal her face and discreetly dried her tears. Her conscience was playing havoc with her. She questioned her actions against Orlando. If these people knew what has happened to me, probably no one would speak to me. Or, worse yet, I would be despised by all of them. Her dark thoughts were getting out of hand. The double hand bells rang loud and clear to gather attention. The priest appeared with his purple garments, making his way to the altar to commence the service. The chatting stopped immediately, and everyone turned silent and serious to participate. The turmoil in Giuliana's heart was slowly dissipating. The singing started and with that the prayers followed and peace seemed to touch her soul. She wanted to see Liliana, Giuliana was concerned about her now. She wanted to know how she felt about Orlando being dead. Was she still angry at him? Was she relieved? With all these thoughts churning through her tender brain, her tormented mind was confused and overloaded.

Once the service was over, men and women gathered outside to continue their gossip and greetings. Giuliana wanted no part in this and wished her mom and grandmother would cut short their nonsense. She was anxious to find Liliana. She was the only one with whom she could openly relate regarding the big news in town. Finally, after pulling away from the crowd, Giuliana turned to her family.

"Mom, Grandma, please," her eyes were pleading, "I would like to talk to Liliana. She told me where she lives with her mom and little brothers. Can we go see her now?"

"Dear, if you insist. We will stop by her house. Do you think she would be home on a day like this since it is a working day at the farm?" her mother asked.

"I am not sure, but we can try," Giuliana replied anxiously.

Gioia sensed the urgency in her daughter's voice. She turned to her mother-in-law and gestured in agreement.

"Let's appease her, Mom."

"I am not sure," Rosa quickly interjected. "Well, I am sure we can find her home, or at work. Where else would she go in this town?"

"I will not go anywhere near that farm, Grandma if that is what you are thinking."

"No Dear, we will not venture to the countryside. That's a long way. If we don't find her home, we will go visit her tonight," reassured Gioia.

"Thanks, Mom. I never want step foot in that cornfield ever again. The thought of that place gives me the chills."

Gioia squeezed her daughter's hand and placed an arm around her waist in a loving gesture.

"Sweetie, don't you worry. You never have to go there ever again, my darling."

As they made their way along, the steps and the cobblestones were uneven. Most of the avenues and the rows of homes were set up on elevated hilly ground. Rosa was having a hard time negotiating the rigid climbing with her asthma. She took a deep breath and found support by slipping her arm under Gioia's.

After having done the treacherous scaling, they arrived in front of Liliana's dilapidated house.

"This is her place, Mom," pointed out Giuliana.

The paint was peeling off the door, which was shut with no sign of anyone around. Usually the folks here kept their doors wide open. The windows were small and therefore needed light from the open door. Everybody knew each other, there was no fear to lock yourself in.

"Oh, well," said Rosa "So much for nothing." She looked at Giuliana. "Don't worry, Dear. You will see your Liliana yet, I assure you."

They turned around. Scaling the steps down was much easier.

As it turned out, Rosa was right. By late afternoon Liliana was peeking through their door, asking permission to enter.

"Permesso! Hello!" she was asking, reluctant.

"Eh! Liliana," greeted Gioia joyfully. "Please, do come in. So glad to see you! We were looking for you this morning after the service. Giuliana wanted to see you badly. I am glad you are here." Gioia said while she gave her a warm hug.

"Thank you, Mrs. Ferrante. I couldn't stop thinking of Giuliana all day. Tell me, how she is taking it? Isn't it awful to think of how Orlando ended up? My God! I hated him, but I certainly didn't wish that on him."

"I know. Nobody did. He caused it himself. Let me get Giuliana, she will be delighted to see you. Please cheer her up. She has been sitting on the floor curled up with a book all day alone up there."

"Giuliana," Gioia called out at the bottom of the stairs, with a much-animated voice. "I've got a surprise. Come down to see who is here."

Giuliana immediately got up, tossed her book away and took the stairs in a giant leap. When she saw Liliana she reached out, hugging her between tears with a smile of both sorrow and happiness.

"Eh! Let me look at you. I have not seen you for some time. You are growing like a weed, girl. You are so pretty, even with your puffy eyes."

"Liliana, what do we do now? You heard the horrible news."

"Giuliana, it's not our fault. Don't you ever think that or blame yourself." Liliana spoke with authority.

"Yes, I know, Liliana. I cannot stop thinking about him and how horrible it must have been."

"Giuliana, stop thinking that. We did not cause it. He did this to himself. Do you know how many women he has hurt? Especially you, being still a child? I think he got what he deserved. If you ask me, as much as I don't like what happened to him, I think God looked after us, and Satan took care of him. Sometimes you pay for your sins."

Giuliana listened to her friend, wide-eyed. She looked up to Liliana. She wished her to be her older sister.

"I want to believe you, but I cannot help but feel bad even though he hurt me badly."

"Giuliana, just think for a minute. His death has saved us. No more court order, no trial, and no witness on the stand to prove him guilty. He is dead, and everything is over. Finished. We have been spared. Isn't that our blessing from up above? The good Lord is looking after you and me. You know, Giuliana, I know much more than you. The molestations of those poor peasants... You know, Sibilla always looked the other way. So, my dear friend, be happy."

Giuliana smiled. One good thing had resulted out of that cornfield, she thought. Yes, I have found a dear, dear friend in Liliana.

Gioia came into the kitchen and reluctantly interrupted the girls. She was afraid to invade their privacy. Grandma had stepped out to chat with the neighbours. They intentionally had been left alone.

"Liliana, I want to thank you for being so kind to our daughter. Tell me, have you heard anything further? What are they doing with his body and all that...?"

"Yes, I accompanied Sibilla to his parents. You know she is related to Orlando? A great –aunt or something like that. I overheard that the body has been taken to the province for the usual routine. The father had to identify the corpse and they plan to ship his body back to Madrid where they come from. There will be no funeral, no shenanigans going on here. Aren't we lucky?"

"I see. That is for the best, I guess."

"All for the better. These folks here have nothing to do, can you imagine the gossip? They are trying to keep everything hushed up. Less publicity, the better. The marshal and the police will keep things confidential."

"I am glad. I see."

"Please, Mrs. Ferrante, keep things to yourself. Don't repeat anything I said. After all, I am Sibilla's assistant. I cannot afford to lose my job. Although Orlando was working on having me fired. I was lucky that he picked the wrong time..."

Liliana said her goodbyes, hugged Giuliana, and made her exit to go home to her family.

As she was leaving, the two bozos approached the entrance with their hunting gear and Spinelli, with her tail wiggling away. Gioia quickly started to get busying herself with supper. They would come with their own report of the day. Rosa would start bickering with Luigi, as usual, and check his loot.

Chapter Twelve
The Rescue Operation

The fire rescue had made their arrival. Four fellows in wetsuits lowered themselves in the deep, green canal. With confidence, they made their way to reach Orlando's body as the helpers on deck were assisting with ropes and other necessary equipment. The rescue was smoothly completed by the experienced and brave man of the rescue squad from the city province of Molise. Nicola and his men had remained the whole time, offering whatever assistance they could. The body would be transported to the city, and the right procedures would be followed according to the requirements of the law.

Nicola was relieved when the ordeal finally came to an end. The body would be released to Orlando's relations according to the rules. The grief-stricken family would take over from there to make the arrangements for Orlando's funeral and burial.

***

First thing that morning, Luigi and Ruggiero had made their way toward the river where they had left off the night before. They saw the commotion toward the electric station, but they could not go anywhere close to the place. A yellow ribbon and posts had been set up. Most of the area was totally prohibited and cordoned off by the authorities. Spinella was going crazy again. The dog barked and barked seeing the commotion way down the hill. She was ready to run and charge in pursuit. Luigi was having a hard time keeping her back. He grabbed her by the collar and almost lifted her off the ground.

"Hush, hush, Spinelli."

The dog was violently resisting.

"Here, here, girl. Stay put. Sit."

With a puzzled look on his face, Luigi studied the situation. A couple of policemen were on the pathway that led to electric plant. They were the guards on duty who had never seen them before. As they got closer, they were immediately stopped.

"Sorry guys, absolutely no trespassing," one of the guards severely cautioned with an authoritative tone, as he brought his hands to his waist where a revolver was belted.

Luigi lifted his hands.

"Sorry, Officer. We are hunters. What has actually happened here, may we ask? We were here yesterday."

The officer wasn't sympathetic.

"You are out of your boundaries. I am asking you to leave this area at once."

In the meantime, the other officer was making his way toward them, sensing trouble.

"These policemen must be from the city," Luigi whispered to Ruggiero under his breath. "We had better turn around and go the opposite way."

"Ok, Officer. Sorry," said Ruggiero. He grabbed his father by the arm. To his surprise, Luigi, being always the more stubborn one, placidly turned to follow.

"Son, I guess your mother's prayers are working. I have been spared from getting my hands on that son-of-a-bitch. I see the pompieri, fire trucks, a car – mortuale, the morgue wagon. He drowned. He is history."

"Papa, I know we were at a distance, but I could almost swear I saw him jump off that deadly rock. He has drowned. They are fishing him out."

"Come on, Son. Let's go do our job. Yesterday was a total loss. Let's see what we can accomplish today." He motioned to move. "Let's explore the riverbank in the other direction, where thick shrubberies and extensions of vineyards could be promising."

Once they returned home, Luigi called out for his Rosa as he entered. As usual, he was ambivalent to her scrupulous behaviour. He was not a churchman and that was the main subject of their arguments. As the head of the family, his priority was to provide in any way he could for them. His customs had been passed on to Ruggiero. These values were the most important in his life. Rosa did not understand sometimes. She would get mad at him for missing church service, but she was wrong as far as he was concerned.

"Rosa, Gioia, Giuliana? Where is everybody tonight?"

Luigi dropped his backpack on the kitchen table, with plenty of pears, apples, some dried grapes, and fresh walnuts bulging it to its seams. Ruggiero followed, proud, with his own provisions. He had gotten a rabbit and a couple of pheasants. When Gioia walked in to greet him, he promptly showed off his loot. She pressed her lips to his smiling mouth for a quick kiss.

"Oh! Thank you, God!" She exclaimed looking up in gratefulness.

"Mother should be happy. It's certainly been a productive day today," Ruggiero exclaimed, smiling with pleasure. "After the rain had stopped, these animals were doing their own prowling, and they were easy to hunt."

Rosa barged in from her room. She took a look at the table.

"My goodness, you have come home loaded tonight!"

Gliding with happiness, she approached the loot. In no time,

Rosa and Gioia had a spread on the table for all to enjoy. After the supper, with their hunger dissipated, the news of Orlando was brought up. As delicately as possible, Trizia was sent to her room to spare her some of the details. Giuliana, like a mature adult, expressed her feelings.

"Dad, Grandpa, I know Liliana and I wanted to stop him and have the law deal with him. It is too bad he had met such a horrible death by drowning, handcuffed."

"Honey, it was never our intention to have him die that way, but sometimes things do happen for a reason. Who are we to judge the will of God?" answered Rosa.

"Yes, Giuliana, your grandmother is right. We resign ourselves to the will of God," her mother said.

Luigi and Ruggiero were listening to how the religious women were reasoning with the matter at hand. Luigi felt it was his turn to say his piece.

"All of you, listen to me. I am not a religious man, but I will tell you one thing: he is dead. It's a shame about how he died. But, his death has spared a lot of grief for you, Giuliana, and that other poor girl. Once the town got wind of the news, you would be ruined for life and so would your friend Liliana. From the court ordeal, you, Giuliana, are blessedly spared. The best thing to do now, Honey, is put this torment behind you and move on."

"Yes, Papa is right, Darling," Ruggiero seconded with a pleasant smile. He was trying hard to convince his daughter to bear no guilt.

Giuliana looked at her family, and without a response she nodded her head in agreement. She did not trust her emotions as they were so mixed up by the chain of events that had taken place in her life.

***

The gossip among the townsfolk continued with the news of Orlando's body being shipped back to Spain. The curiosity of the townsfolk was combined with their disappointment. Rosaria, the neighbour across the street, had opened the window and shouted out to Rosa.

"Eh! Uh, Uh, Rosa, Rosa…"

Rosa knew Rosaria's habit of persistent yelling meant she could not ignore her. She ran to open her own window to listen to what Rosaria had to say.

"Did you hear? They are taking that fellow back to Madrid. Yes, the mother and father, with that woman, Sibilla, have left for the city. They are not bringing the body back here at all."

Rosa had opened her window and leaned out to listen. She was tall and slim and had no difficulty leaning out, unlike the short and stubby Rosaria. It was normal to engage in conversation with the surrounding neighbours by leaning out the windows or balconies since the rows of homes were a short distance across. Sometimes they would even pass items or food across.

"Rosaria, who told you that?" Rosa inquired.

"My nephew had to chauffeur them. That's just too bad what happened to him. He was so young. Did you know he drowned?" she said, twisting her face.

Rosa didn't want to engage with nosey Rosaria. If you knew what I know, you would not feel so sorry for him. But her lips were sealed.

"Oh, yes. That is sad. What a tragedy," Rosa said absently as she shook her head in agreement. She was sure her answer would please Rosaria. It would take a while until all the chatter around town would stop. If they were lucky, something new would happened to capture the folk's attention. You couldn't blame them. After all, their small town did not offer much. What else could they do to intrigue themselves other than delve into the occurrences of other townsfolk?

***

The rainy days and foggy nights of November had ended. The crisp, cold air of December signalled the coming excitement of Christmas. All would attend the La Novena mass at six in the morning and find joy singing Christmas carols and saying prayers alongside the setup of baby Jesus.

***

Giuliana's days were dragging, and she was bored and restless. No one needed or wanted her, and besides – with the residual effects of her trauma she preferred to stay close to home. She had memorised her old books and most of the time she daydreamed. With her eyes closed, she envisioned and wished for some of the beautiful things in life to be part of her own life someday. Now, all she could do was pray. Every now and then she went along with Grandma Rosa to help her dig the vegetation along the country roads and empty fields. It was now February going into March. Nature was waking up as time moved forward into spring. She admired the yellow Ginestra flowers along the road; they were always the first to bloom in February. Just like the yellow Ginestra flowers, maybe, just maybe, the beautiful universe will bud out something for me. Though the bad memory of Orlando's episode was never far from her mind, she was starting to cope. She thought of Liliana and wished to see her. They had run into her mother the other day at the small grocery store, with the twins. The youngsters were vivacious and mischievous, and very hard to control.

"Hello, Agnes. How are things going?" asked Gioia while Giuliana bent down and tried to amuse the little boys. "How is Liliana doing? Where is she working now?"

With a faint smile, Agnes answered.

"My Liliana is still working at the farm. They are turning the soil right now to seed. It is heavy work. She is skin and bones because Sibilla works her hard. She is tired when she comes home. Most night she falls asleep at the table, my poor girl."

"I am sorry, Agnes. Your daughter is a lovely girl," responded Gioia.

"Thank you, I am sure blessed to have her. Liliana is our breadwinner. The twins are a handful for me."

She gestured to the boys, shaking her head. Giuliana understood. She felt sorry for them, but there wasn't much she or her family could do to help.

***

Although time slowly passed, the days were getting longer and brighter. The sun gleamed in the blue sky, warming and transforming nature in its renewal. Spring was in the air and Easter holidays were approaching. The church bells were continuously ringing and the outdoors echoed with the sounds of children's laughter and games. There was definitely life on the streets, but that life didn't always echo in Giuliana's heart. It felt empty. Her playmates were gone and her dear Liliana was being worked to death. As much as she desired to see her, she had vowed not to step on that farm ever again. Liliana's only day off was Sunday and she usually slept all day. In the kitchen, Grandma Rosa had made corn pizza with some pork - a rare treat. It would be nice to share some of this pizza with Liliana.

"Nonna, your pizza is exquisite! I would like to bring a piece to Liliana. Can I?"

Rosa never denied a request from her granddaughter, even if it meant to do without herself.

"Darling, of course you can. I will cut it right now for you so that it is still warm. Look, I will give you enough for her mom and the twins also. How is that?"

"Oh, Nonna! You are precious." Giuliana stood on her toes to plant a kiss her on her cheek.

"My Sweet, the good Lord wants us to love thy neighbours as we do ourselves. Isn't that why we go to church and pray?" she said, as she wrapped it up in a kitchen towel. "Pronto, it is ready for you."

Excited by her small token, Giuliana skipped the hilly cobblestone steps to Liliana's place. It was Sunday afternoon and Liliana's mom was sitting outdoors in front of her home on a stool made from a tree trunk. The boys were kicking an old ball, amusing themselves. Giuliana approached shy and somewhat reserved, but her insecurity immediately vanished after Agnes jumped up to embrace her much to Giuliana's delight.

"Giuliana! Nice to see you! Wait 'till Liliana sees you. She is inside still resting but once I tell her you're here she will be so happy."

She stepped away into the windowless, dark kitchen to summon Liliana. In a flash, Liliana appeared at the door, all smiles.

"Hi there, Kiddo! What a surprise. What brings you here?"

Liliana greeted her friend with her arms outstretched.

"Here, I brought you some pizza from Nonna Rosa," Giuliana said proudly.

"Oh, Thanks! Mom and the boys will love it." Liliana gave the bundle to her mom. The boys quickly devoured it and only the crumbs were left all over their faces. None remained for Liliana and her mother.

"Let me look at you. You have gotten even taller since I saw you last. Tell me, what are you doing these days?" Liliana asked her.

Agnes had brought another stool for Giuliana to sit down on and was rummaging through her kitchen to find some offering for the precious girl.

"Absolutely nothing. I am bored out of my mind. Other than helping my grandmother sometimes, my life is empty. I miss school, I have no more books to read."

"Don't despair, Giuliana. I am sure sooner or later something from this blessed universe will drop into your lap. I know this town seems to be abandoned by God and men, but have hope, Sweetie."

Giuliana furrowed her brow at her friend's description.

"Grandma, in her evening prayers, always states 'Jesus, son of God, guide us, show us the way and keep the love nourished in our heart.' She always says God is with us. But then Pappy rolls his eyes behind her! I prefer to believe Nonna," Giuliana said with a laugh.

Agnes returned, dropping her holdings on the stones.

"Are we abandoned by God? You think?" Giuliana questioned, seeking positive answers.

"Never, my Dear, although sometimes it seems that way," Liliana's mother replied.

"That is how I have felt for a long time."

Liliana nodded her head seriously. She then grabbed Giuliana's hands and looked up at her with a big sparkle in her eyes.

"Wait until I tell you my good news!"

"Ok. Tell me! What's the good news?" Giuliana shook her arm to get her to respond. Agnes was first to answer.

"My prayers have been answered, Giuliana."

"Yes, Mom. Leave it to my mom," Liliana said, as she turned to Giuliana, wide-eyed.

"You see Liliana, God never abandoned you. Now come on… I am dying to know, what is the good news?" Giuliana begged.

"Giuliana, I will be leaving for the big city of Bologna next month. I have been recommended to a family by our church! Mom's connection, of course. A widow and her son are in need of an aide. He is a young man, confined to a wheelchair. The mother is getting old and frail and needs help to take care of him. I will give them my service."

Giuliana took a deep breath before her eyes watered and tears started rolling down her cheeks. Embarrassed, she started to wipe her face with the back of her hand.

"Sorry Liliana, I should be happy for you. I am being selfish. My world will be even emptier once you are gone. I apologise. Yes, if it will provide a better life for you, you should go."

"Giuliana, I cannot continue to work on that farm! The hard labour is too much for me. The clay is heavy to turn, and my back is destroyed. I have no future there. I will be able to provide better for Mom and the twins. Plus, that place holds bad memories for me. The ghost of Orlando haunts me, especially at dusk. At times I feel him approaching, his footsteps behind me, extending his hand for his usual harassment. I can almost feel him grabbing at my rear end or his filthy hand crawling up under my skirt. I know my mind plays tricks on me… It's just my imagination now that he is dead. But the recollection still startles me. I cannot wait to get out of there. Anything is better than working at that cornfield."

In a startled daze, Giuliana listened to her friend.

"You are right, Liliana, I understand. I don't blame you for wanting to go."

"So, cheer up, Kiddo. Maybe I will meet new people being in the big city, and I might find something for you too! I might be able to send for you, eh? How would you like that?"

"Liliana, I appreciate your interest. I don't doubt that you would help me. Believe me, my biggest desire is to continue my studies. I wish I could go to school, but it takes money. My family has none. My poor dad, I watch him sometimes as he holds his head in his hands. Yes, I see despair in his eyes."

"Giuliana, I understand exactly how you feel. At least you still have your dad. For the four of us here, it's hard, especially for the twins. They need a male figure to guide them. I hear my Mom cry sometimes at night in her room when she thinks I am asleep. She still grieves for my dad. As much as I miss him, my heart goes out to her."

Giuliana got up and gave her friend a supportive hug and said her goodbyes. After the announcement of Liliana news, Giuliana's sombre mood returned like a dark cloud in the sky. Like a beat up puppy, she arrived home looking down. She had no desire to see her family and all she wanted was to go straight to the refuge of the four walls in her room. I am glad for Liliana but sorry for myself. My world will be even emptier now with her gone.

However, another surprise was awaiting her.

***

Gioia and Nonna were waiting, sitting on the steps at the front door. Giuliana's Mom jumped up nervously and lashed out.

"Giuliana what took you so long?" she scolded, "You missed your teacher. He came here looking for you. He wanted to talk to you. He couldn't wait any longer and left."

119

"My teacher, here? That is a surprise! What was he doing here?"

"Looking for you."

"Sorry, Mom. Liliana had a lot to tell me and it took me longer than I anticipated."

Gioia, driven by her own curiosity, lashed out again at her daughter.

"He wants to talk to us with you, he said. Since we are going to the parent teacher meeting for Trizia, you are to come along and he will talk to us all then."

"Oh!" Giuliana exclaimed, suddenly animated. "When are we going, Mom?"

Rosa nudged Gioia and mumbled to her.

"Change your tone of voice!" She was protective of her Granddaughter.

"Tomorrow night, Dear" Gioia continued, in a milder tone.

Puzzled by the unknown, a flickering light of hope sparkled in Giuliana's tortured soul. She looked at her mom and grandma.

"We will have to wait for tomorrow."

Chapter Thirteen
The School Interview

Ruggiero and Gioia always looked forward to the school's teacher interviews. It was the spring term and Trizia's teacher, Iolanda Arcana, had sent a notice home. As the trio entered the two-story building and headed down the corridor on the first floor, they soon ran into Henrico Navarra. He had been Giuliana's teacher. A nice man, Henrico was personable, short in stature, and wore his black hair brushed back. He had a kind demeanour and eloquent verbal skills. The townsfolk had only good things to say about him. Giuliana loved his teaching.

"Mom, Dad, he captures my attention, and he is dedicated to his students. I don't want to ever disappoint him," Giuliana had said while under his tutelage.

He had been her teacher for three years, being sent to teach at the school from the lower part of Italy - Agrigento, Sicily. Henrico was an excellent educator that loved his work. Most of his students excelled with his teaching – Giuliana being one of them.

When he spotted the Ferrantes, he proudly shook hands with them.

"Mr. and Mrs. Ferrante, how are you? Tutto bene? All is well?"

"Yes, and you?" they gratefully responded.

With a pleasant smile, he turned to Giuliana

"Tell me how my brilliant student is doing these days."

"The best I can," Giuliana said, bashful. She continued, "I miss school so much."

He turned to her parents.

"She passed the elementary grade five with honours. You mean to tell me she did not go on to write the admission exams to continue high school in the city?"

"No. How can she go, Mr. Navarra? We have no means, and she needs to live there.

Room and board... it's impossible," Gioia responded while Ruggiero looked as if he wanted to hide, feeling his inability to provide for his family's needs.

"Signora! Nothing is impossible. This is why I came to visit and check on Giuliana the other day. The principal and I have been discussing our honour students here at the school and following up on them. If anyone should go on, it is your Giuliana. She has been one of our brightest pupils. We cannot allow her intelligence to be wasted. I must go now – leave the matter to me."

He shook hands and departed. On his exit, he turned back to the family.

"In bocca al lupo - keep it confidential."

***

Mrs. Zicardo always encouraged her daughters to include Giuliana in their outdoor games. The girls peeked in the Ferrante's open front door and called out.

"Giuliana, we need you... We have marked the squares ready to play skipping. Come and join us."

Lately, Giuliana often spent hours sitting in her room reading the old books that by now she knew off by heart. When she heard the girls calling she reluctantly put her book down and made her way downstairs.

"Eh! Giuliana, what are you doing cooped up in your room? Come. We need you. You will be my partner. We will play two against two," enticed Lora, excited.

Gioia and Ruggiero were only too happy when they saw the girls at their doorstep. They encouraged it.

"Giuliana, go darling and participate in the skipping game. It will be good for you."

Giuliana obeyed without hesitation. She put her book down and walked out the door to join her friends. Gioia sighed in relief and turned to Ruggiero.

"Dear, I don't like the way she has been behaving lately. Too much time in solitude in her room. I don't want her to slip into a depression again. We need to do something."

"Yes, I am concerned also. Her seclusion and taciturn behaviour have resumed too frequently. I have noticed it since all her friends have returned to school, and now with Liliana leaving... The gossip around the town of Orlando's drowning, funeral... It's all too upsetting for her. Sometimes I forget she is still a child. I need to see about what to do. I will go to the city on foot and look for a job. I will take anything as long as I get work."

The following morning Gioia had fastidiously tied her bright flowered apron on to her waist. She was about to commence her kitchen duties when a voice from the open door startled her.

"Permesso? Hello? Can I?"

"Oh! Mrs. Zicardo. What a surprise! It's you? Please come in."

Mrs. Zicardo was standing in the entrance harmonious as usual and with a big smile on her lips. She greeted Gioia.

"Buon Giorno, Good day, Mrs. Ferrante, I am on my way to

attend a delivery. Sorry, I cannot come in. I just want to tell you that I have some interesting news for Giuliana. I would like to talk to you and your husband, and Giuliana of course, later when I am done with Martina's new baby's arrival. Va bene! Ok!"

Gioia's curiosity immediately got the best of her.

"Mrs. Zicardo, of course. Anytime. I appreciate your interest and all the help you have given our daughter. We will make ourselves available at your convenience."

Mrs. Zicardo disappeared in a flash with her little black bag leaving Gioia puzzled with much escalating anxiety. Lately, Mrs. Zicardo had been keeping company with Giuliana's old teacher, Mr. Henrico Navarra. He knew of her keen interest in Giuliana. Mr. Navarra had showed Mrs. Zicardo his research into a school for the girl in the north of Italy, in the big city of Milano. He felt the need to inform her since she came from the area and could help with a plan.

"Mrs. Zicardo, we need your influence here for Giuliana," he had said at their luncheon meeting last week. "Your neighbours, the Ferrantes, are fine folks. Giuliana has been one of my best students. She passed with honors. The principal and I want to help her to continue her education. We can handle the fees and have her enrolled. The problem is the room and board..."

Mrs. Zicardo listened attentively.

"I gather you want me to find someone to take her in?"

"Yes, that is exactly what we need."

She put her hand on her chin, seriously thinking.

"I might have the right family for her. Leave it with me for few days."

There was only one telephone in town located at the pharmacy. It served the townsfolk in emergencies to place calls to the big cities. The service was rarely used since no one could afford the luxury. Mrs. Zicardo occasionally called her sister, Amelia, in Milano. She was a gynaecologist. They often consulted one another regarding patients when a difficulty surfaced. Amelia Zicardo was married with four children. Her husband, Roberto, was a judge. They lived on the outskirts of the city in a large villa. They were two professionals, both dedicated to their work. They had lost their only daughter to leukaemia. Life had been a real challenge to them in the last five years. Mrs. Zicardo could sense the grief in her sister's voice every time they talked. Last Sunday, Amelia had broken down in tears when they were speaking.

"I know we should accept the loss of my Maria Teresa, but it's hard. I cannot bring myself to remove anything in her room. Everything has been left the same."

"Amelia, you should know better. Life goes on," her sister responded. "I am surprised at you. It's time you clear her room and give her belongings away to charity," she scowled.

"I cannot bring myself to do it just yet. Her two pet birds are still in there. They keep calling her name. Roberto had them imported from Southern Australia, you know. The two parrots twitch their heads from side to side. Their lamenting noises go together with the sorrow in my heart. When I enter the room, they look so distracted, as if they are waiting for Maria Teresa to return."

"Oh, Amelia stop it. You are torturing yourself."

Her sister continued, sobbing, ignoring her pleading.

As she recollected the conversation with her sister, an idea sparked in her mind. Maybe, just maybe, this would be a solution for Amelia and Giuliana. She shook her head. I can make the suggestion . . . and leave the rest to God's will.

Chapter Fourteen
Broken Soul

As the days progressed, Giuliana was slipping back into her black mood again. Liliana had stopped by to give her goodbyes. Her schoolmate friend Lora had come along too.

"My classes are resuming," Lora had said, "I will be moving to the province soon. What will you do, Giuliana?"

The sad look in Giuliana's eyes said it all. She just shook her shoulders in denial. She lifted her face, and in a low-spirits she asked simply.

"What will you study, Lora?"

"I want to be a nurse someday. That's my passion."

"I wish you luck, Lora," Giuliana said as she hugged her friend, fighting the tears that threatened to obscure her vision. Lora will make a good nurse, she thought.

Giuliana's world was empty due to poverty. She thought of her family and questioned herself. Why is it that all the love in my home cannot compensate for the emptiness I feel deep in my soul? Her restlessness was unbearable.

***

Mrs. Zicardo had been called at the school for a parent-teacher meeting. Her younger child, Sara, was attending the one and only public school in town with Trizia. She had made it her business to request a meeting with the principal and Henrico. She walked in, enthusiastic to relate to the two gentlemen her new idea. Guglielmo Rocca, the principal, was a middle-aged fellow who was dedicated to his students and school. He immediately got up to greet her.

"Buona sera, good evening, Signora Zicardo," he said, inclining his head with great respect.

"Good evening Signori," she replied, saluting both of them with a handshake.

"Mrs. Zicardo, we appreciate your help in any way you can offer it for our students here. Giuliana is one of our brightest students. We are saddened that she cannot continue her education for lack of funds. Our system is failing our young people. I will not give up until an avenue is opened for her."

"I agree with my colleague here. We must persist until we find a place for her," Giuliana's teacher added.

"Signori, Sirs, I might have the perfect family for her. I didn't have to look too far, right in my family! My sister, Amelia, might be the answer. They lost their eleven-year-old daughter last year after fighting leukaemia for five years. After having a long conversation with my sister, I found out that she is not coping as well as I thought. Giuliana might be a blessing for her and my brother-in-law. They have three boys, a large home, a good salary, and they live in Milano. She can attend any school she desires there – all the courses she cares to take! Leave it to me and let me relay it to them." Then she turned to Henrico, "After I talk to Amelia and her husband I will go to the Ferrante's and we might have to do some convincing there. . . Will they be willing to part and send Giuliana away…?"

"Great! It sounds encouraging, let's get busy and move forward," responded Guglielmo.

"I am with you," retorted Henrico.

"Gentleman, thank you for your time. I have a job to do. I can assure you, I will do all I can for Giuliana."

***

It was Sunday morning. Gioia, Rosa, Giuliana, and Trizia had gone to church. Rosa's beads were moving fast in her hand as her lips were whispering the Holy Mary, praying to Jesus for the wellbeing of her family and asking forgiveness for Luigi and Ruggiero not attending mass – a mortal sin in her belief.

When they returned home, the kitchen was cold, and food was scarce. Rosa could not go out much these days rummaging greenery from the empty fields. It had gotten colder and her arthritic hands were aching and crippling her. She went to her spare pantry and found some wheat flour. She would mix it with corn flour and turn it into pasta, put some sparse oil in a frying pan with a little garlic, a sprinkle of salt and pepper, a few tomatoes, and her salsa would be ready. That would be their Sunday lunch and supper. Unless those two return with a surprise,

she thought. Even on the day of the Lord they had to go roaming the hills.

Ruggiero had a bit of luck this morning while wandering the fields by the river with his father. They had spotted the caretaker at the central power station. He was standing on the bridge and whistling to get their attention, he waved them over.

"Eh! Ruggiero, we have a problem with our turbines, I think they need oiling or something. Our mechanic did not get back from the city last night. Would you be able to look into it for us?"

Ruggiero had worked at the station from time to time. He had an engineering mind. He was willing and ready anytime if only they would hire him full-time, but there had been no such luck.

"Yes. Of course I can, Roger," he responded with a big smile on his face. He turned to his father, "Papa, this is our lucky day. It must be Mom's prayers answered."

He dropped his gear and rolled up his sleeves: pronto, he was ready to work. This would give him a few liras to buy some food for the family. He proudly attacked the work at hand.

"Yes, Son. We will stop at the Ponte Aquine and buy some goat cheese. That should cheer up your mother."

"Good idea, Dad. We will see if we have enough for some crusty bread, then the girls will really have a feast."

In no time, with his expertise, Ruggiero had the turbines up and running. Besides the oiling, the wheels needed a lot of cleaning. Debris had accumulated but with dedicated, hard work, it was finished. Luigi had insisted on helping out. Ruggiero was protective of his dad, fearing the danger involved.

"Papa, I prefer if you stand on the edge, and I will hand you the discarded parts for the garbage. No way should you be climbing and hanging on that ladder."

He skillfully cleared the machines in no time. Roger paid him promptly. The pair left joyfully with their precious money and went happily home.

***

Rosa was trying to keep their miserable plate of fettuccini warm by the smouldering fire while bitching as usual about Luigi.

"Oh! That grandfather of yours! Girls, he sure tries my patience. It's getting dark out there. Do you think he will get the notion to find his way home?"

She had just finished talking when the door slammed opened and there was Luigi, weaving a loot of sorts from the bottom of the

130

stairs.

"Rosa, girls, wait 'till you see what we've got for us. Prepare the table, we will have a feast!"

Rosa shook her head; he never failed to amaze her.

"I wonder what he has to show us tonight?" she said to the girls in a low voice. "Go call your mom, Dear. She is at Mrs. Zicardo's. Let her know the jokers are finally home."

Once Gioia arrived, they gathered around the table and feasted on bread, cheese, and wine. Luigi continued with his jokes, trying to keep them entertained. Gioia signalled for their attention.

"I was working at Mrs. Zicardo's this afternoon, and she wants to talk to us. She said it's good news for our Giuliana. Ruggiero, you need to be here in the morning and listen to what she has to say."

They all quieted down, staring at Gioia in suspense.

"Did she give you any idea what's all about?" asked Ruggiero.

"No, Dear. She was all smiles and optimistic. You know she loves our Giuliana."

"It's my prayers! Luigi makes fun of me, but I believe in my prayers. I feel it in my heart.

The good Lord will look after my family," responded Rosa.

***

Mrs. Zicardo had wasted no time getting in touch with her family in Milan. She had called Amelia first, and then her brother-in-law.

"Amelia, I have a solution for your despair. There is a young girl – she is almost thirteen. I know you will fall in love with her. She is bright, intelligent, and smart."

131

"Renalta, what are you getting at?" asked her sister.

"She belongs in your family. Her family is dirt-poor, but they are good people. She cannot continue her schooling. No money. The principal at the school and her teacher are willing to contribute to the expenses required, all she needs is a family to take her in."

Renalta held her breath and waited for a response.

"Renalta, do I understand you right? You want us to take her in? To live with us?"

"Amelia, yes. That is exactly what I am asking you to do. It will give you a new lease on life. You have the room and the means. Your home is perfect. Her name is Giuliana. She will never replace your Teresa, believe me, but she will make a difference in your home. The girl could be good company for you and Roberto."

Silence followed.

"Amelia are you still there?"

"Yes. Yes, I am here."

"What do you say, Amelia? I am trying to help both of you here."

Amelia was surprised to find that the heavy rock that had been sitting hard on her chest seemed to have lifted, and she could breathe a bit better. Peacefulness had come over her body. Smiling, she responded.

"Renalta, I will consider your suggestion. Let me talk to Roberto and the boys. It might be our salvation. The boys miss their sister. My husband and I are heartbroken, as are Teresa's parrots. A new young girl. . . I will get back to you."

"Thanks, Sis. Love you."

"I love you too. A domani, tomorrow."

Both sisters hung up the phone in an elated mood of hopefulness. Waiting for tomorrow, Renalta felt she already knew

132

what the answer would be.

Amelia could not wait to tell her family. There would be some adjustments to do in their life. It might uplift their melancholy, she thought. She had no more tears to shed. Although she was in the medical field where she regularly found herself facing the ordeals of sickness and death, the everyday reality of Teresa's loss had been hard to accept. Their only daughter had left such emptiness in their hearts and their home. Resentful of her loss, she was often turning bitter – blaming the cruel world. She had stopped going to church. Why had God taken her only precious girl away so prematurely? Her doctor friends had tried everything that medical science offered, to no avail. The demons of hell were determined to take my little girl. Her heart had been torn with the loss. Amelia struggled in her daily work. Her sorrow was rooted deep in her soul.

The family meeting resulted in full agreement at Amelia's household. The boys especially were enchanted by the idea and happy for their mom. They fully trusted their aunt's judgment. With renewed hope, she called her sister and happily announced to her that they would be getting ready for their new guest.

"The sooner, the better, Renalta."

"I knew you would, Amelia. Thanks. I will proceed with the plan on this end and keep you informed."

Renalta, delighted by the news, couldn't wait to get to the Ferrante's house to pass it on to them. This new avenue opened for Giuliana was fantastic. She needed to inform Henrico and the principal, Signor Guglielmo. Together they would visit the Ferrantes with their proposition.

Once she passed on the news to the school, she was respectfully greeted and praised.

"Signora Zicardo, you have been a blessing to this town and the help and devotion you have given to these people is immeasurable! I am grateful."

"Oh, well, in my place, anyone would have done the same. Let's inform the family so Giuliana can be off to a better future!"

The three of them were greeted by the Ferrante family clan. Henrico was the first to speak.

"I have had the pleasure to have Giuliana as my student. She has been one of my best. I was saddened to know that she could not continue her studies due to the lack of funds."

He nodded at his colleague to take over.

"Signor Henrico, myself, and Signora Zicardo here are prepared to help your family by sending Giuliana off to school in Milan. She can be enrolled in one of the top schools. We will sponsor her at our expense. Mrs. Zicardo has done a great job assisting in finding a family to receive her."

"Yes. My sister, Amelia, along with her husband and their sons, are willing to receive Giuliana in their home; free room and board. As you know, they lost their only daughter. They will welcome your Giuliana with open arms as one of their own," she said, looking serious at the adults. Then, turning to Giuliana, she continued, "You will be happy there, Dear. It will give you the opportunity to further your studies, and my sister and brother-in-law are good, loving people. I am told the boys are anxiously awaiting your arrival."

The Ferrantes stared at each other with mixed feelings. They were happy and sad at the same time. It was important for their daughter to continue her studies, but at the same time, how could they cope with her absence? It was a big decision.

Chapter Fifteen
Milan

Giuliana, accompanied by her mom, dad, and Mrs. Zicardo, was on the train headed for Milan. With a heavy heart, she had said her goodbyes to her grandparents and Trizia. Trying to be brave, she was looking forward to her new life of studies and her host family. The train zipped them away toward the north furiously fast. In few hours, they found themselves at the grand train station of Milan. Mrs. Zicardo was familiar with the territory – all they needed to do was follow her. Giuliana found the business of the trains from different tracks zooming in and out mindboggling.

"There they are!" pointed out Mrs. Zicardo as soon as Amelia and her husband were spotted. When the couple noticed them back, they ran over to greet them with happy grins on their faces. Behind the couple stood the boys. They had respectfully taken the morning off school to meet Giuliana.

"We want her to feel welcomed, fellows. It's important for all of us to be there," Amelia had ordered.

Here they were: The Sbarro family.

"Giuliana, here is my family, now yours also," Mrs. Zicardo said as she did the honours by introducing everyone one by one.

Amelia, Giuliana noticed, was contrary to her sister as she was a slim, tall lady. Amelia's sparkling blond hair and kind face framed her sunken brown eyes, and she spoke softly with a kind of gentleness. Mr. Roberto Sbarro was shorter than his wife, pudgy, with thick eyebrows. His look was softened by the easy smile that governed his lips.

"Oh! The boys!" Amelia pulled them forward one by one. "This is our son, Dino, the oldest – eighteen. Here is Nino – seventeen. And this… this is our Marco - fifteen."

Giuliana and her parents were taken with these lovely people. They appeared so well-groomed and refined. They could not help but compare them to the poor peasant-folk of their hometown. Mrs. Zicardo had given Giuliana one of Sara's dresses so she could look presentable for her sister's family. Since Giuliana was a natural beauty, it didn't take much for her features to shine.

On their way to the Sbarro's, Giuliana and her parents didn't know where to look first. They had never seen such a big bustling city with so much going on - traffic, people, stores, street vendors, and amazing architectural buildings. There was life here. Ruggiero took Gioia's hand and squeezed it. This is where our daughter belongs. Here there is hope. She could build a future.

Once home, Amelia couldn't wait to show the family around. She was especially enthusiastic to present Giuliana's room. As she walked through the doorway, Teresa's two parrots started to go crazy, squawking and whistling. This had been their way when Teresa was alive, but it had not happened for a long time.

"Giuliana, they like you!" said Amelia. "They have been quiet for so long. We didn't have the heart to part with them, but listen to them now."

Giuliana was all smiles,

"I like them too, Signora Amelia. What a joy to have two parrots in your home." She walked over to touch them.

"Be careful, Dear! Sometimes they are unpredictable."

"No, look. Listen to them. They like me and I like them."

The two crazy birds were twirling in a surprise dance performance.

Once the tour of the house was complete, they settled in

Amelia's huge library. Light and airy, two walls were fully loaded with books that sat on rich, moulded wood shelves. A large desk covered with Italian leather was well-positioned, comfortable and inviting. By a cathedral window, a cozy sitting area with a sofa in white snakeskin leather and two comfortable, relaxing chairs sat, ready for reading in. Giuliana was in awe. My Grandmother's prayers have come true, for sure. What did I do to deserve this and these people?

Ruggiero and Gioia remained for few days to settle in their daughter and check out the school with Mrs. Zicardo. Signor Henrico and Signor Guglielmo had made all the arrangements in advance. The following Monday, nervously agitated by the fear in her heart, Giuliana was ready to attend and discover her new school, to meet her new teacher and her classmates. Her parents were beside themselves with joy. They liked everything they saw and Gioia herself was overwhelmed. She mused to herself. This was heaven sending this boon our way. Giuliana, accompanied by her parents and Mrs. Zicardo, made their way to The Superior School Institute Tecnico so her first day could begin.

The artful, glazed stone building was a whole city block long. The huge double doors with rich brass handles were open and inviting. A white marble stairway lead them to the second floor, and the Carrera marble led them further to several different classrooms. Students and teachers were going in every direction.

La Signora Piglionella met them, as planned, in room four. With her cordial and gentle manners, she welcomed her new student cheerfully. Giuliana took a deep breath. She loved the woman's sweet Milanese accent, but unfortunately she couldn't help but feel intimidated. A heated flow of blood flashed up and down her spine, breaking her into a drenching sweat. Fear suddenly installed itself in every extension of her body. The people in the classrooms were all strangers to her. She wiped the sweat from her forehead with the back of her hand. Her vision blurred, playing tricks on her. She tried to shake herself of the tremendous ugly feeling that had overcome her. Menacing thoughts of Orlando's amused face appeared in a flashback and threatened to consume her when the teacher's voice broke her dreadful spell. She came beside her and placed an arm around Giuliana's shoulders.

"Come to the front of the class with me, Giuliana. I need to introduce you to the class."

There, facing all the classmates, Mrs. Piglionella addressed the class.

"We are fortunate to have with us a new student, Giuliana Ferrante. She will attend our classes from today on. She comes to us highly recommended from a school in Molise. I would like you, one by one, to rise, starting from Antonio on this side, and introduce yourselves, please."

After the introduction was over the students surprised Giuliana by clapping for what seemed like the longest time.

"Welcome to our school, Giuliana."

Her eyes darted from side-to-side and row-to-row checking all the new faces. Their appearances were polished and serene. The room was spacious and bright. The sun rays coming through the large arched windows felt warm and soothing. The cold-hot sweat had vanished from Giuliana's body. Her gaze stopped at a girl sitting in the third row. For a moment, Giuliana's instincts made her want to call the girls name and run toward her. She stood her ground with her mouth open. My! What a great resemblance she has to… she could be Liliana's twin!

The teacher interrupted her stunned revelation.

"Giuliana, we saved a special seat for you close to the front. Would you like that?" She motioned with her hand.

"Yes, thank you."

Before taking the seat, Giuliana, blushing nervously, felt

obligated to address her teacher and classmates. With a shaky voice, she managed to speak.

"I want to thank everyone for welcoming me. I feel privileged to be in this class. I hope I can live up to your expectations. Mrs. Piglionella, as my teacher, and for you, my classmates, my wish is to contribute to you my love and friendship."

Looking around the room, she silently prayed. Please, dear Lord, let me accept all these new people with tenderness and affection.

Her parents had left to catch the late afternoon train back. Although they were pleased with Giuliana's new, miraculous opportunity, sorrow reigned in their hearts at leaving her behind. Giuliana felt for them. But she needed to concentrate on her new life. Shifting her mind to positive thoughts, she assessed her surroundings with a pleasant acceptance.

A tap on her shoulder made her turn. She found two big brown eyes facing her.

"I am John. If I can be of any help, feel free to ask," offered the young fellow sitting behind her.

"Thank you," she responded, forcing a smile. She was not so sure she would be asking any boy for help.

After school, to her shock and surprise, the girl that resembled Liliana was waiting for her.

"Hi, I am Erica," she said, extending her hand.

Erica was of medium stature with blond hair and fair skin. She had big, blue eyes and an infectious smile on her lips.

"Nice to meet you, Erica," she replied, pleased.

"I heard you live with the Sbarro's. I live around the corner, if you like, we can walk home together."

"Oh! Yes! Why not? That will be great."

***

Amelia and Roberto, together with their boys, were delighted with the new addition to the family, but Giuliana felt shy and reserved. Her insecurities made her feel ill at times. Those two birds were hilarious. When they saw her enter the room, they started like two old ladies. They reminded her of the toothless peasant woman of Molise.

"This is Biricchina, the red feathered one, and the blue and yellow is Lola." Giuliana was introduced.

The birds had quickly repeated the line right back, twirling around the cage in amusement as they continued.

"Giuliana, Giuliana!"

"Listen! Listen! Giuliana, are they are calling you? It didn't take them long to learn your name," Amelia said.

At some point the two parrots started to fight with one another in competition to call out to Giuliana.

"Giuliana, I must tell you, you will be surprised to hear they don't like each other. We tried to put them together in the same cage, thinking they might start to love one another. It has not worked. We will probably have to separate them again," explained Amelia.

Giuliana was surprised.

"Why is that? What a shame!"

"There is jealousy between them."

"Really?"

"Oh, yes."

"That's funny!" Giuliana was amused.

Marco had been watching them from the doorway.

"Mom, I am hurt. Those two buggers certainly don't fuss over me, and I have been feeding them! They are yours, Giuliana, from now on," said Marco, indignant.

"Marco, I don't mind. I like them too. Sure, I will feed them. But, in cleaning the cage, I will need your help."

"Oh? The dirty work for me? You can get Costanza, our housekeeper, to help you with that."

"Marco! Costanza has enough on her hands! It's your job to help Giuliana with those two old ladies," ordered Amelia.

Nino intervened.

"Giuliana, don't let this character get away with anything, after all, it was his idea to get a second bird. Lola is his." He squashed his hand on Marco's head.

"Lola, Lola!" As Lola heard her name she sang while attacking and biting Biricchina's head.

Giuliana laughed so hard. They were hilarious, and the boys were amusing and funny too. She had never had brothers, and these guys were funny, like the two parrots.

Dino, the oldest, was tall like his Mother, with wavy brown hair, grey eyes, a high forehead, and a perfectly oval face. He was an attractive fellow. Nino resembled his Dad more: black hair, a soft smile, more reserved with a medium height. Marco had a delicate physic and small stature that concealed his age, but he was charming and witty, with devilish eyes. He hung around more, pestering Costanza, his brothers, and his parents. Giuliana would be an addition, but she didn't mind. He must miss his sister, she thought. Dino and Nino usually came home late. They busied themselves with their friends after class, pursuing and goofing with the pretty young girls around the piazza. The two older brothers seemed in competition courting girls.

Dino had come home last night shouting at Nino.

"Nino, I am warning you, when you see me talking to the blonde by the cappuccino bar, scoot would you? Pretend you don't know me. How many times do I have to tell you?"

"Eh, brother, calm down. Maybe I can help you," he remarked, snarling his face and giggling away. "You are afraid she might prefer your brother, eh? That's it?"

"No. I am warning you, go find your own. Three is a crowd."

Dino was serious, but Nino seemed to amuse himself by bugging his brother. Giuliana sympathised with Dino. He seemed to her like a kind soul. He treated her with great respect. Often he emptied his pockets of change and would dump it on her lap.

"Giuliana, here. I want this weight out of my pockets," he would say.

"Dino, are you sure? I cannot take this money from you. I haven't earned it."

"Nonsense! I don't like digging for change, and it accumulates. I save them for you, Giuliana. Can you make use of them?"

"I can buy stamps to write to my family. At the same time – if you can use them, I don't want to take it from you," she responded with guilt.

The only way she could communicate with her family was by mail – writing letters with the stamps his change provided. She looked forward to receiving any news, although it didn't happen too often because her family had no money for stamps. Oh, how I miss them! She glided in luxury in this home and her beautiful room. The crazy parrots would be fun to show to my sister. If only Trizia could be beside me sometimes. In her dreams, she reached out for her sister at times, but she wasn't there. Occasionally she felt her beside her in her subconscious mind. She was pleased.

***

Back home at the Molise, her mom and grandma had baked bread mixed with corn flour. It had a whitish-yellowish colour, thick crust, and smelled delicious.

"I wish we could send a loaf to Giuliana, Mamma Rosa. Should we try?" her daughter-in-law teased.

"Tell me how? You know it's impossible," the older woman replied.

"You are right, Mom. From what we know of where she is living, she does not need our cornbread!"

Ruggiero was called to the electric plant every now and then. It gave him some money for his family and his pride. He had come home this day with few liras. Waving them at Mamma Rosa and Gioia, he had said:

"I want this money saved in the sealed jar in your room, Mom. Christmas is coming, Giuliana will come home for the holidays. She always wanted new shoes. I will take her to the piazza to get her winter shoes. If I get more work, we will buy oranges and torrone for Christmas."

"Ruggiero, don't you worry. I am a frugal shopper. I can stretch that money and make sure I have a panettone, a special holiday cake on our table," Rosa said cheerfully.

Luigi had not been feeling well. Since fall had rolled around his knees were hurting and his arthritis was getting unbearable. He was having a hard time going through the hills – the slopes were a challenge. He felt useless not being able to come up with much in the way of provisions.

"Rosa, you need to help me. My joints are swollen."

"I will boil some vinegar and salt. Soak a cotton strip and bandage your knees and elbows. You will feel better in no time," she reassured him.

"Rosa, my Rosa! What would we do without you?" He kissed her forehead in devotion.

"You need to get better. Giuliana will be home for Christmas. I don't want you limping around," she teased.

They were all excited, counting the days to Christmas. As happy as they were, Ruggiero was concerned about his dad's health failing drastically.

***

Up in Milan, Giuliana continued to immerse herself in her studies. The school was her outlet, although it was much more demanding than her small-town class and more competitive. She tried studying harder to keep up with the big city people, each with much more experience and exposure. Dora Piglionella, her teacher, treated her well.

"I recognise your efforts. Brava! Clever. Well done," she praised.

The encouragement gave Giuliana the momentum she needed to strive for better.

Amelia was working long hours at the hospital. Often she had patients coming down from Austria and France. She was well known for her skill and a lot of foreigners were seeking her knowledge. The Sbarro's household was filled with high achievers and professionals. Mr. Roberto Sbarro was occupied with his lengthy court cases, which sometimes lasted six months. He was not allowed to talk about his work, and he never did, until they would hear it on the news or read it in the papers once the judgment was passed. The family was unaware of what occupied his time. Occasionally, he would mention needing to do a judgment report, but never a mention of who or what. After dinner, he would retreat in his library to review his papers in total privacy.

Costanza, their live-in housekeeper and cook was up at seven in the morning to make sure she looked after their needs. She occupied a quarter on the third floor. She was a pleasant lady who wore a grey uniform with a white apron and a crispy white collar that exemplified cleanliness. A white net covered her head to keep her hair in place. Every day she would go to the open-air market to buy fresh vegetables, veal meat, poultry and fish, which was delivered to the door, from several speciality stores.

"Miss Giuliana, your breakfast is ready," she would call out.

Sundays were a day of rest. Costanza would have the afternoon off. The family would gather in the big dining room with no exception. Mr. Sbarro sat at the head table and Mrs. Amelia at the other end. One by one, Mr. Roberto Sbarro asked them to report on their week, good or bad, and the plans for the following week.

"We start today with you, Amelia," he announced, playfully.

"I have not lost any lives this week. I am grateful to God and our medical science."

"Your wish and plan for next week, Dear?"

"I have a couple of critical patients; I wish for them that they turn around. My best wish is for myself and my assistants: to give our patients the best care that they deserve."

"Thanks, Dear."

"Thanks, Mom," echoed the boys, with Giuliana following suit in a low whisper.

"Giuliana. Your turn, Dear."

Shy and confused, she was not prepared. Marco even had warned her earlier,

"Have you recapped your week, Giuliana?"

She had paid no attention. Now, here she was.

"Uh? My week… I wake up in the morning with the chirping of the parrots. I admire their beautiful feather colours and their morning singing. I jump out of bed and get washed and dressed. I love my school, my teacher, and my class. Marketing, literature, and philosophy are my favourite subjects. I kneel beside my bed every night in prayer. I thank God for giving me the Sbarro family, and the beauty and gift of my life. I close my eyes. I see my family back home; I pray for their wellbeing. I am looking forward to another joyful week."

"Very good, Giuliana. We are fortunate to have you in our home and in our family. Dino, your turn."

"Mom, Dad, I love my family. My studies went well. I enjoyed all my subjects. Please, Dad, order Nino to stop bugging me. As soon as I approach a girl he appears and barges in out of nowhere to interrupt my world."

They all laughed out loud. Marco was beside himself. He turned to his brother.

"That is funny! Dino, call me next time. Take me with you."

Nino didn't think it was funny and seriously thought his brothers were cruel.

"Now, now! You little squirt. Wait until your turn comes. I will be on your toes pestering you," answered Dino, giving his young brother a menacing look.

"Marco, you have to respect your brother's privacy. That goes for you too, Nino. Stay out. Approaching girls is a delicate matter when you are as young as Dino. My advice to you is to walk away."

Marco and Dino were making faces, acting smart at Nino's expense, when Amelia interrupted.

"Boys! That's unacceptable."

"Yes. I suggest you apologise to your brother," ordered their dad. "Nino, what do you have to report?" He nodded at his middle son.

"Dad, Mom, all of you. I had a wonderful week. I got an 'A' on my math exam, physical fitness was the highlight of my classes, and I am not so popular with the girls at my school. I love having Giuliana here with us. But I wish you would expedite this one to another planet," he said, turning toward Marco.

Marco immediately went on the defensive and started to elbow him.

"What did I do to you?"

"Yeah? What about using my shaving equipment? My deodorant? My aftershave? You thief!"

"When did I do that?"

"A thief and a liar, Dad." Indignant, Nino answered looking at his Father for help.

Amelia winked at Giuliana.

"Boys will be boys! You might as well get used to hearing them argue about their mischief."

With that, Roberto spoke.

"Marco, you do not use your brother's toiletries. You get your own. Do you hear? Don't ever do that again. It's a matter of hygiene and personal privacy."

"Yes, Dad." Marco nodded sheepishly.

"Marco, it is your turn," his father reminded him.

"Uh, what can I say? I did well on my science test. I liked playing cards with Giuliana and having her here. We feed the birds together. I would like to go with her to visit her family for Christmas."

"Thanks, Marco. As for wanting to go with Giuliana at

Christmas… you are getting carried away. We only want to hear the plan for the following week. Thanks, everyone, I want to wish you all good week ahead, with gained knowledge and happiness," said Mr. Roberto, nodding his head.

"Thanks, Dear." Amelia nodded at her husband with a soft smile and added, "and thank you, boys." Turning to Giuliana, she said, "A special thanks goes to you too, my sweet girl. You have brought life into our house since the day you arrived. We love you dearly."

Marco had moved the parrot's cage to the hallway and before Giuliana could respond, they were squawking aloud.

"Love you! Love you! Giuliana!"

The whole family broke into laughter. To their surprise, the parrots were getting along better and had come alive again since Giuliana had arrived.

A great dinner had been served with an antipasto of prosciutto, clear broad beans, spaghetti, veal, salad, roast potatoes, and Tartufo with espresso and liquor. The reports were finished until the following Sunday. Giuliana was impressed. The boys had been gradually growing on her. She was slowly learning to love them as her own brothers, but with caution. The scar deep in her soul surfaced now and again, impairing her flow of free feelings. Mr. Sbarro came across severe at times with the boys. His stiff black suits and big glasses showed authority. But, when he referred to her he spoke respectfully and with gentleness.

The Christmas season was approaching. Giuliana was counting the days until she would return home for the holidays. Her host family was going to pay the train fare as this was to be her Christmas present. All her Classmates at school were making plans to go skiing in the Alps or Switzerland. Most of these young people's families included a mother and father who had steady jobs. Money did not lack here as it did in the lower region. Therefore, there was no suffering. Students could plan for holidays and live comfortable lives. They were close to France, Germany, and Austria. The Northern industries – such as designer studios in clothing, shoes, machinery, and much more – had easy access to import and export. This area had much to offer.

Giuliana would pick up and read the paper with keen interest after Mr. Sbarro had discarded it to the side. The business section interested her. She listened to the reports on the radio and was tuned into the transmissions of the close neighbouring countries. The Germans ranked high on their mechanical skills. The reports on their perfection were an eye-opener. She often would send some clippings in her letters to her mom and dad. Gioia would read the newspapers to poor Rosa who could not read nor write. Gioia herself had only gone to school till grade three. She, nonetheless, managed to read and write letters to her dear daughter. Ruggiero had been fortunate to have gone into the army, where he had access to more schooling and had been trained in constructing machines and maintenance. He was a bright man.

Giuliana's thoughts were always back home with her family. When she walked home from school with Erica, she confided in her.

"I feel guilty living in Milan with so much, Erica. The Sbarro's shower me with good food, accommodation, and designer clothes."

"Stop the guilt. You deserve it, my friend. I am sure you reward them in kind. You are beautiful inside and out, sensible, mature, and studious," Erica commented.

"Oh my friend, you're gracious."

"If you ask me, I think you skipped your childhood. You are always so serious, and worrying. Come on, Giuliana. We are old enough to start eyeing some boys out there and have some fun," Erica said with a wink.

Giuliana totally ignored her statement.

"If I could only get my dad a job up here. Then I would feel better," she replied.

"See! Here we go again. Tell me, what do you think of Johnny? I think he has the hots for you."

"He does not enter my mind except for where school work is concerned."

"I figured, Giuliana. Wake up. Start to notice the boys out there because they sure are noticing you."

"In what way?"

"Have you ever heard of such a thing as love, Giuliana? Romance? Kissing? Embracing? Cuddling with a young fellow? With a handsome boy like Johnny, this should not be hard to do."

Giuliana looked at her friend, surprised. She suppressed her secret deeper in her soul, shutting in the feelings that accompanied it, sealed with a tight lid. My experience with a young man was far from her description.

Chapter Sixteen
Winter in Milan

The days had gotten shorter and the air cooler in Milan. The dark grey sky was overcast; the sun had been hiding for days. The white flakes of snow drifted down in a gentle motion. The Christmas music from the stores and the streets were setting the pace of the holiday season and the spirit of it all was manifesting as the people saluted each other in the piazzas. Giuliana arrived home half-frozen as she rubbed her hands to warm up by the fireplace. She wasn't used to the colder climate of the north. Although the snow melted as it hit the ground, the bitter cold still managed to penetrate her bones. The tip of her hands ached and her feet were numb. The blood in her veins were used to the warmer climate of the south. The walk back and forth to school had become a challenge. Here, people walked everywhere in the city and the streets were always crowded. Most people lived close to their jobs to avoid the horrendous traffic.

Costanza arrived loaded with bags of groceries.

"That wind is bitter cold out there," she puffed.

"Yes. I must have caught a real chill standing at the corner chatting with Erica. I am ice cold and wet. My body is shivering," answered Giuliana.

"Oh dear. I will make you a cup of tea. That should warm you up."

"Thanks, but Costanza don't bother. I will go to my room, get under the covers for a while and rest."

Once she walked into her room, taking her clothes off didn't seem like a good idea anymore. Her teeth were jittering, and she couldn't wait to get under the covers. Her body continued to shake. Soon came the sweating. The covers were tossed on and off.

An hour later, Costanza came to knock on her door and check in on her. There was no response. She slowly opened the door, concerned. Giuliana's fatigued breathing broke the silence of the room. As Costanza moved closer, she could see Giuliana's face was flushed. Costanza placed a hand on her forehead – it felt abnormally hot. It was clear Giuliana was delirious. She was mumbling to herself and wasn't making much sense.

"Oh my God."

Costanza was alarmed. She ran to get the thermometer and soon found out that her fever was over the limit. She immediately uncovered Giuliana, put fresh water in a basinet and proceeded in sponging her down.

"Giuliana, Dear, you are scorching hot."

Costanza wasn't sure her words registered. Giuliana's body was lifeless. Frightened, Costanza called the hospital to page Amelia. It took a while for the nurses to get Dr. Sbarro, and while she waited Costanza's panic accelerated.

"Hello, Costanza?"

Finally! Costanza gave a sigh of relief.

"Signora, you need to come home at once. It's Giuliana. She is very sick. She has a high fever and she is delirious. I am afraid she will go into convulsions."

"Dear Lord! Keep her cool. I will be right there."

Without wasting time, Dr. Sbarro signed off the floor.

"Sorry, I have an emergency at home. Have Dr. Salerno cover for me. I need to go home."

Her heart was racing. She was reliving her daughter's many nightmarish emergencies. In no time, she was at Giuliana's bedside.

"Giuliana, Dear, it's Aunt Amelia. I am here to help you. What brought this on?"

There was no answer. She checked Giuliana's heart rate. It was racing out of control. Giuliana's skin was hot, and her body, lifelessly week.

"Dear, speak to me," she pleaded as she uncovered her completely. That is when she noticed a pool of blood in the bed. After pulling off her clothes, Amelia watched as a lump of blueish blood gushed out of Giuliana. The sheets were soaked, and her panties were blotched with dark, ugly blood.

"She is hemorrhaging. I need to take her to the hospital! She is losing too much blood."

Amelia called the emergency department. In no time, a unit was at the door to take Giuliana to the hospital. Amelia didn't leave her side for the whole trip and ensured that Giuliana got the best treatment possible with her oversight and guidance. Upon arrival, Giuliana needed to be placed on intravenous to replace her blood loss. She was almost fourteen and her body had gone into shock with her first menstruation.

Listening to her lungs, Amelia remarked to her assistant nurses.

"The breathing is definitely abnormal. Page Dr. Romano, the internist, and tell him to get to the emergency department at once. Place a red code signal for an emergency. It's just too much for her body to cope with all at once," she diagnosed. After feeling her pulse, she noted that her heartbeat was fatigued and irregular. The nurse wrote everything down on the chart.

Moments later Dr. Romano was beside them. He immediately got to work checking the young patient.

"Her lungs sound like a racket. We will take x-rays and go

from there," he said solemnly.

"She got her period – from what I gather, her first," Amelia relayed.

"How old is she?"

"Fourteen, almost fifteen."

"Amelia, you are the expert in that department, but don't you think that's a little late?" he asked, shaking his head.

"Not really. It's acceptable and is seen in cases with poor nutrition. Circumstances can delay development. The worrisome part is that the loss of blood is more than it should be."

"She is in good hands with you. The blood replacement should be no trouble. I am told we have plenty in our reserve bank today."

"Let's act fast. You check the seriousness of her lungs," she ordered as she handed the nurses, Matilda and Emilia, the instructions.

Matilda was one of their top nurses. She came to them highly recommended by the medical university of Bologna. Amelia remained vigilant and continued giving instructions. She turned to Matilda.

"You will monitor her around the clock."

Amelia wasn't sure if she should call her sister to notify Giuliana's parents. I don't want to alarm those poor souls. She thought it might be best to wait for the x-rays results and Dr. Romano's diagnosis of the state of Giuliana's lungs. The results would be back soon enough. When they came, the results showed that Giuliana had a severe infection in her lungs. This would need to be cleared, but she could perhaps be stabilised.

A few days went by, and Giuliana's weak body proved to not be responding as well as it should have. Amelia was sweating the possible outcomes. Sometimes she wished she had chosen a different profession in life. The medical sciences were not always rewarding. She put a hand on her forehead, thinking hard. God, please. You took my little girl. Spare Giuliana. She had called her sister to inform her that Giuliana was not well, but she had warned her not to alarm Giuliana's parents.

"Sis, we will have her on her feet and well in no time."

Mrs. Zicardo was always positive.

"Amelia, I am sure you will. I have no doubt. I will put it lightly to her parents."

Amelia had not been home for two nights. Roberto understood his wife's dedication. She had done this a lot when their daughter was in the throws of blood transfusions, but in the end, all Amelia's efforts had been futile.

Another week passed and Giuliana was still hooked up to intravenous for liquid nourishment. However, she was starting to show signs of improvement.

"She has lost too much blood and that has rendered her anaemic," said Amelia from Giuliana's bedside.

"The combination of infection in her lungs and blood loss made her lifeless. We have replaced a few pints of blood," reported Matilda.

The next morning, as Amelia entered Giuliana's hospital room, she noticed the sun rays that beamed, bright and warm, reflecting off the headboard above Giuliana. They bathed her face with an angelic glow.

"How is my favourite patient today?" greeted Amelia, smiling.

Giuliana stretched her arms.

"I am better. The heaviness on my chest has lifted. My legs don't feel cumbersome to move anymore."

"I am glad, Dear. It's such a beautiful day out there with that luminous sun shining. You have got to feel better."

She smiled, and Amelia's heart rejoiced instantly, putting her past days of stress behind her. She didn't mind being Dr. Amelia Sbarro today. Now she had a delicate matter to speak to Giuliana about: the facts of life and the realities of menstruation and puberty. Giuliana's mother and grandmother should have prepared her, but it seemed they had neglected to do so. Amelia had heard tales from her sister that the southern townsfolk were a different breed. Their old-fashioned beliefs did not allow them to talk about such realities. Perhaps it was against their religion. Her sister would often comment on such things with a smirk.

"But, believe me, Amelia, it's not that liaisons don't occur here. There is much going on even in this small town. The woman and men are fast to label a young girl as soon as they see her talking to a young man twice," related Mrs. Zicardo with disdain.

"Sis, don't you wish you lived back here where we are more open-minded?" Amelia would tease.

"Amelia, they love me here, and I love them too. I skip to the main city – which is really only two hours away – when I need a break. I am needed here. I cannot leave."

Giuliana was indeed naive about her period. She had heard Erica talk about it sometimes, but she preferred to walk away or change the subject. It was embarrassing.

Amelia sat beside Giuliana, took her hand, and held it gently.

"Giuliana, what has taken place here is that your body has developed into womanhood. Now you are part of the universal bliss that allows us women to reproduce and contribute with God's will in the unity of love between the two genders – if and when one chooses to. As you may have observed in your family, marriage and love is something that happens to us human beings, and when it happens our bodies endorphin and dopamine levels are elevated, which is favourable to our existence."

Giuliana listened attentively.

"The way you put it, Aunt Amelia, sounds good. I believe you."

"That's my girl. I have a book here about anatomy and development. Read it and you will understand," she handed her the manual.

Amelia put a hand on Giuliana's shoulder for reassurance and continued.

"Let me tell you one thing – remember, it's all part of our universe, Dear. When we let nature take its course… only then it will feel right. Everything in life has its right time, including sex."

Giuliana took the book and couldn't wait to read it. It sounded lovely the way Amelia had put it. Pensively, she reflected. I guess that is why Orlando's actions had been so ugly. It was against nature, and the requirements of two human beings coming together in love. Will my body ever erase that horrendous experience? Will I ever feel the love and pleasure Amelia explained to me? The doubts were a discomfort to her subconscious but she shrugged her shoulders. She trusted Amelia. Right now, I need to get well and strong again and resume my studies.

Amelia wasted no time in calling her sister.

"Sis, good news. Giuliana is coming along well. The episode of the menstruation in combination with a lowered immune system contributed to her complications, which caused chaos in her body."

"Sis, I understand. I am sure she received the best of care."

"Please update Giuliana's parents. She will be fine. She is young and resilient. In no time she will be strong again."

"Thanks to you, Amelia. If she were here, she would have died. The limitations here are frustrating. I try my best to help these people even with these limitations."

"Sis, I admire your dedication. You will be rewarded in heaven someday."

"Thanks. If I didn't feel for these folks, I would not be here."

"Just think, Renalta, all the facilities and knowledge we have here sure didn't save my daughter. We are all at God's mercy."

"Give that Signorina in Milano my best wishes, will you?"

"I will. Ciao." Amelia hung up the phone.

Amelia needed to wait until Giuliana was well and back on her feet, but as soon as she was, she would take her to the best haberdashery in Milan and fit her with the best woollens money could buy. Her mind swirled with images of sweaters imported from Ireland, a camel hair coat, and a fedora hat. She would buy her fur lined booties too, to protect her from the winter's bitter cold. On her last round, Amelia checked on Giuliana once more before leaving.

"Giuliana, hurry up and get well. We are going on a shopping spree when you get out. You will be so warm, Dear. There will be no chance of you being cold or in discomfort up here in Milan ever again! I should have known you are not acclimated."

"Aunt Amelia, you are so kind to me. How am I ever going repay you?"

"You are already – with your presence. And, I am going to get old someday... I know you will be there for me, my Dear."

She gave Giuliana a strong hug and away she went.

The school had closed for the holidays and Erica was missing her friend. Giuliana had become close to Erica since they connected on that first day. A bond had been established. When Giuliana related to Erica how she resembled her dear friend Liliana, Erica was quick to respond with a smile.

"I hope she is beautiful," Erica had teased, patting Giuliana's shoulder.

"Yes, she is. I must write to her," Giuliana said, staring into the emptiness. "She is kind and caring, just like you. Poor Liliana. She has left her family behind to take care of a young, paralysed man and his old mom."

The pair was quick to disclose their true feelings and confided in one another, becoming school chums while walking home together. Erica had related to Giuliana all about her family and how they had moved here from Germany. Her dad was a mechanical engineer in one of the big companies in Milan. Often, he travelled abroad to pass on his skills. Erica lived with a younger brother, Peter, and her mom. She faithfully waited at the corner every morning for Giuliana to walk together to school.

"I will be going to visit my grandparents in Munich for the holidays, Giuliana," said her friend when she reached her in the morning.

"Me too. I will go see my family. I can't wait."

Giuliana always looked down when she mentioned her family, with sadness in her eyes. How she wished her family could move here. But how? It took money.

After school, they hugged before they parted for the holidays.

The next day, Giuliana, with her new outfits, was seated on the train and heading for the meridional region of Molise. She had gotten taller and prettier – her skin in the north had changed pallor due to the lack of sunshine. Her silvery-gray fedora hat gave her an added finesse. The cosiness of the fur collar around her neck brought her comfort.

Her Mom and Dad, as well as Mrs. Zicardo, were waiting at the train station in the city. Her eyes widened when she spotted them. Kicking her new boots high in the air, she ran to embrace them joyfully, greeting Mrs. Zicardo with a much-deserved respect. The connecting bus they all boarded quickly descended the hills towards the small town where the rest of the family waited. The family had no money to pay the fare for everyone, so Mrs. Zicardo's had supplied the fare for her mom and dad.

Giuliana was going to be home for two weeks. Delighted by her return, she vowed to cherish every moment in the limited time she had. Once she arrived, she saw that her grandparents and sister were all waiting for her. Gioia kept hugging her daughter continuously. Rosa's happiness glowed around her as she held her granddaughter for the longest time. Trizia had grown few inches taller and had lost her plumpness. Grandpa was standing behind them all, last to be greeted, waiting with his arms stretched out to hug her.

"Eh! Let me look at you. Our big city girl. Oh! My, my. Don't you look spiffy," he said. The man was all smiles as he wiped away the tears that were rolling down his cheeks. "We have missed you so much, my pumpkin."

He bent over and pulled her closer, taking off her hat to kiss her silky brown hair.

"Grandpa, I missed you too," Giuliana said as she furrowed her forehead with concern. She couldn't help but notice Grandpa's sunken cheeks. He looks malnourished. "Grandpa, you have gotten slimmer. Isn't Grandma feeding you?" She shook her head. Something is not right with Grandpa.

Poor Rosa had been sweating away in the kitchen all day. She had managed to prepare the best supper she could to celebrate her granddaughter's return. She had borrowed some white flour from her neighbour to make homemade fettuccini and white bread.

"No cornbread tonight, but the feast will soon start. Our precious girl has come home," she announced to the family.

Her other sons were joining them later with their wives and children. Rosa's eyes sparkled. Her family was reunited. And, with her other son's families coming to join the gathering, her and Luigi's lives felt complete.

The door opened and the rest arrived.

"Hello! Permesso."

"Come in, come in!"

Gioia was the first to get up to invite them in, followed by Rosa. Greetings were exchanged, and Rosa began frantically shaking Luigi's arm.

"Luigi, Luigi! The accordion! The accordion! Music, that's what we need!"

"Rosa, calm yourself. Give them a chance to settle down and have a drink, for heaven's sake. You are too much."

"You are supposed to have it ready and going," she retorted.

With all the commotion going on and Rosa's incessant requests, Luigi had to ignore his aching body. He pulled his accordion from the kitchen shelf, and with animated energy started to play 'La Tarantella.' His three sons joined in the singing and the fun was enjoyed by all. Giuliana looked around the crowded kitchen. The young cousins were twirling about, her aunts and uncles were singing at the top of their lungs, and Grandpa was cranking that old accordion like a professional.

"Thank you, God, for my precious family." She silently whispered.

The eating, drinking, playing and singing went on late into the night. When Giuliana finally walked into her bedroom, she noticed the shabby bedspread and the thin sheet. What a difference, she thought. The luxury of Milan does not exist here. There was Trizia, snoring away, sound asleep, sharing her bed. She gave her a delicate kiss on her cheek and happily crawled in beside her. She was glad to share the bed with her again.

***

The days were going by too fast. Giuliana had no desire to go back anytime soon. She wanted to visit Liliana. I wonder if she has come home?

"Mom, have you heard any news of Liliana from her Mom? Has she returned for Christmas? I would like to see her," Giuliana asked.

"No, Dear, she hasn't returned. Her mom was saying that Liliana is taking care of that sick young man and cannot leave them. They have no one else. Mrs. Manzana will go visit when Liliana sends her and the twins the train fair."

"I must get her address and make sure I write to her. I really would like to keep in touch with her."

"Yes, Dear, you should. Her mom said she is living outside of Bologna, in the suburb."

"I shall visit Mrs. Manzana and get her address," she nodded.

***

It was Christmas morning. The family was cheerfully gathered in the kitchen. There was no Christmas tree, but Rose welcomed them with a nice crackling fire she had lit up earlier that morning. Giuliana glanced out the window. Fluffy white snowflakes were peacefully coming down.

"What a perfect Christmas, Grandma," said Giuliana, and she gave her a hug.

"The sparkling fire is warm, and that makes everything perfect," said Rosa.

Ruggiero and Luigi barged in from the storage room singing 'Jingle Bells' and carrying a basket each. As the two finished their serenade, Rosa and Gioia took up the charge and launched into more Christmas carols.

"You come down from the stars…Oh, my Signore…"

"Merry Christmas!" The girls clapped and joined in singing along.

Ruggiero and Luigi proudly distributed their torronies and oranges as their gift to share with the family. It was a gift, in and of itself, to be together.

The Holidays would too soon slip away, and on the morning of the 8th of January, Giuliana found herself on the train returning to the north.

Chapter Seventeen
Return to Milan

On her arrival, Giuliana spotted Amelia and Mr. Sbarro stretching their necks on the platform among the crowd, waiting. Marco, hiding behind, was jumping up and down. On spotting her, he delightfully called out, waving his arm.

"Marco!" she called out.

His eyes beamed. He lifted his hand to show a small red box.

"Chocolates, for you!" he shouted, as he playfully held the box up, making her reach for it.

"Marco couldn't wait for you to come home, Giuliana. He insisted on bringing his present here," said Amelia.

"Thanks, Marco. How thoughtful of you."

"Marco is Marco. He has to do whatever he sets his mind to do. He couldn't wait for you to get home to give it to you," commented Mr. Sbarro, with a light-hearted sigh.

"How nice," she responded.

"He acts like a five-year-old at times."

"Oh, Roberto! Don't be hard on him," Amelia retorted, protectively.

Once they arrived home, shiny boxes were revealed, unopened and waiting for Giuliana under the tree.

"Giuliana, you must be tired from your travel. Why don't you go rest up? When the other fellows come home, we will celebrate your homecoming and open your presents."

"Yes, I badly need a shower," Giuliana agreed.

"Eh, Giuliana, if you are not tired, you can help me clean the bird's cage. After, we can play a game of cards!" said Marco.

"Marco, leave her alone, will you?" ordered his dad.

"He can be a pest sometimes," Amelia added, sympathising with Giuliana.

Dino and Nino, too, were happy to have Giuliana back. Marco's pestering was accelerated due to Giuliana's long absence from the home.

"She is always so polite and patient toward him. We owe her for her mercy!" Nino winked at Dino.

Rushing supper at the boys' insistence, Giuliana opened the presents under their watchful eyes that evening. School supplies greeted her from Dino, a scarf from Nino, and from their parents, Giuliana received tickets to the opera at La Scala.

"Oh, My God! Thank you!" She held the tickets to her chest and reached out to kiss them both. "You are way too kind. What did I do to deserve this?"

"Never mind, Giuliana. Stop beating yourself up."

She ran to her room and quickly returned with the one torrone, embarrassed.

"This is to share," she said. Then she retrieved a bag from beside her chair and said, "My Grandma Rosa made these biscuits. There are two of them – also to share."

"Giuliana, you should keep them for yourself," said Amelia.

"Sorry it isn't much, but I would like everyone to have a piece."

"Giuliana, never mind if they don't want any. You and I can

feast on the torrone," Marco said, nudging her with a smirk.

Nino and Dino smacked him on the head with their napkins, and he brought his arm up for cover.

They were nasty and comical in their behaviour. Giuliana loved them dearly.

School resumed, and so too did Giuliana's daily routine. In the evening, despite being blessed as she was with all God's goodness, Giuliana went to bed with her stomach in knots. She tossed and turned, trying hard to fall asleep, but she couldn't. Breaking into uncontrollable sobs, she tried to muffle the sound, as to not wake anybody in the house. I miserably miss Mom, Dad, my little sister, Grandpa and Grandma. Oh! Why do I feel so sad? Trying to appease her misery, she sat up. Pen and paper were always to be found beside her on the night table. She tore a page from her ornate, rose petal stationery. She stared at it for a while in a daze.

"I feel like a shredded rose petal," she muttered to herself. She put pen to paper and wrote of the sorrow she felt in her heart. By the wee hours of the morning, her heavy eyes finally drifted away to sleep. No sooner had she closed her eyes, a gentle tug forced her to open them. The shadow leaning over her was Amelia.

"Giuliana, Dear. You slept in and are late for school. Please get up. My sister called and I need to talk to you." She said with a gentle voice.

A shiver of fright ran up and down her spine.

"Aunt Amelia, please don't tell me something bad has happened to my family? I have not been able to sleep all night."

Amelia held her breath. The shrill ring of the telephone called out and Amelia quickly walked to the hallway to answer.

"Pronto, hello."

"Hello, Amelia"

Quietness followed.

"Hello..?"

"I am afraid I have bad news."

Chapter Eighteen
Sorrowful News

In the small town of Molise, the news was spreading like wildfire. Women leaned over windows and balconies, or outside their front doors, accelerating the blaze of gossip. This means of dissemination was faster than any newspaper or radio announcement.

"Eh! Did you hear? Luigi Ferrante is dead."

"Oh! When? How? Pity."

The whispers jumped from one to another. The church bells rang out in a slow and sombre tone. The folks out in the fields would stop whatever they were doing and make the sign of the cross, asking among themselves who had died.

After Giuliana's departure, Luigi's heart had grown weaker and weaker. As much as Luigi wanted to get out of bed and join his son for their daily routine of roaming the countryside, his body would not cooperate.

"Those hills make my heart race, Son. I lose my breath," he had said, barely audibly.

"Dad, you don't have to go anywhere. Rest, and get yourself stronger. I'll manage by myself. Don't worry," responded Ruggiero as he started on his way, furring his forehead, concerned.

Rosa wanted to go and get Don Francisco – the old doctor. It wasn't in Luigi's character to remain in bed. Rosa was up early, totally consumed with worry.

"For him to refuse to go with Ruggiero is serious – he is

169

awfully weak. I need to go get the doctor," she had said, venting to Gioia before leaving for her own chores.

When she reached the doctor's home office, bad news awaited her.

"He is out of town today, Signora," the girl at the desk informed her.

"When will he be back?"

"Not until Monday."

"It is Friday! Three days away? I'd better look after him myself."

Rosa returned home and mixed then boiled some herbs from her invented remedies. Luigi's heart was failing. Rosa was frantic.

"Why isn't my mixture working?" she asked Gioia, frustrated.

"Mom, he should be in a hospital where they are better equipped to take care of him."

They knew it was impossible, and praying was their only hope.

With great effort, Luigi rolled over in bed.

"Son of a gun," he swore to himself.

***

Before sunrise, he had taken his last breath. His weak heart suffered a massive cardiac arrest at the age of seventy-two. Upon his passing, Rosa's emotions were totally out of control. She sobbed away while mumbling about her beloved Luigi. The rest of the family also were in deep sorrow. The ordeal of a funeral would be a challenge for the family. After the announcement, Mrs. Zicardo approached Ruggiero and Gioia dutifully and with much sympathy. She hugged Gioia, stepped between both of them and

170

then put her arms on each of their shoulders.

"Gioia, Ruggiero, I feel for your loss. My heart goes out to you. Now, regarding Giuliana, I am concerned. I don't think it's possible for her to get home. There has been a terrible snowstorm up north that has brought traffic to a halt. I know your Dad has to be buried today, and I am afraid we will just have to go on without her. I've spoken with my sister twice already. Of course, you are the parents, but I think it might not be a bad idea to spare Giuliana this day and let her remember her Grandfather with only the joyful memories of her recent visit. I will call Amelia again and inform her and you can talk to your daughter on the phone if you like."

Giuliana's parents looked at each other. There was barely any spirit left in them. Ruggiero looked up at Mrs. Zicardo.

"Yes, Signora. I think our daughter should be spared this ordeal."

Then Gioia, holding her husband's hand, forced herself to speak between tears.

"I agree. I want Giuliana to remember her grandfather with only the good memories of our holidays. He was the strong rock in our life. Let her preserve his memory as such."

Ruggiero's mind was filled with thoughts of his father. The man was a hard worker and did whatever he could to ease the burden his children faced. He was never one to shy away from lending a hand. Ruggiero felt responsible at times for Luigi's arthritic bones. Now that Luigi was dead, pangs of guilt set in; he was terribly missed already. Ruggiero cherished their time together – Luigi was his best friend, and now his best friend was gone.

***

Months later, spring was approaching and the days were getting longer and brighter. The direct sunrays were soothing to the skin. On this day, Ruggiero came home earlier than usual. It was a Monday night, and Mamma Rosa greeted him with a sad smile on her face. Once the four of them set at the table for supper, Ruggiero took a deep breath and announced what had been plaguing his mind all day.

"I will walk to the city tomorrow, and I will refuse to come home until I find work. Especially now, with Papa gone, I need to get out of here before I lose my mind. I am ready to accept anything or go anywhere to find an opening."

"Ruggiero, where will you sleep if you cannot come home?" questioned Gioia, furring her brow.

"Gioia, there are benches inside the train station. I will slump on one of them when my body gives up. The next morning my search will continue. You girls look after yourselves while I am gone, ok?" he ordered, with a serious look on his face.

The next morning, Ruggiero was up at dawn. With a light knapsack on his back, he left the house quietly. His footsteps were swift and determined.

"I must conquer the distance before high noon," he muttered. He had a destination in mind, and if he did not arrive on time, they would close for the afternoon break and his day's efforts would turn fruitless. He needed to do one thing first – there was a farmhouse by the river bank. He recalled Papa's advice.

"Son, in this country, in order to get anywhere, you need to oil the wheels."

Ruggiero laughed at his dad's strange logic.

"Papa, what do you mean, 'oil the wheels'?"

"Son, you have to put your hands in your pocket. Otherwise, nothing happens."

"Yes Papa, as much as I don't want to agree with you . . . I have heard of how some of my friends got positions – they bought their way."

"You see, my Son, it's just what I told you. We have no money, and so we remain unemployed. I am not concerned about me. I have had my day, in America. You and your brothers, however, worry me."

Ruggiero had few liras in his pocket. Mamma Rosa had handed the money to him the night before. He recalled some folks by the river that made fresh cheese. He had been there with Papa once when they had gotten a hold on some money. He stopped at the farmhouse and picked up a fresh round piece of mild goat cheese.

"With few extra liras," the lady told him, "You could buy a piece of sheep cheese, which is much stronger and tastier."

Ruggiero carefully counted his loot out of the cloth sack that contained his coin. He responded by nodding his head. This would be his gift to give away. The lady wrapped the cheese in brown paper, and Ruggiero put a cloth napkin around it to keep it even fresher. He guarded the parcel as if it were a precious jewel. He looked up at the sky, and implored. God Almighty, please let me find work. Papa, if you have any influence from up there, help me.

Kicking his feet up, he conquered the distance as fast as he could.

The office of The Labour Department had been swamped in the past week. The peasants from the surrounding towns had gotten wind of work available in Switzerland, France, America, and Australia. They had been coming in in droves. Mr. Jerome Falcone had been conducting interviews as quickly as he could, but the line was endless.

Ruggiero had been lined up for hours, and now he was finally next to be called. He discretely pulled his wrapped treasure from his extra-deep inside jacket pocket and handed it to the man. Ruggiero eyed his surroundings, hoping no one was watching.

Jerome at first hesitated, but then the smell of fresh sheep cheese reached his nostrils. His face folded into a smile. He nodded, encouragingly.

"Ruggiero, come forward please and step aside," he gestured to a spot by his desk and picked up some papers, which he handed over. "Fill these out and hand them back to me."

A surge of energy revitalised Ruggiero's tired body. He quickly filled out the sheet and handed it back to the man.

"Mr. Falcone, thank you," he said, though he didn't have to say anything, as his pleading eyes said it all.

"A presto. Soon, my friend." Mr. Falcone tapped his shoulder, turned his back on the line and in a low voice mumbled, "You will receive a notice by next week."

Ruggiero felt extremely animated as the joyful promise of work gave him the strength to cavalcade down the long road home by foot. He was eager to give Mamma Rosa and Gioia the good news. Tired and breathless, he arrived home. It was late. There they were: Mamma Rosa and Gioia, by the low flickering fire, reciting their beads.

Ruggiero's body was ready to drop from the exhausting and long journey, but when he saw his dearest two women waiting for him, he slammed the front door open with gusto, climbed the four steps to the kitchen and hugged Gioia. Twirling her around he released Gioia only to then hug his Mom with the same vigour, causing her rosary to fly about her.

"Mamma Rosa, I know Papa always teased you about your rosary. I am beginning to think it works. I have good news. I have a feeling that this time I am going to find work and I don't care where they will send me," he said.

He had clearly gotten his second wind of energy and he was all smiles. They, in return, shared in his happiness.

"Tell us! Please! Tells us all about it, Ruggiero!" begged Gioia, hopefully.

"Nothing to tell yet, but there are openings in the foreign countries. I will know by next week."

"Ruggiero, what if they send you far away?" Rosa asked, aghast.

"Mom, wherever will do. I cannot stay here any longer. Look, I practically had to give away my daughter due to our misery. Trizia is coming up. What will happen to her? I have no choice. I am dead here. You girls deserve better."

Ruggiero was so hopeful that he couldn't wait for next week. He had a good feeling about this. The days went by slowly, and finally, one sunny morning a big grey envelope arrived addressed to 'Ruggiero Ferrante' with a government stamp. His hands were shaking with anticipation as he began to tear open the paper, and Rosa and Gioia stood beside him just as captivated. The call had come and the procedures to take were laid out. There would be some red tape to clear, but, yes, he could go to France or America, or other foreign countries where openings were offered to emigrate.

The talk in town was about how glorious America was. The land of opportunity, they called it. America it will be. Yes, Papa had expressed many times how he regretted coming back. He was elated with joy for such an opportunity.

"Mom," he said, "don't let me see you looking down like that. Just think – no more famine or misery for my family and me. The only problem is that since it took these papers too long to clear, it is bringing me into winter."

"Yes, Dear, that's what I worry about," responded Gioia.

"Dear, don't forget about Mom and her beads. With God's will, I will be just fine."

He gave an affectionate hug to reassure her. Before catching his ship in Naples he needed to do one thing: take a train to Milan.

175

He wanted to see and say goodbye to Giuliana.

***

Ruggiero was fidgeting his fingers in the waiting room of the Sbarro's in anticipation of seeing his daughter. She was due to come home soon. She would be surprised. He badly wanted to hold her in his arms before he left. He vowed to make up everything she had endured to her once his fortune was made. I have not been a good provider or father. He kept torturing himself, riddled with guilt.

Giuliana, unaware, bounced in, heading straight to the parrots. They were calling to her incessantly.

"Hello Giuliana, Hello Giuliana!"

Biricchina, with her jealousy out of control, kept biting Lola's head to stop her.

"You silly girls. You are a riot. Hello there," she said as she caressed their wings. Costanza's calls finally got her attention.

"Miss Giuliana, I have a big surprise for you. Come, come. You have a visitor."

"Oh my! Who can that be Costanza?" she frowned curiously.

Costanza opened the door. Giuliana could not believe her eyes. There he was, her handsome dad with his big brown eyes, wearing a navy blue suit, and his dark wavy hair freshly cut and swept back – he did not look like a peasant. He looked like a refined Signore, a Lord.

"Oh, my God! Dad? Dad! What a surprise. What are you doing here? Where is Mom?"

He jumped from his chair, grabbed her hands and stretched them open wide to take a good look at her.

"You have gotten taller and have become such a beautiful girl, just like your Mother. Let me hold you, my pumpkin."

He embraced her and held her in his arms afraid to let her go.

"Dad what's up? Is everything ok?" she said with concern.

"Giuliana, I am to catch the train tonight at eleven. I will be going to Naples and catch the ship tomorrow to America. The government has job openings, and I am one of the lucky ones. I couldn't leave without seeing you first, my darling."

Giuliana was happy and sad at the same time.

"Dad, it is so far away," she said woefully.

"I know, but we will be together as soon as I can call for you."

Giuliana did not respond. The pain in her heart was deep and carving further down by the minute. She was keenly aware of how her sadness would only add to his own hurt and feelings on leaving. I am sure Dad doesn't want to emigrate, but he has no choice.

Her dad had said his goodbyes, thanked the Sbarro's and left. Regardless of her ability to understand the situation with clarity, Giuliana's uncontrollable emotions got a hold of her during the following days. She would often wake up with crying spells at night after her dad left. After school, she would seek the privacy of her room. It wasn't easy, with the parrots and Marco wanting her attention constantly. At times, it was necessary to place the parrots in the hallway. As much as she loved them, with their gorgeous, striking feathers, they were a pain when they would start to imitate her, and her crying was no exception. The first night they heard her muffled sobs it had started.

"Oh, my God!" Giuliana said with fear, "Shush, shush! You are going to wake everyone up...I need to stop. It's not fair to them to be forced into my world of misery."

When she turned the light on, there they were, like two old

ladies. Without blinking, they stared at her, mesmerised. Until she got to them and caressed their heads, their pupils would not relax.

Giuliana remained in her sombre mood, waiting desperately to hear of her father's safe arrival and of his new life in America. After three slow weeks, her long awaited letter arrived.

Dear Giuliana,

I have arrived safe and sound. New York is a bustling City; bigger than Milan. All is well. I am making my way to Buffalo and will update you as to my findings when there. I met two nice fellows on the ship, and they have been a great help.

You look after yourself. I know how much you care about your schoolwork. I know you will make us proud. Be well, I will write you again.

Regards to the Sbarro family.

A big hug, with all my love,

Your Papa

XXXOOO

Chapter Nineteen
The Voyage

No mention of the discomfort Ruggiero suffered on his voyage was included in Giuliana's letter. He certainly didn't want cause any unnecessary worry to weigh on his daughter's wellbeing. God and Ruggiero knew it had not been an easy one. His ship, 'La Saturnia' had left the port of Naples and had managed to cross the rough waters of the Atlantic Ocean. Arriving in New York, weak and hardly able to stand up from the seasickness he had endured, Ruggiero was pleased to be on solid ground. His two new friends, Giacobbo and Billy, helped him during the worst of his sickness and helped him get off the ship. Even in his sluggish state, he couldn't help admiring the lifestyle of the fast moving city of New York.

The traffic flowed at a dizzying rate, the skyscrapers lived up to their name, and there were people everywhere.

"I will say, guys, there is certainly life here," Ruggiero said, turning to Giacobbo and Billy.

Ruggiero was to catch a train to Buffalo and the two fellows were headed for Rochester. Ruggiero's arrangements were such that he was to report to work in a steel factory as head of the maintenance department. Although his body struggled to regain some stability on the unfamiliar ground and overcome the chill climate, he had no time to spare for weakness. His working skills were highly in demand here.

***

The factory was huge, and it employed many people. Ruggiero, grateful for the chance he was given, gave all he had by working day and night. This new place had become his salvation.

"No use to going home. I'd rather watch my machines, and I get a kick from watching the cupola firing the steel, especially with that snow blizzard out there," he would say to his supervisor.

That supervisor, Mr. Jack English, considered himself lucky to have such a dedicated employee. After six months Ruggiero was even moved to a finer department. There they made airplane parts, and now they made them in perfect precision, thanks to Ruggiero. The company was soon shipping all over the world. Ruggiero was proud of himself. He was going home every Friday night with a pay cheque. That was very important to him, as he had been deprived of this for so long. At month's end, he would run to the post office and send a draft to Gioia and his Mother. He would often write to them on his lunch hour. Oh! How I miss them so... if they only knew how much. He would write only about the good side of his new world. He didn't want to worry them.

Dear Gioia and Mom,

I have plenty of work here. This factory is as big as our town, and the money is good. I want you to look after yourselves and buy anything you need. Mom – no more cornbread and dandelions. This is why I came here, to save you, my Dearest. My only problem here is the cold winter and my English. I will conquer the cold with my heavy boots and quilted coat; I look like a seasoned North Pole fellow! I am going to night school twice a week for my English.

Since all my workmates don't speak my language, I am forced to learn. I need to read the blueprints of my patterns, so it's a must to learn.

Gioia, I am kept busy, that will take care of my longing for you, darling. You take care of Mom and Trizia. Of course, I often write to and hear from my pumpkin in Milan. She tells me she is doing well. She is delighted with her studies and she is working hard to make us proud. You know she never complains, but we can rest assured that she is fine.

I will soon consider calling you over, I cannot wait for us to be together again, Dear.

We were not meant to be apart. Await my next letter, my love.

Affectionate hugs to Mom, my precious Trizia,

Hugs and kisses,

Your loving husband,

Ruggiero.

The letters of communication continued regularly to Ruggiero's home and Milan. A year rolled by fast, and before anyone realised it, it was almost to an end. The distance was great between Ruggiero and his family and trips back and forth were impossible.

***

Although the state of living had improved back home, Gioia's heart was sinking with deep pain for her missing husband. Rosa would often notice Gioia's eyes, swollen and red from crying.

"Gioia, I don't see you smiling much these days. What's wrong? You must miss Ruggiero incredibly," Rosa inquired gently.

"Mom," Gioia responded, tearing up, "I know Ruggiero sends us money and we live well now, but my family is divided and broken. Giuliana is in Milan, Ruggiero is in America, and we are alone here. If you ask me, I'd rather eat cornbread and onions, and be together."

"Yes, Dear. I feel for you. I suggest you encourage Ruggiero to get you and Trizia over to America. Even Giuliana. There is no reason now for her to live away from us for her studies. Her own Father can pay for her schooling."

"What do you mean, me, Trizia and Giuliana? You are to go with us."

"Gioia, at my age…I will not go anywhere. My husband is buried here. I want to die here and be buried beside my Luigi, where I belong. Until then, I have my church, this old house, and my friends. But you, my Dear, you must go to your husband. It is not fair to you or him," the old woman mused.

Gioia, disturbed by her mother-in-law's answer, snapped back.

"Mom, do you think we will leave you here alone? Forget it. You have to go with us, regardless of your beliefs."

"Gioia, my mind is made up. You need to attend to your husband and your daughters. Never mind being concerned about me."

A strong knock shook the door, startling both of them and interrupting their conversation.

"Posta, Signora – mail, Mrs. Ferrante," the mailman called out. "I need your signature here."

"Oh! Sure. It is it probably from my husband," Gioia called back as she hustled to the door, almost tripping on the stairs.

"I have a big envelope here, Mrs. Ferrante, and one regular mail. Both addressed to you."

Gioia frantically scribbled her signature, grabbed the mail, and waved the mailman off. Her eyes eagerly took in the two envelopes. One was posted from America and one from Milan Italy. They were from her husband and Giuliana. She held them close to her chest as if they were two jewels.

"Mom, Trizia, I have two letters." She couldn't wait to open them and read what her two dearest people had to say.

She sat at the edge of the chair, opening Giuliana's first.

Dear Mom,

I am writing from school on my lunch hour. I wanted to give you the news as soon as possible, so I am going to mail this letter on my way home. I have passed my all-state exams with top honours! Plus, I will be graduating from high school next month. I want the three of you to be here to attend the ceremony. I will make a reservation at the hotel close to the theatre for you. After the dinner, we will join my Milan family to see the opera (Madam Butterfly). Please, Mom, you must come. I wish Dad could be here, but I know it is impossible for him.

Mom, I love my school. My teachers are great and my family here is loving. My adopted brothers are fun and wonderful. Oh, yes, and my parrot Biricchina nearly killed Lola the other day, biting her head off. Amelia is totally dedicated to her emergencies and often does not come home. I worry about her. The Honorable Sbarro has lengthy and serious trials going on. We are all hard at work. My love to you and Grandma. Hugs to Trizia.

Your loving daughter,

Giuliana

Rosa and Trizia were standing there as she read the letter out loud.

"Mom, when are we leaving?" asked Trizia, with shining eyes.

"Not so fast. I want to see Giuliana, and we should be there, but I am not sure Grandma can handle the business of that city."

"Nonsense!" said Rosa. "We are going. My granddaughter is special, and she deserves us all."

"Oh, Mom. Thank God. You're wonderful," Gioia said with a smile. "I was afraid you wouldn't come. It would not be the same without you. Of course we are going!"

All jubilant, the women hugged each other, elated.

"Next, the big envelope. Let's see what Ruggiero has to say," fretted Rosa.

The envelope was stuffed with papers, but a handwritten letter finally surfaced. Gioia recognised Ruggiero's writing.

Dear Gioia,

I have gone to the consulate of immigration and I have filled an application for you girls to come over to America! They told me you should be called in three months' time. I have sent you copies and instructions for your preparations. I know this is the best for us, and we should soon be together my Dear. All is well here — working day and night.

Regards to Mom, hugs and kisses,

Ruggiero.

"Oh my!" exclaimed Rosa. "Today has sure been a news day: invites to Milan, papers for America. Gioia, how lucky can we be? I feel like opening the window and shouting it out loud to the neighbours! We are going to America! Except...I am not going to America. But, I am ready for Milan!"

Gioia crossed her arms.

"Mamma Rosa! Please don't make my life more difficult than it is."

GINA IAFRATE

Chapter Twenty
Love Struck

In Milan, Giuliana's affection for her family was always at the front of her mind. Having diligently kept up her schoolwork, she was awaiting her graduation and hoped to share it with her dear family. She had been writing letters to her mom and dad, keeping them informed. The weeks and months kept swiftly going by and before she realised it, the last few years had flown by. The Sbarro's were good to her. Every member of the family was absorbed in their obligations so she fit right in as a dedicated student.

Dino was always courteous to her in his shy way. She often caught him staring at her, and couldn't help wondering if he was amused by the way she swung her hair on top of her head to keep it off her face. He would smile and playfully tug at a strand of hair, pulling it up further up.

"I like your hair in a crest like that," he would say.

"Dino, it feels comfortable. It's off my neck," she would reply, rolling her eyes.

He bought the monthly romantic magazines and loved to read stories and look at illustrations. Often he would pass them on to her.

"Giuliana, you are old enough now. Read this chapter. It will teach you how to love."

"I have plenty to read with my school work. Leave it here for my spare time," she replied good-naturedly, smiling at him.

As time passed and she got older, her curiosity got the best of her. She found herself often glancing at the images and the stories.

"Dino, when is the next chapter coming out?" she now would ask him.

"Oh! I got your interest, eh? You like my Grand Hotel magazine!" he teased.

Nino, on the other hand, was peculiar at times. He struck Giuliana as a follower more than a leader. This is why he seemed to get on Dino's nerves. He wanted to do what his older brother did, and copy him in every which way. She liked Marco. Marco was now older but still somewhat immature for his age. He was always getting into trouble with his dad and brothers by getting into their private belongings, one way or another. Plus, his shoes were never shined, he dressed sloppily, and he refused to get his hair cut regularly. Mr. Sbarro was meticulous and demanded much from them in their mannerisms and ethics. He was strict and brought his sons up with a disciplined, military-style. Giuliana had caught on fast after her arrival and she complied in every respect.

Marco had struck a special note to her heart; she tenderly treated him with kindness. He reminded her of Trizia seeking attention. His Mom once remarked to Costanza.

"Poor Marco. Being the fourth child in this busy household, growing up with extremely in-demand parents and a sick sister for many years... he must have felt neglected somehow."

"Mrs. Amelia, I think Giuliana has been a Godsend for him. She is good to him, and he likes her a lot." Costanza responded.

"Yes, I know. He wants to go with her to Molise. God help us when Giuliana moves on. He will miss her terribly."

"He will grow up and find a new interest. Let's not worry about that now."

Their Sunday ritual continued, and it was marvellous to come together that way. Giuliana wanted to implement that to her own family someday.

Her stroll from school to home had continued daily, either with Erica or alone. Sometimes Johnny also waited for her, always with a sweet smile. He recently had been paying a lot of attention to her with a gentle, captivating interest. His gaze lingered to the point of making her uncomfortable at times. She remembered Erica's remarks.

"He has the hots for you."

Her mixed up feelings didn't register 'the hots,' but rather the platonic friendship her soul could handle given her fragile history. This is how she preferred to remain: polite and friendly. In her world, schoolwork was most important. Besides, the boys at home and thoughts of her far-away family kept her busy enough.

***

Time continued to fly by for Giuliana. It was now spring again, 1955. Soon her train ticket would be purchased, school would be over, and she would be bound for the little town of Molise once more for the summer holidays to reunite with her dear family. Giuliana had become comfortable in Milan and had openly confided to Erica as much.

"As much as I love my mom, Grandma, and Trizia, and want to be with them, I don't look forward to going home. The situation is not the same. My dad is gone; Grandpa is not there anymore… It makes me sad."

"Why don't you stay here?" Erica asked.

"I can't. My family needs me. I feel hesitant to impose on the Sbarro's more than I have to. After all, I am only staying here to go to school."

"Giuliana, you can stay with me. If you like, we can go to

189

Germany. Let me tell you something, my brother likes you a lot. He thinks you are the most attractive girl I have ever hung around with. He is afraid to ask you out."

Giuliana was flattered.

"Really, when did he say that?" she asked with a widening smile.

"The other day, when you were wearing that lovely pleated skirt. You had your hair up in a twist, accentuating your high cheekbones. Your big eyes are enough to attract any young guy!"

"Oh! Come on, I am just an ordinary girl from the south...the kind that you people from the north look down at!"

"No, never, Giuliana. You are a real beauty and smart too. Who gets the best marks at school? You have passed the entrance exams for law school! Although, I see you going much further and better than that, my friend."

"Thanks, Erica. Your confidence in me means a lot. You are such a good friend."

"Let me remind you of one thing. You forget I am German. I don't look down at the meridional people. How can I?"

"Yes. We are labelled as peasants: poor, uncivilised, and not worthy of the classy people of the north, especially the Milanese."

"Not all of them do though, only the uneducated. The Sbarro's would never make such a statement."

"Absolutely not."

They parted with a hug every afternoon, always looking forward to meeting the next morning.

When Giuliana arrived home, she did not get her usual greeting by Costanza and the parrots. Today she found only Biricchina alone in the cage, and she looked mad. Squirming, and crossed eyed, she didn't even salute Giuliana.

"Costanza, where are you? Where is Lola?" she called out.

Costanza appeared from the laundry room, covered in feathers.

"Marco has taken her to the corner store, alla tabaccheria," Costanza answered.

"Oh? He wants to show her off to his friends, I guess. Poor Lola needed a break from Biricchina? Were they fighting all day? If you ask me, Costanza, I think they should be separated before something drastic happens."

"I agree with you, Giuliana. Poor Lola was doing circles in the cage all afternoon as her enemy was chewing her head off, pinning her and incessantly screaming at her."

"Oh my! We must discuss it with Amelia and Mr. Sbarro. Something needs to be done."

Giuliana walked toward her room. She was tired and wanted a short rest before Marco returned to make demands of her. She craved privacy. To her surprise, Erica's new revelation echoed in her mind. She found herself standing by the full-length mirror checking her appearance. Is my friend right? Am I really a beauty? Mom and Dad had always raved about my perfect facial structure. She had never considered herself a prize. There was an iron barrier around her heart, especially where young fellows were concerned. Oh? Well, maybe. If Erica and her brother think I am a beauty...am I?

***

Like the blooming yellow rose of Killarney, Giuliana's mentality was slowly changing. She had become a stunning young lady. She was all grown up and going on eighteen. Besides her gorgeous body and her sculptured oval face, the brainpower she possessed had developed also. She possessed more maturity, confidence, and self-esteem. Her self-assurance had been growing in leaps and bounds. The boys at school marvelled at her. When she walked through the street, the men would turn their heads in admiration. She ignored it with a casual lightness, although it would stir some pleasure in her soul. She reminded herself frequently, I am still the girl from the hills of Molise and the cornfield. No one could look down to her. No one could take away her love and passion for literature, math, and her hunger to learn – gifted by the universe itself.

Erica and her other friends often tried to pull her away from her studies. They were all raving about the boys – their escapades to the municipal gardens, the secret meeting places for their liaison encounters, all foreign to her. Her friend Dora once grabbed her aside from the group outside the school.

"Giuliana, tell me, don't you have blood running through your veins? Don't you desire to be kissed, hugged, and loved?" she asked.

"I haven't given it that much thought. No. My love is my work, my family, my studies."

"How boring! Wake up kid. You want to have some fun, don't you? A lot of the guys ask about you. Since you are so stuck up, they are afraid to approach you. Or, are you the other way…?"

The other girls joined in on the attack, aware of Dora's mission and Erica's constant complaints.

"Yes Giuliana, Dora is right. You need to let loose. We are going out tonight. Come with us."

"No. I can't. Friday night I play scopa with Marco. I cannot disappoint him."

"Marco! That little squirt? Why would you sacrifice a Friday night for him when you can have fun with handsome boys? Come on, Giuliana. Something is wrong with you. Are you turning into a nun, or… a lezzie?"

"Yes, you might as well lock yourself up in a convent. You can study there too, you know," said Sofia, contributing her two cents.

They were ganging up on her.

She slowly departed from her friends. Their words and accusations echoed in her ears for the rest of the evening and weekend. She had heard rumours about Dora being the cat's meow with the young guys at school. At home, Nino and Dino were always talking about girls, goofing, and gossiping. Nino was always in competition for the hot girls. It was devilish Nino who would relate to Dino who got whom among his friends. Describing disgusting facts of the easy girls, they would make fun of them and brag about them to their friends. Dora's name had often come up.

***

Erica had gone away for the weekend and not returned. Giuliana was walking home alone. There was a house en route before she turned to her street, which she had always admired. The majestic front structure was refinished with a white glittering stone. Three stories high, the house had thick double doors with heavy brass doorknockers. Balconies from the second story connected up to the third with green Persian louvers. She always wondered who lived there. This afternoon as she passed by, the place was lively with a bunch of boys rowdily kicking a ball. A handsome young man seemed to be their coach. When he saw Giuliana, he suddenly stopped. His eyes locked onto hers in an enduring gaze. Giuliana turned her head quickly and kept walking. She stumbled, catching her footing, and almost tripped on the uneven cobblestones. The other fellows had remained still since the young man in the lead held the ball at his feet, putting a halt to their game. One boy hollered out.

"Eh! Joseph?" waving a hand across the young man's face to break his spell. "Kick that ball! My God, Joe, have you been struck by lightning or something?"

"Ma che'! You strunz, don't you see who struck me? The full moon, right there," he pointed, picking up the ball.

"She lives on the next street. Get over your spell, Joe. She doesn't dig you," said another.

Joe straightened himself up and returned to the interrupted game.

"That girl makes me stir," Joseph said as he grabbed the ball and placed it in a proper setting position before he addressed it in full force. The ball went flying over the rooftop, across the street.

"Oh! Joseph, go burn your energy on the next street. That's where she lives, I am told," said the first boy.

"Guys, I will make it my business to find out who on earth she is and who she belongs to," stated Joseph.

"Good luck. There is a rumour about her. I won't say," one of the guys said, nodding his head.

The new encounter had affected Giuliana immensely. She couldn't help reliving the scenario over and over in her mind. A warm flow of giddy nervousness zipped throughout her body. Then, a stirring, pleasant, and cold shiver followed. She had never experienced anything like that before.

As she opened the door, there was Marco waiting. Immediately he started pestering her. He wanted attention.

"Giuliana, how about a card game? Su andiamo."

Giuliana gave a deep sigh.

"Marco, please give me some time. I am tired right now." She slumped her body on her bed, hoping to be alone to reminisce about the incident of her brief encounter. That fascinating young man… Who is he? They called him Joseph, she had heard, does he live in that house? She had always wondered who lived in that marvellous place. But why in the past had she never seen him before? All these questions were going through her mind. She kept replaying an imprint of him behind her eyes.

She went to bed early that night, dreaming of the stranger that had stimulated her heart. Never imagining that a slight encounter could create chaos in another boy's inner-being also, around the corner on the next street, Joseph De Santis was restlessly tossing and turning in his bed unable to sleep. He too, had been replaying over and over his encounter with the beautiful girl. That mysterious young girl has hypnotized me completely, he thought. Who is she? What is her name? I will do everything in my power to find out.

Chapter Twenty-one
The Graduation

Gioia, Rosa, and Trizia, dressed in their best custom-made attire, were on the train heading for Milan. Gioia, overwhelmed with joy, gently took Rosa's hand in hers.

"Mom you are such a good sport. I appreciate you going with us. Your presence will mean a lot to Giuliana. She needs our support, especially on her graduation day."

"I wouldn't have missed it if my life depended on it. Luigi will be admiring her from heaven."

"Oh, Mom! I hope so. As long as it makes you feel good," said Gioia. She wasn't so sure of that, but she didn't want to spoil Rosa's belief.

The reservations and arrangements had been made by the honourable Judge Roberto Sbarra. Last week, he had returned home waving an envelope in his hand with a big grin on his face.

"Giuliana, I want your folk's to stay here, I want it to be an experience of a lifetime. I managed to get tickets for the opera – centre balcony – with the best view of the stage." He exclaimed.

The judge was well known and highly respected in Milan. With his influence, he had no trouble getting anything he set his mind to. He had booked the family at the elegant Grand Hotel near Piazza Del Duomo.

"I am told how devoted your Grandma Rosa is. Giuliana, we must take her to the service at the church of Santa Maria Nascente." Piped in Amelia.

"Oh, Aunt Amelia, yes!" Giuliana responded, with a big smile. "Wait 'till she sees the white, glittering marble roof peaks, and the sculptured façade, and the Madonna's with the gleaming reflection of the sun's rays."

Gioia, Rosa, and Trizia had now arrived at the busy train station. The fast moving trains were departing and inward bound from every direction in uncountable numbers. Giuliana and Dr. Amelia were already on the platform waiting for them. Affectionate greetings were quickly exchanged as they didn't want to be swept away by the fast zooming trains. Soon they were whisked away by their waiting vehicle. The taxi, almost at the same pace as the trains, was swerving in and out of the busy traffic at a frightening speed. The driver had amazing driving skills, but Rosa's heart was in her throat. She was afraid of crashing with all the traffic and constant movement of the cars, trams, and pedestrians coming and going from every direction. Rosa embraced herself.

"Gioia, I am not sure we will be able to survive here a week!"

She was used to her quiet, isolated remote town down south; this was too much for her. Trizia felt overwhelmed to be reunited with her sister. Gioia was all smiles. She loved the movement of the big city, but her heart ached for her Ruggiero.

"Oh, Mom! I wish my husband were here," she moaned as she placed an arm around Rosa in affection. Rosa only nodded in agreement.

"My Luigi would be mighty proud. Giuliana was the apple of his eye."

"Ma, he knows. He is watching over us from up there. You said, remember?"

The Hotel was not far from La Scala, the biggest renowned theatre located right in the heart of the city. They would walk around and amused themselves with so much to do and see. Rosa's wide eyes didn't know where to look first. Trizia was bursting with joy, mesmerised with the attractions.

***

The school was packed with graduates. An honorary award was presented to the high achievers and Giuliana Ferrante was called up to the podium more than once. Humbly smiling, she held her trophies. She received much admiration from the Sbarro's family members who were all present, including Costanza, dressed and groomed to honour her. Gioia and Rosa, with tears of joy running down their cheeks, and Trizia, simply happy for her sister, cheered on with her friends in support. There was a lot of noise sent in her direction.

While up there, a young man with a fancy camera called out to her.

"Miss, please allow me…" he yelled, coming up front.

He was snapping pictures as fast as he could from behind the camera. Giuliana noticed wavy, curly black hair. The man lowered his camera and in a split second she recognised him. His big, dark eyes captured hers again in the same fashion they had on the quiet street. It was the young man the next street over.

"Joseph," she breathlessly whispered, as she slowly walked back to her family with a flicker in her heart.

She tried to smile to her family and the Sbarro's, while concealing her emotions. She mentally hushed her fluttering heart to stop its rapid speed.

"Someone is in love." Dino whispered right in her ear, making her jump. Distracted and shaken, she stretched her arm to push him away in a sisterly gesture.

Amelia had made reservations at a special restaurant. The celebration was followed by an exquisite seven-course meal. There was everything from prosciutto and melon, to a fine broth, risotto Milanese, polenta with gorgonzola, mushrooms, and breaded veal cutlets, tartufo gelato with espresso, plenty of fruit and cheese – served with figs.

The meridional family lived their week to its fullest. They went on the city tour to get an overview of the most interesting parts of the city. They went shopping in the high fashion district in Montenapoleone, via Dante. The girls had fun admiring the luxe, glamorous styles made by the top designers. To top it all off, the Opera house, La Scala, took their breath away with both the architecture and the performance.

The week flew by and the family found themselves heading back to the train.

"I have seen it all now, Gioia. If I die and find my Luigi, I can talk to him about Milan. What a city!" Rosa said.

"Mama, I am happy for you. You will still have a lot to see once we go to America."

Rosa did not respond. She remained quiet. Those unwelcome thoughts roamed in her brain. When she thought of Gioia and the girls emigrating, the lava of sadness would start flowing, damaging the core of her heart and soul.

Chapter Twenty-Two
Ruggiero's Development in America

Ruggiero's dedication had brought about the great results of higher performance, precision, and efficiency for the company. As a result, the head supervisor had rewarded him with a bonus at year-end. All the merits of a top employee were awarded to him. Mr. Alex Mac Aley had called Ruggiero into his office for a private meeting with his accountant.

"Ruggiero, I want you to meet our accountant, Richard Johnson."

"My pleasure, sir. Ruggiero Ferrante," Ruggiero introduced himself as he offered his hand.

"I am told you are the miracle man for the company," the accountant replied.

"Oh, I don't know about that. I do my job, and I love my work. I am here alone, with no family. Work and my studies are my salvation."

"Well, it shows. You have brought this company from near bankruptcy to an incredible profit, which now rises at a steady pace."

The man showed Ruggiero the graphic scale he had drawn out.

"I couldn't do it alone. I have some good man and cooperation from my patrons," Ruggiero said modestly. Like his daughter, he was humble in nature with no air of superiority or vanity. He was a good man through and through.

"Mr. Mac Aley has instructed me to offer you a percentage of shares in the company as your reward, with the stipulation that someday, should they want to sell the company, you should have the right to first refusal, should you choose to purchase DGB industries in its entirety. You could become the sole owner of the company. Or, should you wish, you have the option to buy or gain more shares, in bona fides."

Ruggiero was taken totally by surprise. Did he hear right? Had his luck turned around that much, to make him believe that the ugly years of famine, pain, and suffering with his dirt-poor family had been a bad dream? He was stunned.

Richard Johnson waited for an answer. Ruggiero remained speechless.

"You need some time to think, of course. I am sure you will want to consult with your lawyer. You let us know. In the meantime, I will get in touch with our legal department to oversee to the transaction of the shares that are to be accredited in your name as an affiliate of the company."

"Thank you, Sir. Thank you, Mr. Mac Aley. I am grateful." Ruggiero managed to say.

He went home to his basement quarters where he had taken up room and board. It was the most economical arrangement he could find, with just the bare necessities. The landlords, Mr. and Mrs. Graham, were pleasant and kind to him. Both in their seventies, Mr. Graham was hard of hearing. Sometimes Ruggiero found it daunting to speak to him. Judy, his wife, was a spunky old girl – vivacious and energetic. She loved to cook and bake. She always left a plate of warm food for him on the stove. The old house felt good and inviting whenever Ruggiero walked through the door. Judy was always by the stove trying new recipes. She reminded him of Rosa, with the exception of the lack of goodies always on hand. The best thing Judy made was her fresh baked crusty bread.

"My Judy is Austrian, Ruggiero. You see, she has never lost

her European flavour." Mr. Graham would say.

"You are a lucky fellow, Mr. Graham. You have a darn good wife if you ask me."

"She sure is."

For Ruggiero, this place was a perfect spot to slump his tired body when he needed sleep; a moment to recharge, which was all he ever needed. He spent most of his time at the factory, always being the first to arrive and last to leave. He didn't entertain anybody. His two friends from the ship were in Rochester, a short distance away. He had no car, and neither did they, so once in a while they got in touch by phone.

Now that he had made the application for his family to emigrate, his life was going to change. He needed to look for a house to accommodate his family. Tonight he felt like pinching himself. Is this for real? I am an associate of the company holdings? Part owner? A shareholder of the company? He was mulling the idea over in his head, trying to believe it in every which way.

"Dad? You up there? Are you aware of this goodness coming my way? Papa, you don't believe in that after-death business, but I am wondering . . . Or is it Mom with her prayers?"

He shook his head. I must be going nuts talking to myself. He opened the door and climbed the double stairs looking for Mr. and Mrs. Graham. He badly wanted to share his good news with them. Maybe he would sit and visit with them. After all, they liked listening to him at times, however, it seemed as if they were not home. They were somewhat like Mom and Papa in a way, which is why he had taken the place. He loved and related well with older people. He needed their advice sometimes. He also sought out Mrs. Graham's advice about shopping for a new home to accommodate his family if they came.

Ruggiero realised it was Wednesday night. Judy Graham liked

to play bingo at the hall down the street. She must have dragged her husband along. Disappointed, Ruggiero returned to his basement, flopping on the bed thinking of his family back home. Tomorrow at lunchtime, he would write a long letter to Gioia and Mother and another to Milan. Slowly, his heavy eyelids closed and sleep took over. When Mr. and Mrs. Graham returned home, his snores could be heard upstairs.

"Uh, that Ruggiero with his music!" complained Judy.

"He must be tired, poor fellow. Fallen fast asleep with his clothes on, I bet!"

"Good thing you can't hear. Otherwise, you would have a sleepless night." Judy pulled off his hearing aids. "I hate his darn snoring."

"Judy, place these plugs in your ears and go to bed. Problem solved. Let that poor soul sleep."

She shut the door behind her while her husband settled in front of the TV. His snoring would soon join Ruggiero's. Judy had gotten used to the double dose since Ruggiero had joined their household.

Chapter Twenty-Three
Back in Milan

Once Giuliana's visitors left, she immersed herself totally in her studies and resumed her daily routine. Whenever she passed by the impressive house around the corner, her heart skipped a beat and her eyes flickered as she found herself searching in vain. There was never any sign of the young man that had invigorated her emotions.

It was June, summer fever was in the air. The days were warmer and longer and the school term was coming to an end. Most of Giuliana's schoolmates were planning to leave for their summer homes or vacation destinations. Erica was heading back to Munich. Giuliana had been asked to remain in Milan through the summer. Judge Sbarro, with his good intentions, had sat her down in his enormous library and advised her:

"Giuliana, the decision is yours, of course. We are proud of you for being accepted into law school. Amelia and I feel that during these summer months you should remain here so that you may be tutored by my colleague, Professor Aristide Quadrino. He will prepare you for the first year of law school. Once you master the basics, you will be fine as you move forward."

Giuliana listened attentively.

"Yes. I like that. I need and want to excel. I am indebted to you, Judge Sbarro, and to Aunt Amelia. How will I ever repay you or make it up to you?"

"Giuliana, you forget, we lost our Teresa. You have replaced our daughter. You are our daughter sent to us by the divine almighty. Amelia has regained her self-worth, she is able to function and help other people since you came into our lives. There, you see . . ."

"When will I start?" Giuliana asked, extending her hand with a big smile, in agreement.

They shook hands. It was understood. The tutoring would begin in a couple of weeks. Giuliana thought of her family. Down in Molise, they would be disappointed. Likewise, she would miss them too, but her studies were important to her. She needed to remain. The young man came to mind. Maybe I will see him again. Why haven't I seen him anywhere? Where is he?

She discarded those thoughts to concentrate on her task at hand. She had remained in Mr. Sbarro's library and now climbed the dark oak ladder, checking the big heavy volume from the collection on the upper shelf. They are impressive and intimidating. Her eyes scrutinised the pages. Suddenly, the door slammed open. It startled her, and she jerked her body around. She lost her footing and tumbled over to the floor. The ladder had tilted along with her, and as she hit the floor it landed on top of her. Lost in the confusion, she didn't know what had precipitated the occurrence. When she looked up, the boys were looking down at her.

"Giuliana! What on earth were you doing up there? Are you hurt?"

"Strunz, never mind! Remove the ladder from her," Dino ordered.

"Nino, get out of the way, let me do it." Responded Marco, I care for her more than all of you.

"Guys, will you stop arguing and help me, I cannot get up."

"Oh my God! Maybe her bones are broken," retorted Nino.

"You two, get out of my way. You imbecile, let me take care of her, You, Marco, go call Mom, but don't alarm her."

Nino ran for the phone.

"Not you, strunz, you will scare Mom. Let Marco do it. Help me here, although, I am afraid to move her. What if she broke something?"

"You guys, will you stop it! My leg hurts badly and my shoulder too."

Amelia arrived, breathless, in no time.

"We need to take her to the emergency. She needs x-rays." She said after checking her out.

The ambulance came, and Giuliana ended up in the hospital. The radiologist showed Amelia the x-rays.

"She is a lucky girl. Look here: a small fracture on her clavicle for which she will require a sling for six weeks. She must have hit the floor sideways. See the trauma to her leg? I think she can get away with an elastic bandage on her leg to keep the bone together since it's minor. Some rest and not much weight on the leg will do. Dr. Sbarro, it will take six to eight weeks, but she will be fine."

Amelia was relieved, but still upset for the unfortunate mishap.

"Giuliana, Dear, with your good nature you accept whatever life sends your way. I am so sorry."

The boys, once home, were bickering, blaming Marco for causing the accident. Giuliana although hurting, still got a kick out of their banter. She placed herself in the midst of them to help alleviate their concern.

"I will be okay guys, lighten up. You, Marco, are elected to nurse me. I will live like a queen with you guys serving me!"

They were lively as rocket ships when together and even Dino was acting juvenile and silly, although he was twenty, and typically much more sensible than his brothers. Nino turned the record player on as loud as he could. The music was blaring. The boys continued kidding and teasing her and one another. Giuliana joined right in with them. They were her friends. How could she complain?

When Amelia walked in she covered her head, shielding her hearing from the noise.

"Oh my God, you guys! The walls are shaking." She turned to Giuliana, "Maybe I should return to the hospital. It's quieter there, even with the ambulance sirens."

Giuliana laughed. Marco was coming back from her room with a big grin on his face. He was carrying Biricchina in one hand and Lola in another.

"Lordy, Lordy! God help me!" exclaimed Amelia when she saw him. He was heading straight for Giuliana stirring the parrots into the chaos. He was talking to the birds, trying to get them to repeat after him.

"Giuliana is not leaving. She is staying with us for the summer, eh girls?"

"Everyone to the supper table! Dinner is ready." Costanza called out from the other room.

Dino sat down beside Giuliana. He winked at her, trying to make light of the situation,

"Have you seen your Romeo lately?"

"Dino what are you talking about?"

"Giuliana don't act so innocent. Joseph De Santis. I hear he is obsessed with you."

"Dino I am glad you know, because I don't. I have not even met Joseph De Santis."

Nino's ears perked and he lifted his head from his plate.

"Giuliana, your friend, the slut, was at the Piazza St. Leonardo with a bunch of boys. She was telling everybody about how Joseph has been digging for information on you. He is head over heels for you, she said."

"Guys, it's news to me, honest."

"I would watch that Dora, she tries to get anyone she can, Giuliana," Nino cautioned.

"Oh! Giuliana, don't pretend with us. The guys told me he digs you," said Dino.

She hoped it was true. Was this Joseph the same Joseph that popped up out of the crowd to take pictures at the auditorium? Who was he? Where did he come from? What did Nino know about him? He had electrified her body once with his stare alone, but he was still a mystery to her.

***

In the past couple of weeks, the boys had kept her occupied while Erica was gone. Judge Sbarro had also given her permission to go to his library and familiarise herself with anything she wished. A particular series of corporate law books had captured her interest. She had been buried in research to enrich her knowledge and reassure herself of her career path.

Some of the girls had remained in Milan, but these school friends weren't close to her, so she had not been out much. With her new injuries, her fun and games were limited to the Sbarro boys.

Amelia was called to the emergency room often. Mr. Sbarro mostly would excuse himself and retreat to his library. There was a lengthy murder case going to trial in his court; he had been totally devoted to it.

After dinner, the boys remained with Giuliana around the table. Often times she kept them in check, but tonight she found them amusing. She wanted to know more about Joseph. God forbid if they got wind of my genuine interest...

Marco, again playing innocent, called out to his brother.

"Nino, who is this slut? Why do you refer to her like that?"

"Yeah, Nino. Watch your terms. Mom and Dad wouldn't be too pleased with you," schooled Dino.

"Yeah, Dino is right. That isn't nice," added Giuliana.

Nino gave Marco a slap across his chest with the back of his hand.

"Oh, stay quiet, you penguin! What do you know? Dora goes with everybody. I know. She is an easy lay. Giuliana should not be seen with her."

"My God, Nino! You make her sound really bad. Poor Dora. She has no father. I feel sorry for her," defended Giuliana. Nino is judgmental and pessimistic, she thought.

The very next day, when everyone was out except Costanza and Giuliana, there was a knock on the door. When Costanza went to answer, she found a young girl standing there.

"Good morning. I am Dora. I would like to see Giuliana. Is she home?"

"Yes, she is. Come in please. Giuliana, you have a visitor," called out Costanza.

Giuliana was feeding seeds to her two old ladies. She stopped, curious, and hopped her way to the front entrance. She wasn't accustomed to having visitors.

"Dora, what a surprise! What brings you here?"

"You, Kiddo," she replied and gave her a hug. When Dora saw the sling she exclaimed, "Eh? What happened?"

"Oh! Nothing serious, I fell from the top of the ladder. I will be fine in few weeks."

"I am sorry! When did this happen?"

"Just a few days ago. I am fine really; just a freak accident."

"Giuliana you are optimistic. No wonder everyone likes you."

"Dora, come in," Giuliana said with a warm smile.

Giuliana was glad Nino was not around. Shame on him for bad-mouthing Dora. Dora did have a certain sex appeal. Her short black hair was in wispy layers that wrapped her lovely pear shaped face. She wore a short skirt, and V-neck sweater that accentuated her long neck and her breast. She walked in with a wiggle.

"Giuliana, I haven't seen you since graduation. Do you know that you have a big admirer? You are one lucky girl."

Giuliana did not know what to make of it.

"What do you mean? Who is my admirer?"

"Who is your admirer? Giuliana, don't play dumb with me. Joseph! Didn't you see him take pictures at the graduation? He lives up the street from me. As soon as he found out we went to the same school, he has been bombarding me with questions about you. I told him the little I know. He has framed your picture. He told me he has it on his night table. He wants to meet you and talk to you."

"Dora, honestly, while I have heard this name 'Joseph,' and I have seen a young man, I am not sure if he is the same person. I never spoke to him."

"Now you are hurt, limping, and in a sling. Can you go out? Tomorrow we can go to the piazza for a gelato."

Giuliana thought of Nino's accusations. Dora seems like a genuinely sweet girl. Why shouldn't I go with her? Deep down she was anxious to find out more about this Joseph.

"Dora, I would love to go with you to the piazza. I can't just yet. It's my leg. I need to take it easy for a while."

"I understand. That's just too bad," she answered with sincere sympathy for her friend.

Giuliana was hoping she would say more about Joseph, but she didn't want to let on she was interested. Grandma had brainwashed her about boys.

"Never make yourself available and keep your legs covered. They are after one thing, and then they make fun of you," she would say.

After her horrible experience, Giuliana wondered how anyone could trust them. She loved her adopted brothers – they were genuine, although she sometimes wondered about Nino. No. She would not allow any sinister thoughts cloud her mind. The power of your thoughts attracts what you're thinking. She was determined to let only good thoughts be entertained. The bad ones she wiped away in denial. She didn't dare inquire further. Dora made her exit promising to check in with Giuliana in a few weeks. Joseph was going to remain a mystery for now.

Chapter Twenty-Four
The Encounter

One of the many benefits of living with the Sbarro family was that Giuliana had access to a tutor. Aristide Quatrini arrived with his thick, silver-rimmed glasses. He was a giant fellow with a strong voice and a serious demeanour. He was wearing a polished light-grey suit with a turquoise tie. He removed his briefcase from under his arm and pulled out some notes in an orderly manner; it was clearly time for serious teaching. The afternoon tutoring was ready to commence.

Professor Quadrino was professional. Mr. Sbarro paid him well. He was to deliver the best of his knowledge and teach law like nobody else could. His assignments for Giuliana required a lot of research and reading that she paid attention to with all her might. She needed to make all the people she loved proud, especially Mr. Sbarro - more than anyone.

Giuliana's continuing recovery was long and tedious. The afternoon lessons helped her keep sane and occupied. Under Amelia's watchful eye, and with Marco's assistance, eight weeks had passed and the summer was nearly over. Now, close to being fully healed, she was starting to get back into the swing of things.

She had recently asked Mr. Sbarro and Amelia if she could take a short trip south to see her family. Her dad had faithfully been writing and often sent her money. She insisted on paying for her train fare. Marco wanted to go with her, and to make him happy, his parents obliged. Together, they got on the train headed for the province city. Next, they boarded a connecting bus that took them to the small town. Marco, wide-eyed, admired the sights in amazement. He had never been anywhere so remote before. He was delighted to play with his cousins and see Mrs. Renalta Zicardo.

Gioia and Rosa were beside themselves in having their big city girl home. Giuliana noticed how the family's food supply had changed. There was white bread on the table, fruit, and ground beef for meatballs. Rosa had graduated to creating the best southern dishes. It was all available thanks to Giuliana's dad's work in America.

"Nonna, it makes me happy to be with you here, and I am glad things have improved for you too. We needed to get out of here, in order to survive. Dad feels the same. I am not selfish to say this, but it is miserable to be poor. What a sin it is for those with the upper hand to take advantage of the poor souls here," Giuliana mused one afternoon. She thought of herself from years before. Turning to her mother, she said, "Liliana, her Mom, and her twin brothers…what has become of them? Do you know? I have never forgotten about them. I think of them with a pain in my heart. Liliana was victimised for being poor."

"I know, Dear, I know. Liliana has gone away. Her mom and brothers moved and went to live with her."

"Oh! You see, Mom, Liliana could hardly write. We could not communicate. I got a letter or two from her at the beginning. She needed someone to read and write her letters. Then there was no more news. My letters to her were unanswered. I wrote two more, but they were returned, so I lost touch with her."

"Life isn't that great for her, I am told. The old lady that hired her died and Liliana married the invalid son she takes care of, in order to have access to the inheritance. However, he is quite abusive. A beautiful girl like Liliana, stuck taking care of this quadriplegic all by herself… Then her Mother moved there with the twins. We heard no more."

"Mom, I am studying hard. I want to become a corporate

lawyer. God willing, I want to dedicate myself to aid the poor. I want to help young people like me that cannot afford to get an education. I want to build schools. I want to help the Liliana's of this world. I wonder if she got a break in life. Someday I will look for her. Mom, I feel doubly blessed: God sent me my adopted family and my own humble family."

Gioia was afraid to mention what was on her mind. Her daughter was enthusiastic about her studies and her life goals. How could she mention immigration? She was tired of being without her husband, and she wanted to be a family together - her husband and Mamma Rosa too.

***

Two weeks soon flew by and Giuliana returned to her metropolitan life. Her university courses were heavy, but she plunged into the work with full force and determination. She vowed to Mr. Sbarro that she would be the best in her field.

"I don't doubt that, Giuliana. You will definitely make us proud. We love you regardless. Dino, Nino, and Marco have other interests. Amelia and I are sure they will excel in their choices."

Amelia and the judge, more than once, had encouraged her to go out more.

"Take a break from your studies, dear. Go out with the boys, or your friends. It will refresh your mind."

It was Saturday night. She had agreed to go for a stroll to the piazza with Dora. Erica had made herself unavailable lately. When she returned from Germany, she had announced that she had met and fallen in love with a young man from Munich. It must have been love, her eyes gleamed and she came alive when describing Otto. She would now run off to him every weekend. Giuliana was happy for her friend, but it made her all the more aware that she had yet to meet that famous Joseph.

They decided to go to the fashion district to the Piazza Montenapoleone. They could admire the latest styles and the elegant shops, stop for an ice cream, or indulge themselves with an aromatic espresso from The World's Import. As always, it was crowded in the square. Being a spring night, the climate was warm and comfortable.

"Everyone has chosen to come here tonight, it seems," said Dora, with approval.

"Why not? Look up there, Dora. There is a full moon, and the sky is bright! The stars are sparkling like jewels – our planet is illuminated."

They had bumped into many people they knew. They were attentively admiring a mannequin in a stylish window with the bright new colours for spring and summer when Giuliana felt a tap on her shoulder. She turned around and found herself face-to-face with her mysterious fellow. She was breathless, and evidently speechless. Dora broke her spell with her voice, loud and clear.

"Joseph!"

Dora leaned over and reached out to hug him, hanging onto his neck longer than normal.

"When did you get back? Oh, excuse me! This is my friend, Giuliana. You've never officially met."

Giuliana was totally struck and struggled to recapture her composure. She extended her hand, as he had been waiting for her reach for some time already.

"Giuliana Ferrante. My pleasure."

"Pleased to meet you, Giuliana. I am Joseph De Santis. Yes, I have seen you, if you remember? I am glad to finally have the pleasure of meeting you."

"Oh!"

Giuliana didn't know quite what to say. It was Dora who finally broke the silence and came to her rescue.

"Giuliana, Joseph divides his time between Milan and Vienna. He appears and disappears from us rather often. I wish he would spend more time in Milan, but I think his heart is in Vienna," Dora smoothly interjected. She turned to Joseph, "How long have you been gone? When did you return . . .?"

"Since our companies are scattered all over, I'm often pulled from one place to another. I would like to have some more stability. I need to talk to my parents about that."

In the meantime, a young man holding two cups of ice-cream made his way to join them. It was Paolo, a friend of Dora's.

"Dora, nice to see you!"

The two exchanged hugs. Paolo handed Joseph his gelato with a big smile on his face.

"Joseph, do you want to introduce me to . .?" He gestured toward Giuliana. Paolo came across as comical and confident. He turned to Dora, "He wants to keep both of you girls to himself."

"Paolo, this is my friend Giuliana. She is from Molise, studying here in Milan," Dora butt in.

"Piacere, pleased to meet you. Paolo Grandin," Paolo assertively declared as he shook Giuliana's hand.

A flash of recognition rolled across Paolo's face as he made the connection. He remembered Joseph mentioning having discovered a stunning beauty that he intended to pursue a while back. That was before Josephs parents had shipped him off to Vienna and the trail had gone cold. Back only a few days, Joseph had already confided in Paolo that he wanted to find the girl. No wonder! She is a hot dish. I would not mind her for myself. Discretely, he admired Giuliana. I will let him have his quest, he thought

"You girls don't mind if we stroll together, do you?" asked

Paolo.

"No, not at all. Please do," answered Dora. She was open and friendly.

"Can I get you girls some ice cream?" Joseph asked.

"No thanks, we have already treated ourselves to one," replied Giuliana.

Joseph, completely absorbed, walked beside Giuliana. Her voice stimulated his senses. Dora and Paolo were good friends, and he was walking beside her. The foursome pleasantly strolled the piazza under the illuminated sky and surrounded by the embrace of a warm, soothing breeze. Giuliana and Joseph were getting acquainted as she glanced at her watch, shocked at the time. It was late, and time to call it a night. The Sbarro boys came to her mind. God forbid if she were to run into them and be seen with Joseph, on top of Nino's disapproval of Dora - she wouldn't hear the end of it.

Before they parted, Joseph had gained enough confidence to ask her for a date the next day.

"Will you meet me by the fountain at the public garden tomorrow at one in the afternoon? I'd love to see you again, and to talk some more with you."

His eyes were pleading and his smile contagious. He grabbed her hands as they separated, and in agreement, she nodded.

"That would be nice. I will see you tomorrow."

Joseph was infatuated with the southern girl, and she with him. Giuliana's warm heart felt as full of renewal as the springtime. When she arrived home, she went straight to her room, flopped on the bed and lay there still, staring at the white ceiling. If this is love, it's the most pleasurable feeling I have ever experienced. Joseph De Santis has magically awakened a volcanic eruption in my heart and soul that out measures Mount Etna itself! Giuliana closed her eyes, impatiently waiting for tomorrow to arrive.

Chapter Twenty-Five
The Encounter

It was Sunday. Giuliana never missed mass – a trait that had been implemented by her Grandmother. The Sbarro's were not practising Catholics, and while Giuliana's hosts didn't condone religion, they knew better than to force their views on Giuliana. Marco even occasionally joined her, but this morning Giuliana preferred to go alone. After all, she wanted to keep her rendezvous with Joseph to herself. If Nino got wind of it, he would immediately have something negative to say. No, I don't want anyone to damper this magic in my heart.

Giuliana heard a ruckus in the living room. Peeking around the corner, she spotted Marco with the two old ladies.

"Oh! Marco, I was wondering where you were."

"You came home late last night. Mom and Dad had gone to bed. These guys were out and guess who ended up with these two? Me! They kept me awake all night. I guess they couldn't sleep, and Biricchina was bothering Lola to death."

"Thank God you had them because I sure needed peace and quiet when I came home," Giuliana said.

"Where were you anyway? It's not like you to stay out that late. Mom and Dad were wondering. Dino said you were out with Dora. You know what Nino thinks of her…"

"Let me tell you, that Nino is dead wrong. Dora is a nice girl. People misjudge her due to her friendliness," Giuliana defended her friend.

Marco was easy to talk too, never insistent, and she loved him for it. She had taken him under her wing since she had joined the family. She smiled at him now, fondly.

"I will go get ready for church. I guess you are not coming?" she asked.

"No, Giuliana. I need to attend to these two. My friends are waiting for me at the park. It will be good for them to go out. They compete with their performances and my friends love them."

Giuliana let out a big sigh of relief.

"It's fine with me, Marco. I don't mind going alone. I have seen you get bored sometimes. It's OK."

Giuliana walked away in a hurry, off to get herself together. This morning she carefully looked in her closet and decided to wear her favourite sky blue dress. She rolled her hair up in a French roll twist and let her bangs asymmetrically cascaded at the side of her forehead. She had never put makeup on, but today she was going to. Her eyeshadow complimented her dress, accentuating the corner of her eyes with glittering mascara. When she finished and glanced at the mirror the reflection looking back at her was unrecognisable. Giuliana's appearance, along with her personality were changing. Dora is good for me, she thought. She is bubbly and loves people. Just for being forward with her embraces, she is labelled. What a shame. All she is doing is expressing her emotions.

As beautiful as a picture, Giuliana left the house for the church, and to meet her beloved Joseph. Church had always been a place of peace. To her surprise today, as she knelt down, she could not focus on the service or pray. She found her edginess disturbing. She put her hands together in prayer and brought them close to her heart. Why is the devil interfering with my calm? Go away! Her eyes kept glancing at her watch. The restlessness was unbearable. She decided to discretely walk out, to put an end to the unpleasantness that had taken over her.

As she approached the gardens with their charming fountains, she spotted Joseph sitting, waiting for her in a mist from the waterfalls. The white gravel stones on the path seemed to slow down her footsteps. These darn shoes! The wedge is too high for my comfort.

As soon as he spotted her, he was all smiles and moved forward to greet her. Dora had been a good example for her. Spontaneously, they embraced, rocking each other like old friends. Is this for real or do I imagine things? She felt like she might wake from a dream. They moved out of their embrace, and Joseph held her arms.

"Giuliana, are you a vision in front of me? You have no idea how I had dreamed of this moment since that late afternoon when I first laid my eyes on you."

Giuliana's heartbeat was going crazy. The mysterious fellow was really here, touching her, holding her hands. She looked at him. A few strands of dark brown curly hair were teasing his forehead. His impeccable white shirt was lined with glittering black buttons and he wore a light sky-blue blazer of the purest combed wool. It complimented his tall, slim body, and his big, dark eyes. His elegance was alluring.

He gently guided her to a bench at the side of the fountain. The sweet smell of yellow roses and white lilies drenched the air.

"It's a little quieter here. We can talk," he said. "You look astonishing, Giuliana. Now that I have you near, your beauty makes my head spin. I am mesmerised."

"Stop it, Joseph! It's embarrassing."

"Never! You are a picture that no artist can paint. I have been lucky to discover you, right in front of my door."

"Never mind this gallantry, Joseph!" Giuliana said with a laugh and a dismissive wave of her hand. "Tell me about yourself." She was surprised at her easy and spontaneous response.

221

"Yes. I want to know all about you, too." There was a short pause before he continued, "Who is going to go first?"

"Joseph, tell me about you; your family. My life story is not that great, except that I was given a break in life. I come from a loving, but poor family."

"I don't care where you come from. I have found you, and I never want to lose you. I implored my guiding star to lead me to you."

They were both absorbed in each other, and deliriously happy. The uneasiness Giuliana had felt in the church had left her, and she was now in the bliss of love.

"Giuliana, is it ok if I put my arm around your shoulder and hold your hand? Please forgive me, but I need to touch you," Joseph asked her.

He was gentle. How could Giuliana refuse him? She smiled up at him and nodded, grabbing his hand. This must be love. He is the most handsome young man I have ever laid eyes on.

"Joseph, after I first saw you…you disappeared. Where did you go?"

"I know! Right after I saw you my family and I had to go to Vienna. We live there sometimes. My mother is Viennese; Dad is Milanese. To make matters worse, some weekends we fly to Bayside. We have a home there for when the winter gets bitter cold. My dad needs me as a co-pilot. Mom insists that I go with them. My two sisters are the liberated ones. Since I am the only son, I feel obligated to comply."

Giuliana listened, before pressing further.

"Joseph, what's your profession? What does your family do for a living?"

"Have you heard of De Santis Conglomerate Industries?"

"No, forgive me, but I have not," Giuliana said.

"We manufacture and supply textiles all over the world from here in Milan. Then, in Vienna, we have two manufacturers. One for ladies and one for men. Our garments are made of the finest quality and we supply the most affluent retailers in the main cities in Europe and abroad."

Giuliana was impressed.

"Joseph, can I ask you something?"

"Anything"

"What are you doing talking to a dirt-poor girl?"

"Giuliana, don't underestimate me, please. I have been searching for you since day one. I couldn't wait to come back to Milan. When Dora told me you were her friend, I pestered her to tell me about you. Our piazza encounter was not by accident. Dora appeased me."

"Joseph, I live with Judge Roberto Sbarro, Dr. Amelia Sbarro, and their three boys. They took me in and gave me a break. I come from a peasant family that could not afford to send me to high school. With God's help, the Sbarro's found kindness in their hearts to take me in and treat me like their daughter. They have been good to me in every way."

"What about your real family?" he asked kindly.

"You want to know about my real family? You would never understand. My mom and Grandma and younger sister are back home. They are living and eating better thanks to Dad. He was forced to emigrate for work and he sends some money. He works in Buffalo, New York, in a steel plant. He wants us to join him there."

"No! You cannot do that," Joseph suddenly looked heartbroken.

"I am in a strange situation. I have two families now. One that wants me to be the best at my studies and the other wants to reunite our family." Giuliana looked pained as she recalled her dilemma.

They talked for hours like they had known each other all their lives. Their souls were one. The comfort of being so close was immeasurable. Giuliana gave a deep sigh and put her arm around Joseph.

"You see, my life is complicated."

Joseph turned to her with longing in his loving eyes.

"Giuliana, we will work it out. So long as you don't leave me, because I will search this entire globe until I find you again!"

"Tell me all about you some more, Joseph," Giuliana said with a laugh. "Have you finished school?"

"I graduated in business administration this past year. I work with my dad in the family business. The companies are doing well. By being involved in the actual management, one learns more than one ever could in the classroom alone. I have firsthand practice from all the different departments! My dad has mastered it all from his father, and his father from his grandfather. The business has been passed on to each generation. I am the youngest to take on the challenge."

"Your mom? Does she work? Your two sisters?"

"My mom? No. She is occupied with her own interests: her clubs, her charities, her travel. She is busy. Dad would not want her to work."

Giuliana listened and shook her head. What a difference.

"What about your mom? Does she work?"

Giuliana didn't know if she should answer him.

"Joseph, do you really want to know what my mom does? I will tell you. She is a cleaning lady. She does household chores: laundry, ironing, shopping, she fetches water. She does this for whoever calls her. It is barely enough money to buy food – corn flour if she is lucky, but wheat flour usually, to make homemade bread, pizza, and pasta."

Joseph grabbed her hands while attentively listening. He didn't know the world of the poor.

Giuliana took a deep breath.

"Do you want to know about my Grandmother?"

"Yes. Tell me. I am here to listen," he replied.

"She pretty well does the same thing. She is a maid and in her spare time, she goes picking dandelions in public places to cook with and feed to the family with a mixture of whatever else she can find. Since Dad immigrated to America, they can afford to buy a little more. My grandma has a hard time abandoning her old habits though. My grandpa died from... a lack of everything... malnutrition, no medical intervention... everything combined."

As Giuliana spoke of her family, Joseph could detect the love she had for them in her voice and the pain she carried for them in her heart. He put his arm around her shoulders and pulled her close to him, rocking her with affection.

"Joseph, now you know. You sound like you are a rich boy from the north. Do you still want to hang around this girl that you discovered walking by your house?"

"You have been the miracle I have been searching for. Lucky that Joseph De Santis followed the star because here she is, beside me!" he teased lovingly. "I cannot wait to take you into my arms and love you with all my heart." He grabbed her hand and placed it over his heart. "Can you feel the beat in my heart? This ticker will stop beating if you ever leave my side, girl!"

The two had been absorbed in their own private world for four hours when Joseph made a suggestion.

"Giuliana, forgive me. Are you hungry? Why don't we go get a bite to eat? The place across the street serves great panini. Let's go."

Joseph was happy as they made their way to the shop, but Giuliana was pensive. Talk of her pending immigration unnerved her now more than ever. Little did Giuliana know, the barriers from this day forward were going to be as high as the mountains. They were from two different worlds, and their path forward together would not be easy.

Chapter Twenty-Six
Gioia's Suffering

Back in Molise, Gioia was struggling to deal with her own conscience as she was tugged between duty and desire. Rosa was stubborn, still refusing to leave her old nest. The papers Ruggiero had sent for them had an expiry date. They were sitting in the drawer of the bedroom, dormant. No effort had been made by Gioia to move forward.

"Mom, we cannot leave you here alone, you must go with us. Ruggiero will not have peace until we are reunited. He has been gone a long time now. We must make a move. Trizia is ready to go. Giuliana can't leave now, but later she is willing to make the transition, as long as she can continue her studies."

"How can she? She would have to start all over again. What about the language barrier?"

"Mama Rosa, Giuliana is taking English as her second language. She is young and smart. I don't worry about her. My Ruggiero needs his family. He has done enough sacrificing by himself, all alone."

"Gioia, I want you to go. You are right, Ruggiero needs his wife. As for myself. I insist… you leave me here where I belong."

So much time had gone by and nothing had changed. Gioia was tired of living like a widow with only the occasional letter from her husband. Receiving the mail was the only highlight in her life. Slowly, resentment had started building in Gioia's heart against her mother-in-law. She felt cheated in life. Bouts of depression were hitting deep, followed with crying spells. She needed to put an end to her miserable sadness, and that meant she needed to make up her mind and abandon Rosa to go join her husband. It was where she should be. I have reached my early forties. My life is being wasted away respecting Rosa's wishes. Rosa's other two sons, with their families, had since immigrated. One to Australia, and the other to Canada. This complicated the matter.

As Gioia was grappling with her duties, a letter arrived from America. It was from none other than Ruggiero.

My dear Gioia and Mom,

I hope my letter finds you well, including my dear Trizia. I miss you terribly. I can't wait for you guys to join me here. Gioia, I have good news again! As you know, work is my salvation here. I have nothing to go home to, my darling, as you and the rest of the family will not be there.

My supervisor thinks highly of me. I am glad to report to you that I got another promotion. I am now the head of the export department. I got a raise, and the money is good! But, what good does it do me without you my Dearest? My English is improving. I manage to read and write better every day, which is great. I still live at Mr. and Mrs. Graham's in a room down in their basement. I need to improve my status before you come. I would like to buy a home of our own, but I cannot do that without you, my Dear.

Please decide. Your papers have expired by now. I will gladly send you the third request. You know I cannot return there. Life can be good here, all I need is you beside me.

Love to you and Mom. Hugs to Trizia.

Yours forever,

Ruggiero.

P.S. - As for our Giuliana, I keep in touch with her regularly. We can be mighty proud of our Milanese!

***

Gioia was getting sicker with each passing day. Her legs were in such pain, and the old doctor had diagnosed her with chronic rheumatism. Rosa kept taking her to the quacks in the country for massages. Rosa also rubbed her aching knees with a mixture of herbs of her own invention, but the remedy wasn't working.

Ruggiero's third application had arrived with a letter:

"This is the last one I am sending to you. Mom, if you want to be stubborn, then Gioia will have to leave without you. I cannot cater to your wishes. If the townsfolk criticise us for abandoning you, so be it. It's your choice..."

***

A few months had passed, and it was time to go to the American Consulate. Gioia was going ahead with her resolution to leave.

"Mom, it's your last chance. You will make us very unhappy if you force us to leave you behind."

"Gioia, my dear, go to your husband. I have my church; my neighbours. My Luigi is waiting for me, and I have my space here beside him. Where am I going..?"

Gioia, for her own salvation, needed to be strong. She would not feel pity for her mother-in-law that could overtake her and change her mind. She brushed her hand through her hair to clear her thoughts. Preoccupied, her mind floated toward thoughts of Giuliana. I need to write to her, not only to inform her of my decision, but also to tell her what is expected of her.

Dear Giuliana,

Our suffering has to end. It is time for us to live like decent human beings. Dad wants us with him. I have decided to go to America. I want you to go with Trizia and me. Your grandmother has decided to remain here. If that is her choice, I cannot do anything about it, but you, my dear, belong with us. You must go with us.

As for your studies, you have learned English. Dad will see to it that you continue in America. He must have let you know about his promotion. Those kind people you are with have been your salvation, and I know how much you love and respect them. But dear, you are our daughter. We belong together. I beg you to go with us.

All my love, with kisses and hugs,

Your mother,

Gioia

Hugs from Grandma and Trizia.

Giuliana, sitting on her bed, had opened and read her mother's letter. She brought it close to her chest, fighting the tears that were spilling freely from her blurred eyes despite her best efforts. Joseph. What about Joseph? Mom does not know of my new-found love. How can I leave him and break both our hearts now that we have found each other?

Chapter Twenty-Seven
Tormented Emotions

Giuliana had a hard time concentrating on her work in class the next day. Amusing enough, Professor Quadrino was strongly implementing in his trademarked crescendo tone.

"...the most important thing is to control your attention span. You need to listen to your client's dilemma. Absorb the facts with your utmost concentration. Only then you will be in a position to offer advice and to think of strategic moves..."

Control my attention span? That's exactly what I am having trouble doing now! Giuliana thought, as her eyes kept filling with Joseph's image, and her ears with his voice. Her mind was playing tricks on her these days – her concentration was poor. In a daze, the class dragged on.

When it was finally over, Giuliana rushed out into the fresh air to invigorate her unfocused body. However, as she stepped out she was met by the very ghost that haunted her. There, by the main path, with his hands in his pockets was Joseph, waiting for her. As soon as he spotted her, he waved. With quick steps, he reached her side.

"Giuliana, I couldn't wait to see you. I decided to come and meet you here."

Her heart rejoiced.

"Joseph! Wonderful. What a lovely surprise. I love seeing you too," she replied, as she slipped her arm under his. How soothing his touch feels!

"How was your day? Dad wanted me to go to Vienna. I found an excuse to remain behind. Otherwise, I would not be able to see you for few days. You would think I disappeared on you again!"

"Yes, I would wonder, wouldn't I? How did you manage it?"

"I told Dad our place here in Milan needed my attention. I had unfinished paperwork, a couple of contracts to wrap up. Sorry, Dad!" Joseph said with a laugh. "It wasn't a total lie. I did have a couple of contracts, but no emergency. My emergency was a certain girl coming out of class that I wanted to see."

"You are too much! Am I supposed to believe that? You are neglecting your father's affairs for this girl?" Giuliana was all smiles. She was beside herself with happiness.

"Giuliana! I want you to come to my place in the next few days. You must meet my mom and my dad. My sisters are in California – they come and go. I cannot keep up with those two. I want you to meet my parents. They will fall in love with you as I have done."

"Not so fast, Joseph. Let's get to know each other first. Let's leave your family out of our world for a little while."

Giuliana was nervous and not so sure of the famous De Santis family. Dora had told her they were not too friendly. She bumped into them sometimes as she lived down the street from them. She had seen them coming and going. Her salutations were not reciprocated, especially by Mrs. De Santis.

"Why? You have doubts? I cannot wait to share you with them, darling."

"Thanks, Joseph. I take it as a compliment, but we should take it easy."

Giuliana's mind was churning in turmoil. She just wasn't sure what her future held. She had to deal with her mother's letter when she got home. If she obeyed, the plan to immigrate would jeopardise her dream, her love, her Joseph. One thing at the time. But, why now? Now that I have found some happiness. The dark clouds were invading her bright blue sky. Haven't I endured enough storms in life?

They walked, holding hands, never wanting to part. They were wrapped in their need of togetherness as they wished to be the only souls on this planet, with no one around to disturb their unity.

"Giuliana, you were made for me, my love. Do you know how many times I dreamt of your lovely face? I was getting impatient at times, as the girl of my dreams did not appear on my horizon. Then, one day, there you were!"

"Oh, Joseph! You are exaggerating. The problem is, I love you too. You are my first love and my soulmate. You have awoken my dormant body. I must confess, I have never felt this complete. I'm so glad I met you."

Joseph knew her words were sincere. He sealed her lips with a long, passionate kiss, holding her close to him and never wanting to be let go. She felt warm all over, and her body responded with pleasure. This is true love, and it feels so right.

Soon, they reluctantly parted, counting the hours and the minutes until they could be together again. Joseph had totally swept her off her feet. Her face sparkled.

The Sbarro's noticed the change in her. Amelia was happy to see her girl in a vibrant mood.

"I hear our Giuliana is in love!" exclaimed Mr. Sbarro. He was a good, rational man.

Marco wanted to know about Joseph. Dino didn't say much, but he handed her the weekly romance magazine.

"Giuliana, now you can practice what you read. I hear you got yourself a good one. Well, my girl, you deserve the best."

"Thanks, Dino. It means a lot to me, coming from you."

"The De Santis family are quoted in the paper often. They are high society. If you become Mrs. De Santis, will you still talk to us?" he asked, joking.

"Dino, I am far from that. How nasty of you. I would never think of myself as high society, to snub my dear family, my adopted brothers!"

"I know. Sorry. I am only joking. I like to ruffle your feathers sometimes! I do love you like a sister. I must say, you are every young man's dream," he paused, before continuing, "You are beautiful. You are smart. But more than anything, dear sister, you are kind with a big heart."

Giuliana smiled warmly.

"Thank you."

She got up and kissed him on the cheek. Nino walked in, and as he did, he saw Giuliana giving Dino a peck on the cheek.

"What was that all about, you two?" he asked, with eyebrows raised.

"We were discussing Giuliana's new boyfriend. You must have heard of Joseph De Santis?"

"If you ask me, he is a strunz and a schmuck."

"My God, Nino. Do you have anything nice to say about anybody? For heaven's sake. Why is he a strunz and a schmuck?"

"Him and his wicked mother, they think they own the world! They have the best balcony at La Scala and that mother of his always digs me. When I usher her at the opera, she comes in and walks with such an air of arrogance. She talks with a Viennese accent. She treats us like dirt."

"Nino, could it be your own perception?" Dino asked, incredulous.

"Yeah? My own perception? Ask my friends. They cannot

stand them either. Last week Mrs. and Mr. De Santis, with their dinosaur daughters, came to see Rigoletti. I was escorting them to their places, as usual, while I held the curtains at the entrance. Suddenly the mother dropped her binoculars. She ordered me: 'Boy, pick them up, will you?' As if I were her servant! She didn't even thank me. I bumped my head coming up. Those two chimpanzees laughed their heads off. I was pissed."

"Giuliana, pay no attention to Nino. He makes things bigger than they are," Dino said.

"Believe what you want. I know better and so do other people around Milan. That lady might be rich, but she is not kind. My friends talk behind her back. They are going to beat her up one of these days."

"Now we have heard it all, Nino! Shame on you! I hope you don't participate."

"You know, Giuliana, when certain people look down at the rest of the world it bugs me. If my friends are going to beat them up, they deserve it."

"Ok. Nino. Let's change the subject."

Giuliana remained stunned. My God. What if Nino is right? Joseph wants me to meet his parents. He is a kind soul. Nino must be wrong… Giuliana kept tossing her hot and cold thoughts around her head.

***

The next day, faithfully, there was Joseph waiting for her. The minute she saw him come toward her, the cloud of uncertainties vanished.

"Here is my favourite Molisana girl, sent to me from heaven."

"Joseph you are exaggerating. Come now… Just tell me what you have been up to today."

"The same as usual – checking orders to be shipped out. No pressures. We have plenty of help. Never mind about my work," he turned to her teasing, "Ok, girl. Tell me, when are you going to come and meet my mom?"

Giuliana's heart tightened with a flashback to Nino's words. Joseph shook her hand.

"What do you say? You don't seem too enthusiastic. Is something wrong?"

"No, not really. Let me see… how about next Sunday?"

"Darling, I am at your mercy. I am ready when you are."

He pulled her closer to him.

***

Amelia had come home earlier than usual that night. Giuliana badly needed to talk to her. She wanted to admit to her dear Amelia about her nervousness to meet Joseph's Mother, and eventually the rest of the family. She needed her help to learn about how to dress, how to behave, what was expected of her and more. She always called her Aunt Amelia. The first day she had arrived at their home, Amelia had said to her:

"Giuliana, you have your mom, I cannot expect you to call me Mom, although I would love you too. I will love you as much as I loved my Teresa. Do you think you can call me Aunt Amelia, Dear?"

"Yes, of course. Thank you. I feel privileged to do so."

"That will make me feel closer to you. "

She had hugged Giuliana, vowing to love her as her own.

She felt close to the Sbarro family. And now, Giuliana and Amelia sat at the kitchen table sipping on camomile tea prepared by Costanza, with warm scones.

"The boys have been blabbering about your Joseph. Now you tell me, Dear, do you like him a lot? I hear he is a good-looking chap and a nice fellow. I am proud of you Giuliana, as long as you are happy."

"Aunt Amelia, I have never been happier. Yes, I like him a lot. If this wonderful feeling is love, then I am in love."

"I am happy for you, Dear. Did you hear that song... how does it go? 'When love comes the bell will ring?' The song says that when you find love bells ring in your heart." They laughed together.

"I am to meet his mother first. The sisters are away. The father is away. Have you ever met them?"

"I have seen them but not met them directly. Mrs. De Santis contributes to the hospital a lot. She is on the board of the Sick Children Foundation and many others... she is well respected and recognised."

"Nino scared me the other night. He said she is cruel. He detests her."

"I don't know about that." Amelia kissed Giuliana on her head, sensing her unrest. "Don't listen to Nino, Dear. I am not sure where that son of mine came from. He is different... Sometimes I feel guilty. Did we neglect him when we were totally devastated with our little girl? I don't like it when he gets nasty."

"I want your opinion and approval Sunday when I go to meet Mrs. De Santis."

"Oh, Giuliana. I am honoured that you trust my opinion. I am no fashion suave, what with my white tunic every day... I don't get jazzed up much. I am sure you will look beautiful. Besides, my

Dear, your inner beauty shows in your eyes. The kindness on your face will make anyone gravitate toward you."

***

Sunday arrived sooner than she wanted too. Here she was, ready for Joseph, wearing a three-quarter length royal blue dress, adorned by a white shimmering shawl thrown over her shoulders. Her hair was swept up in a bun. Glancing at the mirror, she thought of the bun: it adds more height to my stature. The sling-back white sandals complimented her well-shaped long legs. Amelia walked in and handed her a set of pearls.

"Here, Dear. These pearl earrings…pin them to your ears. Here is a matching string of pearls. This small pearly white purse goes over your right shoulder. There! A picture perfect to admire."

Amelia had taken time off to aid her favourite girl. She had loaned her the jewellery and had taken her shopping at the best fashion district. They shopped together, laughing and giggling like two best friends.

Joseph arrived to pick Giuliana up and took a long look at her.

"I can't wait to show off my beautiful princess."

They got into his Ferrari and off they went.

Chapter Twenty-Eight
The Introduction

Joseph suggested they take a country ride first.

"I want to take you to the lake, it is one of my favourite places to go on a Sunday afternoon. This place has the best espresso and pastries you have ever tasted," he said as he pulled her close to him. "I want to have you to myself for a while. If you don't mind, Darling."

"What about your mom? Won't she be waiting?"

He gestured with his hand as if he didn't care. Are you stalling on purpose, Joseph?

"Darling, when I am with you, I want the rest of the people in this world to disappear." The car rolled to a stop. "Here we are."

A placid lake swamped with white swans that were moving in groups greeted their eyes. Joseph, with his polished manners, promptly got to her side to open the door.

"Come, my love," he said, gesturing with a deep bow.

A warm breeze caressed her face, as the bright sun rays glowed. They were surrounded by wisterias in full bloom. To their right, in a half-moon shape, a fabulous establishment set majestically. It was terraced in three levels with ornate wrought iron chairs and elegant tables set up. Giuliana admired the scene in awe.

"Joseph, this place is mesmerising. That fresh aroma of baking and coffee is stimulating my taste buds. Listen! That alluring music is pulling me in its direction."

He smiled, pleased.

"I wanted you to see this place. Many times, I have come here alone; dreaming of sharing this sight with the love of my life. Aren't those swans something else? Come. Let's go for a cappuccino, and some Viennese apple strudel."

The leading path to their destination was covered in pearlized white river stones, beautiful but challenging for her highheels. Joseph, with his gallantry, held her secure with his arm around her waist. The fresh greenery that lined the way was a vivid ash colour, which was new to Giuliana.

"They are flowers sent here from the North. Holland, I think. They derive from the family of hydrangeas. They are hardy plants that change colour with the climate."

Joseph looked at his watch and jumped up. His mother came to mind. Absorbed in the pleasant atmosphere around them, Giuliana realised he had totally forgotten about her. She would be waiting. Or, perhaps, he is a bit reluctant? Giuliana did not want to pry.

***

At the entrance of the mysterious home, Giuliana thought of the many times she had admired the home in lust, never imagining she would ever gain entry to the opulent place. This was the world of the rich and famous. How Joseph De Santis could be a part of her life, she would never understand.

A marble staircase led to the second floor. A butler dressed in a black uniform with a crispy white shirt and gloves opened the enormous double doors. He tipped his head and bowed his hand.

"Come in, please."

Giuliana entered a large room with many arched rectangular windows. It was long and spacious, with many sitting sections decorated in fine antique furnishings. Furniture was richly cushioned in fabrics of plush velvet with matching draperies. The paintings and portraits on the walls were much to admire. The colours were soft and soothing to the eyes. Giuliana didn't know where to look first. She was trying to remain calm and composed.

"This is beautiful, Joseph."

"It's too much if you ask me. Mom and her Austrian charm… My Mother is an opera buff, she likes antiques. This room is a replica of the Marie Antonietta style. She turns our house into an opera house!"

Before Giuliana could open her mouth to comment further, the door opposite to them opened. An elegant lady appeared, making her way toward them.

"Oh, Mom! This is Giuliana" Joseph exclaimed, excited. "Sorry, Mom. We are late. We were making our way to you when I got sidetracked by your favourite hideaway. I was explaining to Giuliana about your Viennese charm here and your love for the opera."

"Oh!" the woman kissed her son, turned to Giuliana and shook her hand. "Much pleased to meet you, Miss…?"

"Please, Giuliana will do! I am pleased to meet you too, Mrs. De Santis." Giuliana was speechless, but she pushed on. "This room is magnificent, Mrs. De Santis. Joseph tells me it's your décor."

"Thank you. I try to reproduce a home away from home, mainly for myself. I am not sure my family appreciates it."

She gestured ahead, and they walked forward into the next room. The table was set, and the maid was at their service. Prepared were appetisers and a selection of foreign foods, strange to Giuliana. Mr. Sbarro had implemented good manners at the table, and she was grateful she had mastered them. Today, she could come across as a refined lady.

Mrs. De Santis was a lady of distinction. Tall and slim, she moved swiftly. She was born with good features, including her blond hair which she had wrapped in a chignon that made her look a little severe, but she had a pleasant smile, which compensated and added to her loveliness.

"Giuliana, Joseph has not stopped talking about you. I would like you to tell me all about yourself. I must tell you that my son gave me strict orders not to ask any questions today."

"Joseph, you are mean! Why not?" Giuliana said, kidding him. Smiling at her hostess, Giuliana replied, "Mrs. De Santis, please feel free. Ask me anything you like!"

"Giuliana, Joseph tells me you are from the South and that you are here in school? What are your studying? Your favourite subjects..?"

"Mom! Stop it. Here you go..." Joseph looked bothered.

Giuliana, ignoring Joseph, answered.

"I started with general law. But I want to focus on corporate law."

"That's interesting. I thought you might like the courts – litigation – to put forward and argue your cases could be exciting. You are a good-looking girl. Litigation, to me, is like reciting on the stage."

"Oh, Mom! Here you go with your stage. You should have been an actress." Joseph turned to Giuliana, "My Mom loves to be in the limelight. Yes, Mom. You just love the stage in any way possible."

"On the contrary. Mrs. De Santis. To answer your question, I plan to bury myself in the calculation of debits and credits – in figures. I want to specialise in mergers and acquisitions.

I will research and bring companies together; big or small. I will work to locate these companies in places where they are badly needed. The results need to be beneficial for both the people and the company itself."

"Darling, you come alive when you talk about your plan. You're dead serious," said Joseph.

"You bet I am! I have a goal in mind. With determination, I want to bring it to fruition – someday."

"I am sure you will, darling." He pulled her near.

Mrs. De Santis listened, and she was impressed. Joseph noticed his mother's scrutiny. He had not come home with many girls in the past and was aware of his mother's nosiness when it came to any girl he might be interested in. This only happened if they were of his choosing, unless they were daughters of her aristocratic friends from the high society of Vienne. Only then is Mom all smiles and sweet as honey…encouraging. Otherwise, she would get on his case. Today was no different, Joseph thought, with her interrogations, and oh God help me with her possessiveness! How can Mom find anything sinister with Giuliana? She is a perfect angel, and I am absolutely crazy about her.

He got up, reaching toward Giuliana with his hand to pull her up and to usher her away. Joseph's patience had run out. He stretched his body and swallowed hard, restlessly holding back. His mother had done a good job of unravelling his nerves to embarrass him.

"Come. Let's finish the tour of the house," he suggested to Giuliana.

Any excuse would do to break away from his mom. He wanted to stop her inquisitions before she got out of hand. She was notorious for digging into his private life. Today, he feared, was totally premature. He would not let this go any further with the girl he loved. Besides, he wanted to keep his precious Giuliana to himself. He was filled with the strong desire to hold her close to him and seal her lips with kisses until their heartbeats merged as one.

They moved on to his home office, and he closed the door behind him. Mrs. De Santis remained at the table with a stern look on her face.

"Joseph has disrespectfully cut me off," she mumbled to herself, indignant.

She shook her annoyance off, promising herself that his behaviour would be taken up with her husband. Joseph will be disciplined.

Chapter Twenty-Nine
The Tour

"This is where you hide, Joseph?" asked Giuliana, almost scolding.

Without a word, he locked his arms around her in a breathless embrace. Their lips met longingly, with an affectionate kiss. Shivers radiated up and down their spines. Giuliana broke the magic.

"Joseph! Please allow me to admire another lovely room!"

"My mother's work, with her decorator."

"Joseph, you are spoiled, my Dear. You don't appreciate it. You sound ungrateful. I must say, it is tastefully decorated." She glided around, touching things and feeling their texture. "The polished cherry wood is rich and soothing. Your desk is fit for royalty. Your filing cabinets, with their bright leather trim and the bookshelves, loaded with sections from your businesses, all look very proper!" She sat down and swivelled the chair. "This chair is made of beautiful silk leather from Firenze; soft, like a glove." Her eyes glanced at the ceiling. "Oh my! The same leather is accented on the crown moulding trim! I could be in this room all day and night just to browse through the contents. Excuse me, that chandelier must be custom made! Never saw anything like it. Just lovely. All for King Joseph."

She tried to be funny to cheer him up. She had noticed the air in the previous room had gotten too stale for him. As far as she was concerned, she wasn't intimidated by Mrs. De Santis.

After all, she was studying to be an attorney. Punches in life would come with the flow. She had many conversations with Mr. Sbarro as to the challenges the job presented. One needed to be one step ahead of the game.

Giuliana was twenty-one now. Surviving her background, struggles with famine and drought, the molestation, and poverty, she had skipped her childhood entirely. By now she had flowed from the abandoned hills of Molise to the Metropolitan city of Milan, with its people's contrasting customs and natures, and she had learned so much for two lifetimes. Now, with her precious Joseph, she was happy. Except perhaps when she thought about her family. Then Giuliana felt torn.

***

Back home, Gioia was getting ready to immigrate. She was going to rejoin her Ruggiero. Only Trizia was following her; Rosa was remaining behind. Stubborn as a mule, she would not change her mind. Several letters and a couple of phone calls to Giuliana, arranged by Mrs. Zicardo, had not convinced her daughter to go with them. At first, she was bitter, resentful and upset. She couldn't understand why her daughter would not leave Milan now and go with them to resume their family in America. Her Ruggiero was making money and progressing successfully – he could support them. Why? Why? Giuliana is being disobedient. Mrs. Zicardo, in her wisdom, convinced her of the possible merit of the girl staying behind.

"Gioia, your daughter is in the midst of her studies. She is not a child anymore, and she has love and support around her. It's unfair for you to strip her of her world right now. I am sure she is torn between love and duty. When the time is right, everything will fall into place. You will see."

Gioia's emotional health had been deteriorating, and Rosa was getting worried about her daughter-in-law. Once more she went to Mrs. Zicardo.

"I need your help signora; I have already talked to old Dr. Don Francisco. You must come and advise Gioia. She is close to a nervous breakdown. She is refusing to go do errands. I hear her crying at night. Her eyes are swollen and red. She looks pitiful, always with her head down, and she walks in a daze. She misses her husband and her daughter, and she is mad at me for not wanting to go with her. Mrs. Zicardo, I am eighty-two years old. Where am I going at this age? Luigi is waiting for me; I will go beside him when God calls me. I cannot bring myself to go to America, I am too old."

"Rosa, I know exactly what you mean, I have seen Gioia myself. To be honest... I am worried about her too. Is she at home? I will come over and talk to her."

Good, reliable Mrs. Zicardo grabbed a shawl, placed it on her shoulders, and off she went to speak to Gioia.

Rosa thought everything was possible through her Jesus. She walked holding the beads in her hand, whenever the opportunity presented itself, and her lips would murmur the Holy Mary. Thank-you God for sending us Mrs. Zicardo. Here she is at the door already. . .

"Gioia, Dear," Rosa called out, "come down, amore, my love. You have a visitor."

In the past couple of months, Gioia had been spending a lot of time in her daughter's room. Rosa had seen her holding some of Giuliana's items close to her chest with a pathetic look on her face and tears in her eyes. She must miss Giuliana immensely, thought Rosa, but we all do, don't we? This family has been torn apart by death, immigration, misery. Our poor Giuliana had to be given away due to poverty and to save her. No wonder Gioia is losing her mind. Can anyone blame her?

Sheepishly, Gioia came down stairs, embarrassed by her dishevelled appearance. Mrs. Zicardo, with her charming smile, was gifted at putting anyone at ease.

"Hello there, Gioia. How have you been doing lately? I haven't seen you out much."

Gioia burst into tears, without responding. She had been doing that a lot lately.

"Now, now, Gioia, my Dear. You need to get a hold of yourself." She hugged her. "I advise you to go join your husband with or without your daughter or mother-in-law. Your nervous system has reached a fragile state, Dear. You need to save yourself. The sooner, the better."

"How am I going to do that?" she answered, wiping her tears away.

"You will. I will help you. I suggest you see Dr. Don Francisco. He might prescribe a mild sedative to relax you a little. You might be able to rationalise better. Rose tells me you are up all hours of the night. Your brain and body need to shut down to recharge, Gioia. You look stressed out if you ask me."

"Mrs. Zicardo, I can make some camomile tea for all of us. That should help, do you think?" Rosa promptly offered.

Mrs. Zicardo agreed.

"That sounds fine, Rosa, but I think Gioia needs a little more than camomile."

***

In America, Ruggiero now drove a company car. Life had improved indeed, as he had been previously walking to and from to work in the bitter cold winter air. Mr. and Mrs. Graham had recommended a realtor, and after house hunting for a couple of weeks, he had bought a two-story older home in the hopes to receive his family soon. Mrs. Graham was going to help him with the bare necessities, the rest was going to be left to Gioia to make it their home.

***

Four months later, Gioia and Trizia were ready for their departure thanks to Mrs. Zicardo and Rosa, who had been busy making the arrangements. Gioia, being in a lethargic state, was not motivated to take any initiative on her own. Rosa had managed to stash away enough liras under her mattress to pay the fare for both of them, although she knew that Gioia had money from Ruggiero. Rosa, in her kindness, felt duty-bound to pay for the trip for two reasons: Gioia was not motivated to actually go and get her travel ticket, and thinking of Giuliana remaining behind, it made sense to leave what funds Gioia had for her daughter. It wasn't fair for her to depend totally on her sponsors. She should have a legacy from her own family, Rosa thought.

What about a wedding someday? Rosa was old fashioned but cared deeply for the family with good intentions.

It was time for the dreadful goodbyes. Gioia embraced Rosa, lingering with emotional devastation as her heart was breaking and her soul tormented. Gioia truly loved her mother-in-law as if she were her true mother. Her own had died in childbirth leaving Rosa to perform double duty for her. The bond between them was hard to break, but now life was separating them.

***

In Milan, Giuliana had a train ticket and was accompanied by Amelia and Mr. Sbarro. They were going to meet Giuliana's

251

mother and sister in Naples, to see them off and to say their goodbyes.

Giuliana's life was demanding these days. Her studies were getting increasingly challenging, and the precious little time she had was devoted to her beloved Joseph. She couldn't dwell much on her mom and sister embarking on a long voyage. She was happy when Joseph offered to accompany her, but when he arrived last night with a sombre look in his eyes as he tenderly embraced her, she knew something was off. Nearly in tears, he buried his face in her side.

"Darling, I am so sorry, but I cannot go with you tomorrow. My mother has to go to Vienna for a serious medical checkup. It's her heart. I need to fly her there. My dad is the keynote speaker at a conference in Miami. My sisters are in California. That leaves me to accompany her."

His mother has changed his plan, Giuliana thought. She had a dubious notion but kept it to herself. He is upset enough, no use insinuating anything further. Giuliana was not the type to complain. A sharp pain crossed her stomach, sending acidity up her throat. She wanted her mom to meet him, and for him to meet her since Gioia was going across the ocean. So far away… She didn't want to ask further questions.

"I am sure your mom needs you badly, especially if it has to do with her heart. I understand, Darling. Don't you worry about me!" She gave him a big hug and held him tight until he released her with the saddest eyes she had ever seen.

"I will miss you, my love. I can't wait for you to return."

His body trembled releasing her, regretful to let go. He walked back home to dutifully attend to his mother. His feverish thoughts were invaded by his adorable Giuliana.

Chapter Thirty
Naples Farewell

The next morning, bright and early, Giuliana was ready to go catch the train.

"Let's go, girls! The train isn't going to wait!" called out Mr. Sbarro.

"I know, Dear," said Amelia. "The way they zip through – in and out – God forbid if you don't hop on swiftly!"

Mr. Sbarro had taken the weekend off to go to Naples. He had suggested to Amelia that they show Giuliana the city and book a tour of the Amalfi coast. If time was favourable, they could take the ferry over to Capri.

"Yes, Dear. A good idea. That will distract her from her mom and sister leaving. You think of everything, my darling." She gave him a quick kiss and off they went.

Gioia and Trizia were waiting for them at the port. Once Giuliana spotted them, she ran to embrace her mom like the little girl of days gone by that she once was.

"Mom, you look marvellous. Wait 'till Dad sees you!"

"Oh! Tesoro mio. My treasure, nevermind me. Let me look at you. What a sophisticated young lady you have become." Gioia's face immediately lightened up upon seeing her daughter.

"Trizia, you are growing like a weed!" Giuliana measured her, putting her hand over her head. "Look, you have passed my shoulder. Eh? Slow down! I bet Dad will not recognise you."

253

"I wish you were going with us. We will not be complete without you and Mamma Rosa," stated Gioia, teary-eyed. In anticipation of her emotional state, Gioia had taken a mild tranquillizer to keep her emotions under control.

Amelia and Roberto stood aside, observing in delight the emotional exchange of affection. Mr. Sbarro looked at his watch.

"We have time for a quick bite. Why don't we settle at La Conca Dora across the street? Listen to that song… The Neapolitan music is alluring even in the morning. Let's go."

He allowed the girls to walk ahead as the traffic was almost as bad as it was in Milan - he wanted to assure their safety and wellbeing. In their limited time, Gioia couldn't stop admiring her daughter and the God sent family that had taken her in. I wish my Giuliana would come back to us. Her glance switched to Amelia who was joyfully chatting with her daughter, and a bout of jealousy snapped through her. Shame on me! Jealousy destroys the mind. Mamma Rosa would scorn me. She forced herself to be kinder.

"Amelia, honorable Judge Sbarro, I do love you both. How can Ruggiero and I ever repay you for what you have done for our daughter?"

"Gioia, on the contrary, Giuliana has given Amelia back her reason to live. She has brought laughter in our home once more. We all love her dearly," Mr. Sbarro answered.

Time was up. Gioia and Trizia climbed onboard the ship. They made their way on deck to wave their goodbyes as Giuliana, Amelia, and the judge, remained on the port platform waving. They stood still watching the Vulcania disappear across the Mediterranean Sea. Once the ship was totally out of sight, Judge Sbarro put his arms around the two woman he loved.

"Ok, my girls, on to our next adventure!" It was time to break the focus from the infinite extension of the sea.

A private car, with a tour guide in a blue uniform and an impressive beret, was waiting for them. He introduced himself as Bruno and courteously helped them settle in. Off they went! Bruno was familiar with the city and the area, so his negotiations with traffic and the narrow roads were slick and professional. His proclivity for narrating their expedition was apparent from the moment the ignition was turned on. He spoke in perfect Italian, without a hint of any dialect. The honourable Judge Sbarro looked at Giuliana and was pleased to see that the tour was offering the young girl the distraction she desperately needed. She had never been here before, and her eyes were totally engulfed by the beauty of the city as they swirled along by the sea. Once they got to the Amalfi coast, Giuliana was really beside herself.

"This is breathtaking," she whispered.

The scattered homes seemed to be hanging on the cliffs. Well kept, they sported terraced outdoor gardens. The sea was spellbinding, as the low tide gently caressed the sand. Bruno kept pointing out the homes of famous people: actors and actresses from abroad and other celebrities.

"This is heavenly! Look at that blue sky. It merges with the sea in total harmony," pointed out Amelia.

"Can I open the window slightly?" asked Mr. Sbarro. "I want to take in that fresh breeze, the rich iodine is good for the glands."

"Yes! That soft breeze feels refreshing," said Giuliana.

"Oh! Giuliana, look at those loaded lemon trees lined up on the slopes above the sea. Do they tell you anything?"

"It makes me think of limoncello. Those are cultivated fruits."

The Sbarro's were having fun. They took great satisfaction in showing Giuliana around the lower part of the country. Milan had a lot to offer, but it lacked the beauty of the seashore. Wide-eyed, Giuliana was totally captured by the expanse of exquisite nature.

"Just wait until you see Capri," Bruno encouraged.

They took the ferry. The sea was calm. A jeep picked them up and they started to climb the hilly, narrow road. Going higher and higher, they were now overlooking the cliff down to the sea.

"This is frightening, looking down. How much higher are we going?" asked Giuliana.

Finally, they were at the top. The biggest attraction was the blue grotto.

"Amazing! This is a fantastic creation by nature itself!" Giuliana marvelled.

Suddenly, she found that Joseph surfaced in her mind. How romantic, this place! The lure of nostalgia pulled at her heart. Joseph, the love of my life!

***

The fabulous trip had been a good break and fruitful. Once back in Milan, the family's usual busy routine commenced relentlessly.

The next day, Giuliana rushed to get out of her class, ignoring her classmate's chit chat in her haste. She was anxiously looking for Joseph. She strained her eyes and stretched her neck, searching among the crowd. There was no sign of Joseph. He had not come out to meet her today. Giuliana had not seen him or heard from him for four days, which seemed like an eternity. Oh! He must be still in Vienna. I miss him so. Walking alone, her thoughts shifted to his Mom. I hope it's nothing too serious regarding Mrs. De Santis and her health.

Giuliana arrived home in a sombre mood. The house was quiet. She headed straight for her room. Good. The boys are still out. Her tired body was craving a lie-down and rest. She flopped on her bed, staring at the ceiling. Her eyes blurred with tears. She wiped them away with the back of her hand and cleared her throat. Stop this feeling sorry for yourself, girl. Cherish the goodness in your life. The walls in her room seemed to close in on her. Her restless mind was darting everywhere. She wondered about her mom and Trizia. They would be mid-ocean by now. A cold shiver shook her body, then she broke in a hot sweat. What on earth is coming over me? To calm herself down, she put her hands together in prayer.

"Please God, keep my mom and sister safe."

Her mind drifted everywhere. Grandmother has been left all alone now. That brought sorrow to her heart. I must take some time to go see her soon. She rolled over, face down, fighting to find calm, and remove any unpleasant thoughts. Joseph, my Joseph. Thinking of him always brought her pleasure. She smiled, closed her eyes, and guided her brain to relive the last moments she recalled being with her beloved. Right now he was the most enjoyable thing in her life. Her focus was in deep meditation and the concentration brought her some relief. She relived his embraces the night before they parted. The chemistry between them was unbearable. When their bodies touched, they both struggled with love and passion.

Giuliana had been brought up to observe the commandments as a devoted Catholic. Her grandmother's voice always resonated in her ears. She wished to be freer with her feelings. But no, it is forbidden.

"Giuliana, when you get married, you need to walk down the aisle worthy of your white dress. The veil covering your face is a sign of purity and virginity. Only then you can walk with your head held up high. Remember, my Dear, never give yourself away before marriage." Puzzled, she had listened to her in years back, not quite understanding what she meant. Since she had met Joseph and been swept away feverishly – madly – in love with him, she understood. It was easy to get carried away and give into temptation. No. She would not.

The flash back of Orlando and her trauma played back,

disturbing her immensely. She thought of her grandmother's words. Have I committed a mortal sin? No. Giuliana strongly refused to believe that the event in the cornfield could be attributed as her sin. It wasn't my fault.

Giuliana adored her grandmother. She had been taught that certain actions were a venial sin, but the graver ones were a mortal sin. With a mortal sin, you would find yourself trapped in purgatory, or you would burn in hell. God almighty! Giuliana didn't want it to come to that.

So, these emotions aroused in both of them that sent their entire bodies into a trembling spin...was it a sin? Giuliana wondered. Sometimes it seemed questionable. However, she would never give herself away – this had been so vigorously implemented deep in her existence and in her soul. Her conscience would never forgive her. Giuliana's upbringing dictated that she was not only to honour her grandmother but to respect her body.

Joseph, complied whenever she pulled back. He would stroke her shiny brown hair, run a hand down her back, look her right in the eyes, and grasp with deep desire.

"Darling, I love you too much. I want to marry you. Our love can wait." He would whisper in her ear.

Brought back to her bedroom with a jolt, Giuliana opened her eyes. Where is he? Why isn't he back? Tomorrow, she would go by his house. The butler and the housekeeper would be there. She needed to know.

Her anxiety was too much to bear. She grabbed the extra cushion and pulled it to her chest, desperately looking for comfort. Begging for sleep, slowly, her heavy eyelids closed, and she drifted away.

Chapter Thirty-One
Mrs. De Santis's Drama

In Vienna, Mrs. De Santis was far from suffering a cardiac arrest. She had insisted that Joseph fly her to her trusted doctor.

"My heart is skipping beats and jumping out of my chest. I need to see my cardiologist, Joseph," she had wailed, with a melancholic voice, while holding her chest and gasping for breath.

Joseph was worried. He cared for his mom. In his alarm, he immediately agreed.

"Mom, I will cancel with Giuliana. I need to attend to you first. Especially with Dad being away. I will make arrangements for our Cessna to be ready to get you to your doctor as soon as possible."

She weakly smiled in relief. Internally she thought, it worked. I am still in control. Good. That peasant girl from the meridional has not taken over my son yet. She never will. Mrs. De Santis had her own plans for her son. This romance is lasting too long. At first, she thought this was just a passing fling for Joseph. She had seen so many girls go after him. What was he doing wasting time with this insignificant girl?

She had hired a private investigator from Vienna. He had served her in the past. Her husband travelled a lot, so she needed to be vigilant of his involvements. They were, after all, billionaires. Their companies were worth a fortune. Sleazy girls would always be eyeing her husband when she accompanied him on business conferences and ventures. The nerve of them, totally ignoring me at his side! Mr. De Santis was an honest business man. Totally dedicated to his affairs, he was not a womaniser at all.

With their marriage, they had combined their assets, and he had seen to it the results multiplied with large success through dedication. She had come from a wealthy aristocratic family so they matched well because they were of the same class. Now, she worried about her son. Was he protected? As a mother, she felt the need to interfere. The report had been completed last week and she had lunch with Carlo Delgato, her private investigator.

"Carlo, you have worked for me a long time. I have been patiently waiting for this relationship to blow over. It hasn't. I am afraid this girl has a good grip on my son. I need to stop it."

"Mrs. De Santis, all I can do is report to you my findings."

"I am listening, tell me. I need to know all about her."

"She comes from a poor family in a small town deep in the rocky hills of Molise. They are good people, but penniless. The only seasonal work in the region is picking corn. The biggest employer is a woman with lots of lands. She grows and exports corn. I was told this girl had found work in the cornfield, for a short time. The father has emigrated to seek work in America. Since then, he has been working in a factory, and sending his family money. I imagine they are living better. I will not go into the small details of how they managed before this because it's sad. You see there are zero industries there - there is no hope unless you get away.

Now, as for the girl, I have been told she is brilliant. The parents could not send her to school due to lack of funds. Apparently these people from Milan took her in as their own and they have supported her in every way. Her school principal and teacher have paid for her education, and now she has excellent credentials. Soon her mom and young sister will emigrate to join the father if they have not already. Her grandmother has remained home in the remote town to die; from what I gather."

"Can you believe it? My son is in love with a southern peasant!" she shook her head from side to side.

"Mrs. De Santis, if you ask me, the girl is an honour student and hard worker. I have had nothing but praises from her teachers. She is an attractive girl. I think Joseph may have found himself a wonderful woman."

"Well, Carlo, it is easy for you to say that because he is not your son. We happen to belong to a society where my son will be scorned for getting involved with a southern peasant, regardless of how bright she is."

"Mr. De Santis, how does he feel about this relationship?"

She made a hand gesture pushing it away.

"You men are all the same. You see a lovely woman and as long as she has a good body – busty. and a nice pair of legs – she charms you over and there you go."

"I think you have nothing to worry about for Joseph, with this girl."

"No. I don't trust her. I see the way she hangs around his neck. There are many other girls out there that are better suited for him – his equals."

"Mrs. De Santis, there is nothing more I can add to this matter. It's up to Joseph. I leave it to you. I did my job. I was happy that I had nothing sinister to report."

He wanted to part from this woman as he had no sympathy for wicked rich ladies. Interestingly, they seemed to make up the majority of his clientele.

Mrs. De Santis got up, shook hands with Carlo, and forced a thank-you with a particularly perturbed look. She did not want to hear praises for Giuliana. The girl came from peasants. She was a peasant. Therefore, not for my son. She needed to put an end to this and the sooner, the better. Her first plan was faking the heart failure. The rest of her plan would follow. She needed to get him away from both this girl and Milan.

Chapter Thirty-Two
The Transatlantic Journey

Gioia, taken over by sea sickness, was having the worst time of her life. Her battered body was weak and confined to her cabin for most of her travelling time. After the ship had passed Gibraltar, the ocean had gotten choppier. Once they hit the transatlantic, the unforgiving tides were rocking the ship as high winds blew fiercely. Trizia was attending to Gioia the best she could and often needed care herself when the ocean was particularly vengeful.

"Where are we?" Gioia asked.

They occupied a cabin down below. It was a long way from the upper deck.

"Mom, all I see is blue water and sky! No land in sight. If you can make it upstairs on deck, you will probably feel better."

"My stomach is upside down. This nausea won't leave me."

"Mom, the fresh air might help."

"Trizia, I know what you mean, Dear. But, I feel so weak."

"Mom, you have to try. You worry me."

Poor Trizia felt helpless with a sick mother and no one else around from the family to help her. She thought of her grandmother. If only Nonna Rosa were here. She would know what to do. They had never been this far out of the hills of Molise and it was overwhelming for them.

After what seemed like an eternal journey, Trizia emerged on deck only to find an animated commotion among the passengers.

They were all admiring land! Trizia pushed her way through the crowd to get closer to the rail. Finally, land! And buildings! Excited, she ran down to the cabin.

"Mom, we have arrived! You must try and come up. They tell me it's New York."

It was chaos for over an hour as everyone clamoured to find sure footing on soil once again. As they finally left the ship, there, on the port, stood Ruggiero. He spotted them first as he carefully watched the tide of people pushing down the ramp. He ran to grab them both with open arms. Tears of joy and sadness crested his eyes, running down his cheeks. He couldn't stop kissing his wife and his adorable Trizia.

"I am so happy you are here. Oh! How I wish Mom and Giuliana could be here with us also."

"Darling, at last, we are here! We will make the best of it, the three of us together."

He led them to his car.

"My darlings, here we are. Hop in."

"Ruggiero, this is your car?" Gioia was speechless.

"Yes, Dear. My company's. At our disposal."

Ruggiero brought them to the two-story home he had found for his family. Mrs. Graham had helped him to get all the necessities to welcome them warmly.

"Dad, this is great!" said Trizia. "We have everything here. Does it mean we are rich now?"

"Dear, I have a job – a good paying job. Countless hours of work have meant that I can now provide everything for us."

Gioia smiled, darting her eyes from her Ruggiero to Trizia. She softly spoke:

"My darlings, we have each other. God's bounty from Mamma

Rosa's prayers will guarantee that we will be just fine." With open arms, she hugged Ruggiero tenderly. "We are reunited. I am happy."

"So am I, Dear. You have no idea how much. But, Giuliana... I need to see her and be reassured of her wellbeing. The guilt haunts my conscience. Back then I could not provide for her..."

"Darling don't beat yourself up. She writes to both of us. Has she told you about her Joseph? She is in love, Dear. I am happy for her."

"She barely mentioned. Girls don't usually confide in their fathers about their romantic relationships. You will have to pass it on to me, Dear."

"Well! I was excited he was coming with her to meet us in Naples. Unfortunately, his mother had an emergency health issue that needed to be looked into – some heart problems. He had to attend to this and fly her to Vienna, she is Viennese. Giuliana tells me Joseph is a kind young man. Dear, don't despair. Besides her studies, she adores the family she is living with. I think Joseph has a lot to do with keeping her in Milan."

"I stressed to her the importance of the English language. With us settling here, it is a must for her."

"Darling, stop being such an overprotective father. Let Giuliana do what she wants at this time. Her destiny will guide her."

"Oh! Mom! How did she take your departure? I cannot think about her alone in that house without any family members around."

"Ruggiero, it broke my heart to leave her. I probably never would have left. You know what she did? Our tickets! She came home with them and made sure they had an expiry date. It boggles my mind to this day – how did she manage to save all that money? She had it stashed under her mattress!

Ruggiero, my Dear, I couldn't leave her penniless. I took some of the money you sent me. I went to the post office and opened up a registered saving account with interest in her name. I told Mrs. Zicardo and the notary to distribute the interest to her every six months. She is illiterate but smart. Can you imagine what she could get up to if she could read?"

He hugged her.

"Mom has always loved you like a daughter. You deserved each other. Too bad she remained behind."

***

Ruggiero was busy settling his wife and daughter in their new world. They were adjusting well. Trizia had been enrolled in school and gracefully accepted by her peers. Her teacher praised her intelligence and complimented her as a fast learner. Gioia, eager to master her new language, was attending classes to learn English. Ruggiero was much happier with his family near. He was excelling even better in his job. Life for them was taking a new turn and shaping up all around. The only sorrow, Ruggiero thought, is my mother.

He had every reason to be worried.

***

Since Gioia and Trizia had left, Rosa wasn't a happy camper in her empty house. Her courage had vanished. Her good intentions at having encouraged Gioia and Trizia to go for their own wellbeing had ultimately backfired for her. The empty house that followed their absence was devastating. She was torturing herself – walking from room to room, calling out their names, going insane, pretending they were there and that they would appear any minute. She kept watching the front door. Yes, Gioia is going to come up those steps to return home anytime.

As she would hear the chatter of the children outdoors, she would open the window to look, leaning way out – almost falling out – lifting her feet off the floor with the heaviness of her head. She had come close a few times.

"Where is my Trizia? Where is my Giuliana? Eh! Sara! Have you seen my Trizia?"

Her mind had gone into a stupor. She imagined things. At night, she would check the bedrooms. When she saw them empty, she would break down, hysterically.

Her seat at morning service had remained empty. Some of the parishioners started to get suspicious. They whispered to one another, "We'd better check on her."

Mrs. Zicardo and the neighbour across the street had the same idea.

***

The door opened, and Rosa was found sitting on a chair by Trizia's bedroom window staring into the emptiness. Her eyes flickered up and down. They stood behind, trying to figure it out. What was she looking at or searching for out there? From here, one could see the infinite horizon, with the earth and the sky meeting at a distance away. Rosa was mumbling to herself

"Where are they?" she asked to no one in particular, with a faint twist of her lips.

"Rosa? Hello! How are you?"

She didn't respond. The look on her face was a distant and questioning expression.

"She is in a state of shock. We'd better get the doctor," said the neighbour.

"The doctor? Don Francisco is sick in bed himself. He had a stroke. I am all you have here. The doctor from the next town will take two days to get here by mule. Someone has to go for him. We need to take her to the city," Mrs. Zicardo chirped.

"By the look on her face … she has lost her mind."

"What can we do?"

Mrs. Zicardo put a hand on her forehead assessing the situation.

"We'll get that chauffeur by the piazza. He has a car; we'll take her to the city. But, I need to make a couple of phone calls."

She ran to the square to the pharmacist. He allowed her to place a phone call to Amelia and Giuliana.

"Giuliana, Dear. I don't want to alarm you…" she paused, "it's your grandmother. She is physically ok. But lapsed into some kind of mental disorder – a shock maybe, or a nervous breakdown. I am no expert; just guessing. You should go down, Dear. It might do her good to see you. We will take her to the city hospital. Try to get here as soon as you can."

"Yes. Oh my God! Of course. I will get there as soon as I can make arrangements. Mrs. Zicardo, thank you. Please, please do everything you can for her."

All shook up, Giuliana turned to Amelia.

"I need to go. My grandmother needs me."

"Yes, darling. We will get you a train ticket. I will have one of my colleagues cover for me. I will go with you."

"Aunt Amelia, I appreciate that. It will be good to have you with me." She hugged her. "I think we need you."

An idea sparked in her head. Joseph! His Cessena! She wanted to get there fast. He had been kept terribly busy in the past while, his heart ached for not being able to be with her as much as he wanted to. He had been apologetic about his absence. She needed him badly this time. She dialled his office number in Milan at the textile factory. His secretary Hilda answered.

"Hello, De Santis and associates."

"Hello, Hilda. It's Giuliana here. May I talk to Joseph, please?" she asked with a shaky voice.

"Sorry, Giuliana, he is not in."

"Oh! Do you know when he will be back? How can I reach him?"

"I am not at liberty to say. He left this morning with his Dad."

"Please, Hilda. This is an emergency I need to talk to him. Or, can you pass on a message for him to call me immediately?"

Hilda was an elderly woman and a faithful secretary – she liked Joseph. He had proudly confided in her about his love for his priceless Giuliana. She hesitated, then responded.

"I am not to disturb him, Miss Giuliana. But, I will do that for you; because he might not forgive me if I don't," she chuckled reassuringly.

"Thanks, Hilda," Giuliana managed to say, frantically.

She started to grab a few things to take with her while she impatiently waited for the phone to ring. Then it came. Joseph was at the other end of the receiver. She frantically grabbed the phone with a high-pitched voice.

"Darling, I am so glad you called. I am in a state of panic here." Before Joseph could get a word in, she continued, "It's my grandmother. She needs me. I must go to her. I need you too, my Darling. You must go with me. I wouldn't ask otherwise, but since it is an emergency. . . Your Cessna… can we fly there fast?"

She was blurting away, not giving Joseph a chance to speak.

"My Darling, I am in Vienna, in a boardroom meeting. I will excuse myself. My dad will understand. As for flying there, it is questionable. Where would I land?"

"I don't know; you are the pilot! There is a soccer field. Could you land there?"

Giuliana was not thinking rationally.

"My sweet I cannot go and land on some soccer field out of the blue. It needs to be arranged in advance. I will get back to Milan, and I will get you there somehow and as fast as I can. Bye, see you soon, my love."

He hung up and called Mr. De Santis aside.

"Dad, I must go. Giuliana is in despair she needs me. Her grandmother is ill."

"Son, do what you have to do. I will take care of things here." He put a hand on his son's shoulder and motioned him away. "Go. Take care of your Giuliana."

"Thanks, Dad. I knew you would understand."

Joseph had no doubt his dad approved of his relationship with 'the southern girl,' as his mother referred to her. As for Mom, I am not sure.

His twin-engine, five-seater plane was fast up in the sky flying toward Milan. On landing in Milan, Joseph rushed to grab the bare necessities and run to Giuliana. His Mother walked in as he was leaving.

"Joseph? What's going on? Where is your father? You are supposed to be in Vienna."

"Mom, I have no time to explain. I am in a mad hurry. I need to get to Giuliana's. She needs me. Her grandmother is gravely ill."

Blood flushed her face, leaving her looking like a red lobster.

She shouted like a fish vendor at the market square.

"Joseph, I have had enough with you! How could you leave your affairs – your father – behind to run to this girl's grandmother? You are out of your mind!"

"Yes, Mom. I am out of my mind in love with my girl. She needs me. I have no time to argue with you. I must run."

He ran out, skipping down the stairs to get to Giuliana. He arrived with his Ferrari ready to leave.

"Darling, this machine will take us there in no time," he said, as he sealed her lips with a passionate kiss.

"Oh, Joseph! Sorry I took you away from your business. I selfishly need you. I am glad you came, Darling." She couldn't control her tears from freely rolling down her face. "If something happens to my grandmother... She is the only family I have in this country."

"Now, now. Where is my positive girl? Don't jump to conclusions, my Dear, she will be just fine."

Amelia promptly joined them, and they were off. They arrived at the province city at St. Margherita Hospital, where they were met by Mrs. Zicardo. Giuliana searched her face for answers. She wasn't smiling as usual. They made their way to a small private room of the hospital where Grandma had been admitted. Giuliana panicked once she saw the pale face of her grandmother. Her pallor was that of a dead person.

"Grandma?"

She bent down to kiss her and reached out for her hand. Rose remained motionless, staring at the emptiness, lost. Giuliana's fear escalated.

"What has happened to my vivacious grandmother? So strong and caring, always putting others first? This is not the Grandmother Rosa I know."

"Dear, I am sorry for you to have to see her like this. Hopefully, she will come to," said Mrs. Zicardo.

Putting her concern for Grandma Rosa first, Giuliana had neglected introductions.

"Mrs. Zicardo, this is Joseph, my boyfriend."

With a smile, she extended her hand.

"My pleasure to meet you, Joseph. I hear great things about you from Rosa."

"How sad. Now that I am here I don't have the pleasure to talk to her."

Amelia had made her way to the front desk to inquire about Rosa's condition.

"I would like to talk to the doctor if I may, please," she told the nurse.

"Professor Santelli should be here shortly. He will talk to you."

"Thanks."

She made her way to the room. From her understanding in simply observing Rosa, her pupils told Amelia she was in a grave state of neurosis. Dr. Santelli arrived a short time later. He methodically explained Rosa's condition.

"Your Grandmother has been diagnosed by our Geriatric Psychiatrist with severe psychoneurosis – an emotional, mental disorder that affects the elderly. The patient usually improves with therapy and medication." He hesitated and went on, "I want to be frank with you. We think she suffered a stroke. The stroke has left her speech impaired and immobilised her extremities. We are keeping a close watch on her, trying to give her the best care we can.

"Dr. Santelli, what are her chances?" Amelia interjected

"Only God can answer that, Dr. Sbarro. In the medical field, we never know. Miracles do happen that beat our science from time to time, as you must have experienced."

Amelia kept her mouth shut. Rosa's condition was bad. She had experienced it often and knew grief well. She turned to Giuliana, and put an arm around her shoulder

"Darling, there isn't much you can do here for your grandma now. She can rest better if we leave." Then, calling to Renalta, "You must know a good place for us to get a bite to eat. Let's go, we will be back later."

Giuliana lingered around, afraid to leave. She bent over to kiss her grandmother, but there was no response. Joseph pulled her away gently.

"Come, my Darling, we will be back soon."

They did return a couple of hours later. As Giuliana walked into the room, a nurse with her back to the door turned from covering her grandmother's face.

It hit Giuliana like a sword to the heart.

"No, it cannot be! No!" she screamed, throwing herself on her grandmother's lifeless body. The touch of softness and love was there no more. The nurse put her hands on Giuliana's shoulders and eased her up.

"Sorry. She serenely expired one hour after you left. She was in peace."

Chapter Thirty-Three
The Funeral

No words could ease her pain. Giuliana had lost the dearest person in her life. The void was too much to bare. Joseph embraced her for the longest time.

"Darling, I am so sorry. I will try to make up her love for you."

Amelia understood her pain from her personal loss, as did Mrs. Zicardo, having known the family and their close-knit ways since the day she had arrived in this strange, hilly town.

Amelia and Mrs. Zicardo, with the help of some neighbours and Joseph, made arrangements for the funeral. As was the tradition, the dead were buried as soon as possible – it would not be long before Rosa would be put to rest. The Sbarro clan had arrived from Milan to support Giuliana. Judge Sbarro had his secretary send telegrams to America, to the Ferrantes, including Raniero and John's families. The church bells rang out news of the passing, but the traveling sound of the bells were no match for the speed word of mouth traveled in this town. The townspeople came in waves to the funeral. Giuliana would be the only family member in attendance, but as Rosa was well-loved, her funeral was heavily attended.

Joseph stood beside his love. He was her rock. He gave her love and strength and holding on to his arm gave her courage. Thank you, God, for my Joseph, she meditated. The thought of Liliana came to Giuliana's mind and she looked around, searching for her among the crowd, but she wasn't anywhere to be seen.

Giuliana was brought back swiftly as the eulogy was initiated. The priest, full of praises for Rosa, was accompanied by the angelic gospel singing of the church choir. Their heavenly verses touched everyone's soul. The Sbarro boys and a deacon served as pallbearers. The procession followed Rosa's casket as it moved from the church to the outdoor platform. There, a thirty-piece band was waiting, and the musicians started to play as they fell in step behind the casket. This was most unusual and came as a surprise for everyone. The townspeople erupted in soft whispers.

Rosa was laid to rest beside her Luigi as she had planned all along. Joseph tenderly clung to his beloved, wishing to alleviate her pain with his nearness. The crowd, after paying their respects, slowly dispersed. Giuliana's head was in a fog. Her legs were ready to buckle with exhaustion. She had no more tears left to cry. Joseph, the Sbarro's, and Giuliana advanced toward the black iron gates of the cemetery when a lady appeared from behind the stonewall.

"Excuse me. My condolences for the loss of your grandmother. She was a grand lady. It is a big loss for everyone. She helped many people with her herbal remedies. Everyone loved her. She will be greatly missed."

"Thank you."

Giuliana's smile felt forced as she battled back fatigue and wiped at fresh tears. The woman's face looked familiar to her, but she couldn't quite place her. Truthfully, Giuliana didn't really care at this point.

"I am Sibilla, from the cornfield," the woman said. "You were young when you worked for us, and you did for only a short time. Do you remember me?"

A dark cloud passed behind Giuliana's eyes.

"Oh. Yes! How could I forget?"

"Do you remember Liliana?"

"Liliana? Of course. I will never forget Liliana."

"Poor Liliana," Sibilla answered.

Giuliana took pause at this response.

"My apologies, I have been away too long. Sorry, I didn't place you at first, Sibilla."

Giuliana observed Sibilla had aged immensely, visible even with her tear-blurred vision. No wonder she hadn't recognised her. But, she questioned, why would she take the time to attend Rosa's funeral? Why humble herself to speak to me now? She knew Sibilla lived in a world of greed. She didn't give a hoot about her workers. To her, we were all illiterate peasants. Giuliana made a point to gracefully thank her and part with Joseph's arm around her waist.

***

Back in her childhood home, Giuliana walked from room to room. As she opened each door, she was greeted with an eerie feeling. The empty rooms echoed with the ghosts of her former life. The battered furniture was tired and ready for the dump. The indents in the chairs were haunted by the memory of their former occupants. Once this place was full of life and felt crowded, now the walls seemed to close in on Giuliana. No wonder my poor grandmother went berserk. She died of a broken heart.

The kitchen smelled musty. The fireplace was mounded with ash from a crackling fire of a time long gone by. The aromas from Grandma's cooking no longer lingered in the air. How sad. We may have been dirt poor, but we were happy together.

The front door squeaked open, startling Giuliana from her thoughts. There was Joseph with the neighbour from across the street behind him and a slew of other folks after them. They were all carrying food plates of different sorts.

"Darling, these people are all here to see you," Joseph said cautiously.

"Oh my! Please, come in."

The people Giuliana recognised from scattered parts of both the town and the church. The table, covered with a dusty tablecloth, was full of food in no time: cornbread, lasagna, ravioli, meatballs, sweets, and cakes. The last in line was an elderly lady holding a bowl of salad. She had a paisley kerchief tied behind the braided loop of her hair. She wore a ruffled apron, crisp and bright, tied around her waist.

"I used to go pick dandelions with Rosa in my younger days. My knees are old and achy now, but I had to go and find some to bring here for Rosa's sake. This is a fresh dandelion salad, for old times'," She said through her missing teeth. Her eyes glittered, proud of her offering and accomplishment. Joseph looked astounded. Giuliana's heart was melting. She didn't know how to thank these kind folks. They must have scraped together their last liras to prepare this food. It brought tears to her eyes and warm emotions inundated her soul. It's all about 'la figura,' her Mom and Grandma used to say.

"You make sacrifices in life, always going without, but when the call of need comes from another, you need to put aside sacrifice and act with generosity."

She remembered those words.

The folks didn't stay. They dropped off their loot, gave their condolences and away they went.

"Joseph, you need to go a few doors down and fetch the Sbarro clan, Mrs. Zicardo, and her girls to come and enjoy God's offerings."

"Yes, my Dear. I am moved myself from the actions of these townsfolk. They are the kindest souls I have ever witnessed."

A short time later, the families arrived. The young guys greeted

Giuliana, but the aroma of the food drove them quickly to check out the abundance on the table. Marco was the first to dig in.

"Guys, I don't know about you, but I cannot wait to start eating."

"Yes, I am starving!" Nino promptly followed.

"Guys, have some respect. Control your voracious appetites," cautioned Dino, being sensible as always.

When the rest arrived, they were more than happy to feast on the southern food. Mr. Sbarro sat down with a full plate.

"Giuliana, I must say this funeral has brought faith back to me. These people, humble as their lives are, must have thought a great deal of your grandmother and your family. The entire town has come together to pay their respects."

"Yes, and what a shame none of our immediate family could be here with me," Giuliana replied sadly.

"Your dad, Giuliana, he is doing well from what you tell me?" Amelia responded.

"Yes, Aunt Amelia. I am sure Dad and Mom are devastated and wanted to be here."

"Giuliana, I want you to know, your father sent a telegram to the Mayor instructing him to find and hire the band for Rosa. It was both his wish and his expense." Mrs. Zicardo responded.

"My Dad would do that. The church had a feast one year with a band. It was her favourite. Grandma sang along. They played her music."

Amelia got up.

"Giuliana, we have to head home. You take your time, Dear. Joseph is with you. My sister is only two doors away should you need any help."

"Thanks, Aunt. I will decide what to do here with the house

and come back as soon as I can. There is nothing left to keep me here."

"Darling, I hate seeing you so sad. Cheer up, Dear, and give me a smile. You know we all love you."

***

Giuliana sat with her head in her hands by the crackling fire Joseph had created. She had decisions to make. What do I do with the belongings? The cleanup? The property itself? Joseph had gone for a stroll, he would be back soon, and she planned to ask for his advice. She made her way to her old room and opened the window wide. The view was mesmerising and the fresh air from the mountain of Matese that invaded the small room was bright and refreshing. The valley was blooming in lush greenery; the top of the mountain was covered in snow. Joseph's heavy footsteps sounded behind her. Giuliana turned around, offering him her lips. She needed his touch and love right now.

"Darling, look out there. I want you to see what I see when my mind is far away. My heart right now feels exactly like that mountain. My love for you, Joseph, wants to flourish in Milan while this place torments me. This abandoned, sleepy town holds me in its grip. I need to uncover that thick frozen ice; melt the snow. I need to bring warmth and prosperity to these people, just like that blooming greenery sprouting out there at the base of the valley, overpowering the rocky terrane."

"What do you mean, my Darling?"

"I will keep this house. My roots are here. You promise you will be with me? Without you, Darling, my life will be meaningless."

He silenced her by sealing her lips tenderly with a kiss, leaving her breathless.

"My Darling, I will follow you to the end of the world."

The sincerity of his love filled her heart. She trembled when their bodies touched.

Chapter Thirty-Four
The Ferrante's Grief

In America, Gioia, Ruggiero, and Trizia were all trying hard to cope with Rosa's loss. It had been barely a year since Gioia had left. The horrible guilt that haunted them all gave them no peace. Blaming herself for leaving, Gioia seemed lost, but Ruggiero tried to reassure her.

"Gioia, you belong here with me. We need to live like husband and wife. I know the tradition is never to abandon the elderly, but, Dear, stop blaming yourself."

"I can't help it, Ruggiero. I know she died of a broken heart."

She buried her face in his chest, and they cried together. Ruggiero gently pulled her away. "Gioia, listen to me. I want you to stop your crying for Mom. We need to be considering Giuliana. She has to come and live with us in America. Only then is our family complete."

Gioia had resumed the dose of tranquillizers that she had taken in the months leading up to her emigration. Once more, she was sleeping most of the day and walking the floor at night in a daze. Ruggiero was worried sick. His loveable young wife was withering away in her sorrow. Slipped into an unmotivated state, as she had, it was hard to make animated conversation with her. In an effort to coax her out of her sad zone, her husband had brought up Giuliana, a favourite topic. He rambled on.

"Gioia, when our daughter has finished her studies, after her bar exams, she will officially be a lawyer. Since her English is good, I would like to see her continue in America – to be licenced here – to practice. Wouldn't you like that?"

"Ruggiero, your daughter will come when she is ready. We cannot dictate to her what to do. She will decide in time when she is ready."

***

Joseph and Giuliana, back in Milan, were having the same discussion.

"My Darling, all you need is your bar exam, and you are a legal corporate lawyer. Knowing you, Giuliana Ferrante, with that smart brain of yours, you will take over the world with your career."

"Thanks for the encouragement and for believing in my abilities. All I need is luck. My dreams are many; my goals immeasurable. With you beside me everything is possible."

"Sometimes I feel as if I am being dragged along by my parent's companies, with not much enthusiasm. But being the only son, I have to carry on my duties."

Secretly, Joseph felt Giuliana had it better, living her life with her own achievements. She was the best thing God had sent his way. He had never lacked for anything in his life. The several companies initiated by his ancestors had been passed on, and carried on, by generations. Every company was well set up in its structure long before he arrived. His input was unnecessary sometimes as they had the best people working in every department. Their wealth had surpassed their fame. But, to him, it was all meaningless. Only his priceless Giuliana mattered now.

He pulled her toward him.

"Darling, I sometimes wish I really needed to work. Before I met you there was a big void in my heart and my life. Now I am kind of happy with my ability to come and go as I please. You see, my love, I can be at your side whenever you wish and whenever you want me, darling."

"How lucky I am, Joseph. You were sent my way from heaven."

He was in a talkative mood. She listened attentively as he went on. He was pouring his heart out to her.

"My Sisters prefer California; they are well established there. The high fashion stores we supply for that region are highly acclaimed by their Beverly Hills clients. They are one-of-a-kind items. We have the top designers from Paris, London, Roma, Milan, Austria, Prague, you name it. Our companies create only signature garments; such unique work as one cannot even imagine. There, my Sisters have the best of both worlds: exclusive supply, and tremendous demand from their clients of choice. I cannot blame them for not being interested in living in Milan. Here I am with my parents. My dad is great. My mom sometimes can be hard with her demands, but she is my mother, and I love her."

"And I adore you, no matter what."

"What do you mean by 'no matter what?'" He asked, with a mischievous sparkle in his eye. He pinched her cheek.

"Mainly because you are humble, kind and generous. Unfortunately, I must admit, my impression of your mom is not as... generous."

"Oh? Why is that, my Darling?"

"The feeling I get from her isn't that pleasant for me. I get the impression she has you saved for one of her rich friend's daughters. Maybe you would be better off Joseph? After all, by her measures, I don't fit into your category."

A lawyer, but just a lawyer from the south. A girl from the cornfields of Molise who leaves a lot to be desired.

Chapter Thirty-Five
Giuliana Ferrante Attorney at Law

Six months later, Giuliana celebrated her twenty-sixth birthday. She was now officially an attorney. She was highly acclaimed by the many law firms in Milan, and truth be told, wherever she cared to practice, even in the big cities of the north. Mr. Sbarro and Amelia were very proud. Nino was somewhat jealous; he would act strangely at times. Marco had presented her with a little gift, a pen with a sparkling fake diamond. Dino had a gift for her as well. He handed her a subscription to a romantic magazine, with a rascally look in his eyes.

"I am sure you are practising the scenes with your Joseph," he said with a smirk on his face. He winked at her.

From his seat nearby, Nino scoffed. Giuliana furrowed her eyes.

"Nino, what's that supposed to mean? Do you resent Joseph? I thought you were happy for me?"

"It's nothing, just the way you carry on. Your entire being revolves around him. We have become secondary."

"Nino, are you jealous? You are always making smart remarks about him, and not to mention Mrs. De Santis... although as far as she's concerned I cannot really blame you," Giuliana said with a laugh.

They were startled by the doorbell. Nino ran to open it, and there stood Joseph with the biggest bouquet of red roses money could buy.

"Come in," Nino said, wide-eyed. He was enjoying his conversation with Giuliana, but he knew it would now be over. Here is her priority.

"Darling, these are for you." Joseph kissed her tenderly.

"Oh, Lovely! What's the occasion? What are we celebrating now?"

"Shhh! Too many questions. Tomorrow is Sunday. I will come to pick you up. I will take you for lunch at Lago Maggiore. We will go to the lake, then we will join my parents for dinner at my house. My sisters are flying in tonight, from Los Angeles. A family dinner is planned. I want them to meet you."

Giuliana didn't know if she should be happy or puzzled. She liked the lake part. She was less enthusiastic about joining his parents and meeting his two sisters. Another discovery, she thought. Oh well. Don't be judgemental. I will enjoy my wonderful Joseph and worry about tomorrow, tomorrow.

"How is my new, stunning lawyer? I am taking you to this exquisite place tonight. You will love it. Let's get going."

Nino, busied himself in the kitchen getting a drink of milk. He was mainly doing it to get out of the way – to give them privacy – but he resented it.

***

As they entered the restaurant La Ronda, famous among the elite clientele of Milan, the serene classic music struck Giuliana as not only soothing, but sensational. The elegant singer at the microphone had a rich, deep voice, and the lyrics revived her inner spirit. The hostess cordially greeted Joseph with high regards.

"Mr. De Santis, your table has been reserved. Follow me, please."

They were escorted to an elegant table that was both private and secluded. White orchids sat on the table. A shimmering silver bucket was filled with an aged champagne bottle. Three flickering candles were arranged in a heart shape and illuminated the sheltered corner of the restaurant. Once comfortably seated, a waiter arrived wearing an impressive navy blue uniform with bright silver buttons and white gloves. He introduced himself and placed a round tray with delicacies before them.

"Your appetisers of choice, Sir."

The waiter poured their champagne and excused himself.

"To us, Darling," said Joseph.

Giuliana's emotions were raw. She was more worried about tomorrow than she wanted to let on. Joseph pulled a shimmering box from his pocket. With a mysterious look in his eyes, he lifted her hand and softly placed the white box in her palm.

"Open it, Darling."

"Oh! Joseph, it's for me?"

When the box was opened, the diamond ring caught the light from the candles and seemed to blaze as if it were on fire. She was breathless. He took the ring from its holder and placed it on her finger.

"Darling, with this ring, you are bonded to me forever." He took both of her hands in his as he implored, "My Dear, sweet Giuliana, will you marry me? I will be the happiest human being on this green earth once you become my wife."

She didn't say a word, but took his face in her hands and sealed his lips with her own. Without a sound, she declared her love.

"You are everything to me," said Joseph. "I love you for you. I am proud of you and your achievements. I admire you for being yourself - the most wonderful human being."

"My Darling, yes, I want to marry you. I want nothing more than to be your wife. But, you have to know that I have a mission to accomplish. My drive to achieve is not for me. I chose this field because my desire is to build an empire for other people. My hometown has given me the strength. I want to serve the people. Since I was a child, I have been exposed to misery that has scarred my heart and anguished my soul. I am not alone in this suffering. I feel for the people, for my family, my friend, Liliana. I read the despair in all of their faces in my formative years."

He took a deep breath.

"My love, you are a remarkable creature. Where did I find you? Right in front of my house. Fate brought you there. How lucky can one be?"

"Joseph, I am not sure, but we belong to two different worlds, you and I. My plans are huge. I might have to travel a lot. How is that going to work with us being married?"

"As I told you before, the beautiful part of my situation is that I am my own boss. I can travel with you. I can be available for you. You name it, Mrs. De Santis, and I will be at your service to help in any way I can."

"Joseph, my dear Joseph. I feel privileged. But, I have a feeling your mother does not want me around you. She has other plans for you."

He became irritated.

"I don't care what my mother thinks. We don't have to live anywhere near my parents. We can be in Paris, in the U.S.A., Austria... wherever you choose."

"Darling, don't forget my practice. I need to go see my own family, it is way overdue. My parents are begging me to go to them. I have to go soon. Yes, we will decide how we will work things out. As much as I love you... I need to be clear about what is in my heart. My career is the most important thing to me right now."

"My Darling, I understand, and I will never stop you."

***

At the De Santis home, the table was luxuriously set. The girls had arrived from California. A family get-together was a joyful event for Mr. De Santis, and he had taken the day off and ordered his secretary to let through absolutely no calls. His three children were home, reunited, and Joseph was with his love. He was happy.

Mrs. De Santis, in the family room, was chatting away with her two daughters, Silvia and Tammy. They were in their thirties and not in any hurry to be tied up in marriage. Mrs. De Santis was inquisitive as to their relationships and private affairs, much to the resentment of both sisters.

They had both chosen to be away from their mother to gain their independence. Silvia was the spitting image of her mother, although she had inherited her father's personality. Tammy was tall and slim, with black hair that she kept rolled back in a knot that aged her and gave her a matronly look. She walked with a slight limp. Her mother had insisted on having her shoes levelled to camouflage the fault from childhood. She was a down-to-earth person, but her appearance was distinguished, and this was all that mattered in her industry. Tammy treated people with respect and expected the same in return. She had no sympathy for shallowness.

"Mother, don't put too much weight on stupidities, please," she would reprimand her mother when she pushed too hard.

Silvia wanted to be more compliant with her mother's wishes, but she found it hard sometimes. She often lamented this to her sister.

"Mom has such a grip on Joseph. Poor Joseph, I hope he will be strong enough to cut loose."

It was only this morning the maid had told them Joseph had left orders to announce that his girlfriend was joining them for dinner.

"Does Mom know, Zila? She has not mentioned anything to us."

"No. Master Joseph left before your mom got back. He is excited for you girls to meet her. She is a lovely girl. I think Joseph is a lucky young man to be dating such a fine girl."

Mrs. De Santis managed to overhear the last part of this conversation. Her face flushed with her rising blood pressure. In a squawky voice, she called out.

"Will you come here, Silvia?"

"Mom, I was having a little chat with Zila. She was telling me what a lovely girl Joseph has."

"You listen to her? What does she care about your brother?"

"Mom, you sound irritated. Does that mean you don't approve?"

"Silvia, judge for yourself. She is a peasant girl from the meridian. Her parents are dirt-poor and gone – immigrated to America. She has been taken over by a family here in Milan to educate her and support her. She was given to them because her parents had no means whatsoever!"

Tammy overheard her mother from the other room, and she stormed in.

"Mom, shame on you! You condemned her because of poverty. She is an honour student graduated in corporate law. Joseph tells me he is madly in love with her. Do you have to spoil it for him? Mom, I am warning you, one word against her to Joseph and I will never come home again."

Silvia, jumped in.

"Mom, you have a problem. You didn't like anyone I was dating when I was young, and you didn't like anyone Tammy talked to. We had to get away from you – you drove us away! You are obsessed with your flawless noble friends. Mom, your phoney friends are empty. They ride on their inherited wealth and they haven't gained anything for themselves in life. You leave Joseph alone. I feel sorry for him, to be under your jurisdiction."

"Oh! My my! Did you girls come home to attack your mother? I am a wise woman, and I know what is good for my children's wellbeing. You girls were born yesterday – you are green! I have lived among royalty. Foundation in a marriage is important. You marry people at your level. You associate with people in your circle."

"Mom, sorry, but we don't agree. You need to abandon your old mentality and wake up to today's world."

The girls were irritated. Their Mother was equally frustrated, and the air was thick around them. It was at that moment that Joseph and Giuliana pulled up in his red Ferrari. Joseph blew the horn, playing like a child in a burst of happiness, to announce their arrival to his family. He put an arm around his fiancé's waist and moved his left hand to cover Giuliana's hand and conceal the ring. He could not wait to show them the rock and give them the big news. The time had finally come to announce his engagement. He hoped they would set their wedding date at the table with his beloved family.

Chapter Thirty-Six
Progress

In America, Ruggiero, with his love and devotion, had managed to finally uplift Gioia's spirit. They had moved to a newer home that required Gioia's attention, and the distraction motivated her back into action. There was always the hope of Giuliana joining them sometime soon. Gioia's English was getting better and she had made some friends at night school, mostly newcomers like her. She participated in every event that took place at Trizia's school. She volunteered at bake sales, book sales, or whatever took place to raise money for charity. The staff at the school admired her dedication and work ethic. She interacted well with the other moms. To appease the guilt in her soul, good deeds and church involvement were the most fulfilling preoccupations she turned to. Their new life in America was getting happier in all occasions where her thoughts were not focused on the loss of Rosa and her Giuliana. She prayed that they would soon reunite with their daughter.

Trizia's life was full and kept her hopping. She was involved in tap dancing, swimming lessons, music, and school sports.

"What a busy girl we have here!" Ruggiero would say, smiling proudly.

Gioia would relate their daily excursions with pleasure. Ruggiero had bought his wife a white Buick. She had learned to drive and was proud that she owned her own car.

Every morning when they parted she would say:

"God bless America. We would have never had these

opportunities back home."

"This is why we had to leave, my Dear."

"Darling, I know. But the pain of being alone shortened Mamma Rosa's life."

"We had no choice. My only wish now is to have our Giuliana near."

"Have faith, Dear. That too shall happen someday. In the meantime, she has made us proud. She has graduated. She tells me she is going to night school, studying French now."

"I have to admire her ambition. Can you imagine how relentless she is? She said to me, 'Dad my new goal is to learn French and Spanish. I need to be fluent in these languages to do my job well.'"

"That's our daughter. I miss her so much, not an hour goes by that I don't think about her."

"The young man she is involved with from Milan – I hope he does not keep her away from us. As much as I want her to be happy, I want her to find happiness close to us."

"Darling, let nature take its course. We wish her happiness. Love is kind. We cannot afford to be selfish."

"You are right, Ruggiero. I cannot help myself sometimes. Selfishly, I yearn to have her near."

"How about sending her a plane ticket for Christmas? She might come."

"Good Idea. I will look into it."

Ruggiero returned that evening with another proposition.

"Gioia, I have been approached to buy a section of our operation, the Foundry Department. I am running it now practically on my own with my crew. What do you think? I am seriously considering it."

"My Dear, where will we get the money?"

"The bank."

"Darling, you know best. Since I got here, I have become a kept woman, thanks to you. I trust your judgment, my love," she hugged him.

"I need to get in touch with my buddies from the ship. To be successful, a company has to be organised with good leaders. I cannot do it alone. I will have to put a plan in place and go from there."

He pulled her close to him. Her warmth instilled strength in him. He left for work the next morning with his head full of big business ideas.

***

In the meantime, at the De Santis house, Giuliana and Joseph were about to announce their engagement. Zila, the maid, had the dining room set up with the best china in the house. She had whipped up a special dish for the De Santis young adults, an old favourite: polenta topped with tomato salsa, green rapini, and chunks of veal sausage – it would be a real treat. Veal cutlets with brown roasted potatoes and a green salad were ready for the table. For dessert, Zila had crafted a sponge cake filled with chocolate and liquor.

Joseph, feverish with joy, lead Giuliana to the family room, proud to show off his adored girl to his sisters. Joseph introduced Giuliana to Silvia and then Tammy. Silvia stood up and extended her hand.

"My pleasure, Giuliana. Glad to meet you."

"Likewise, Silvia. Joseph has spoken well of you."

"That's my brother." She bent over and smacked a kiss on his forehead.

Tammy made her way to them, smiling away. Extending her hand to shake, she was undoubtedly pleased with the lovely girl her brother had brought home.

Mrs. De Santis sat quietly in the corner of the room and swallowed hard. She would make a conscious effort to be pleasant in response to the tense conversation she had earlier with her daughters. Mr. De Santis could not help but admire Giuliana and be pleased by the apparent joy radiating from his son.

Zila entered with a tray of drinks. Joseph could not hold on to his announcement any longer. Once everyone held their Martini and Rossi, Joseph asked for their attention.

"Hold on, everyone. We have a great announcement to drink to here." He held Giuliana's hand, exposing the sparkling diamond. "Giuliana and I are engaged!"

Silvia and Tammy squealed and jumped at the news, and quickly moved to admire Giuliana's ring.

"Congratulations! It is marvellous. Joseph, you have good taste."

They both hugged Giuliana and showered her with their well-wishes. Mr. De Santis did the same, sharing his joy readily.

"Son, Congratulations! I am so happy for both of you."

Mrs. De Santis was overwhelmed and felt the room closing in on her. She remained frozen.

"Mom…" Silvia gently beckoned for her mother to respond. Her mother looked disoriented.

"Sorry…" Mrs. De Santis finally croaked out, "I have a splitting headache. Congratulations Giuliana, Joseph," she murmured as she forced herself to hug them both while looking as if she were in pain.

The pain wasn't in her head but in her heart. Silvia broke the atmosphere of her mother's anguish. Cheerfully, she asked to the conversation.

"When is the wedding? Have you set a date?"

"It's up to Giuliana. I hope she doesn't make me wait too long," Joseph said with a broad smile. He was over the moon and oblivious to his mother's behaviour.

"I would like to consult with my parents. I cannot wait for them to meet you! I am not sure how we are going to work it out... but my parents will love you, and you will love them. Just like my family here!"

Mrs. De Santis listened hard, and made a concerted effort to control her tongue, but her brain shifted gears intensely.

GINA IAFRATE

Chapter Thirty-Seven
The Intruder

The biggest law firms in Milan had sought Giuliana out. She ultimately chose a position with the law firm R & S International, founded by Gianni Rolando and Nardo Sforza. Specialising in business law, the company's main areas of practice were in finance and business transactions. They often dealt with international contracts, mergers, and acquisitions. Their services didn't stop there; they employed one hundred-fifty lawyers total. The attorneys from the different departments were each judiciously selected. Each was specialised to provide service in various areas of law. The firm was well equipped to handle whatever their clients needed. Giuliana was chosen for Mergers and Acquisitions and Business Transactions. This was her preferred focus.

Mr. Gianni Rolando was the head of the firm. A man in his fifties, he was well-spoken and had a Milanese accent. Always professionally dressed, he preferred dark suits and crisp white shirts accessorised with flawlessly selected print ties. He always presented himself with an aura of authority, but he was equally courteous and pleasant. An attractive, mature man with good features and broad shoulders, he was a formidable image at the helm of the company. Giuliana had been hired after a brief interview. Her high marks readily revealed her extraordinary intelligence. She had been assigned a moderate size office, overlooking Piazza Verona, on the fourth floor.

She was eager to work and apply her knowledge. Joseph's demands with his companies had increased lately, but she didn't mind as her new world of actually practising law was already challenging. Also, her night language courses were time-consuming. When she got home at night, her drained body was usually ready to drop.

On this Friday evening, Amelia and Roberto Sbarro were away for the weekend. Marco had insisted on going along with his parents. Giuliana had later plans her beloved, but those plans were derailed when Joseph rang the house.

"I am sorry, my love – I have been detained. I cannot return to Milan until next week. Business calls…"

Giuliana, being overtired, didn't really mind even as much as she did miss him. The house was quiet; Costanzo had gone home. Giuliana grabbed some food that had been left on the stove, took a few bites, and decided to roll into bed and get a good night sleep. Dino and Nino were out. Being the weekend, they would probably get home late. She clicked the bedroom door shut, and her tired body slipped into the comfort of her plush sheets.

Giuliana was in a deep sleep at the edge of her consciousness, when suddenly she felt her covers being pulled away from her body. The unpleasant chill prompted her to reach out and reclaim the blankets.

"Oh!" She cried out, surprised and half asleep. "I am totally uncovered."

She grabbed the covers to pull them back over her. Rapidly, hurried footsteps were audible, moving on her porcelain floor. She sharply held her breath, trying to convince herself that she was still dreaming. Her eyelids felt heavy, half asleep, resisting her beating heart's command to wake up. Adjusting to the darkness of the room wasn't easy. The hinges on her door squeaked as they closed. A terrifying jolt rushed through her body, and she sat on the bed trembling. I'm not dreaming! She couldn't scream – her voice was gone. Petrified, she remained there, afraid to move. Her heartbeat was racing out of control and her teeth began to chatter. What is the matter with me? I am dreaming? There she remained, waiting for dawn to appear.

Chapter Thirty-Eight
Manipulations

Joseph had been entrusted to stop in Paris on his way back from London. Mrs. De Santis had called the head supervisor of their operation in Milan with instructions:

"Peter, I have received notice that our new cutting machinery with the extraordinary sewing machines have arrived and are being installed in our new plant in Paris. I suggest Joseph stops in on his way home to oversee the operation. The company has supplied us two mechanical engineers from Munich. It's a good idea for Joseph to meet these fellows. They will give instructions to the operators; my son needs that knowledge first hand."

"I will pass it on immediately, Mrs. De Santis."

She had done a good job lately of keeping her Son out of town, indirectly giving orders for him through the internal branches of the company. By mounting her schemes from inside the company, Joseph could not refuse her or even understand her role in his movements. If he knew it was her idea, he would rebel. Ever since the news of the engagement, her manipulations had increased. She put down the phone and smiled, satisfied, like a mollified cat. So far, every plan had worked to her advantage. Luca was a good administrator, and Joseph could learn from him. His focus was where it belonged.

***

At the law firm in Milan, Giuliana was hard at work in her demanding new. The files on her desk were accumulating. Her clients, passed on to her by the senior lawyers of the firm, were mostly simple business transactions to start. Once the senior partners recognised her capabilities, they challenged her with bigger and better cases.

Gianni Rolando walked into her office with a grin on his face.

"Miss Ferrante, congratulations! I have received praises in your regards from my clients, and here are some thank you notes." He pulled three cards out of his pocket and set them on her desk methodically. "We have our employee recognition for high achievement this Friday night. We would like you to attend."

"Thank you, Mr. Rolando! I will be there."

On Friday night, as no plans had been made with Joseph, she made her way to the boardroom after work with the rest of the staff. Mr. Gianni Rolando and Nardo Sforza gave an eloquent but brief speech, thanking everyone and mentioning the merits of some key individuals.

"This month, our top achiever award goes to…Giuliana Ferrante!"

Giuliana was caught off guard.

"Oh my goodness!" She was sincerely surprised and walked up to receive her award, hardly believing her worthiness to receive this honour.

"Read the cards, they speak for themselves!" said Mr. Gianni Rolando, as he congratulated her.

"Thank you," she responded. "Our clients are a pleasure to work for."

"Your name will be placed on our bulletin board with a gold star."

Giuliana humbly smiled with her happy heart.

"Miss Ferrante, since they tell me you speak French, we have been contacted by a company in Paris and we would like you to join Mr. Sforza and myself for our meeting. We hope, eventually, to be taking many international cases."

"I feel honoured. Thank you, Mr. Rolando."

That evening she shared the news with Amelia and Judge Sbarro. They were overwhelmed with joy for her, right on the heels of the wonderful news of Giuliana's engagement. Next, she called her parents. She wanted to share the news with them too. It was costly to call the state of New York from Milan, but now I have a salary and commission, so why not splurge with my own money? Gioia was at the other end of the receiver.

"Mom! It's me. How are you? How is Dad and Trizia?"

"Oh! My Giuliana!" Gioia broke in tears at hearing her daughter's voice.

"Mom, I called you because I am so happy. I wanted to share the good news."

"Sorry, Dear. You know I cannot control my emotions. We miss you so, Darling. I can't help myself."

"Mom, it's all good! I want you to know that your daughter is the star employee of the month at the firm of R & S International! I have more news: Mr. Rolando and his partner have invited me to go to Paris with them on a new case – my first international project, Mom!"

"Darling, we are proud! And here I thought your engagement would be the biggest news I heard this month! You don't stop! You are our angel. Don't you forget how your grandmother prayed for all of us. She is undoubtedly still looking after us, Darling."

"Mom, I am not so religious here in Milan anymore, but I think I believe you. Where is Dad?"

"He comes home late these days. Has he written to you regarding his company acquisition? When are you coming, Dear? Did your Dad send you the tickets?"

"Yes, he has. He shouldn't have. I can buy my own, Mom. Can you imagine I get a salary? Plus, commission bonuses too!"

"Good for you, Giuliana. Tell me, how is Joseph? We long to see you and meet him."

"He is fine. Terribly busy. We have not been able to see each other much due to our work. He has been travelling a lot. You will love him, Mom."

"I'm sure! Dear, this phone call will cost you a lot," she cautioned. Her old money-conscious habits had not left her.

"Don't worry, Mom," Giuliana reassured her.

"A big hug to you from us all. We love you, darling." Gioia hesitated to hang up, throwing a kiss in over the phone.

"I love you too, Mom. Bye. A big hug to Dad and Trizia."

The day had been exciting. Tomorrow she would talk to Joseph. It was time to plan to visit her family soon.

My Dear Joseph. Where is he tonight? She knew in her heart he loved her just as much as she loved him. He was only away as he was obliged to do diligent work.

Chapter Thirty-Nine
International Movement

The firm was expanding, opening offices in other European countries. The requests from every department kept pouring in. Giuliana's keen interest and enthusiasm were addictive and this made her a popular employee. The trip to Paris had been an eye-opener for her, from the elegant offices she was received in, to the city itself.

"Paris is marvellous - the Eiffel Tower, the Seine River that runs through the city,

the night lights, the elegant shops, and the Parisian fashions." Mr. Rolando had said to her before they departed. "Miss Giuliana, do combine business with pleasure whenever possible," he encouraged.

That evening, to celebrate their new account and their arrival in Paris, the partners took her to a quaint bistro for dinner and then for a tour of the main points of interest in the city.

"Giuliana, is this your first time in Paris?" asked Mr. Sforza.

"Yes. What a city! Thanks for asking me to participate in this assignment."

"We must show you around a bit. It's a must!"

Giuliana thoughts went back to the small town where she was born. Oh! There is just so much here. I must write Mom and Dad and describe Paris. She couldn't wait to share her pleasure with them.

The work engagement was to acquire the laboratory department of a cosmetic manufacturer, and the wholesale distribution giant R.W. Company Limited. The amalgamation of the two wholesalers was to benefit the distribution side. The principals of the manufacturing clinic were getting on in age and less interested in the operations of the large company. The influx of young blood was needed to keep up with the times. Innovations had started to ebb noticeably in recent years and the company was slowly declining and showing a loss of profits and productivity. An analysis was conducted by the Consultation Department of R & S International concluding with a recommendation to offer the production company to the distributor. With the new restructuring, hiring and creating new products, alongside a planned launch of a professional promotion campaign yearly, the red ink should turn into the blue in no time with soaring sales. The distributor would be in control once the domain of productivity was under their jurisdiction. A new company would be created and named Moriche Laboratories and Distributors Company Limited.

Giuliana sat in on the meetings that worked towards the executions of registering and putting the proper documents in place with the right stamp of registration for the company. The principals, from the president to the vice and the directors, were all present. Giuliana was invaluable as her tongue switched easily from Italian, English, French, and Spanish. She had to admit, German was still hard for her to grasp.

Few months after her return to Italy, Mr. Rolando had given her permission to take some time off. She badly desired to visit her parents. She needed to book Joseph's flight to New York. Her dad had written to her asking advice for his new venture and Giuliana was anxious to look into the matter. She carried his letters with her from time to time to read over, it made her feel closer to him.

Dear Giuliana,

Since you are now an expert in corporate law, I would appreciate your advice. An opportunity has been offered to me by my supervisors at work: they asked me to buy out the rights to a division of the plant! They want to eliminate the fabrication of the machinery parts we now supply worldwide. I have been in charge of this division for a while and I know it well; It employs one hundred and seventy-five people.

They are asking a fair price for me to buy it outright. I could arrange finances. The government would offer a grant should I consider moving this operation to a rural area to create employment where the industry is suppressed.

I am seriously considering this opportunity. As you know, a successful business needs good structure with the right principals – I think I need a couple of partners. I would love you to come. I will show you the operation, and go over it in more detail.

I hear you are doing well, and your work is rewarding.

Looking forward to embracing you. All my love,

Papa

XO

She read the letter once more and put it down, trying to visualize her dad's kind face. Funny how Dad should consider helping people in rural places. My biggest dream in my life is to bring hope, life, and employment to the less fortunate living in those remote, forgotten places. That's my dad. She dialled Joseph's phone number. His mom answered almost immediately.

"Mrs. De Santis, how are you?" Giuliana greeted, pleasantly.

"Fine. You want to speak to Joseph, I presume?"

"Yes, Mrs. De Santis. May I?"

She heard her put the receiver down, and off she went, calling Joseph. Why does she have to be so cold and dry? Giuliana couldn't understand. Joseph, pronto, was on the receiver. Once she heard his voice, her controversial thoughts of his mother vanished.

"Darling, I will be right over. I cannot wait to see you."

"Me too, my love."

She put the phone down. She turned around and bumped into Nino, who was unexpectedly right behind her with a disturbed look on his face.

"Nino, what's the matter? You look troubled?"

"Wouldn't you be? While Mom and Dad are gone to the opera, Dino ordered me not to appear anywhere near him, Marco has gone someplace, and you have your Romeo! You don't pay any attention to me. Yes, I am agitated!"

Giuliana didn't know how to take this.

Thankfully, Joseph arrived in no time. He picked her up, twirled her around and their lips sealed in thirsty, long kisses. Nino left for the kitchen. There he spied, watching them kiss away, with much resentment as he stuffed a big bite of an apple in his mouth. Giuliana pushed past the door, giggling and dragging Joseph by the hand behind her, startling Nino.

"We are going to the piazza for supper, then for a stroll," she said to Nino. "Would you like to join us?"

"No. I don't. I don't need charity. I don't want to hold your candles," he responded, in a nasty tone.

"Nino, you are in a bad mood," she scolded.

It bothered Giuliana. Better to let him brood on whatever his problems are tonight. Probably he's mad because he's had an argument with some girl.

Joseph was secretly relieved. He had not seen Giuliana for a week and wanted her all to himself. Tenderly, his arm slipped around Giuliana's waist, and he lead her to his waiting Ferrari.

At the main piazza by the opera house, they sat at their favourite bistro. He pulled her to him longingly.

"Giuliana, I cannot wait much longer for you to be my wife."

"Joseph, be patient. We need to go see my parents first. Let's book your flight and go! I can't wait to show them my ring."

"You mean we will be together for a couple of weeks? I have not seen you all week, and I thought I was going insane."

"Good thing I have been terribly busy at my office. The files keep mounting on my desk. It's a good distraction. You have been away a lot lately. I missed you too."

She stood on her tiptoes to reach and gently rub her lips on his, teasing him.

Lost in his own world, Joseph was totally unaware of his mother's wicked activities. At home, she was planning out where to ship her son next. The further away, the better. She considered dangling other females in front of him, but previous attempts had totally been ignored. Giuliana couldn't help but catch onto the coldness of her treatment. She might have come from the cornfield, but she was determined to win the woman over and her feisty personality combined with her brilliant intelligence was worth more than anything these aristocrats possessed. The love in her heart was given without expectations. She practised what she had been taught by her mother and grandmother. That was important to her.

She had vowed to love and nurture Joseph without pressuring

him with selfish demands. Her career was demanding. In order to excel and serve her clients well, she also needed space and freedom from Joseph. Mrs. De Santis' scheming to keep them apart was actually having a reverse effect and was strengthening their love; absence had made their heart fonder.

Chapter Forty
Devious Plans

Nino wished Joseph would disappear with his red Ferrari so Giuliana's attention would return to him. For some strange reason, Nino had felt short changed by his family. Deep down, he was desolate. His confused, mixed-up thinking resulted in his lashing out. He had disclosed his feelings to his friend, Heinz, the other night after Giuliana and Joseph had left. He had called his friend over. He needed to talk to someone before he would explode. Heinz had been his friend since high school. They both didn't seem to have much luck with girls. In the depths of self-pity, he poured his feelings out to him.

"Dino, handsome Dino, has it made. Being the first son, he had more attention and adoration from my parents. He graduated as a mechanical engineer with a position waiting for him at Fiat in Milan. No sweat. The girls crawl at him. He is charming and popular. My brother Marco is the youngest and he was babied and showered with adoration. Teresa had been ill for so many years; Mom and Dad were consumed assisting her. She died and their heart went with her, until Giuliana arrived and then their interests changed. The novelty was good for all of us, including me. Giuliana paid attention to me. Dad said we should love her like our sister. I think I loved her like a sister and more."

Nino was nearly in tears as he made this confession.

"I was just there, lost in the shuffle. A middle child! Mom and Dad were busy with their demanding jobs. Romeo doesn't want me around, and forget about Marco - he has his birds. I enjoyed spending time with Giuliana. We used to have a nice time together chit-chatting. Now she is busier than Mom and Dad! Whatever little time she has, Joseph appears during and the world revolves around him once more. 'Nino, get lost!' He doesn't actually say it, he tries to be polite, but I know it is what he thinks, and I feel it. Like tonight – Giuliana asked me to join them. I know he was holding his breath for me to refuse. He was all over her, kissing and necking, nibbling at her ear. I wanted to slap him."

"Nino I get the feeling you are jealous. Are you? Do you have the hots for Giuliana? After all, she isn't really your sister."

"I love Giuliana like my sister, yes. But… It is hard for me to stomach his advances on her."

"Nino, she's your adopted sister. Chill it, will you?" Heinz slapped him on his shoulder. "How about getting out of here and going to the piazza. Let's court some chicks of our own. That will change your mood and your mind, buddy."

"Heinz, you don't understand. This guy has totally taken over Giuliana." Nino cautiously replied.

"He is in love, what do you expect? Your Giuliana is a knockout, if you ask me. Why wouldn't he be all over her? Come on, Nino. Let's go dig for ourselves and have some fun. I am rusty and so are you."

***

The trip to America was scheduled. Joseph had helped Giuliana shop in preparation. He had picked the best travelling suit for her. It sculpted her body, perfectly revealing her curves.

"Joseph, how much is this suit?" she had asked.

"Darling, that's not your worry. You deserve the best."

Upon arrival, Giuliana and Joseph were picked up in New York by Gioia, Ruggiero, and Trizia. The family was ecstatic. They

314

hadn't seen Giuliana for a long time. The reunion was a blessing from the sky.

Ruggiero hugged his daughter, afraid to let her go.

"You are the famous Joseph?" he asked, as he hugged and kissed him on each of his cheeks.

Gioia, with her uncontrollable emotions, buried her face in her daughter's shoulder, covering her tears.

"My love, I am filled with joy. Since we arrived here, we have been waiting for this day."

"Me too, Mom. This is just the beginning. Don't worry – from now on, we shall see each other more often, I promise."

Then, Giuliana turned to her sister, who grabbed her hand, admiring the big stone.

"It's beautiful! Breathtaking! We are so happy for you!"

"I'm elated!" Giuliana stepped back from her sister, eying her up. "Trizia, you are a teenager! My goodness! You are hardly recognisable. You have gotten taller and absolutely stunning."

Joseph admired the affections among the small family. Gioia's languid eyes were full of love and admiration.

Since it was Giuliana's first time in America, the Ferrantes didn't know where to take her first or what to show her. Ruggiero had bought a new home with an acre of land, lavishly landscaped with an abundance of flowers and shrubberies. It sported a large kitchen with a sunken family room, an inviting dining room, a library for Ruggiero, and four bedrooms on the second floor. Lavish bathrooms with Italian marble were found on both storeys.

"Mom, this is great! I am happy for you, Dad and Trizia."

"Darling we want you here too. Your dad works hard. He is doing well. There is no reason now for you to be away from us.

Darling, we never forgave ourselves for having to send you away to get a better life."

Giuliana kissed her mother.

"Mom, you had to. If hadn't gotten away what future would I have? Dad too. We had to."

She opened the kitchen cabinets and had a look inside. They were loaded with food. The fridge could hardly close with the bounty it contained.

"Mom, Dad, I don't want to look back. Do you remember what we had to eat? Before?"

"Yes, Dear, how can I forget? Your poor grandmother would see what she could scrape together."

"It seems so long ago now – we forget. Mom, I have had it pretty good in Milan with my adopted family. I see you guys have it even better here!"

"This is America, Dear, the land of opportunity. If you are willing to work, there is plenty of work."

"I must vouch for all of us. We are go-getters."

Ruggiero was happy to take Joseph around. The first place he showed him after his home was the plant. It was large and interesting and he was proud to show off the operation. When they gathered around the table at night, Giuliana couldn't help notice how her mother had adapted to America. There were fresh flowers on the table and scented pine candles. The table was also covered in fine china and crystal glasses. Mom has come a long way. Thank you, God. Their kitchen and wood chairs back in Molise flashed behind her eyes.

"Mom, Dad, when I think of our hometown and the people there, I have this strong desire in me to change things for the town and the people in it. We have been lucky to have prospered with help. I will not find peace until I can do something for the people too. Mom, I go there sometimes by train. It's sad. The desperate folks are still living the same way we did."

"Your friend Liliana, did you ever see her? Did you hear from her?"

"No, Mom. I have not heard from her or seen her for a long time. I often think of her. I wonder what ever happened to her. Poor soul."

"Too bad you lost touch."

Gioia changed subject to focus on her daughter.

"Your job must be exciting. Tell me about it – our Giuliana the attorney."

"Mom, I love my job. The people I work for are incredible! It is nothing like Sibilla and those poor souls at the cornfield. I am lucky, Mom, in every way. I love the Sbarros almost like you and Dad. Amelia asked me from the first day to call her Aunt Amelia. Mom, no offense or disrespect to you, but she has been like my mom."

She turned to see Gioia wiping her tears.

"Darling, this is why we feel guilty. We had to give you away."

"All for the better, Mom, and now I have Joseph, my pride and joy."

"Yes. He is such a refined young man. When we see the way he looks at you … Dad and I love him already."

"Thanks, Mom. I am glad. We wanted your blessing. He is pushing to set a date to get married."

"What about his family, Dear? Do they like you?"

"I will be honest with you," she sadly blinked her eyes, "His

Dad is wonderful, his sisters are delightful, his Mom is… questionable? I don't feel loved by her."

"I am sorry, Dear. Why not?"

"I don't know. Joseph and I are fine together."

"That's the most important thing, that you two love each other! Anyone outside of you two doesn't count. I was lucky your grandmother was so lovely to me. She was my mother and mother-in-law."

Ruggiero and Joseph arrived home, like two old friends, engrossed in talking business.

"Joseph, has Dad been boring you with his business talk? What have you seen, tell me?"

"What an operation! Impressive."

"Anything close to your manufacturers?"

"No way, two different worlds! Your Dad is ingenious. He reads those blueprints with no problem. I wouldn't know where to begin."

"To each his own. You know fashions and textiles. You know how to design patterns and the right fabrics for the right garments. Your companies are intricate in their own way."

"I agree, Miss Ferrante, my expert fiancé and attorney at law!" he teased her.

They gathered for their sumptuous meal prepared by Gioia, and after they retired for liquor in the living room.

"Giuliana, is there any chance you would consider practising in the state of New York, Dear? I know you would have to go through the legalities. With your intelligence, that should be an easy task." Ruggiero asked his daughter.

"Dad, I will not say never. For now, I will stay in Milan. My firm is international, we are opening offices everywhere in Europe, and this is why I needed to study new languages. I am glad, I prefer not to work with a translator. My English is almost as good as my Italian. French is excellent. Spanish is no problem. God help me with German and Russian! You know, Dad, the best machineries with good engineering come from Germany."

"I agree. I should know, with our operation."

"Ok. Getting back to you, so there is hope that someday you will be near?"

"Dad, I have some accomplishments to do in Italy. With my merger and acquisition requests from certain companies, I travel everywhere. Milan is a great place to be."

"I need your advice for my venture. I would like you to go over my proposal and make sure every issue is well addressed. I don't want to miss anything. My lawyer here has overseen the contract, and I would like you to look at it. Especially because I am taking in two partners."

"You know, Dad, partners in business are beneficial for certain reasons and not a good idea for others. Individual partners usually end up dead weight to carry. It depends on your situation. I would prefer to see you as the sole owner, if you can be."

"I know what you mean, Dear. You are right – one hundred percent. As you said, it depends on the situation. The situation is this: the anchorage of the principals. In this case, I need a salesman to travel, call on clients, and to bring in orders. He has to be a darn good sales person to know his product, and it is imperative that he has a personal interest in the company. For the income and expense control, again, someone with keen personal interest is a must. As for the production, blueprint reading and manufacturing, I can handle that with a foreman overseeing the staff and productivity for delivery. There you have it. The three owners are officially involved with the responsibility of their investment and interest in the company's success."

"It sounds good, Dad. You are a smart business man. You have it thought it all out, all right. You would not be choosing these fellows if they were not qualified, I know."

"I have always stressed to my fellow managers the importance of getting the right person for the job. These fellows are experts for their positions."

Joseph listened to the father and daughter talk with much confidence and know-how about their topic. Mr. Ferrante impressed him as a man of great knowledge. Giuliana, with her education, was one bright girl. Listening made him realise he had been passing orders to one of his supervisors while not sufficiently being knowledgeable of the design and fashion department. He now wondered if he had made a big mistake. A cloud of worry came over him. He looked at his adorable fiancé and put his concern away. After all, he was in America now. He would see to it on his return.

Chapter Forty-One
Urgent Demands

The two weeks flew by and Joseph and Giuliana were back in bustling Milan. Worry greeted Joseph on his return, as many a crisis suddenly seemed to require his attention in the De Santis empire. Joseph found a notice on his desk. He was to leave for Los Angeles immediately. The CEO had ordered him to get down there to calm an irate client. He had been threatening to sue their company for millions of liras, plus a big shipment had been returned to them. The result of these two happenings potentially meant a significant loss for the enterprise. The business seemed to be in an uproar as different departments were placing blame on one another. In light of this, Joseph didn't mind the thought of getting away, even if it was to visit an incensed client. Maybe things in Los Angeles wouldn't be as bad as the atmosphere around his current workplace. He ordered his Cessna to be ready, and he would take off as soon as possible.

Giuliana walked into her office and opened the window to let in some fresh air. It feels stuffy in here having been absent for two weeks. She peeked out at the street as the noise of the avenue, the traffic and the people made her think. She couldn't help but compare, Buffalo is quieter. If I want to concentrate on the files piled on my desk I had better close this window and find some quiet. She sat down ready to get to work, when a firm knock on her door startled her.

"Yes?"

Mr. Rolando appeared at the door holding more papers in his

hands.

"Oh! Do come in, Mr. Rolando."

She got up to greet him.

"Welcome back, Miss Ferrante. How was your holiday?"

"Wonderful. Great to see my family."

"We missed you here. We were swamped while you were away. I took in a lot of work for you. Here is more. Everything saved for you."

"Ok. I will roll up my sleeves and tackle them one by one."

"I will brief you on some new clients that we have taken on. You will have to meet with them once you analyse their files. They are mostly business transactions, your forte'. Should you have any difficulty, I will be glad to assist you."

"Thank you, Mr. Rolando. I will certainly let you know."

"This client from Switzerland wants to set up a cheese company in Italy. We have been selected to represent him in the entire set up," he said, pulling out an unusually large file.

"Interesting. He must think highly of our firm."

"This is one of them. I got another call from a sheep farm in Killarney, Ireland. They would like to find a textile company to supply their sheared wool too. They would buy back the refined yarns to manufacture their thick woollen sweaters. There is a local market, plus export to the northern countries where their woollen goods are highly in demand. I believe you are connected with the De Santis conglomerate? Maybe they can help us help these people."

Giuliana listened to her boss and jotted down notes as he spoke. When he was finished, she put her pen down. She smiled pleasantly and assured him.

"Mr. Rolando, give me a few days. This workload doesn't scare me. I will digest your requests with much consideration. Now, I need to get busy. Oh, am I glad to be back! I do need to go over these previous files first."

She slapped her hand on the folders piled on her desk, anxious to get started.

"You can count on me to consult with you as soon as I am finished. I promise to research some new leads for our clients."

"I suggest you have my secretary take notes for you, to help."

"Thanks for the offer. However, I work better by myself; I concentrate better."

"Miss Ferrante, you are a different breed. My partner and I are lucky to have you on our team."

She slowly walked him toward the door.

"Thank you, Mr. Rolando. I will do my utmost to live up to your expectations."

When it came to business, she didn't want waste any time. With grave seriousness, she sat at her desk and attacked the files one by one. They had been reviewed and noted by her secretary, but the follow up would be re-noted with precision by Giuliana only. The more homework she did, the better the results she got. Once Giuliana was well prepared, she would meet with her clients.

A few weeks later, she picked up the two big clients' files that had been placed aside for review. Giuliana decided to consult with Mr. Rolando first. It was imperative for her to meet with one of her clients. The rehearsal had been keeping her awake at night. With God's help and her strong wishes, Giuliana planned miracle had to materialise.

She went to work earlier than usual. Reading over her notes

once more, she impatiently waited for nine o' clock to arrive. She wasn't willing to wait for the arrival of the secretaries to engage in the formalities of patching calls through. Waste of time. They don't realise I come from the school of hard knocks. She picked up the phone

"Good morning, Mr. Rolando. I want to discuss with you my ideas for your client."

"Good morning, Giuliana. It's your client now. You are in charge of the case."

"Thanks, I am grateful for your confidence. All the same, I would like to discuss it with you. I have done a lot of thinking about the company. We need to meet with Emilio Baldone from the Baldone and Son's Company Limited. I have their proposal ready, in proof copy only.

Once I discuss it with them, and I get your approval as well as theirs, I will have it drawn out and go through the legalities and move forward."

"Fine. Arrange the meeting. I will make myself available."

"Don't you want to familiarise yourself, and go over it before we meet with them?"

"Giuliana, if you insist. I totally trust you. Your ideas are always in the best interests of everyone involved."

"Thanks for your kind words, Mr. Rolando. I will place the call and set up the meeting."

She dialled a number in Switzerland and asked for Mr. Emilio Baldone, Senior. After waiting few minutes, a man picked up the line.

"Emilio Baldone, here. Hello?"

"Mr. Baldone, I am Giuliana Ferrante from R & S International, in Milan. Mr. Rolando has assigned me to your case. I have a proposal ready and I am eager to discuss it with you. Can we make an appointment to meet?"

"Yes, of course, Miss Ferrante. When? My son and I will be in Milan next week. Can we set up something for next Wednesday, say? Ten in the morning? Your office?"

"Very good. I will ask Mr. Rolando to be present. Looking forward to seeing you then, Mr. Baldone."

"Likewise. Very well. Bye."

Mr. Baldone's voice sounded confident, short and to the point. Giuliana appreciated when clients were the straight-to-business type.

This weekend she was headed to her hometown. It was still so easy for her to bring the image of that place to mind: the town and the hills sloping down to the river. I must go there and walk those roads. I shall re-experience those abandoned hills and valleys. I must go stand at that place I have in mind and breathe that fresh air, hear the roar of the river, absorb the reddish rocky terrain covered by the wild wisps of nature. Only then can I regroup these thoughts.

***

Joseph was still away in Los Angeles, trying to resolve his company's problems. He wasn't used to fighting adversaries. The fellow they had assigned to him to pacify did not want to hear any excuses or reasoning. He had instructed his attorney to sue the De Santis conglomerate with no benevolence. Attempts from Joseph to talk peace were straight out refused with menace, despite his compensation offer for their negligence. However, Antonio Delgato was attacking Joseph personally, like an insane lunatic.

"Do you guys realise what you have done to my clients and

me? I have lost the season! You cannot compensate me with those orders I had sold to my retailers. I have not only lost millions, but my reputation. Me! Antonio Delgato! A man of my word!"

His outrage was painted all over his face. He lifted his fists as if ready to fight with his nerves in an uproar. Joseph was scared. This individual was no human being to talk to with any semblance of reasoning. Joseph was innocent, and the actions of his company were really not to blame for all that this man attributed to them. He couldn't understand why this character wouldn't give in to peace.

Joseph called his mother, who responded with an exasperated condemnation.

"Joseph!" she screamed into his ear, "It was your job to oversee that account. You have been too busy catering to that precious girl of yours. You cannot deny having neglected your responsibilities. Now you have to face the music. I will tell you that this is a darned big account to lose. God forbid if they sue. You had better find a solution. This is why we sent you personally down there. It's time you take your business seriously."

Joseph felt miserable already, and his mother had made him feel guiltier. His stomach ached, and his heart was torn. He had been taught to be strong, but he suddenly found his eyes were teary.

Mother is cruel, insinuating that my going to America with Giuliana is to blame here. I thought she would be happy for me, but Mother resents my time with her. She didn't seem too thrilled about my engagement either. I bet she doesn't approve of Giuliana. The Ferrantes entered his mind. How kind and gentle they have been with me. Mom has never been that kind to Giuliana. Her remarks about the people of the meridional, the south, don't make sense. The Ferrantes are genuine and kind. Mom has a mean streak.

He picked up the phone and dialled Giuliana's number.

Quickly her sweet voice was on the phone.

"Pronto! Hello?"

Her voice soothed his ears.

"Darling, it's me. How are you?"

"Sweetheart! I am fine. I could be better if you were here with me, but it's ok. My love, I am so…busy!"

"Darling, can you come down here?" Joseph's voice became a low, pleading tone. "I need you."

"Joseph, you sound serious. What's wrong?"

"I told you about this client. He threatened to destroy our design department. I didn't tell anyone this, but he said he would contact the local newspaper and have them run damaging stories on us, plus the Milan paper, and news media everywhere! He plans to sue our company for millions."

"Oh! Can't you talk to him? That sounds damaging. Can you reason with him?"

"Giuliana, he is so enraged. I cannot get a word in. I held back, keeping my cool. He wanted to fight! He had his fists on my face!"

"Darling! I am sorry! Who is this fellow? That's no way to react about a business mistake. Mistakes are inevitable."

"It's money. He said a year's income has gone down the drain due to our negligence. Can you come?"

"Joseph, my darling, my heart wants to. I am working on a business plan and I have to go to my hometown this weekend. Although I need to do a lot of thinking by myself, I was hoping you drive down with me."

His mother came to his mind. All she needs to hear is that he had left the mess down here and gone gallivanting away with Giuliana into no man's land.

"Dear, I cannot leave here until I find a way to stop this Antonio's vendetta against De Santis Fashion Design."

"Tell him you will counter sue for slander if he goes through with his threats."

"He won't hear me out. He doesn't let me talk. Can you come, Darling? I need you. Please come."

"I will try. Let me check the flights. I can only stay the weekend. I must get back. My meetings are set up and I need to be prepared. Otherwise, I risk losing my job. Besides, I cannot disappoint my clients."

"Giuliana, I will count the minutes. I can't wait to see you."

She was torn between her love and duty. She was to meet Baldone in just a few short days, and she had vowed to be fully prepared. By deviating to Los Angeles, it would set her back. However, her dear Joseph needed her, and she wondered, how can I ignore him?

Chapter Forty-Two
To the Rescue

Giuliana arrived in Los Angeles determined to save her beloved Joseph from this impossible character that was determined to destroy him and bring harm to the very company his family had built over generations. The arrival of Giuliana reenergized Joseph's body with a spirited vitality. She was his saviour and automatically instilled in him so much self-esteem. The warmth of her touch and her tender affection melted his heart.

They cherished their moments alone. This trip was purposeful and such a short time. Giuliana wanted to find out as much as possible about this Mr. Antonio Delgato. She had a plan. The next morning, she placed a phone call, took a taxi and walked into Mr. Delgato's office. She was well groomed in her power business suit with her hair half up in a roll and half cascading down her shoulders. Her leather briefcase was ready with papers for taking notes. Her plan was to keep the visit amicable, and go from there.

"Mr. Delgato, it is a pleasure to meet you."

She extended her hand in a charming way. He looked tough, but like nothing she couldn't handle. Antonio Delgato answered her back, and she quickly noticed that he spoke with an accent. Good, she thought to herself. By the name, he must be Italian.

"Mr. Delgato, I am a friend of Joseph De Santis. I am told you are ready to kill him for a mistake the company has made, gravely damaging your suppliers. Mr. Delgato... can I call you Antonio?"

She said his name with a sweet Italian inflexion. Antonio

mellowed instantly.

"Sit down, Miss, will you?"

"Thank you, Antonio. Let me tell you, it might seem catastrophic for you and I sympathise with you. Let me reassure you, Antonio: for every problem, there is a solution."

She gently put a hand on his shoulder and with her head bent, looked him straight in his eyes. In a quiet whisper she went on:

"You can gain by the mistake."

"How? Tell me how. They made me lose all my orders. I could not supply my retailers with the junky stuff they sent me. Totally wrong – the styles, the material… a disaster."

"I understand. I feel sorry for you, Antonio. We will have them pay you for it. What is your gross income for the year? Put the figures together for me."

"My gross income? What about my expenses?"

"I've got news for you, I would have them reimburse you; the gross income, plus compensation for the expenditures and damages."

"I have lost all my accounts."

"Antonio, you will get a good sum of money. There is a way to get your clients back. The manufacturer will have to give you a grace period for promotion. They will have to do it at their expense."

He smiled.

"Antonio, where are you from in Italy?"

"Oh, you've probably never heard of it. I came here when I was five years old. My parents came from Molise, a small town out of the province. No one knows it."

Giuliana brightened up.

"Oh! My God! Don't tell me you are from my area?"

"Your area? Where are you from? You speak good English, but I detect a sweet accent. What do you know about Molise?"

"What do I know? Plenty? I am a Molisan."

His eyes lit up.

"Really? A paesan?"

"Yes! A paesan, a fellow from the same town!"

Before long they were deeply engrossed in details of their old village, and the vibrant glare in his eyes had melted into a charmed glimmer at having found a paesan from his hometown. Now that they had something in common, Antonio could not be callous to this sweet girl. Giuliana couldn't stop talking, and neither could Antonio. Her mom and dad had warned her that the old Italian-Americans were passionate about their homeland. They held on to their culture by reliving and treasuring their memories.

"I like you," he said after a short pause in their conversation. "You are a smart girl and beautiful too. You must come and meet my family."

"Antonio, you are sweet. Thank you."

Antonio Delgato had transformed from a wild lion to a sweet lamb. Giuliana imagined –with a smile – that this was far beyond whatever Joseph could have dreamt of when she left this morning.

"Getting back to business, I will leave you my card. I am a lawyer from Milan. I don't expect you to put figures down today. Take your time. Jot down the numbers and we will go from there. Your problem will be resolved in an amicable way. You start to fool around with the courts…. you will both lose out, even if you are in the right. I have seen it before. I can reassure you, you will be a winner when you allow the company to make it up to you."

He looked at her with admiration.

331

"You are a real sweet girl; you know that? I am glad we met."

"Joseph is a good friend of mine. When he told me you were an infuriated Italian fellow, I said to myself, 'I have got to meet this guy.' No offence but my grandfather was a hothead, and things got out of hand sometimes. I guess it comes from being born on those hilly sides of Molise. By the way, I got deviated to Los Angeles this weekend, but I was to be in our hometown. I have grand plans to revamp that place and bring life back to the people left there. Monday is another day. I should be standing on those hills then."

"You are kidding me?"

"I am dead serious! Antonio, can I interest you in opening an outlet at that historical, abandoned place? You have done well here. Wouldn't it be rewarding for you, opening a place? 'La Moda Fashions by Antonio Delgato' – in honour of your heritage."

"You are amazing. Tell me, what are your qualifications in law?"

"Only corporate. My forte' is business transactions, mergers, and acquisitions."

He stared at her for a minute, as if studying her. Then, he twitched his eyes and asked her, with a hand holding his chin:

"Listen to me for a moment. I find you fascinating. Can I invite you to my home with your friend for dinner? I want you to meet my wife and children."

"Antonio, are you sure? Shouldn't you check with your wife first? I am flying out tomorrow."

He wasn't listening.

"My wife is a good woman. She will be pleased. Tomorrow at lunchtime, after church. You cannot say no."

They embraced like old friends. She liked Antonio. He reminded her of the old folks back home from her childhood days.

Joseph waited, pacing the floor of the hotel lobby as he held his breath. Continuously vigilant of the entranceway, as soon as he saw Giuliana approach, he ran and embraced her.

"Darling, I was worried about you."

"Joseph, I am a big girl! I can take care of myself. We are invited for lunch at Antonio's tomorrow at one in the afternoon. I am catching the plane in the evening."

"Are you joking? Why are we going there? Is it a conspiracy?"

"Antonio is a lamb. A gentle soul from Molise, my hometown."

He looked at her in disbelief.

"That horrible guy has a heart? I am confused."

"Darling, all is well. Antonio is our friend," Giuliana reassured him.

In detail, she quickly explained to him how she convinced Antonio to comply with no trouble. Her intuition told her that she had also put a bug in his ear. She wouldn't be a bit surprised if he considered her idea. Antonio certainly possessed a nostalgic love for his place of origin.

"Joseph, I suspect I will be hearing from Antonio after tomorrow. Business ventures are in his blood. Why do you think he was so angry? His eagerness drove him berserk. He is right, though; his business has been terribly disrupted."

"You didn't tell him that, I hope?"

"Joseph!" she said as she looked at him cross-eyed. "I know how to get around my arguments."

"Sorry, Darling!"

Joseph's crisis was resolved. Thanks to Giuliana, the De Santis Corporation would be spared bad publicity, lawsuits and loss of further clients in addition to Antonio Delgato.

Later, Joseph recounted the story to his mother.

"Mom, Giuliana is the best of the best. I cannot wait for her to be my wife. I hope she makes up her mind soon and we are wed."

On the other line, his mother almost choked on her saliva. There was no verbal response. She gave him no credit, and especially would not have attributed any of this to Giuliana. Her strong resentment was such that she saw no other truth but the one that wanted Giuliana out of her son's life in the worst way.

After her conversation with Joseph, she had called her friend in Vienna.

"Rosalie, how are you? I am calling you to vent my frustrations. My son announced his engagement. Now he is waiting for this girl to set a wedding date. I will go to any length to make sure this marriage doesn't take place. He just got back from Los Angeles. Can you imagine my son reported to me that this – I don't know what to call her – was in Los Angeles with him. Thanks to her, evidently, his problem has been solved. We have lawyers representing our companies. Why would we need her? Oh, Rosalie! My son has lost it. Ever since she came into the picture…"

"Gisela, what can I do?"

"Since Joseph and your Anna were children we had them matched up. They played nice together, remember? How we admired the two of them! Joseph dated her occasionally before 'pretty face' came into the picture. Now, ever since this girl has appeared, he has gone stupid on me! You have to help me to get this son of mine away from her. She boils my blood. 'Pretty face' is going to marry him over my dead body."

"You are determined."

"You bet I am," she responded, seriously infuriated.

"My Dear, it would bring me joy to see my Anna and your Joseph together. But how are we going to make it happen?"

"Easy! Ask Anna to call him. Find any excuse for her to spend time with him. Get tickets to the opera; anything. Anna is young and beautiful – her charm should do it. She will seduce him, for heaven's sake!"

"Gisela, you and I can talk. When it comes to actions, these young people have a mind of their own. I can mention it to Anna . . . I do not promise anything."

Disappointed by the conversation, Mrs. De Santis was thinking of another scheme she could come up with.

Rosalie, her best friend, knew Mrs. De Santis well and was well aware of her reactions whenever Joseph dated a girl for more than a few minutes. She would jump in to interfere with any relationship Joseph initiated. Poor Joseph, he is destined to remain single, Rosalie thought as she hung up the phone. Mrs. De Santis wanted to keep her one-and-only son to herself.

Giuliana's relationship had lasted surprisingly to long already. Mrs. De Santis knew beyond a doubt that the marriage definitely needed to be stopped – one way or another.

Chapter Forty-Three
The Second Invasion

Upon her return from Los Angeles, Giuliana found herself totally drained of energy. She happily rolled into bed earlier than usual and pulled the covers over her head. Tomorrow would be another travelling day. She needed to catch the train first thing in the morning, and then the connecting bus ride to reach that God-forgotten land.

The meeting with Emilio Baldone was set for Wednesday. Her research was still incomplete. It wasn't her style. She was keenly aware that every angle of the investigation needed to be done methodically. Her restless mind and her fatigued body kept tossing around refusing the sleep she craved, but it eventually came to find her. Again, a strange force slowly peeled the covers from her body. A cold shiver flowed across her bare legs. Her loose nightgown slowly peeled up. Her body felt exposed. Her hand reached to roll down her nightgown. She sought warmth, and the discomfort of being uncovered was annoying uncomfortable in her dream state. The covers were out of reach. Groggily, her brain tried to rationalise, where have the covers gone? This nightgown of mine has rolled up? She shot to consciousness as the rustle and soft tap of footsteps pulled her into the world. Frightened, she held her breath to listen hard. Someone is in my room! She held her breath to smother her scream. Terrified, she plunged toward her lamp and switched on the light. No one! She couldn't see anyone. Whipping her head toward the door she noticed a minute, but undeniable movement as the door softly shut.

"Oh my God! This is no dream; someone was in my room,"

she spoke into the empty space.

Her bedcovers and sheets were at the bottom of the bed on the floor. Flooded with an incensed rage that brought her strength and courage, she got out of bed and opened the door to look out into the corridor. Silence, darkness, and the snores of her family could be heard from the other rooms that lined the hall. A doubt touched her again. Was I dreaming or hallucinating? She closed her door and rifled through the drawer of her vanity table and found the rusted key to her bedroom door. After a few attempts at working the key in the keyhole she managed to lock it, and she went back to bed. Daylight will soon be here, and I need my rest to function correctly, she tried to convince herself. She wanted to rationalise this experience, but she was definitely spooked.

The next morning, she made her way to the train station, dragging her overstuffed briefcase with her. While travelling, she planned to continue her work, but before long her body slumped to the side of the seat and her eyes closed. Her papers lay scattered on her lap and by her feet. She had given in to the much-needed sleep.

When she arrived at the front steps of her old house, cobwebs welcomed her. They stretched from one side of the frame to the other, ornamenting the peeling door. The place looked unsurprisingly neglected and abandoned. At one time Gioia and Nonna Rosa kept this place immaculately. Well, it's my fault. I have not been here for a while. What did I expect?

Back in Milan, her Joseph had plenty to contend with. She didn't dare ask him to come with her this time. Besides, she had homework to do. Therefore, it was wise to go alone. Since she had slept on the train, her energy had been replenished. The walk through the empty house was always painful. This time, she didn't indulge in her past memories due to the lack of time. She hurried to the site in the country to investigate locations. There was a lot riding on finding an impeccable site. Where will I set up the cheese factory for Mr. Baldone and Sons? This is what she needed

338

before moving forward. Location was her number one concern. Next, she needed to ensure there would be a stable water source for the operation. The factory would need power. The power plant was not far, which was ideal. Immediate access to the main road would guarantee swift export and deliveries. She jotted down notes to pass on to the selected architect.

The few folks left here watched her carefully as she went about her business. They were staring at her inquisitively, trying to figure out who she was and what she was up to. She passed by the cemetery and although she had not planned to, automatically, her footsteps found the path toward that black iron gate that lead to her grandparent's graves. Their pictures were covered with dust and debris. She pulled a hanky out of her pocket and polished until their images became visible. She recited a prayer and shed a few tears. The loving memories of her beloved grandparents resurfaced vividly in her mind. With sadness, she moved on.

As always, dedication to her work was her salvation. She buried herself in her notes with deep concentration. No question, she thought, the facility should be close to the river. This was the best spot.

Once back in the town centre, Giuliana walked the avenues, climbed the stairs and wandered. She soon found herself at the front of Liliana's house. Perhaps her soul was reaching out in the hope someone would be there. No. No one had lived here for some time. Old debris were mounded in front of her door with no sign of life. She sullenly returned to her own family home and sprawled her notes on the kitchen table. The quietness felt odd in this house that at one time had been crowded and full of life. Ghosts of the past started to invade her mind. Her usual clarity in doing calculations of figures became obscured by her preoccupied thoughts. She placed her papers in her case got ready for bed.

In the morning, Giuliana wasted no time to get to the bus to connect with the train and find her way back to Milan. On the train, her mind started to wonder with flashbacks of her last night in Milan. Was there someone in my room, or had I been dreaming? If someone or something was there, what was it? Am I in danger? Was it a ghost like Grandpa's stories used to warn of? She discarded such unpleasantness from her mind with a shake of her head. But, her gut was sending out a danger signal. Amelia. I will talk to Amelia. If she told Joseph, his alarm would be endless and he would relentlessly press her for a wedding date so she would be safe by his side at night. She loved him, but she was not ready for the wedding yet. Her career right now was more important to her.

If her presentation went well with Mr. Baldone, this would mark a successful first step toward her dream. She had carefully rehearsed every angle of her presentation because she was keenly aware that if they agreed, the first cheese factory would mark a turnaround for her town. Once her thoughts turned to business, the terrors and questions from her previous night in Milan vanished from her brain.

Wednesday morning, well-groomed and meticulously dressed, she was ready. Her pictures of the location were enticing. She was all ready to present it to Mr. Baldone and his sons. She insisted Mr. Rolando be present too.

"I am happy to assist, Miss Ferrante. I know you can handle it," he had said, assuredly.

As scheduled, Mr. Baldone entered the boardroom with his two sons in tow. An impressive businessman, he was tall with wide shoulders, a high forehead, protruding long nose, deep blue eyes and dark brown hair. His features made him appear slightly intimidating. She led their greeting with a firm handshake and complimented his appearance.

His sons, although physically they resembled their father, seemed young and timid by comparison, but appeared easier to talk too. Once Giuliana cordially introduced herself to everyone, she invited the men to sit down. She chose to initiate her meeting standing, slowly leaning on the sprawled papers on her desk. A clear glass ruler helped her hand guide the directions here and there. She wanted them to absorb the scene through visualisation first, then she would unroll the rest. Her philosophy was sell to the eyes first, lay down the facts after, and the cost last. Mr. Rolando didn't say a word throughout her performance. The Baldone's listened attentively.

"Miss Ferrante, your research has been skilfully handled," Mr. Baldone said at her conclusion. "I like your idea. My question to you is about the employees. How are we getting them back and forth to work? The young people will be okay. Some of the older, mature folks cannot read or write. How are they going to learn recipes? There are many ingredients involved. It's necessary."

"Mr. Baldone, there is an easy solution to your concern. I can solve that problem in no time. I have connections to set up a night school for those folks wanting to learn. Believe me, they will be so happy to have work they will go to any length to get and keep the job once you send some of your fellows to teach them. They are intelligent people that have been denied opportunities. I can assure you, they will learn in no time. As for the transportation, we need a shuttle. The land is close to the main road and therefore within easy reach. To top it off, you will never have to worry about absenteeism. You will have the whole town at your service."

"You make it sound stress-free. Let us take the information back to our office. We will discuss it amongst ourselves. We will decide if it's favourable and if it will work to our advantage."

"Mr. Baldone, I understand. I didn't expect you to make up your mind today. Definitely, digest it, discuss it with your sons, your company supervisors, and get back to me when you are ready."

She handed him the extra copy of the file. She shook hands

with everyone, and they left. Mr. Rolando had served only to make the initial introductions. He was amazed by what had occurred. He had watched Miss Ferrante at work. As he sat silently through the meeting, he had to make a conscious effort to not grin wildly, ever so proud of the young lawyer. She is a genius.

Giuliana was on a high from the presentation. As soon as the door shut she turned to Mr. Rolando.

"Mr. Rolando, did you say you had another company from Ireland you needed assistance with regarding textiles?"

"Yes, I do. I thought you might want a day's rest after your travel and all the work done in this case," he said with a soft chuckle.

"Mr. Rolando, I am fine. I am anxious to get to my next case. I will call my fiancé, and while I have lunch with him, I will make the necessary inquiries as to which of his departments can handle that kind of textile work."

She called Joseph's office. Promptly, his secretary put him on the line.

"Hello, Joseph. I finished early with my client from Switzerland. Would you like to meet me for lunch?"

"Darling, how could I refuse the best girl in my life? Of course! Where are we meeting?"

"At the bistro around the corner. Moro's Cuisine."

Mr. Rolando had left and returned with his file. A quick glance inside had given her some idea of what she was dealing with. When she arrived at the restaurant, Joseph was waiting for her.

"Darling, I have missed you. Sorry I couldn't accompany you to Molise."

"Joseph, as much as I would have liked your company, I needed to work alone. As for yourself, you needed to look after your affairs. You don't want another irritated client on your agenda."

"Yes, I know. Thanks to you I have one less."

"Joseph, I have a client to discuss with you."

"This is lunchtime, my love. Can we have a break from business? I want to hold you in my arms and bask in my love for you. To hell with clients."

"Joseph, this can be business and pleasure, my Dear. I have a goal to reach. Time is precious, and I don't want to waste it."

"When are we getting married? You can be on our staff, work as much as you like – protect our companies."

"Joseph I have no intentions of working for any of the De Santis companies."

"What about me? I will be less fortunate without you at my side, Darling."

He stretched his neck, begging for a kiss.

"Joseph, my love, I hate to tell you this, but you have no idea what it is like to be less fortunate. When you get up in the morning, there is water to wash your face with, it is not cold, and your body does not shiver. You do not have broken shoes to wear, and you have no lack of warm clothes. You indulge in coffee and know nothing of being limited to eating but a single dried piece of cornbread, that has been left sitting on a dusty kitchen shelf for you as your only food for the day. I could go on forever to spell it out for you, but I will stop right here. You were born in luxury. How can you understand?"

Just then the waiter arrived at the table.

"Sorry, Mr. De Santis, but you are wanted on the telephone. The caller said it is urgent."

Before Joseph could properly form a response to Giuliana, this had snatched his attention.

"Excuse me, Darling. I will be right back."

He let go of her hand, frowning his forehead. What is so urgent?

On his return to his seat, Joseph obscured eyes, disturbed as hell. The call was from his mother. She needed to fly to Paris at once. Her friend and her daughter were to meet her for the day. She had forgotten they were waiting for her.

"Joseph, I am in a mad hurry. I cannot catch the train; you must fly me there at once. I cannot disappoint these people."

Joseph relayed the situation to Giuliana.

"I have to get back to work, Dear. It's fine by me. Go and make your mom happy," encouraged Giuliana.

"Sorry darling. I will call you as soon as I get back. Give me a hug and your lips to last me until tonight."

He regretfully left, genuinely annoyed with his mother's antics. Giuliana watched him walk away, shaking his head, as her beloved young man disappeared from her sight. He sure wasn't happy. Sorrow came over her. A sharp pain flashed through her stomach, and her heart ached. Joseph is in the clutches of his mother, and in the shadow of his father. Is he actually living his life trapped between these two forces? She could never imagine. She valued her independence.

She did not know that this afternoon was the last time she would watch Joseph walk away and still taste the freshness of his lips on hers.

Chapter Forty-Four
The Storm

Back at the office, Giuliana initiated dealings with the company in Ireland. She gave Mr. Brian Fitzgerald a phone call.

"Hello, Mr. Fitzgerald? It's Giuliana Ferrante, from the law firm of R & S International, in Milan. I am the lawyer assigned to looking after your requests. I have gone over your file. I believe I have the perfect textile company to meet your needs. I will work out the details and get back to you with all the information. Once my research is complete, we shall meet in my office, or I could come to you at your convenience, Mr. Fitzgerald. We will go from there."

"Thank you, Miss Ferrante. Looking forward to meeting you and discussing our new venture soon. We have just completed a major shearing. My foreman is anxious to move forward."

"I will do my best. Leave it with me. I should have an answer for you by next week."

She hung up the phone and dialled the De Santis Textile Department switchboard.

"Good afternoon, De Santis Textiles," a female voice promptly answered.

"Good afternoon, this is Miss Ferrante, from the law firm of R & S International. I would like to talk to someone in charge of the Yarn Department."

"Miss Ferrante, we have several. What yarn department would

you like me to connect you to?"

"Oh! Sorry. Sheep wool?"

Promptly, a male voice came on the phone.

"Mr. Leonardo speaking. How can I assist you, Miss...?"

"Hello, Mr. Leonardo, Miss Ferrante here. I have a client interested in shipping you sheared woollens from Ireland. He wants to make a special arrangement with your company. The agreement would use you to refine the textile and supply it back to him. Any surplus would be yours to sell to your clients, sharing a percentage. You would supply to him at wholesale cost."

"It sounds complicated, but I am sure we can accommodate him, somehow."

"Mr. Leonardo, I will list everything on paper, spelling it out as simply as possible. It won't be complicated once we meet and go over what my client requests."

"Do you want to set up an appointment, Miss Ferrante?"

"Yes, I do – as soon as possible. I need to get back to my party by next week."

"Miss Ferrante, please hold on for a minute. Let me check with my secretary as to my schedule." After a pause he was back on the line. "How does tomorrow afternoon sound, at two, in my office? I will take you for a tour of our department and show you the operations and samples."

"Wonderful. I like that. See you tomorrow."

The tour would enrich her knowledge. The more well informed she became in her cases, the easier things went for her and her clients. Usually, she liked to handle two cases at a time, especially when they were both challenging. She loved a challenge, and with dogged determination she would always successfully accomplish whatever she set her mind to. That is how she worked. No files were neglected or left unattended. Judge Sbarro had warned her about this.

"Giuliana, you want to be successful. Do your homework thoroughly. Be well prepared, memorize every individual case – your dealings are the most important. I have no sympathy for unprepared lawyers. One good bit of advice is to always be early for your appointments. Lateness is disastrous and a sign of unpreparedness."

Giuliana was disciplined and lived by these rules.

Excited about tomorrow, she arrived home happy as a lark. The fellows were munching on popcorn. The aroma enticed her. Encouraged by Marco, she joined in to munch and drink coke with them.

Amelia was at the hospital again tonight and Mr. Sbarro was secluded away in his library, probably working on some papers. Giuliana had been hoping to talk to Amelia about her two episodes experienced in the past nights. Now that she found herself at home without Amelia, doubt crept into her mind. Why should I? Why alarm Amelia with the idea that there was an intruder in the house when it could very well be my imagination playing tricks on me. Lately, she had been very tired. I will keep it to myself. God forbid I mention it to the guys, they would make fun of me and all the house would be in an uproar. In denial, she ignored the feeling deep in her gut.

Costanza came in from the kitchen to serve their special risotto Milanese, anise salad, and a platter of mixed fruit.

"Good for the digestive system," she said as she set down the platter.

Nino pulled his chair back, making an irritating screeching noise.

"Where is your lover boy tonight?" he asked, sarcastically.

She hesitated. Nino's tone of voice didn't come across right to her, and whenever he referred to Joseph his eyes flickered with anger.

"I am not sure . . . I was having lunch with him today when he got called to an emergency."

Mr. Sbarro's door opened, and he walked in.

"Guys, have you heard the thunder and rain out there?" he asked the group.

"Dad, with Marco's music blaring, who can hear anything?" responded Dino.

"The news is predicting a severe storm tonight. Your mother is not home yet. We should go pick her up. It's getting late. I don't want her on the road alone."

"I will go with you, Dad," offered Marco.

"You go to bed; school tomorrow. Dino and I will go."

"Yes, Dad, I will go with you," agreed Dino

Giuliana started to yawn. Remembering her big day tomorrow, she thought she had better get a good night's sleep. She had just gotten comfortable under the covers when the rain drops on the roof got heavier and louder, playing havoc on the old home's clay shingles. The storm seemed to advance in crescendo. Flashes of lightning followed by thundering explosions suddenly illuminated the entire room. Her body tensed. The wind rattled the windows and threatened to break through. She rolled into a fetal position, terrified. Her chest was pounding. The storm was in full swing. Lightning increased the bright pops of light and jarring thunder like fireworks in the last draw of explosion. Suddenly, a firm knock on the door startled her. She didn't move.

The beats turned to pounding. Hesitantly, she got up to open the door. There stood Marco, clutching his birds, frightened as a poodle.

"Giuliana, can I stay in your room? I am scared and so is Lola and Biricchina," he begged her, his face was as pale as a ghost's.

She put an arm around his shoulder and guided him in.

"Marco, yes of course! Do come in. It's a nasty storm out there. I am worried about your Mom, Dad, and Dino still out there. They should be home soon," she reassured him. Joseph crossed her mind. He was in France somewhere, missing this awful storm. Why hadn't he called?

***

In Paris, Joseph had been arguing with his mother.

"Mom, I will gladly pick you up tomorrow afternoon. I left Giuliana at the bistro to have lunch alone. I want to surprise her and go back tonight."

"Joseph, you are ignoring your duty toward your mother and showing disrespect toward my friends. It doesn't make sense for you to go back and come back for me tomorrow. You are snubbing them. Is that the way we raised you?"

"For heaven's sake, Mom. I have my own plans. I flew you here. Enjoy whatever you want to do with them and allow me to live my life. I want to see Giuliana in the worst way. Many obstacles have kept us apart lately. Mom, I love her; I choose to be with her."

Her patience had run out and her tongue lashed out, unchecked. She slashed at him, snapping viciously with her cruel words.

"You are such a fool, Joseph! That girl is nobody to lose your head over. If you ask me, you are not rational anymore. You have closed your eyes and your mind and tuned the rest of the world off."

349

Joseph's couldn't believe his mother's accusations. His natural reaction was to run. Let me get away from here! How dare Mother talk that way regarding my adorable Giuliana?

"Mom, shame on you!"

He slammed the door behind him and headed to his Cessna. The assistant attendant, Fransua, had questioned his taking off.

"Mr. De Santis, a storm has been predicted. Are you sure you want to fly?"

Joseph, in his disturbed state, didn't even respond, totally ignoring the man's inquiries. It was to be a short flight. Joseph turned on the engine and up he went.

The anticipated happiness at reuniting with his adored Giuliana had been diminished by his Mother's malicious statements. The sky was his now to get lost in, and there was plenty of space to get away from the cruel, evil world he left on the ground. He climbed to the maximum altitude.

The innocent, fluffy clouds in the sky that afternoon had risen. With the heat of the day and their rising, they had developed a foreboding look. In less than ten minutes a storm had formed, and there were lightning and thunder in full force, which began to cause serious turbulence. Joseph found himself flying through the Alps, struggling to stabilise his Cessna. Things got out of control fast. Panic had awakened his senses. I need to land somewhere, but where? How? The gusting winds were overpowering his efforts to stabilise the plane. The mountainous area below him was another problem; his plane was no match for Mother Nature. He was veering left and right against the force of the storm. The turbulence was getting worse. Joseph felt like the plane would soon tear apart. Something was going to have to give. Empty air pockets were sucking him down. His small, five-seater plane seemed light as a yo-yo as it rolled out of control. The radar was scratchy and all communication systems broke down. God help me to land somewhere in this mess! Joseph was spiralling down, rolling swiftly. The mountain rose to meet him at an alarming speed. The Cessna slammed hard against the side of the Alps on the left side, reverberating in Josephs skull upon impact as the plane skipped and slid down the ridge, cracking both wings into pieces. With the second impact, Joseph was tossed out. Once the Cessna met the valley, it exploded in a ball of fire.

Joseph was sprawled between two large boulders on the side of the mountain. His eyes fluttered, trying to open. He sensed his head was lower than his body, but his awareness was limited. He struggled to move his heavy frame, but he remained motionless. There he stayed, laying in the ice and snow as his consciousness blurred away into darkness.

Not far from the crash, a night watchman from the Lorenzine ski resort had watched the Cessna come down in disbelief. He alerted the facility and hastily advanced to the location to help. When he arrived, the plane was shattered into pieces and still burning. He searched for survivors and was soon joined by a band of men from the resort who had come to assist in the effort. One of the new men noticed some colourful clothing on the ridge. All efforts turned to rescuing the pilot.

To reach Joseph was difficult. The climb was treacherous and took some time. Once the first climber crested the ridge, it quickly became apparent that their efforts were in vain. Joseph's motionless body showed no vital signs. The climber signalled the loss to the men below. The burning aircraft had now been reduced to ashes as it finally completely lost its battle with the raging storm.

***

Giuliana hadn't slept a wink that night as the pounding storm mingled with a panicky Marco and the two petrified birds. When the phone rang at dawn, it was Mr. De Santis. His voice was strained.

"Giuliana, Dear. I will send one of our fellows to pick you up. Please, you need to come to our home."

She didn't like the tone of his voice.

"Mr. De Santis is anything wrong? Where is Joseph? He promised to call last night. He didn't. Did he come back from France?"

"Dear, we will talk when you get here."

A premonition told her something was terribly wrong. She got dressed, and the De Santis chauffeur was at the door before she had even made it down. She didn't know what to make of this mystery.

Amelia had slept in later than usual. She turned the radio on and tuned it to the news broadcast. They had announced news of a small plane crash, but the details they had were sketchy. The name of the victim would not be revealed until next of kin was notified. Amelia meditated on this for a moment, but pushed dark thoughts aside and left to attend to her patients, unaware that Giuliana had already left the house.

Once at the De Santis estate, Giuliana was greeted by Zila, who seemed guarded. A few people were mingling around with gloomy faces, but there was no sign of Mrs. De Santis or Joseph. Mr. De Santis was on the phone. When he saw her enter he hung up and made his way toward her. He greeted her, throwing himself at her, hugging her and crying.

"Giuliana, we have lost him! There has been an accident...a crash. Joseph is no longer with us."

Giuliana's hearing went and her legs buckled out from under her as she slid to her knees. "Oh my God! No!" she croaked out. Her voice seemed to be broken, like her heart. "It cannot be true! Not my Joseph! We were to get married..."

She broke down hysterically, unable to control her emotions.

"How can this be? Life is unfair! He gave me strength. He was my reason for living."

Mr. De Santis lowered down to the floor next to her and squeezed both her arms in support. His face was twisted in pain that echoed the pain in Giuliana's heart.

"I know, Dear. My son was madly in love with you. He was the happiest when with you. He told me. He admired you and your family."

Giuliana looked up at him, shaking.

"Mrs. De Santis?" she asked. "How is she? How is she coping?"

"Mrs. De Santis has suffered a cardiac arrest, and she is in the hospital in Paris. She blames herself for the mishap. I should be beside her. I am waiting for the girls to arrive. They are on their way from California."

More people kept coming in the room. Giuliana felt like the walls were caving in on her. The emptiness in her heart had torn the centre of her core right out of her. She felt limp and powerless. How can I go on without Joseph? She cried openly, and violently until no tears were left.

***

The funeral service was a blur; the sadness suffocating. Amelia stayed beside Giuliana like an extra limb, protective and ready with love and support. Her parents took a flight to Milan as they were genuinely concerned about her well-being. They all mourned the loss along with her. Joseph was a gentle soul to love. The sorrow of their daughter extended to them easily. It was indeed a great loss. Gioia knew her daughter well.

"I have to pray with all my might. Only God can alleviate the pain Giuliana feels right now," she said to her husband.

"I can feel her pain. He was a wonderful young man. God must have needed him up there," her husband replied, sorrowfully.

"He takes the best, your mother used to say," mused Gioia.

After a couple of weeks, Gioia and Ruggiero had to return to America. They hated to leave Giuliana behind, but their life now belonged to the other side of the Atlantic. They still had hope that their daughter would join them someday.

Giuliana, with the help of Amelia, found ways to cope. When the hurt was hitting deep and threatened to pull her apart, she resorted to mild tranquillizers and conversation.

"Aunt Amelia, sometimes I wonder…why my Joseph? I am bitter…no,

angry, toward God. Then I feel guilt. Am I selfish?"

"Darling, don't despair. Maybe God has something better saved for you in your life. I know you are hurting right now. Time is a great healer. The sun goes down; the sun comes up. After the darkness of the night, the brightness of the morning appears. That is our life, Dear."

She hugged her.

"You are young. Someday you will re-experience that glow of love again."

"Aunt Amelia, part of me has died with Joseph. You know I didn't trust the opposite sex much. Joseph, with his sincerity and love, restored all faith for me. Now he is gone. There is no love left in my heart, only sorrow. Who will I ever trust again?"

"Love is patient and kind, and you are beautiful. Someday, sweetheart…"

When Giuliana returned to work, she noticed the people from the bustling city went on as usual, as if nothing had happened. She felt like running away to the peacefulness of her sleepy town. There she felt she could indulge in her sorrow and mourn her loss. Milan, once loved for the opportunities it provided for her, seemed now meaningless without her Joseph.

Amelia and Mr. Sbarro were showering her with much attention. They were genuinely concerned for her. Often Giuliana would pretend to be cheerful when she saw how hard they tried. Her soul, deep down, wept in despair. The seclusion and solitude in her office gave her some comfort. All her energy was consumed by her work.

Mr. Rolando knocked on her door. It was late. He had noticed Giuliana was always the last one to leave lately.

"Miss Ferrante, are you working late again? I am just leaving; would you like me to give you a lift instead of having to catch the tram?"

"No thank you, Mr. Rolando. I am fine. I want to finish off the file on the cheese factory. My client is eager to know the complete cost and details of the involvement. When I wrap it up, I will leave."

"If you insist. You have been working long hours lately. Maybe you should take a break."

"My job is my saviour. I don't want to have time to think about myself. Mr. Rolando, feel free… whatever cases no one else wants, I will take them. Since my Joseph is gone, I am in no hurry to go anywhere."

"Would you like to take on some foreign affairs? Travel might be good for you, Miss Ferrante."

"I am ready to travel anywhere. Actually, I was considering taking another trip down to Molise. I had limited time when I went a few weeks ago. I need to oversee a few things."

"I trust your judgment, Miss Ferrante. Whatever is necessary on your part is ok by me. Good night. See you in the morning."

Giuliana sat there holding a pen in her hand and staring at the document. She had not been able to work efficiently lately. I need to pull myself together. This is not good. The last thing she wished was a lapse into depression.

She brought her hands up to hold her head. A strange desire surfaced in her mind. She picked up the phone and dialled the numbers. Zila picked up the phone.

"Pronto. Hello?"

"Zila, hello! It's Giuliana. Good evening. Sorry, it's a bit late. Is Mrs. De Santis available? I would like to speak with her."

"Giuliana, yes, she is home. I can try," Zila hesitated. "Since the accident, she won't talk to anyone. I will ask her if she wants to pick up the phone."

Chapter Forty-Five
The Inauguration of the Plant

Giuliana held the phone waiting. A strange, involuntary force had made her dial the number. Giuliana was gifted with proficient verbal skills, but in her company, Mrs. De Santis had always managed to make her stumble. She wasn't sure how this woman had so much power over her. Well, I will test the waters and be a sucker for punishment. Joseph's Mother may be a hard woman, but she loved her son. If love meant anything, she is feeling as miserable as me right now.

Mrs. De Santis's weak voice came over the line.

"Hello Giuliana, how are you, Dear?"

Shocked and encouraged, Giuliana thought: Is it the same person? Animated, she answered.

"I am fine, Mrs. De Santis. How are you doing?"

"Oh! Giuliana, Giuliana."

Giuliana's name sounded sweet coming from her lips. This was the first time Giuliana had been acknowledged by Mrs. De Santis by name.

"I dread the sunrise in the morning. I prefer to sleep than to wake up and face another day. It's the worst pain to endure. I cannot believe my vibrant Joseph is gone. What about you, Dear? How are you coping?"

"The best I can, Mrs. De Santis. I choose to work hard to keep busy. By keeping my mind occupied, I don't think much. I have, however, been thinking of you and Mr. De Santis. This is why I called. How are you both managing?"

"My Dear, my husband is beside himself with deep grief. He has aged, his heart is broken, just like mine."

Oh my God! Giuliana thought, that's twice she's is called me 'Dear!' Does she really feel for me?

"Mrs. De Santis, my heart is torn too. I fall into a dark abyss when thoughts of Joseph overtake me. I guess tonight I am reluctant to leave my office, and my own pain prompted me to call you. For some strange reason, I wanted to hear your voice. I knew in my heart you are one of the few people who feel what I feel, and more."

The other side of the phone went silent.

"Dear, I would like to see you. Can you come over sometime? Soon, I hope."

"Yes, of course. I would like to see you too, and Mr. De Santis. How are the girls? Please give them my regards."

"I will, Dear. When can you come?" she persisted.

"How is tomorrow evening?"

"Great," her spirit seemed to rise. "Will you join us for dinner? I will ask Zila to set an extra plate."

"Thank you. That will be ok. What time would you like me to come?"

"Six. If you come earlier, we can visit."

"I'll see what I can do. See you tomorrow night."

"Goodbye, Giuliana."

The phone went dead. Giuliana felt relieved. She closed her files in the cabinet and gathered her things. She couldn't wait for tomorrow night. The thought of Joseph not being there gave her

358

the shivers. A sharp pain flashed through her chest, bringing tears that she allowed to roll down freely. In a daze, she left the office knowing her beloved Joseph would not be anywhere waiting for her tonight. She walked to get the tram, without any spirit left in her. It seemed to bring some hope knowing tomorrow night she would be with the people that were part of him. She knew they missed and loved him just as much as she did.

***

The next day, at work, she was deprived of any quiet moments. The phone calls at the office were relentless all day. New client requests were coming in from everywhere.

Giuliana decided she would leave by the weekend for her hometown. It was time to seriously take action with Emilio Baldone. She didn't like to keep her clients in limbo by stalling.

Before leaving the office for the De Santis estate, her nerves started to get to her. As much as she hated to resort to drugs, she knew it would offer instant relief. She reached into her purse, pulled out a tranquillizer, swallowed it in one gulp with a glass of water and sat back and waited for calm to restore her body.

***

Zila greeted her at the door, followed by Mr. and Mrs. De Santis. Affectionately they embraced her, as all three broke down in sobs. The light conversation was effortless as their sorrow was so shared, present and raw that it required no acknowledgement amongst the three of them. Mrs. De Santis absently rubbed her eyes, which were red and swollen.

Later, Zila called Giuliana aside.

"She has been crying all day," she whispered.

Mr. De Santis sat in an overstuffed leather chair. His face appeared tired and withdrawn, and there was no zest left in his body. It was hard for Giuliana to be in this house – the vibrant spirit of Joseph resonated everywhere. She half expected him to appear, bouncing in at any minute, with that sparkling glow in his eyes and easy smile.

At dinner, Giuliana could hardly eat. She toyed with her food. Mr. De Santis turned to her and cleared his throat.

"Giuliana," he called out, "My wife," he gulped down some wine from his glass, "she has a confession to make." He cleared his throat again and turned to his wife. "Go ahead, Darling." He nodded. Mrs. De Santis was hesitant and looked anxious.

"Go ahead, Dear. You will feel better."

Mrs. De Santis set down her fork.

"Giuliana, I...I feel responsible for Joseph's death. I blame myself. My son paid with his life for my selfishness."

Giuliana was taken aback.

"You must not do that, Mrs. De Santis. It was obviously an accident."

"Giuliana, you need to hear me out. There is no gentle way to tell you this... I resented my son being in love with you. I was unhappy about your engagement. When Joseph kept mentioning marriage, well, I was determined to break you two up. I didn't have to go to France, Vienna, and all other places. I was making demands on my Joseph to get him away from you."

She looked up at Giuliana, surprised to see her calm and not furious.

"Mrs. De Santis, I knew that. It bothered me somewhat . . . But I loved Joseph too much to give him up. We were happy together. We were meant for each other."

"I cannot help but feel that God took him away for my sins, to punish me. Now I have lost him, forever. I am paying for it with my pain."

"Mrs. De Santis, you mustn't do that. It was an accident. God sometimes takes the best. It hurts. I hope someday the pain gets easier."

"Giuliana, my son loved you more than life. We had an argument before he left. I didn't want him to go. I had arranged to meet some friends, but he ignored my plans because he wanted to surprise you with a bunch of roses. He wanted to beg you to set a date for your wedding. His last words were: 'Mom, sorry, I must see Giuliana tonight. I will come back and pick you up tomorrow'."

Giuliana was thankful that her tranquillizers kept her emotions in control. Although, the sorrow felt like a sword piercing her heart and no amount of numbing could prevent her from feeling it.

"Giuliana, if you find it in your heart to forgive me, I want to be your friend and make it up to you. I know you hurt as much as I do."

"Mrs. De Santis, Joseph wouldn't want me to resent you." Surprised at her calmness, Giuliana continued, "Don't give it a second thought as far as I am concerned. You are forgiven. Please don't blame yourself."

After that evening, Giuliana became a regular guest of the De Santis estate. In a strange turn of fate, Mrs. De Santis grew to love and need the girl from the cornfield.

***

361

Mr. Rolando and Mr. Nardo had approached her with a proposal to make her a partner at the firm. The big project in Molise was well under way and had taken a lot of research on her part. The electric power line had been easy to arrange and with its arrival those dark desolated hills were finally illuminated with the life of electricity. The funds were in place, and Emilio Baldone and Sons were ready to move forward. Three architectural firms had submitted quotes for designing the new plant. Giuliana had gone over the drawings with the architect, builder, and engineer. She picked the best to be hired based on a criteria of performance, reputation, and delivery. The first cheese factory would provide work for five hundred people as well as benefit the landowners that owned cows, sheep, and goats. After construction, the first supply of milk had to be purchased from local farmers who had the right of first refusal. Any overflow would come from the surrounding area. The factory would benefit locals, the surrounding towns, and the province at large. Giuliana was the talk of the town. She was God's gift to the locals. The priest preached about her to the worshippers at Sunday Mass.

"We will pray for our saviour, Miss Giuliana Ferrante. Her hard work and dedication, with God's grace, has provided for us all. Where there was only famine, there is now hope. Our long desolated area is finally going to know thriving."

The Mayor had worked closely with her from the beginning of the project. He cooperated to the fullest. Because of this, any red tape was easy to overcome. Together, the people of Molise felt compelled to do something in recognition of their benefactor. The Mayor visited Giuliana in her humble home, personally, to deliver what had been entrusted to him.

"Miss Ferrante, you are highly esteemed by our people. We would like to show our gratitude."

He handed her a rolled paper tied with a striped ribbon in green, red, and white – the colour of the Italian flag.

"This is an invite for you from the dignitaries of our province as well as our folks here."

Giuliana was humbled as she didn't expect any fuss over herself. Whatever she had done and intended to do was part of the work that she loved. She unrolled the script gently.

Miss Giuliana Ferrante,

Your honoured presence is cordially requested at the City Hall balcony on Sunday, the tenth of June at two o'clock in the afternoon, where a bronze sculpture made in your image will be ceremoniously revealed. The likeness will be formally erected at the Piazza Marcone in celebration of your significant contributions to the people of Molise.

Signed,

Guglielmo Ambrosi

Justice of the Peace

From the province of Molise,

Alberto Valdano

Mayer of Molise

Rizzieri Fonta

La Questura, The Law Enforcement Dept.

Giuliana was speechless.

"Signor Mayor, Thank you. I am... so moved by your people's recognition. My intentions were only to give the people a chance in life, as others gave me."

"They will expect a few words from you. The folks want to do this for you. A committee was formed to collect the funds, plus the province contributed. These poor folks dug deep into their pockets and gave every lira they could to donate toward the sculpture. It means a great deal to many."

Giuliana's eyes blurred as she fought back tears.

"My God! I am deeply moved. Signor Mayor, it is the least I could do. My heart is here, with them."

"Thank you, Miss Ferrante, you are a rare breed."

***

On Sunday afternoon, accompanied by Mrs. Zicardo and escorted by two Carabinieri, Giuliana entered City Hall through the rear door. The room was full of people in uniforms, unknown to her. Everyone cordially greeted her in turn.

"Miss Ferrante step in here please," gestured the Mayor as he opened a door to his private office. Giuliana was in total shock as she realised the group gathered in the room was composed of the dearest people in her life. Among them, her eyes quickly found her mom, dad, and Trizia, together with the rest of the Ferrante relatives that had come: Uncle John, with his family, Uncle Raniero, and his wife. The Sbarros were present. Marco stood with Lola, the parrot. Mrs. De Santis, wearing a large hat that shaded her face, stood next to Mr. De Santis and Zila.

There were tears of joy and sorrow exchanged. These people had been personally invited by the Mayor using a list provided by Mrs. Zicardo. Giuliana was received like a celebrity. She heard music play, followed by folk songs. Her skin erupted in goose bumps.

What is taking place out there? She recognised a folk song as one that Grandpa Luigi would sing to Giuliana as a child while holding her in his arms. The Mayor led her toward the balcony to step out. The piazza was packed with people, wall to wall.

"There are people here from the surrounding towns, Miss Ferrante, they have all come in in celebration of the hope you symbolise," said the Mayor.

The people erupted in cheers and applause, elated with enthusiasm. The band she had heard playing before was now visible in the back of the square, dressed in black and white uniforms. Their berets made them look distinguished. Their gold instruments were held in their white-gloved hands.

Quite suddenly, the noise of the crowd faded to total silence. They were waiting, expectant. The Mayor launched smoothly into an eloquent speech. His voice carried loud and clear through the microphone. Giuliana stood slightly behind him, sandwiched between the two escorts. She was mesmerised by the pomp and formality of it all. The afternoon sun was comfortable, and a gentle breeze caressed her warm cheeks. The sky was a bright blue, with far faded, unthreatening white clouds. She took a deep breath. Am I going to be able to speak? Is this for real? All for me?

"...We are honoured to have with us, the figure behind all of these ambitious and far-reaching plans, Giuliana Ferrante, a native of our town. For those of you who have never met her, you are privileged this afternoon to hear firsthand from our distinguished guest who represents hope and fidelity to so many in this town. Without further ado, I present to you, Miss Giuliana Ferrante."

The crowd broke into a roaring applause as Giuliana stepped forward and took the microphone. She marvelled at the crowd. Her dear ones had moved to take their places among them. Mrs.

De Santis, with her large hat, stood out vividly.

A sense of serenity filled her once she started to address the assembly. Her sincere thoughts and feelings were effortlessly accessed.

"I thank our honourable Mayor for inviting me here. My thanks and gratitude goes to you folks for having taken the time to attend and generously support this event. I am humbled and honoured by your recognition. I thank all of you for placing your trust in me. My dear folks of Molise, I am one of you. I was born and lived here with my dear family. We suffered from hunger, thirst, abuse, and humiliation from individuals that had power and held it over those who did not. I am very well aware of how all of these things are intimately tied to poverty. Some of us – and I count myself among them – were lucky to have the opportunity to get away, to immigrate, or move to more prosperous places. Through the kindness and help of others, we were able to prosper. But we are few, and our privilege is great. As I grew up, I never forgot this place, or the real people here, dear to my heart. So many were left behind, governing this corner of the world, without a chance.

I chose my career with you people in mind. I dreamt of possibilities to provide noble work for the people of these hills. We, together, need to regenerate our area. I will do my best to drive industries in this way. My goal is to eradicate famine and suffering for the families here. The factory is complete. It is up and running, ready to fulfil many contracts to date. The company of Emilio Baldone and Sons is a reputable organisation. The operation will not only benefit the owners, and shareholders, but all of you, the folks of this town.

Careful regulations of labour laws, well implemented and registered with regular health mandates, will mean a safe and prosperous future for you."

Applause erupted. Giuliana was on a roll. She was telling

them the truth that had resided in her heart for so many years. Once quietness resumed, she continued:

"This is only the beginning. I promise to direct more companies to this area. With job creation, many of you should find work, right here. Now, for our young people, who are the hope of our future: as you are aware, our new school is already in progress. I have been working with Mr. Henrico Navarra, my old teacher, my mentor. The construction should be completed by fall next year. Every student should have the choice to continue their education right here, with qualified teachers. Education should not be denied to anyone, regardless of status or location. Rich or poor, everyone should have a chance."

Once more, the crowd broke out into applause and interrupted her speech. Mrs. De Santis lost amongst the swarm was equally moved.

When Giuliana's speech was over, she was escorted back into the building. She was uncomfortable with this formality and protested.

"These are my people. I belong with them."

Sibilla was among the crowd. Her health had been failing for some time and as the labour laws became stricter, her industry, outdated and coarse, was failing too. She had not been able to keep up with the revolution of time. Her fields were wilting as her poor crop was invaded by weeds. So many of the people that surrounded her had suffered in her fields, under her domain. With a sorrowful heart, she was forced to confront her legacy. An inner voice spoke from deep in her soul and shook her with fright. You chose to ignore the pain of many of these people, including Liliana and young Giuliana. Remember? In despair, she watched the compassionate girl walk into the crowd. Maybe she can help me sell my land to one of her clients?

Chapter Forty-Six
The Mystery

Henrico Navarra may have been bent over and feeble, but his senses were sharper than ever.

"Giuliana, we are so proud of you," he said, from behind his old wooden desk. "You are an asset to the world at large and to our people. What a sinful loss it would have been for everyone if you had not been given a chance, if we hadn't intervened, or that blessed family refused to take you in."

Giuliana flashed him her biggest smile. Something about being here, in front of his old desk made her feel child-like again.

"Thank you, Mr. Navarra." She reached forward and kissed his soft, papery hand.

Whenever she ventured back to town, visiting her benefactors had become her duty. It was a matter of respect, taught to her as a child by Nonna Rosa.

Her biggest admirer of late was Mrs. De Santis. Before she left for Molise, she stopped in for one of her usual visits at the De Santis Estate. No sooner had she entered was she greeted warmly by Mrs. De Santis herself. She walked over and hugged Giuliana.

"Giuliana, my Dear, did Joseph ever mention to you that I sponsor many charities and organisations?"

"No, Mrs. De Santis. He didn't."

"Please, allow me to do something for my son. I would like to share a percentage of his textile profits to an organisation of your choice."

Giuliana was speechless for a moment.

"Mrs. De Santis, I cannot thank you enough. How kind of you! I can tell you what this place badly needs: once our high school opens, there will be a growing number of unfortunate students that cannot afford to go to university. I would love to set up a bursary in Joseph's name to sponsor deserving students in need. You see, this school will not only benefit our town, but also the surrounding towns."

"Giuliana, my dearest, whatever you suggest. You draw out the papers. I will follow your instructions."

They embraced again, and Giuliana was struck by the clear affection in her heart for Mrs. De Santis. Mrs. De Santis is not as cold as I thought. Too bad my Joseph is not sharing her kindness. According to Grandma Rosa, he knows. I need to believe that in my heart. She made the sign of the cross.

It was nice for Giuliana to have the family-like relationships she had forged in Milan. Her parents and sister had long left Italy to return to their duties in America. Ruggiero, with his two well-established associates, had purchased the entire department of his steel operation, as planned. Business was thriving. To keep up with his orders, Ruggiero had recently created a night shift. He now employed two thousand five hundred people. There was plenty of room for Giuliana in his operation to be his legal aid. Ruggiero missed his daughter dearly, but he believed in freedom. He was unable to sleep one night thinking of his daughter.

"Giuliana needs to come to her own decision to return to us someday. I will no longer push the issue." He said to Gioia in bed.

***

Back in Milan, Giuliana was hard at work. It was time for her to concentrate on the Ireland account. The manager of the De Santis Yarn Department, Leonardo, had taken her for a tour and upon hearing the details of the arrangement, he promised his utmost cooperation and signed the contract. The contract now sat ready, in a brown envelope, to mail to Aiden McCauley for approval. He had indicated his pleasure at the arrangement by phone earlier that day. However, this morning, upon returning to her office, the envelope and the papers were suddenly nowhere to be found. Giuliana experienced a flash of panic. The filing cabinets were locked; the office undisturbed. Am I losing my mind? Did I put the contract somewhere else? She tried to reassemble her thoughts and retrace her footsteps. A certified cheque had been among the papers on hold. She had left them out as she had been in a hurry to leave for Molise. She panicked. Her secretary had called in sick that day and could not have collected them. The information was strictly confidential. What has gone on here?

There was no sign of a break-in or anything out of the ordinary in her office. She eventually decided that she had no choice but to summon Mr. Gianni Rolando, her superior. He joined in the search, but they came up with nothing. The night watchman had not seen anything strange.

Two days went by with no sign of the file. With much scrutiny, Giuliana studied everyone's face, suspiciously. Everyone had begun to look guilty in her eyes. The loss caused her several sleepless nights and much agony. She could re-draw the contract, but it was unsafe for private, privileged information to be out there.

When something starts to go wrong, other mishaps seem to follow. Giuliana, after a stressful day at the office, went home, ready to drop. She retreated to the privacy of her bedroom, drowning in her thoughts. Not much later, her tired eyes got heavy and shut closed. She didn't know how long her inert body had been immobilised, half sitting up against the headboard. Darkness had fallen over the room. The dim light, coming in from outside, created shadows on the wall. Her window curtains were left open. She was a light sleeper these days and, therefore, when her door made a low creaking noise she was quick to startle awake. Her lids were still heavy and her vision had yet to start cooperating. She tried to adjust to the darkness and straighten herself to a more upright position. The noise guided her attention toward the door. She could see that the handle was being directed by an unseen force, turning it to open. Giuliana remained paralysed, frozen in fear. This is real, she thought. Who, or why? She licked her lips, but couldn't speak from fear. The door opened. At first, she couldn't make out the hunched over figure tiptoeing close to the floor. Breathless, she watched as it made its way toward the bed. Past trauma caught up with her and Giuliana's mind temporarily blacked out. Her eyes rolled back in her head, and she fluttered on the edge of consciousness. She sensed someone close to her, uncovering her. The fear tugged her and out of consciousness like a wave lapping at the shore. Suddenly and abruptly she came to. The invader, with quick footsteps, made an exit, pulling the door behind.

Giuliana forced her body up and wiped her eyes to clear her vision. A surge of energy flowed through her, and she forced courage to reign as she jumped out of bed. She pushed herself out into the hallway, half crazy, ready to attack whoever was out there. The hall was empty. She paced and looked in the adjacent bedrooms. Everyone was snoring, fast asleep. She stood in silence, holding her breath; fearing; listening; keeping vigil.

Suddenly, a noise came from the end of the hall. She proceeded slowly. A grey sock lay on the floor. She continued further and found another right by the door. She had a hunch but didn't want to admit it to herself. A dim light appeared under the door. She slowly grabbed the silver handle and turned it. To her surprise, it opened. It wasn't locked.

The outline of Nino's body could be seen under the covers in the dim light. She walked powerfully right up beside his bedside making no effort to conceal her presence.

"You dropped these, Mr.?"

As if she were possessed, an uncontrollable angry force had taken over her body. She was now out of control. With both hands, she grabbed the covers from his bed and ripped them onto the floor. There he lay, naked, with only his trunks. She furiously slapped him right and left and punched and scratched at him as hard as she could. Nino rushed for cover, trying to save himself. "Giuliana, have you gone crazy?" he screamed.

"It's been you!" she screamed, right back at him.

He was out of his bed now, running around the room. He had no place to hide.

"What were you thinking, Mr. Peeping Tom? What was the plan? Sneaking in my bedroom!"

Trying hard to control her voice, she lowered her tone. She did not want to wake up the rest of the house.

"What are you talking about? I never came to your room!" pleaded Nino.

She lunged forward and put a hand on his throat, half choking him.

"It's not the first time. I thought I imagined things until tonight. If you dare come close to me or step in my room once more, I swear... I will kill you with my bare hands. You perverted creep. What do you want with me?"

Nino's eyes flashed with fear.

"Giuliana, please! I didn't mean anything! Please don't tell Mom and Dad. I find you attractive. All I wanted to do was watch you. You are lovely when you are asleep."

Her gut clenched, and she feared she would get sick. She squeezed him a little harder.

"Nino, I don't find that amusing. I am not afraid of you or anybody. Anyone making advances on me without my consent will see that I will retaliate with all my might. Shame on you! I loved you like a brother."

To her surprise, he was now sobbing like a two-year-old child. She let go of her hold on him. Pitiful.

"Look, Nino, you have a problem. I suggest you get some counselling."

She backed away from him, and he slumped to the floor.

"Go to sleep. We need to talk about this seriousness tomorrow."

Like a wounded boy, he retreated under the covers.

Giuliana walked out of the room. She actually felt sorry for him. He needed attention, in a bad way, and the matter needed to be dealt with by a professional. She would talk to Aunt Amelia. Despite her anger, she sincerely loved Nino like a brother and cared for his well-being.

Back in her room, with both hands on her chest, Giuliana took a deep breath. She returned to her undesirable bed. Her mind raced. She was relieved by the discovery of her mystery but not by the results.

***

The mystery that remained was the disappearance of her files. She replayed in her mind all possibilities. Who would want to mess up my affairs? Everyone in the office was cordial. Was it jealousy? But who? She was popular in the office, but she was getting the better cases of late. Other lawyers were being handed stuff they didn't really enjoy.

She decided to call her dad and ask his advice.

"Dad," she said, "do you think people are envious of my success?"

"Darling, what makes you ask such thing?"

"A strange thing has happened to me. Someone has stolen my files. I can redo it, no trouble. It contained a certified cheque they cannot cash. Why anyone would want to do that?"

"To copy your ideas, perhaps? Modify the contract? You could add complex contingencies? Start over and go from there. It happens all the time, Dear. Put it behind you. It's not worth the aggravation, Dear."

"I agree, Dad. I will sit down and start all over again, as you say, with improvement."

Ruggiero was happy that his smart daughter had picked up the phone to seek his advice. A week later, her binding contract was redrawn. The deal came to a close and would be up and running within a year with great success.

Soon the venture became so successful that Aiden McCauley couldn't keep up with the demand of the growing market. McCauley responded by initiating plans to increase his herd. Giuliana suggested to move some of his operation to the hills of Molise, where nature itself would provide feed for the sheep and acreage costs were substantially lower.

Giuliana's hard work was paying off. Her work requests involved a lot of travelling. Often she would fly privately to attend meetings or conferences, or just sit in on meetings, as an adviser. Mrs. De Santis had become her best friend. Sometimes Giuliana went on excursions with her eager benefactor. They opened many schools together in rural areas. Now scores of underprivileged students had a chance in life. News of Giuliana's efforts spread. Often she was met by dignitaries and escorted by the local securities. She made a difference where it was badly needed.

***

Addicted to her work, Giuliana's years were slipping by without her realising. Gioia and Ruggiero's concerns for their daughter never ceased. Especially, her mother wished for her to meet someone and share the love she deserved. Trizia had found a soulmate and married. Now Gioia and Ruggiero were expecting their first grandchild. Giuliana had all the glory, but her lonely heart was not fulfilled. She was now in her thirties. The young corporate lawyer had met many people on her path. Most of them admired her and some were intimidated by her. The few that had enough nerve to approach her were rejected with no reservation. The men in her office wondered who would be the lucky man to have a relationship with this untouchable girl. The fellows often made smart remarks when she walked by. She moved swiftly with a twist of her hips, and they found her striking.

A new fellow, Aldo Doriano, had joined the firm. He replaced a retired lawyer in the Litigation Department. The staff had been asked to welcome him at the lower-level restaurant for a champagne breakfast. He was speaking with the partners in the corner of the restaurant when he spotted Giuliana and admired her with a firm gaze. He turned to Mr. Rolando.

"Who is that radiant girl? She sure walks with an aura of distinction!"

"Don't get any ideas, my friend. She is one of the most talented girls I've ever worked with. As far as romance, and relationships…she rejects everyone's advances. She lost a boyfriend years ago in a plane crash. They were to be married. I think she is still grieving her loss."

"How sad. Someone needs to bring her out of that haze. Grief isn't good for the body or mind."

"Well my friend," said Mr. Rolando skeptically, "you are young and vibrant. Good luck."

"I shall try," he replied with a big smile.

Aldo proceeded to walk in her direction. His eyes took in her high-heeled shoes, perfectly shaped legs, and the tweed, navy-blue suit that accentuated her body. She was at the cappuccino bar leaning on the counter as she waited for her coffee. Aldo was an old pro at approaching women. He was assertive and confident. He marched up to Giuliana and extended his hand.

"Miss Ferrante, we haven't been properly introduced. I am Aldo Doriano. Molto piacere, my pleasure."

Giuliana smiled at him and offered her hand to shake in exchange.

"My pleasure as well, Mr. Doriano. Welcome to our law firm."

"Thank you."

When her cappuccino was ready, he offered to carry it for her.

"Please allow me," he said as he led her to a table.

"Would you like to join me?"

"Love too. Allow me to grab an espresso."

He signalled the waiter for the order. He was pleased with himself so far and ready to pursue this further. She seemed receptive.

"Tell me about yourself, Mr. Doriano. You are in litigation; I believe?"

"Yes, formerly from the firm of Dante Mantovani, from Bologna. I joined your firm for a change. Milan, I am told, is more stimulating."

"There is no shortage of work if that's what you are looking for."

"Just work and no fun? I like a mix of fun with business. It makes life more interesting."

"You are probably right. I seem to willingly drown myself in my work."

"Tell me about yourself. You must find your work fascinating: juggling numbers, bringing companies together. This is not an easy task."

"Every job, as with life, has both the good and the bad. If the results are rewarding, then the hard work is worth it."

She started to get up.

"Mr. Doriano, it was nice meeting and chatting with you. I wish you the best of luck. I must get back to work."

"Miss Ferrante, could we go out for lunch or dinner sometime? Am I too forward in asking you so soon after meeting you? I am new to the city, I could use a guide," he said with a hopeful smile.

Giuliana paused. He wondered if she would just turn and walk away without answering him.

"Good idea," she said, slowly, after a moment. "I would love to show you around. The only problem is I am leaving tomorrow morning. I am not sure when I will be back."

He wasn't sure if she was blowing him off or interested. He was pleased and disappointed. Nevertheless, his first move had been successful.

Chapter Forty-Seven
The Visit to America

Giuliana's flight to America was scheduled for the next morning. A large company had requested an analysis of their operation. Despite overwhelming sales, the bank accounts were continuously running into the red. The company was situated in the state of New York. Excellent, she thought. The opportunity would allow her to see her family and look into the client's dilemma at the same time.

She had called her mom.

"Mom, I will be in Rochester for a business consultation. I will see you in few days since I will be not too far from you. Can't wait to see you both!"

Gioia's heart vibrated with happiness

"Oh, my Darling! You really mean it? Your dad will be ecstatic. I can't wait to see you. When will you arrive?"

"Tomorrow night. Can't wait to see you too, Mom. Bye."

Giuliana was in a hurry to hang up.

"Wait! wait, Giuliana!" Gioia was trying to stall. "There is a play at our church Saturday night. Will you go with us? I will get an extra ticket for you."

"Mom, that sounds great! I would love to do something with both of you."

"Thanks, Dear. I will call your dad right now to give him the good news."

"Love you both. Bye Mom."

She hung up the phone and held the receiver for a while, reflecting on her mother's words and joy. In the past while, her parents had been on her mind more than ever. She wanted to be closer and spend more time with them. They were getting on and it was time for her to consider her family. The transformation of her hometown was well on its way and doing fantastic. She had been in Milan for many years now. She wondered: Maybe I should shift gears?

***

When she arrived in Buffalo at her parent's new home, she was flabbergasted by the impressive structure. Professionally landscaped with pine trees, the gentle aroma of green spruce filled the air. A majestic gold and black iron gate surrounded the property, rendering it both impressive and prestigious. The home had an elaborate front entrance that led to a white marble staircase, connecting to the upper level. The first floor was spacious and cosy with all the necessities. Giuliana's room, elegantly decorated, was saved for her like a museum chamber. It was a lovely room with glass double doors that opened up to a terrace that faced the back of the house and overlooked a large heated pool. The greenery of the pine trees made Giuliana feel as if she were in a northern paradise island. She was proud and impressed by her dad's achievements. He was, without question, a dedicated, hard worker.

Once here with her family, she realised the void that had been present in her heart. How much I have missed them. Although Amelia had been good to her, her mom's tender love touched her heart as nothing else could. The doorbell rang. Trizia had arrived with her husband, seven months pregnant.

"Oh, my God! Let me look at you! My little sister, ready to have a baby! I cannot wait for the occasion." Giuliana laughed with pure joy.

"Yes, Sis. You will have to be here for the birth and the baptism."

"I wouldn't miss that for the world!"

Ruggiero was reluctant, but he needed to speak to his daughter. She was a mature adult now, and he needed to choose his words carefully.

"Giuliana, we are well off now. You don't have to work so hard. I can support my family with no trouble, Dear. We want you near."

"Dad! Do you think I do it for money? No way. It's not about money. It's about love and passion for my work: helping people out there."

"Darling, I understand. Forgive us for wanting you for ourselves."

The Sunday meal was served in the elegant dining room. Gioia walked in from the kitchen with a basket of warm toasted bread.

"Giuliana, your sister had a craving for… cornbread! Can you believe it? I had to make it. I have improved the recipe I think. Taste a piece."

"Mom, it's delicious! What did you mix into it?"

"I mixed some sausage meat. It's a meal in itself. Does that not bring you back? The memories…"

"Mom, Grandma never had sausage meat. Poor Grandma, she tried so hard to feed us. She was such a mother hen."

"God rest her soul."

It felt good for Giuliana to be with her family. She promised herself that she would take more time off for her dear ones and come to visit more often.

Gioia checked the time.

"It's getting late. Let's leave everything and go see the play. People are waiting for us at our church hall."

Ruggiero and Gioia knew a lot of people by now, and they were greeted by everyone. They proudly introduced Giuliana to all of their friends. The group had sat down in centre seats that had been reserved for them. The announcer called out to the audience:

"We have a special guest here tonight, from Milan Italy, Miss Giuliana Ferrante! Will you please come up to the stage? We want to introduce you to our congregation."

Giuliana, surprised and reluctant, made her way to the stage. As she stepped on, the room erupted into applause. The deacon addressed her with a short speech.

The way they are going on you'd think I was Mother Theresa. She took the podium to thank the people in few words. Before the play started, she began to hear the whispers circulating the entire room. For a moment she thought she was back home in her hometown. The play lasted an hour and a half. Afterwards, three musicians started to perform: one on the accordion, one on the violin, and the third on the guitar. It was a lovely melody and it filled the room, pulling some folks to start dancing. Ruggiero and Gioia got up to dance. Giuliana smiled, admiring them joyfully. They make a lovely couple. While rejoicing solitarily, a young man approached her. He seemed to have appeared out of nowhere.

"Would you like to dance?" he asked.

Spontaneously, she got up and there she was in this stranger's arms in the middle of the floor doing a moderate waltz. The young fellow had a good grip on her, leading her well, without any difficulty.

Her mom and dad looked at each other, overwhelmed with pleasure. Their daughter was dancing! The fellow pursued her to dance again, and again. Giuliana glowed in his arms, loving the music and the dance. The young man was totally concentrating on the music and spoke few words. Although from the few words he did speak, Giuliana noticed he was well spoken in both English and Italian.

"I am Lucio Albano. Are you new in town?"

"You could say that. My parents live here. I come occasionally."

"I have never seen you at our church before."

"I don't live here," she responded.

"Oh! I wish you did!" he replied with a slow smile.

He resembles that singer with the terrific voice; what's his name? Elvis Presley, she thought. He had the same features: big dark eyes and jet-black hair. He was well dressed. The cloth of his blazer resembled the quality goods the De Santis Company produced. She rubbed her hand on his shoulder. The fine-combed woollen was smooth as silk. Ah! It's fabric from the U.K or Milan. Joseph had often played guessing games with her to identify the materials. She had learned to distinguish them with ease.

It was midnight when the music stopped. She had danced with the mysterious man all night. When they parted, he seemed unsure of himself, glancing at her shy and blushing. She waited for him to ask for her number. He remained silent. Oh well, she thought. He knows my last name and I have introduced him to my parents, who are no strangers to the church. Perhaps he will find my number in the phone book.

Giuliana was intrigued by the young man, and she went home

that night with a strange, warm feeling in her heart. He is mysterious…

Gioia, as a mother, was always concerned.

"Ruggiero, I wish our daughter was involved with someone. She is getting on in life…"

"Gioia, give her time. When she is ready, she will."

"Her clock is running out, Dear…no grandchildren."

Giuliana's suffering had left her feeling, at times, like her soul was empty. This fellow had revived some life in her. She sat at the kitchen table the next morning and told her mother:

"Mom, that guy last night, I hope he calls. I find him… interesting."

Gioia smiled and perked up.

"In what way, Dear?"

"Everything about him: his mannerisms, his doubts. He is distinguished without pretence."

Gioia listened quietly, hopeful. Thank God, my daughter is waking up!

The time for Giuliana's stay ran out, and the phone call never arrived. She returned to Milan where her desk was mounded with work. The strange fellow surfaced in her mind every now and then, but once immersed in her work, he slipped away.

A firm knock on her door startled her.

"Come in."

There was spiffy Aldo, cheerful and confident as ever.

"Miss Ferrante! Since you forgot your new-comer here, would you give me the pleasure of your company for lunch?"

"I would love too, but I have a lot of work to catch up with."

"Come on, what do I have to do? Get on my knees?"

He walked to her desk and dropped to his knees. Giuliana laughed.

"I am working on a serious, complicated case. I need to lift my spirits with a beautiful girl like you, Miss Ferrante. Please!" He put his hands together.

"Only for an hour," she said, throwing her hands in the air.

The street was full of people coming and going. The outdoor vendors were competing with their respective aromas.

"Would you like some roasted chestnuts? We can get them on our way back for your afternoon snack," Aldo asked.

"No thanks, I don't snack."

"Tell me, do you ever indulge in any pleasure?" he asked with a grin.

Giuliana increased her speed, ignoring him by changing the subject. A young man at the corner was hollering, offering the daily paper for sale.

"Read 'La Voce' today! It's the newspaper with the people's voice! Learn more about the thrilling murder case of Liliana Manzana, featured on the front page!"

Giuliana's footsteps came to an abrupt halt. Upon hearing that name, she grabbed Aldo's arm and picked up the newspaper from the young man.

"I don't believe this! Is it the same Liliana I know? I wonder…"

She handed three hundred liras to the vendor and glanced quickly at the paper.

"I used to know a girl from my hometown. Her name was Liliana Manzana, and she was dear to me. We lost touch. I have thought of her many times over the years. I promised myself I'd find her someday. As my hectic life took over, it was never done."

Big and bold, the printed headline stated: 'Liliana Manzana Convicted of Murdering her Disabled Husband.'

"Dear God! It cannot be! She did marry a paralysed fellow. But, maybe it is a coincidence? Could it be someone with the same name? The Liliana I knew was not a murderer. There must be a mistake of some sort."

"How long has it been that you have not heard or seen your friend?" Aldo asked.

"I don't know. Many years, I think. My letters were returned unanswered. She couldn't write. Someone had to do it for her. We lost touch. I know she married this fellow to take care of him, and his feeble old Mom."

Giuliana scanned the paper.

"My goodness," she said, with her face obscured by her hand, "I hope it's not her. This woman has been convicted for life without parole."

"Let me run an inquiry into the case. Criminal law – litigation – is my speciality. Giuliana, let's not jump to conclusions. Put the newspaper away, let's have lunch."

Giuliana nibbled at her food having lost her appetite. Throughout the years she had wanted to look for Liliana, but never took the necessary steps, due to the demands of her own life.

Giuliana stared and listened passively to her colleague, but her thoughts were elsewhere.

Chapter Forty-Eight
Research and Discovery

Aldo showed a keen interest in Giuliana. Not only had he wanted to help Giuliana find as much as possible out about her friend, but he also wanted to impress her with his capabilities as a criminal lawyer. His true motive was his interest in her. This matter will give me a good excuse to be in close contact with her and she with me. He was attracted to her. The fellows in the office had warned him not to bother pursuing the iceberg of Mount Bianco of the Alps. He was determined to prove them wrong, more for his own ego than anything else. No girl refuses Aldo Doriano. Giuliana's disinterest was motivating him even more; driving him crazy. After all, she was highly regarded as the most famous lawyer at the firm.

The case of her friend's conviction was a good opportunity for him to be more in touch with her. In the meantime, he was curious himself to find out about what had taken place with this Liliana. By late afternoon, Giuliana's phone rang. It was Aldo.

"Giuliana? Let me ask you: what on earth could have motivated your friend to kill her husband? Motive... the first thing to look for is the motive."

"I don't believe she would. The Liliana I knew would not be capable of murder. She was ready to sacrifice her life for this fellow, knowing he was an invalid, in order to survive herself and provide for her family, her mom, and twin brothers."

"Maybe she had a lover? You have not heard from her for so many years. People change. He was probably in her way. Maybe she needed to get rid of him."

"Now you are talking like a prosecutor, not a defence lawyer. No. People don't change. We are brought up with deep morals in the south. We are faithful and duty bound. I will never believe her capable of such an act. Someone has framed her, or committed the crime, and she has been wrongly convicted."

"Ok. I will find out as much as I can."

"Please do. I will run an inquiry also. I must go see her. I have to see what I can do for her. I will have no peace until I talk to her."

The research revealed that Liliana Manzana had been convicted of murdering her invalid husband by the Bolognian Court judge, Abramo Dante. The accused had been sentenced to spend thirty years at an undisclosed location. Giuliana returned home and knocked on Judge Sbarro's library to ask for his help.

"Please, Mr. Sbarro, I need you to look into the disturbing ordeal of my friend. I need to know where she is being held. If she is incarcerated, I have to go visit her as soon as possible."

"Giuliana, I am sorry about your friend. I will do all I can to help you, just give me some time."

A few days passed, without much progress either by Aldo or Judge Sbarro. Giuliana was putting off travelling abroad until this heavy burden saw some answers. She recalled how Liliana was ready to help her with Orlando, putting her reputation on the line to convict that monster that molested her.

"Poor Liliana. I wish I had known. I could have been there for her. I can't wait to see her. Please, God, don't let it be true. This must be a big mistake."

She picked up the phone and dialed Aldo's number.

"Hello? Aldo? It's Giuliana here."

Happy as a lark, he cheerfully replied:

"Good morning, Miss Giuliana. It's a great pleasure to hear your lovely voice first thing in the morning! What can I do for you?"

"Aldo, I was wondering if you might have any news of my friend. I am troubled. I can't wait to find out and see her."

"Be patient. I will have all the details for you before you know it. My friend is away on holiday. I will try someone else. I promise you, we will get the details."

"Sorry Aldo, I am just anxious and impatient, I guess."

She felt foolish for her insatiable demands.

"I don't blame you. She is lucky to have such a caring friend. Hey! Speaking of friends, would you like to have lunch again with this friend?"

"Aldo, sorry, I would love too, but honestly, I need to tackle the work on my desk."

"If you change your mind, let me know."

He liked to be seen and looked forward to showing off to the other guys by walking out with Giuliana.

***

In America, Gioia and Ruggiero were enthusiastic. Trizia was to deliver their first grandchild. They had called Giuliana to fly over for the birth but she didn't come. Trizia was in labour. After many agonising hours, she finally gave birth to a bouncy, nine-pound healthy boy who arrived to meet his overwhelmed father – Trizia's husband Glen – and his delighted grandparents. Gioia and Ruggiero tried to hide their disappointment to Trizia but were beside themselves with Giuliana's absence. Nevertheless, they called her to give her the good news.

"Giuliana! Why are you not here? That is disrespectful toward your sister. Dad and I are disappointed," Gioia blurted out.

"Mom, I am so sorry. You are right. I can't wait to get there and see my new nephew. My apologies to Trizia and Glen. You won't believe the news I got a few days ago. It was all over the news here and in the papers. Remember Liliana? She has been convicted of murder, Mom! Can you believe that?"

"Murder? Liliana? Who did she kill?"

"Her husband. Mom, she has been convicted!"

"How can that be? Unless she went insane... Her mom came home a couple of times when I was still in the old house. She cried to me and your grandmother about her daughter. The marriage – It wasn't a great arrangement. Lovely Liliana was to take care of the handicapped fellow and the mother. The mother died not much later. The fellow, her husband, was very difficult, a mess – hard to handle. This is crazy to say, but Agnes said she felt like killing him sometimes. To watch her daughter put up with him was torture for her."

"Mom, did she really say that?"

"Yes! She moved in with them, and she took the twins along after the old lady died. Liliana accepted that position mainly to provide for her mom and young brothers."

"Oh my God! Mom, I forgot about them! Where is her mom? Her brothers? Did you ever hear from them?"

"Giuliana, remember the gossiper across from our window? Her daughter lives here. She said Agnes died. God bless her soul."

"Mom, I need to find out. I have a friend in criminal law. We are investigating. Poor Liliana! I will be there as soon as I can be, I promise."

"I understand now, Dear."

Giuliana put down the phone. Judge Sbarro was sitting in on a case out of town. He was going to be busy for some time. The next morning, she would pester Aldo again. After all, he had better sources coming from Bologna. The last Giuliana knew, Liliana lived in a town in the vicinity of Bologna. She was getting antsy. This is why she had chosen business law over criminal.

Her restless body wouldn't relax. She got up, got herself dressed in her favourite blue power suit and pumps. She would call Aldo again. If he wanted to go for lunch, so be it. She needed the info. She sat at her desk, totally absorbed in her files. She looked at her watch. She was about to pick up the phone when the knock on her door stopped her.

"Come in,"

The door opened, and Aldo bounced in with a smile on his face.

"Madam Ferrante, Buon Giorno!"

He walked to her desk. Giuliana began to get up.

"Remain sited, Mademoiselle, please. You need to remain seated."

"Aldo, what's up?"

"You are not going to believe it."

One hand was hidden behind his back holding something.

"Giuliana, it's going to cost you. Will you go for dinner with me tonight?"

"Aldo, stop the nonsense! Please, have you made any headway?"

"Have I?" He lifted his hand up and waved the envelope around. He continued, "Make sure you are sitting. Your friend was transferred here, to a prison in Milan. Here is the report of the court case."

She was breathless.

"Are you serious?"

"Here it is. Now, will you allow me the privilege to indulge in your company for tonight?"

"Aldo you are something else. Thank you. I am dying to read the report. I want to see my friend."

"I have taken the liberty of making an appointment for you. It needs to be confirmed. Shall I accompany you, my Dear?"

"When?"

"Are you available tomorrow, at ten in the morning?"

"I am as nervous as hell. I will be ready."

"Dinner tonight – at the Austrian bistro at Piazza Renascent."

Giuliana felt obliged to comply with his wishes. He was a charming character. He had delivered what she needed.

"About seven. I want to get as much done as possible."

He grabbed her hand and kissed it delicately, while wishing for her lips sometime soon. Maybe tonight? He would not rush it. Giuliana politely walked him out and closed the door behind him. Rushing back to her desk, her trembling hands picked up the envelope, eager to read the contents.

There it was in, black and white: 'Murder Conviction.' 'Liliana Manzana found guilty of murder.' The horrific report came from the Court in Bologna. She glanced through quickly. The story was reported clearly with listed details. The file was thick, and Giuliana was too anxious. Impatiently, she kept flipping the pages upside down. The names, addresses, places of origin, the defendant, the offence, the plea and the court where the case was heard were all outlined alongside the name of the presiding judge and verdict. The name of the prosecutor and the defence lawyer were there; the punishment recorded.

I will concentrate on the crime, she muttered to herself. Aldo Doriano has definitely done a good job on such short notice. The security passes for visiting Liliana were in the file. Aldo's homework was perfect. She would soon learn from Liliana about what had taken place.

Chapter Forty-Nine
The Meeting

When Giuliana got home that evening, Amelia was in a talkative mood. Judge Sbarro was still away on his case. Giuliana felt obligated to sit and chat with her dear Aunt Amelia. After all, Amelia deserved her devotion.

"My goodness, Dear, everyone in this household is consumed with substantial obligations. How about you and I get away to your sleepy town for few days? I could use a break. If it's the weekend, we can take Nino with us as a chaperone."

"Oh, Aunt Amelia, my sleepy town is hardly a sleepy town anymore! But, just the same, there is nothing I would like better. As you know, I have been distressed by the news of my friend, Liliana. We now know where she is. Tomorrow my colleague and I have made an appointment at the prison to see her. My family is waiting for me to get to the US. However, I cannot leave Liliana unattended now that I know about her fate. I must talk to her first. I hope we can help her somehow. I had planned to stay abroad for six weeks to be with Trizia and the new baby. Now I am troubled."

"I am sure you will sort it out, Giuliana. You are a smart girl."

"Thanks, Aunt Amelia. Also, now that you have mentioned Nino... I am concerned about Nino. We are all so busy. I think Nino could use some counselling. You are the doctor, but I get the feeling that, for some strange reason, all our actions have left him feeling left out. He needs more attention and better coping strategies."

"What makes you say that?"

Giuliana wasn't going to reveal the real cause of her concern.

"He has complained about how Dino gets all the girls. I could be wrong, but I think he lacks self-esteem. He seems unsure of himself."

"You could be right, my Dear. It is Roberto's department to talk to his sons when it comes to courting girls."

"If you ask me, I think he turns to Dino. But, Dino wants him out of the way when he chases girls. Nino is hurt. He hangs around with that Heinz fellow. One time they were planning on beating up Mrs. De Santis! If you ask me, I think it was because for jealousy of Joseph. I was taken by Joseph, and because of that, he felt abandoned."

She tried to put things mildly, but somehow get the message across.

"Giuliana, thanks for opening my eyes in regards to Nino. I must confess," she frowned in recollection, "at times I did notice some peculiarities in him, but I shook it off. I must talk to his father. Some Saturday nights he doesn't go out. He sits in his room listening to music. That is not right for a young man."

"He has never had a steady girlfriend. Young Marco is even flirting with girls now. Dino is Mr. Don Juan. It won't hurt to have one of your psychiatric friends over for dinner one evening for observation, without mentioning anything to Nino."

"Giuliana, you're a bright girl. I am always running, turning a blind eye to my own family. I will try to be more aware. It's a good idea to have him checked out."

Giuliana's soul felt lighter, and she was relieved. Her thoughts had been clouded by Nino's behaviour.

***

Once more, Giuliana's restlessness kept her awake. This time, it emanated from the anticipation of seeing Liliana. She couldn't wait for daylight to appear. At six in the morning, she pulled out a simple suit from the closet and comfortable pumps. She tied her hair back in a twist. By seven she was at her office, going over Liliana's file. It wasn't easy, and she struggled to concentrate. Aldo arrived at nine to pick her up in an upbeat mood.

"How is my brilliant lawyer this morning?"

"Aldo, you are such a charmer. Talk like that would lift anyone's spirits."

"My girl, this job isn't easy, especially when dealing with criminal cases. You have to find joy to survive."

"I am glad you are the expert. My friendship makes me biassed. I am concerned for her well-being. You will be the one to analyse objectively."

At ten in the morning, they pulled up to the prison checkpoint. In no time, they were ushered into a room. They were told a guard would bring the convict to them. Giuliana took a deep breath. Never had she imagined she would see her friend in prison. Aldo always knew what to do and what to say at the right time in the process. His keen eyes switched from the door to Giuliana's face. He put an arm around her shoulders and brought his face close to her ear.

"Everything will be ok. Have faith. With faith, there is hope," he whispered.

His arm brought comfort to Giuliana's shivering body. His words provided a distraction from the intimidating environment that was overpowering her brain. The door opened. A frail inmate wearing an orange striped jumpsuit was accompanied by a female guard. They entered. Giuliana, wide-eyed, stared hard. The woman hardly resembled her beautiful friend. Her straggly hair hung over a wrinkled face that was punctuated with dark circles around the eyes. Her sunken cheekbones made her appear so much older.

Upon seeing Giuliana, Liliana's appearance shifted as a look of recognition lifted her face. Liliana burst out crying, uncontrollably. The prison guard looked at her watch.

"It is now ten thirty. Visiting rights are thirty minutes only. Since you are both attorneys, you are allowed two hours. Your meeting is over at twelve-thirty."

Giuliana quickly took the lead.

"Liliana, this is my friend, Aldo Doriano. He is a criminal lawyer. I want you to tell us, in your own words, what has taken place."

Liliana continued her sobbing. Giuliana adopted the same manners Liliana used when Giuliana's body had been violated.

"Now-now, Liliana. I couldn't wait to see you. We are here to help. We shall see if there is anything we can do for you. My friend here handles the Criminal Defense Department at our firm. He is as smart as they come, from Bologna. Liliana, I only found out about your conviction in the paper recently. I lost you for years, but I always thought of you. Now, you need to tell me everything. We are allowed two hours. Let's use the time productively. With Aldo here, together, we'll try everything in our power to get you out of here."

Giuliana nodded toward Aldo.

"I will jot down notes. You do the questioning." She turned to the guard, "Are we allowed recording? I brought a recorder just in case."

The guard only nodded. Aldo Doriano was serious now and got right to work. The guard left to grant them their confidential rights.

"Liliana, try to give us, in exact in detail, your account of what took place. Even if it's hard, we need the truth; nothing but the truth."

"I did not kill my husband."

Her first words were spoken with absolute certainty.

"Fine. You did not kill your husband. Do you know who did?"

"No, I don't. I was the caregiver. I was the one feeding him. I found him dead and everything pointed to me. The autopsy performed on his body revealed traces of poison in his system."

"Liliana, who lived with you? Giuliana mentioned your mother and twin brothers. What happened to them?"

"My poor brothers had just finished high school. My husband, in one of his tantrums one night, ordered them out of the house in a storm and they left. I eventually found out one went to Switzerland and one found a job in Munich. Mom, devasteted, remained with me. Later, she had a massive coronary and died a month before my husband. I lost my husband and my mom in a month's time. Then, to top it all off, I was arrested and charged with his murder. The interrogations were endless. They bombarded me with so many questions. Who cares Giuliana, if this is how I end up; if I live or die? I have never had anything to live for. Now that my mom is gone, and my brothers are gone, I am all alone. The sooner I die, the better."

Giuliana interjected Aldo's questioning.

"Liliana, stop talking like that. Stop feeling sorry for yourself. God takes you when he is ready for you, no sooner. Just tell us. I care for you. My letters to you were returned, undelivered. I thought of you all the time. I was going to hire a private investigator to find you."

Liliana cried heavier.

"Liliana, if they found poison in your husband's remains and you didn't do it, who else could have done it? Tell me about your relationship with your spouse. I need to know every detail if I am to help you," asked Aldo.

"How can you help me? I have been convicted and found guilty."

"That is my job, my profession. We can ask for an appeal."

"An appeal? What for? Even if by some miracle I got out, where would I go? What would I do?"

Giuliana jumped in again.

"This is not the feisty Liliana I used to know – ready to fight any monster in our life. Remember, Liliana?"

"I am tired of fighting people. That is all I have done in my life. I have no more strength left in me."

"Aldo, are you thinking what I am thinking?" Giuliana asked.

"Tell me first, and then we'll know."

Giuliana turned to her friend, thoughtful. Aldo continued:

"Liliana, your husband, tell us about him and his mother before she died. He was abusive, even though he was in a wheelchair, right? He was demanding. From what we hear, you were a slave at his mercy. Did anyone help you with him? Did anyone else put him to bed? Clean him up? Did he ever show affection toward you? Did he ever make love to you? He was paralysed from his waist down; actual intercourse was impossible for him, right? Did you resent him?"

Giuliana interjected.

"Aldo, stop it and listen to me. I am furious. Liliana has been abused all her life. She has given up. Before us sits a beautiful girl that has been the subject of one abuse after another. She sacrificed herself in accepting the offer of marriage in order to feed her family, to provide for her brothers and her mother."

Aldo raised his eyebrows.

"No wonder… I don't blame her. She has given up."

Aldo had handled many criminal cases, but looking at Liliana, his heart went out to her.

"Liliana, your mother lived with you?" Aldo asked, gently.

"Yes. Mom wanted us to leave. Afterwards, when we heard from my brothers, she kept asking them to take us in, to take us out of our misery, but the boys were young and just scraping by themselves with their own problems. They told us to stay where we were and be grateful we had a roof over our head and food to eat."

"Your husband, how did he abuse you? Was it physically? Verbally? Tell me," Aldo pressed.

"I was taking care of both of them – Mother and Son. Both needed twenty-four-hour care. I was supposed to live there as their maid. Then, my mother suggested that I had better marry him in order to inherit the house, the money, and the disability pension when his own mother passed. We were married. He was fine at first. The marriage was never consummated. The abuse began in earnest about a year after his mother died. He accused me of sleeping with other men. He called me a slut. He timed me when I went shopping for food, and he would be waiting by the door with a bat, slashing at me and chasing after me in that wheelchair. He would tell my mother to get out of his house. Mom cried a lot since she didn't want to leave me alone with him."

"Did you poison him?" Aldo asked bluntly.

"No. I was miserable. Mom begged me to go back to our hometown and abandon everything. We would be dirt poor again. But you see, sometimes he was calm. If I did not leave the house, things would be almost tolerable for a short while. My life has always been hell. Then, when Mom died, I just didn't care anymore."

"How did she die?

"Her heart gave up. She died in her sleep."

"Your husband, how did he die?"

"He wanted polenta, a corn flour delicacy from the north. That evening, he ate until he couldn't eat anymore. A couple of hours later, he tumbled out of his chair. He was dead on the floor."

"You never put any mixture or anything in his food to harm him?"

"Absolutely not. There was only me and him in that house." She let out a long sigh. "The prosecutor kept insisting I did it. At a certain point, I gave up. They could believe what they wanted. I just did not care anymore of what would become of me."

Their time was up. The officer escorted Liliana away. Aldo sheepishly turned to his friend.

"I believe she is innocent but I am challenged by this case. Giuliana, my friend, I will do everything in my power to bring life back to your friend. I will make it my business to appeal her case."

She turned to him, lifted herself up to reach his lips, and gave him a warm kiss.

"Thank you, Aldo. You are the best."

They left the prison, both planning their next move. Giuliana finally broke the silence.

"Aldo, I must leave for the US. I trust you will continue with this matter. We will keep in touch with any new developments. I have been putting off my trip. Now that I have seen Liliana and I know I am leaving her case in your capable hands, I can go feeling relieved. With you, her case isn't dormant.

"Giuliana, trust me, I will do all I can. Time will tell if I can help her."

Chapter Fifty
New York

In the sweltering heat of July, Giuliana arrived in New York. Ruggiero and Gioia, with Trizia and the new baby, welcomed her joyfully at the airport. Overwhelmed with bliss, Giuliana affectionately greeted her dear ones.

"Oh my! Let me see the new addition to our family!"

The baby was her first interest. She was all smiles, gazing over baby Ben. He was a perfect boy with blondish hair and big blue eyes. He took after his Dad's Scottish-Irish decent.

"Trizia? Does he have anything from our family?"

"Yes of course!" Trizia said with a laugh, "His temperament! When he is hungry, watch out. Let him have his father's features for now. Babies change as they grow. Glen is delighted when people comment on the resemblance."

Giuliana shrugged.

"Eh, Sis… If his hair doesn't turn black, we can always dye it later!"

"Oh! Poor child in the hands of you two," chuckled Ruggiero, as they all broke down in laughter.

"Oh, Trizia," Giuliana gushed, "black hair or blonde, he is beautiful."

Gioia and Ruggiero had planned all kinds of events trying to make their daughter's visit as pleasant as possible. They wanted to amuse her and keep her entertained. Giuliana was just happy to be with them and was not looking for much more. The baptism of the baby was the first thing to take place since it had been postponed while the family waited for her arrival. It was to be held following Sunday mass. It was a big event for the baby and the family.

The church was packed, and the priest announced the religious festivities that were to take place. Gioia wanted to make sure her daughter would participate.

"Giuliana, there is a feast of St. Anna at the church by the falls. We must attend the devotion. There is a procession, music and all that sort of thing. I would like you to come along and see what they do here."

"Mom, I am here to please you and Dad. I will go where ever…"

"You are such a darling, Dear."

Gioia hugged her.

The heat of the summer seemed unbearable, even in the late evening. Giuliana decided to put her bathing suit on and go for a swim in the family's pool. She stepped out the back into the dark yard. The air felt calm and the atmosphere serene. A warm breeze caressed her bare arms and legs. As she glanced at the sky, she noticed the full moon illuminating the earth and she felt surrounded by the sparkling stars. A placid music could be heard in the distance from next door. Her bare feet slowly crossed the warm deck. The wood was still hot from baking in the sun that day. She stepped onto the cooler softness of the green grass as she was drawn toward the music. There she stood between the two back yards, listening to the melody in a hypnotic state.

In a daze, she moved around, admiring the beauty that surrounded her. The large outdoor pool looked both refreshing and inviting. Pensively, she continued walking, assessing her surroundings. This is a heaven on earth, she thought with a sigh.

The sculpted, Roman-style flowering pots were bursting with flowing geraniums. The white impatiens, planted in the surrounding flowerbed, seemed to glow in the dark. I am so happy for my parents. They sure live in luxury. They had a lucky break. Milan offers a lot, but this place is incredibly peaceful. Her comparisons were making her fall in love with this place. She couldn't help but admire the different lifestyle of the USA. Liliana surfaced in her mind – she would call Aldo tomorrow.

The music from next door seemed to get louder and closer. The lyrics were romantic and pleasurable. Voices could be heard. The cedar fence created privacy, blocking whoever was out there. She didn't care. She wasn't nosy as she, herself, cherished privacy. This is what she liked about America's people. They didn't pry or invade. It suited her. That inviting blue clear water urged her to dive in. She took the leap and started doing laps vigorously. The swim revitalised her body. Her proud parents came out to check on her.

"Giuliana, I am glad you are making use of our pool. We don't enjoy it as much as we should."

"Mom, why on earth not? What a shame! It is lovely. The water is refreshing."

"Yes, that is what Mike next door tells me. He comes with his friend Lucio sometimes to swim. Remember that fellow that you danced with in the spring at the church?"

"Oh! Yes, that mysterious individual." she paused to recollect.

"As a matter of fact, they are always out there, with music resounding through the air for our comfort. Nice fellows."

Gioia walked over to the fence.

"Hello Mike," she called out.

A male voice responded promptly.

"Hello, Mrs. Ferrante! Beautiful evening out tonight. Is my

music bothering you? I will turn it down."

"No, No. Actually, it's pleasant. Our daughter, Giuliana, is here visiting. She loves music. Why don't you come over for a swim?"

"I have my cousin visiting here. I am not sure."

"You are both welcome if you want to."

So much for my privacy, thought Giuliana. She wished they would not come.

"Oh Mom, I was just enjoying my quietness and indulging in my own thoughts," she whispered.

"Giuliana, indulge in your thoughts when you go to sleep. Young blood is good for you."

In no time, the two arrived at the gated entrance with towels and in bathing attire. Mrs. Ferrante hurried to enthusiastically let them in. She liked to have young people around, especially now that Giuliana was visiting. She wanted her daughter to make new friends.

"Giuliana, Dear, you met Mike before, and his friend Lucio."

She made her way to the edge of the pool to acknowledge them, trying to hide her displeasure to please her mother. She had met the neighbour before, briefly. He seemed friendly enough.

Mike was a young man of medium height and a slim build. He seemed both polite and kind. She recognised Lucio from that night at the church. He was the strange young man she danced the night away with. He was the one that never called.

Mike, full of confidence, shook her wet hand.

"This is my cousin, Lucio," he said, stepping aside.

The man behind him was all smiles.

"We've met," he said as he extended his hand. "Remember

that evening at the church?" He shook her wet hand tenderly.

"Oh, yes! I remember perfectly," she replied.

She wondered about the phone call that never came. His big eyes appeared locked on her face. Then, timidly, he looked down, blushing. His smile sent a shiver down Giuliana's spine. To her surprise, he didn't waste any time getting into the pool. While Mike was chitchatting with her parents, like the old women from back home, Lucio dove in.

Gioia and Ruggiero were overjoyed with happiness to see that their daughter had company. They were fond of Mike – he was an honourable young man and a good neighbour, and they trusted him. By the time Mike found his way into the pool, Lucio seemed well acquainted and comfortable conversing with Giuliana. Mike, in a bit of envy, got right in between them to carve out some space near the lovely Giuliana. She sensed his claim. For a split second, the fellows reminded her of her boys at home in Milan.

As the evening moved on, she found the two men absorbing. After the swim, Mike invited Giuliana over his place for a bonfire, and a drink. This was a real novelty for her.

"A bonfire in July? That's interesting," she remarked.

Lucio held his breath, secretly hoping she would accept the invite.

"Why not? I have nothing else to do. That cool water from the pool has totally woken me up."

"We will be waiting for you. Mike has invited few other friends to come over. You will get to meet them," said Lucio with a big smile.

"Mr. and Mrs. Ferrante, you are welcome to join us, also," said Mike.

"We will watch a movie instead. You guys go ahead and have fun. I will make some popcorn for you to munch on."

"Oh, Mom! Even here? As if I haven't had enough of the corn!" Giuliana said with a hearty laugh.

"You will love it! The way I make it... well, you wait and see."

Giuliana arrived next door with a big bowl of popcorn prepared by her mother. It was steaming, with butter and fancy pink sea salt. Even Giuliana thought it looked delicious.

Lucio's big eyes widened as she arrived, jumping up to accommodate her and beckon her to sit beside him. Other young people came. Giuliana found herself among a bunch of strangers. But, they were fun, friendly, and made her feel like she was part of their group. Lucio, in his own peculiar way, warmed her heart. It is all strange... and different, she thought. When it was time to leave, Lucio walked her to the door and asked if he could call her. She smiled gracefully and nodded.

Gioia was waiting up for her. Giuliana sat beside her mother and grabbed her hands in her own.

"Mom, this is strange... I don't know how to explain this, but I know I have met the fellow I am going to marry."

Gioia jumped up.

"What are you saying?" She hugged her, shaking with joy. She went on, "Are you serious? This is a miracle! Dear, you know we want you close to us. This sounds promising. Who is this fellow?"

"You will find out soon, Mom."

Chapter Fifty-One
Dreaming of Love

Giuliana went to bed with Lucio in her dreams. The next evening, the phone rang, and there he was on the other end of the receiver. His deep voice stimulated her existence. He wanted to see her. Without hesitation, she said yes – she couldn't wait to see him too. He called every night after that. By Sunday afternoon, he had arrived to pick her up and take her for a country ride. He wanted to show her the beauty of Lake Erie and the surrounding parks with their lush gardens.

In hers, his hand felt warm and strong. Giuliana's agony from Joseph's death seemed to ease into the sweet memories of a lingering dream. Lucio was replenishing the love that had been missing in her long-pained heart. He gently held both her hands and sat her down on a wooden bench. Together they watched the calm, slow flow of the lake. He turned her chin to look at him with much sincerity in his big eyes.

"Giuliana, can I kiss you?"

Tears filled her eyes.

"How gentle of you to ask."

Without a word spoken, their warm lips met in a lasting, warm kiss. His lips were luscious and his embrace tender and warm. Their chemistry magnified, uniting their souls

"I want to marry you."

"How can you say that? You hardly know me?"

411

"I know. But, I have been waiting for you all my life. Now that I have found you, I will not let you go."

Oh, how he sounds so much like my lost love reincarnated!

"I live in Milan. You are here in the USA. How are we going to work that out?"

"You feel what I feel. Our bodies tremble when we touch. Our hearts are one and our souls belong together."

She knew he was right but she kept it to herself. A lot of changes needed to take place in her life. She found his eyes were irresistibly fascinating. She responded to him with a spontaneous warm kiss. His lips felt soft and magnetic with a vibrating energy.

They spent as much time together as they could since her days were numbered and she would be returning shortly. She learned much about Lucio. He had studied architecture. He had not been able to land a steady job, and he had been forced to take whatever was offered to him to survive. Giuliana could relate to him and felt a profound sense of understanding. Since his life wasn't prosperous, he confessed it affected his well-being. Lucio poured opened his heart to Giuliana easily.

"I have been going through a rough time since I arrived here. I have no right to be even talking to you. But, I do have big dreams. I promise if I can put my knowledge to work, I will create an empire just for you."

"Lucio," she responded, staring at him, "I feel as if I have known you all my life. I don't need an empire."

Observing from afar, Gioia wasn't so sure of what was going on. In her sharp scrutiny, she usually didn't miss much. Although she liked her daughter's new friend, it worried her that at times he would appear pensive. She wasted no time passing her concerns on to her daughter. "Giuliana, your friend at times takes deep breaths. He looks troubled."

"Oh, Mom, Lucio is just fretful. He worries about not having a proper job."

The following Sunday afternoon, a church function was taking place. Gioia suggested that the family should go. Giuliana didn't mind. Her parents, again, were greeted by many people. Everyone here was gracious and kind. Once the Saint Service was over, they walked around the church grounds, socialising with people her parents knew. The place was packed. An orchestra was playing typical church music, and there were two singers: a man and a woman. Food stations were set up that offered pizza, drinks, coffee and sweets sold by volunteers to raise money for the church. A lady, her husband and their two teenagers approached the family.

"Giuliana, remember the neighbour across the street from Liliana's house, in our hometown?"

Giuliana needed to think for a minute. The woman in front of her looked like a typical Italian lady from the town. She had tightly permed hair, and she hadn't lost the peasant look.

"You probably don't remember me," the woman said with a smile. "You were young. After we had gone away, I ventured back several times until my mom died."

Giuliana wasn't sure she could place her, so she politely responded.

"Oh! I see. Nice to see you again."

She extended her hand. The woman and Gioia began to make conversation. Some time later, she turned back to Giuliana.

"Isn't it sad what happened to poor Agnes's daughter? Agnes cried a lot for her girl. She hated her crippled son-in-law. After she had sacrificed her beautiful daughter to that invalid, Agnes told us he ordered the twins out of the house late one night in a pouring rainstorm. Oh! It brings tears to my eyes. I cannot even recount what that poor woman and family went through." She made the sign of the cross. Giuliana paid attention. This woman talked a lot. My God she knows a great deal. Is this gossip or real? Liliana is in prison; the boys had not come forward to support her. Are they mad at her?

"Signora, who told you all that?"

"Agnes, God Bless her soul. She hated him, her daughter wouldn't leave because of the inheritance. Agnes felt it wasn't worth it."

"Do you have any idea who poisoned him?"

"I have an idea, but I am not saying anything."

"You know, Liliana has been convicted, but she maintains she is innocent."

"I wouldn't be surprised if she is. I have said too much already. I don't like to get involved. My lips are sealed. Signori, Miss Giuliana, excuse my over-chatting. Have fun in America," she said as she quickly excused herself and departed, waving her hand goodbye.

"Mom, I am surprised to encounter the same tattlers here as back home. Even after moving halfway around the world they don't change, do they?"

"Some of them cherish their old ways and indulge in their gossip."

"I must consult with Aldo when I go back. He needs to unveil the case from every angle."

Lately, being so taken with Lucio meant that she had felt sidetracked from her work. The break had done her good, but even with her newfound love, she felt duty-bound to help her friend. Her thoughts switched back to her attorney state-of-mind and to the search for clues. An idea surfaced in her brain. She needed to consult with Aldo.

Chapter Fifty-Two
Marriage and Miracle

First thing Monday morning, Giuliana checked the time and picked up the phone. Before dialing, she rehearsed her mental notes of the tattler's comments. Liliana, her dear Liliana was a thorn in her heart. Aldo, in his wisdom, would help her.

Aldo swiftly answered as if he had been waiting for her call.

"Eh? Where is my girl? I have been counting the days until your return. Are you back in Milan? How about dinner? Same time? Same place?"

"Aldo, hold on," Giuliana quickly interjected. "I will be back in a couple of days. I need to talk to you."

"Don't sound so mysterious. Forget about clients and cases, let's talk about you and me for change."

"Aldo, you are such a joker. See you Wednesday. We will have lunch then at the bistro."

"I can't wait. Can I pick you up at the airport? Carry your suitcase? I will be a slave at your command."

"I need your relentlessness to be redirected into research for Liliana's case. That is how you can help me," said Giuliana, trying not to be agitated.

"My Dear, anything for you. I am at your mercy."

"Fine. We have a date: Wednesday at noon. I will arrive on the morning flight and meet you there."

"Can't wait."

Aldo shook his head. Why does this girl play so hard to get? I guess I will have to prove myself to her first.

Giuliana had scribbled some notes while on the plane. When she arrived at the bistro, she was ready to pursue her hunch with Aldo. Their greeting was more business-like on her part as she immediately launched into what was on her mind, but her criminal lawyer friend had other priorities.

"Aldo, listen and listen carefully," Giuliana quickly interjected as he attempted to change the topic to his admiration of her outfit. "You are the criminal lawyer, and I am interested in your intuition, but I think I have a suspect. I had to go to America for it to click in."

"Thanks for the confidence," he said.

"Aldo, I think Liliana's mother killed her husband."

"The dead mother? What made you come to that conclusion, may I ask?"

"Aldo, I come from Molise, don't forget. The townsfolk's favourite pastime there is gossip. Well, I met a lady in America that lived across the street from where Liliana lived. Her mother, Agnes, used to talk to this woman regularly. This woman stated how much Agnes hated Liliana's husband. The lady also mentioned how Agnes expressed more than once she was going to kill him."

"Giuliana – talk, even threatening speech, is far from murder. Do you have any proof that she actually committed the crime? There is also the small issue of her being dead when the death occurred."

Giuliana continued, unshaken.

"Motive one: besides abusing Liliana, the man ordered the twins out of his house in the middle of a stormy night. Apparently

416

the ordeal was messy; another episode in a continuing nightmare. I bet any money that Agnes plotted the murder, and Liliana doesn't even know it."

Aldo listened attentively. So far this made sense.

"But where is the proof, my Dear? You need proof," he insisted, grabbing her hand.

"I have been thinking back to my childhood. My grandmother would always concoct herbal remedies for all that ailed our family. Ancient knowledge is still strong in the older generations in that town. There are many helpful and poisonous things growing in the countryside and my grandmother knew them all. Maybe Liliana's mother did too? You are a smart lawyer," she said, "It's up to you to dig it out. I challenge you, my friend. Look after Liliana will you?" She looked him straight in his eyes and held her gaze.

"You are deadly serious. Aren't you?" he asked.

"Yes, I am."

Aldo remained thoughtful. This case was getting more mysterious by the day, and it was arousing his interest. In all fairness, he had to admit that Giuliana certainly had a good point. He liked being challenged by her. If Liliana was innocent, she shouldn't be behind bars. He put a hand on his forehead and seriously scrutinised his notes once more.

"Leave it with me," he assured her.

"Thank you!"

She jumped up and excitedly hugged him.

"We will come up with something interesting."

***

417

As Giuliana tried to settle back into her daily routine in Milan, her dear new friend in Buffalo was dealing with serious health issues. Since Lucio was not the type to confide his sorrows in others, he had kept his pain and suffering to himself. His cousin Mike finally had had enough and decided to place a phone call.

"Giuliana, I want to inform you that Lucio has been taken to the emergency department during the night. He was in excruciating abdominal pain. The doctors had to perform surgery to save his life. I was told not to call you, but I just wanted to let you know. It seemed like the right thing to do."

"Oh my! Thank you for calling. How is he doing? Is he ok? What has happened to him?"

"They were hopeful going into surgery, but there were some complications. He is holding on. I am optimistic he will pull through."

She was shocked at the turn of events. Giuliana couldn't believe how troubled she was by the news and how this revealed how much she cared. This person had become very dear to her in such a short time.

She was on the next plan available to Buffalo. With much concern, she had rushed to see him and be at his side. After a week of holding a vigil at his bedside, the doctors finally concluded he was out of grave danger. She still postponed her return to Milan until Lucio was solidly on his way to recovery, afraid that her absence would cause him to spiral. The fear of losing him surpassed any other concern in her life. As she cared for him, his eyes brimmed with love, without words and demands. She sensed all his needs in the gentle tenderness of his manners. Giuliana took his cold hands into the warmth of her own.

"Call it fate, or God's will, but your episode has confirmed for me that my place is here, with you, my Darling."

His eyes lit up, and his lips enveloped her in an inviting kiss. His pale face glowed with pleasure. That was exactly what he wanted to hear. His recovery progressed well, which Lucio attributed readily to the stimulating endorphins flowing through his veins as a result of the desire he felt for his new love. Unfortunately, Giuliana's obligations did not cease even though the world seemed to stop when she gazed into Lucio's eyes. The firm and her clients were eager and impatiently waiting for her across the ocean. Their goodbye was painful when it came, and they were both longing for one another before they even escaped each other's sightlines. Giuliana had returned to Milan, but her heart was left in America.

There was no question in her mind now: she had to make some significant changes. Milan had so much to offer with its industries, opportunities and neighbouring countries. It had been good to her. But when she looked into her heart, Lucio captured more real estate than Milan. Now that she had finally found love once more, she found some humour in the fact that it was on the other side of the ocean. Nevertheless, I must go to him, she decided with a firm nod.

At the office, a few bits of unfinished business needed to be addressed. With her expertise and efficiency, it would be no problem. Liliana was still the big thorn in her heart. Recently, Aldo had convinced the old quack in her town to sign a declaration. He confessed to seeing Agnes collecting dangerous herbs near the riverside. Aldo is smart, she reminded herself. Surely he will continue to make more discoveries.

***

Preparations for Giuliana's exit took longer than anticipated. The farewells were sorrowful. Her colleagues at the law firm held a big bash for her. Her supervisors presented her with many

419

offerings to celebrate her contributions and merits. The tears spilt freely as her emotions were running high. The Sbarro's were getting on in years now. Amelia had been her second mother, and she would miss her terribly. The Sbarro brothers were busy with their new endeavours. They now were all involved in love pursuits of one kind or another. Even Nino was happier these days. He was dating a girl from the south and totally infatuated with her.

To everyone's surprise, Mr. and Mrs. De Santis had become part of her weekly visits in the last few years. They affectionately saw her off.

"Giuliana, you are the dearest thing we have in our lives without our son," Mrs. De Santis had said.

"Giuliana, what a lucky girl you are," said Aunt Amelia. "You are blessed. So many people love you here. But, you, my Dear, must go where your heart takes you. As much as we like to have you here, it is a wise choice to be near your mom and dad. No one can replace your biological parents. And, your new love Lucio is there! Dear, follow your heart in all things, and you will never go astray."

"Thank you, Aunt Amelia. You are the most logical of souls and forever unselfish. I am only a flight away from Milan. I shall be back often."

As much as it pained Giuliana to leave these adorable people that had played such prominent roles in her life, Lucio had an effect on her that surpassed all other obstacles. The distance between them would soon be closed. The burning desire to touch him and be near him made her body quiver. Lucio's thoughts, day and night, revolved around the true love he had found. He knew in his heart that once their blissful union was fulfilled their souls would become one.

***

Lucio and Giuliana were united in marriage on a splendid summer day in August that year. The Ferrantes, with their many friends, celebrated the wedding in the richness of the American custom. All of Giuliana's friends from abroad flew over, including some of the folks from the old town and her dear, disappointed Aldo. Giuliana's new life had begun with her husband. Lucio, with his new bride at his side, felt encouraged to conquer any endeavour life presented.

On their honeymoon, after making love to her, he declared:

"Darling, I want to get all the best things life can offer for you. I must confess, when I saw you for the first time, I never thought I would be worthy of you. Now, I can proudly state that you are my wife, and I want to live up to all of your expectations and more."

"What a shame," Giuliana crooned. "How wrong you were. You thawed the ice around my frozen heart and brought it back to life."

"That first night I met you, I had gone home and began to think I had only dreamt of you, Darling. I feared rejection. I was sick, broke and unemployed with nothing to offer. Michael always talked about the great girl next door. When fate directed me to you a second time, the energy you sent through my veins broke all the barriers in my mind."

"How wrong and foolish you were!"

She met his lips in a long, breathless kiss.

"You are the only one that has awakened my senses like this. You are the only one I want to love, and you have made me feel alive again. But, most of all, you have inspired me to trust again."

Lucio sat silently for a moment.

"I was told you lost a boyfriend in a plane crash," he said, softly.

"Yes, I did. Joseph was dear to me. But, it was a different kind of love. You know – young love. It didn't feel the same. We belonged to two different worlds. He belonged to another class, and I was just the poor girl from the cornfield. But, you, my Darling, are at my level and have managed to melt the iceberg in my heart. With your meek personality, you have totally captured my world. I can honestly assure you my heart and soul have surpassed boundaries I never thought they could."

He looked at her with his big, brown eyes and sealed her warm lips in real passion. They fell asleep in each other's arms. Giuliana's world revolved around Lucio and his around her.

***

Giuliana had kept in close touch with Aldo about all developments regarding Liliana's case. On a recent phone call with Aldo, he reassured her that he had a few new leads moving forward.

"I will fly to Milan if I can help, my friend," she offered.

"I have embarked on a broad investigation. Yes, my smart girl, leads are pointing toward the mother. She is still very dead, so the twists and turns keep twisting and turning. This is a fascinating case, to be sure. I have total faith that everything will eventually surface and be sorted out. She might have her day in court once again. Giuliana, your friend deserves to be rescued. I believe she is innocent. Now I am determined to pursue this to the end."

"Thank you, Aldo. We must save her. She deserves a break in life."

She hung up the phone. In the meantime, her hands were tied

from here. All she could do was wait and pray.

***

The two newlyweds became inseparable. Operating on a high from his marriage, Lucio's projects flourished and he began to be recognised. Giuliana had no trouble passing her equivalency exams and soon was fully licenced to practice in the state of New York. She had mastered business development and administration in Europe, in America, it was really just a matter of adapting to the American laws, regulations, and customs.

As time passed, the couple's affections grew deeper as their love bloomed. Two years later, they were blessed with a healthy baby boy. Giuliana was thriving, showered with all the goodness life offered. Later on, a little girl was born – a carbon copy of Giuliana's features, but with the sparkling big eyes of her father. Now, with a son and a daughter, and his talented wife, Lucio felt like the richest man on this planet.

They were in the habit of discussing everything together. One night when Lucio arrived home, Giuliana sat on his lap as she greeted him.

"Darling, I have been thinking, with your expertise and my vision and hard work; what do you say we form a company and work together?"

"Darling, whatever your heart desires! I would love to work with you."

And so, the journey of their chain of business creations began. Lucio and Giuliana each occupied an elegant, well-furnished office adjacent to one another. Large windows brought in natural light from sunrise to sunset. Giuliana stood faithfully beside him with her support and expert advice. Together, they built an empire of wealth. She was in charge of marketing, finance and all legalities, along with her bookkeepers and accountant. They always made sure their assets and liabilities balanced.

Their success had benefits that spread to others, and their profits were often shared with ones in need. They contributed to medical research, donated to hospitals and Giuliana continued to contribute to an education fund for children overseas. Eventually, her scholarships overflowed to high achievers in America as well.

Their dedication inspired many, and their office was repeatedly called. They were continually approached by publishing houses to write about their success and secrets. The couple kindly refused.

A few years had passed since Giuliana and Aldo began their investigation and the time had come when Giuliana would finally get the call she had been waiting for, since the day the saga began:

"Giuliana the appeals court reviewed the evidence and overturned the conviction. She is fully exonerated! Our strong evidence acquitted Liliana of any wrongdoing. Turns out Agnes did kill her son-in-law. Our signed declarations, witnesses, and evidence has prevailed. The poison came from the Belladonna plant that grows by the riverside. You were right! It is used for medicinal purposes but too much will kill any man. She placed it in a peppershaker, which he poured with his own hands long after Agnes's death. She knew Lilian would never touch pepper due to chronic stomach trouble and she would be safe."

"Oh my God!"

"I will help her get settled on the outside. I have become fond of Liliana and since you are taken, my friend, I would like her to be my wife."

"Oh, Aldo! Do I hear right? Thank you. Thank you so much. I knew you could do it. Liliana will be the best wife for you."

Giuliana put down the phone. She was over the moon.

"Thank you, Lord!" she whispered, relieved.

She ran to find Lucio, to hug and kiss him and to share her happiness.

"Oh, my darling! The miracle I have prayed for has happened."

***

The years passed, and the two inseparable soul mates continued to live their lives fully into a ripe old age, with a wealth of experiences and wisdom. When the news media interviewed them at their home, Lucio, holding his Giuliana, answered the question posed to him:

"Mr. Albano, of all your successes; which do you cherish most in your life?"

"My most valuable possessions? Well, those are my wife and then my children."

"What have you to add, Mrs. Giuliana Albano?"

"Spread your love, share your wealth. Believe in God, and when in desperation, turn to your faith. Be true to yourself. Regardless of my life's possessions and accomplishments,

I can honestly declare that in my heart I am still the humble peasant girl from the cornfield.

The End.

www.ingramcontent.com/pod-product-compliance
Lightning Source LLC
Chambersburg PA
CBHW070931100726
47908CB00001B/179